All the Little Guns
Went Bang, Bang, Bang

All the Little Guns Went Bang, Bang, Bang

Neil Mackay

FREIGHT
BOOKS

First published June 2013

Freight Books
49-53 Virginia Street
Glasgow, G1 1TS
freightbooks.co.uk

A CIP catalogue reference for this book is available from the British Library

ISBN 978-1-908754-28-8
eISBN 978-1-908754-20-2

Typeset by Freight in Garamond
Printed and bound by Bell and Bain, Glasgow

CREATIVE SCOTLAND

the publisher acknowledges investment from
Creative Scotland toward the publication of this book

Neil Mackay is a multi-award winning investigative journalist, newspaper executive, non-fiction author, radio broadcaster and film-maker. He has won around two dozen national and international awards for his newspaper journalism. He was a launch editor of the *Sunday Herald* newspaper, and has subsequently been the paper's Crime Editor, Investigations Editor and Head of News. His last film, an investigation into the rise of the far right in Europe and America, was nominated for a BAFTA. His book, *The War on Truth*, which investigated the roots of the invasion of Iraq, was published in the UK and USA. He has written for the *Sunday Herald*, *The Observer*, *Scotland on Sunday*, Ireland's *Sunday Tribune*, Australia's *The Age* and most newspapers in Northern Ireland.

With love to Nicolla, for being there too

The Ballad of Two Moths

There are two moths tonight in my garden,
and the garden is a bad place to be –
with owls and spiders and those black night-birds –
but the moths flying free – them's you and me.
The moths Roma dance round the lilac tree,
flirt like fools, duck, dive and ride wild.
The man-moth grabs his girl-moth by her dust-wings,
the girl-moth brushes her man-moth's hair aside.
In a hole in a hedge hide lost moths there,
webless and owl-less, unscared, and bird-free.
So only two moths fly by night in my garden;
mollyed moths secret-safe ain't you or me.

by Katie Cloaky
TOOMEBRIDGE, IRELAND, 1905

PART ONE

Back in the time of Giants

Years ago now, in a town called Antrim, on the eastern shore of Lough Neagh in Northern Ireland, there were two kids from an estate named Parkhall. The kids were Pearse and May-Belle, of whom people have heard a lot, but know little.

When they were wee – and this was a very long time ago – these children did a whole host of terrible things, so some say, and were punished and sent away. Part of the rules of their sending away had it that they could never see each other again – whether free or at large, no matter how old they grew, inside or out.

Now, two such people as Pearse and May-Belle were not meant to be apart – depend on that. And so, when they could, throughout their lives, and no matter where they were, they worked and wended their way towards each other, regardless of who said what: the courts, the police, social workers, prison guards, government ministers, doctors or probation officers, let alone the newspapers and the great general public at large.

For no other reason than it seems to go that boys always get their say in first, Pearse's story begins when he comes to consciousness – as he would put it – sometime around the age of two; early for most, granted, but he remembered it all.

In Pearse's house back then there was a long hall, front to rear, that seemed to have no end to it – just a fizzing black hole at the very back of the house – a kitchen, a cubby-hole place under some stairs for the coal and bad kids; rooms, a door, paintings of horses and men, little brass bells, a polar bear mat and TV.

Around this time, young Pearse carries out what he considers to be a great act of heroism. The great act of heroism is this: he walks into the kitchen, goes to a drawer, gets out a fork, returns to the living room – where the father fella, Da, will not stop shouting and swearing and hitting, and Mum won't stop screaming and crying and hitting back – and Pearse stabs the fork into Da's leg, pretty deep for the thrust of a little arm. 'I kill you,' Pearse said. He was still too young back then to have a proper sense of the future tense, or perhaps he thought that words had to back up deeds to make the action happen, like magic. Whatever the reasons for the grammar, Da dropped him with a bop to the face, a lion paw cuff, which, before Pearse hit the ground, realigned his wee body in space, so his feet swapped places with his head.

Often Pearse would be told about this by Mum and Gran, but never by Da, of course; for Da it never happened. But for years this was proof of Pearse's future character. The day Pearse showed him.

After all of this terrific bravery, there didn't seem to be anything very much of anything going on for a while, just a grey bobbing along of Champion the Wonder Horse, the news, playing in the park; food, mostly beans and Smash.

Things start to jellify a little, though, around the Time of the Beehive. The beehive is a mound of stones – or maybe bricks – piled in the back-yard, pine-coned like an old-fashioned beehive; an attraction he has never seen before. Barky the dog is there too. Pearse declared to everybody that he loved Barky – and hardly ever hurt him.

Pearse picked off a few stones from the top of the beehive and looked inside. A shiny black gun was nestled down there – with a butt with the wee-est of wee nobbles all over it and a revolver barrel that span if you flicked it with your palm.

And this moment – Pearse always felt – was the true start of the jellification process.

The beehive was about the size of his arm. Pearse put in a hand and pulled out a gun – like he put in his thumb and pulled out a plum. Granny read poetry all the time and constantly rhymed things. Nappy, happy, clappy, snappy. She sang songs about how far it was from Tipperary, and the Auld Dog Tray – how loyal the poor critter was before he died and all that. It's a dog's lot really.

This gun was oily and cold and clean and heavy, and sat wrong, but right, in his wee hand. He couldn't grip it by the butt and wrap his Peter-Pointer round the trigger at the same time.

Pearse tottered into the kitchen. Mum took the gun away. She looked like she was about to shout, but then changed expression – scared of the gun's import for her wee man, not of him blowing her head off with it.

She said it was a toy gun. That Da had hid it for a joke. Good auld Da, she said – trying to sound Irish through her funny English accent. What mighty crack he is.

This was summer time. Centuries ago, it feels like. Back in the time of Finn McCool and the Ulster giants; back when we still had stone axes. Pearse was three or so. Long before May-Belle, long before Martin and Galen, long before Muckamore Abbey and the Weary Woods – and all the other children and people and places.

*

Gran lived on a housing estate in a flat up some stairs. There was a wee stinky bin place underneath the block where Pearse played with other children during the day. Gran would sit chewing her face for hours and watch the kids. Mum and Da lived nearby in a house. They had a garden at the front and back, and next-door neighbours who had horrible children called Philip and Lizzie – even though they were Catholics. Mum called the children the no-necked-monsters. Da called Mum a stupid fucken bitch for insulting the neighbours unnecessarily.

It couldn't have been those wee brats, though, who started the biggest physical fight Pearse had ever seen, because the family of the no-necked-monsters had moved away come the day Mum

3

decided that was that, alright, and threw a sideboard at Da.

Da – sometimes known as Fuckface, Big Neb, Papa Pickelino, Unresolved Business, Ironsides, Death Wish and so on – Da walked into the bedroom and hit Mum and then hit Pearse a whack too for no reason. That's when Mum picked up the sideboard and threw it over the bed taking the legs from under Da. She shouted, 'Leave him alone', and chucked a lamp at Da's head. Da ran round the bed and pulled her about by the hair for a while. She freed herself, then jumped on top of him and slapped him and chewed his ear and ripped his hair and then he pushed her off the bed and punched her twice, with two sharp raps on the temple. Da ran out of the room and Mum sat on the floor with her hair all over her face and screamed her bloody head off. It was some quare show.

After that, with the jelly nearly readying to set, it's off to live with Gran and Mum at Gran's flat.

By Christmas, though, Mum and Da weren't split up anymore, and it's back to the family home proper. The jelly is still a bit wobbly, so it's hard to remember leaving Gran's place. It's mostly grey fizz for a while, but then there are two pretty bad things which happen and both are about toys.

The first's like this: it's a few days before Christmas, and thanks to Mum or Gran there's an early present. Pearse always worried that he'd die before the Big Day, so they'd buy him a toy to shut him up and stop him fretting about becoming a little angel in the Great Beyond.

This time the toy is a cowboy wagon with Apaches chasing it, and gunslingers hanging on the sides, defending it from attack and shooting the Red Native American Indians or whatever they are called. Pearse is playing with the stagecoach and the cowboys and Indians on the sofa, which is a daft place to play, granted, because stuff doesn't sit right and everything keeps falling over.

Da comes in with his friend Hinley. The Christmas tree is on and the living room lights are off and they're laughing and joking with Mum. Hinley stays talking to Mum in the kitchen because she hasn't finished making dinner.

Da walks over to the sofa. His suit's too tight. He smells hot and like drink. He sits down – his fat arse lands on the cowboy wagon smashing the wheels off it. It's impossible to get it out from under him as he's watching the news and says stop fidgeting about him for fuck's sake.

Pearse gets up and walks into the kitchen and tells Mum that Da's sat on the cowboy wagon. She says, 'Dan, did you sit on Pearse's cowboy things?' And Da says to Pearse, 'Stop being such a wee fairy and get away from your fucken mummy's apron strings.'

Pearse turns a look to the living room and, you know, imagines shooting Da dead with a Colt .45, the auld Peacemaker. Da stands up and grabs Pearse and flings him about a bit, saying, 'Get in here and take that sleekit expression off your face.'

So, it's sit-on-the-mat-and-be-quiet-time; the mat that looks like it was made out of a polar bear skin. If you turn it over though, there's no red underneath, no bits of meat clinging to the weave. The news is on TV. There's a girl being carried round a mound of rubble in a city by some men. The city's blown to smithereens and there are helicopters. The men are holding the girl up over their heads – the chopper blades whirring; her stomach is hanging out of her. The tubes of her guts are purple and she must be dead. Everyone looks Chinese.

Then a plane has gone down on the news and there's a drawing of a map and a circle where the plane fell and lots of people have died, children too. Pearse is outraged about the destruction of his cowboy wagon – and for being flung about and called a wee fairy who hangs on mummy's fucken apron strings – so he says 'good' when the pictures of all the dead folk come up on the screen. And laughs as well.

Da gets up and picks him up and tans Pearse's arse like he's never tanned it before. Pearse screams at him to leave him alone, that he's a horrible auld bastard and he hates him, and Da hits him a wallop that bleeds his nose and throws him onto the settee, onto his busted up cowboy wagon.

Hinley's not seen leaving, but he certainly did not crucify Dandy Dan on the Christmas tree like he was meant to – he just dissolved into mist and disappeared out through the letterbox.

So Pearse has a bit of a knocked-in lumpy circus head after all that battering, but he still gets his tea. No-one goes without their tea. It's beans and mashed spuds made from Smash, by the little yakking robot Martian men on the ads. Mum stirs it up. Da looks while she stirs it up. And Pearse's auld nose goes drip drip with red.

*

Around the time that Pearse was poking a finger up his bleeding nose, May-Belle's mind was starting its own jellification process, although of course she never used that expression – it was something she picked up from Pearse much later.

To May-Belle, Scotland was the strangest of memory places. Big free open cities, and then glens followed by lochs followed by mountains and islands and sea like long dark iron grass. A country far greener, she still remembered, than even Ireland. Scotland was just pretty pictures; then Ma and Dad took her and headed back to Larne on the ferry – its floors awash with sick, and the vomit making her vomit. For a while, May-Belle would introduce herself to people saying, 'I was born in Scotland and stayed there until I was four years old'. Then Scotland faded.

The Mullhollands – her family name – the Mullhollands moved into a house near her grandmother in Antrim town, and Dad got a job in a tyre factory, turning old wheels into new ones. May-Belle's grandmother died a few months later and then it was just the three of them, forever.

Scotland, the family story goes, had been idyllic. Dad and Ma told May-Belle it was a joy back then. They travelled around the country, working casually on the land or in bars, getting digs here and there until they got bored of where they were and decided to move on.

In Ireland, though, the beast came out in the family. One day Dad got May-Belle dressed up for nursery school: a portacabin near the shops. This recollection is prima facie – real; perhaps the first memory not received through a story told by another person.

It was springtime and there was a fete at this kindergarten.

She woke with Dad standing over her, going, 'Shush, May-Belle, get up.'

She got up and Dad dressed her in a checked blue and white pinafore. They had breakfast, and about a quarter of an hour before play-group began Ma came in through the back door. She started cooing and saying, 'What a wee doll, how pretty you are.' Then Dad said something along the lines of, 'So why weren't you here to get her ready?'

Ma goes, 'And why have you dressed her like a hoor?'

And Dad got up and left.

After he walked out the back door, Ma said to May-Belle, 'Did you hear that? Click. The door went click. Say goodbye to the fucker.'

She didn't pull the clothes off May-Belle or knock her around – she just told her she wasn't going to nursery.

They got into bed together and Ma started to tell stories of what Scotland was like when she and Dad just started going together, and how driving around in a car they'd found by the side of the road was the greatest time of her life.

She got May-Belle to zhoozh her to sleep – May-Belle patting her on the head, and humming with her mouth like a wee bee, lulling.

Ma started to nod off. She twitched, and reached out, pawing and patting – and said, all murmury, 'Your father is an evil cunt and there is no-one but me in this world looking out for you.'

*

The second story about Pearse and toys which is bad goes like this: during that same Christmas, 1974, Pearse got a proper Hornby railway set with a tunnel and a junction box and a wee house for the little Station Master man and rails that went two ways. It was hard to set up and get working with electricity. Mum couldn't figure it out and she had to cook the turkey anyway for Christmas so she told Da to do it.

Pearse was sitting beside Da on the floor talking about turkeys and asking why we ate them at Christmas only and why America was called the New World – for isn't that where turkeys come from originally – while Da took a screwdriver to the railway set. He couldn't get it to work. Pearse asked him when he was going to get it to work and Da said soon and Pearse said how soon because I want to play with it and then Da said shut the fuck up and laid out such a slap on his leg that the thigh went red, and finger-marks came up in white lines as if nettle stings had grabbed ahold – welts like little broken train tracks.

Mum must've heard. She came in and screamed standing in the doorway between the living room and the kitchen. Da said you're a wee cunt and called Mum a fucking hoor and went upstairs slamming the door.

Later that night everything seems okay, though – all floaty and drowsy. The vampire bats are elsewhere; the moon's not bleeding; the dead are in their graves, it seems. It's all good. Pearse must've fallen asleep on the couch and been taken upstairs to bed. It's the middle of the night – and he's come round from sleep, half awake. The sheets have been rucked off the mattress and are all scrunched up on the floor. Da is slobbering on Mum and they're both naked and have more limbs than they should.

Beside them, in their bed, it's quite dark and their moving about keeps sleep away but there's a little bit of blue light from somewhere out in the hallway drifting into the room. Mum is sitting on top of Da. There's her fanny, and her diddies too. Pearse claps his hands over his eyes, and then squints through his fingers.

Mum says, 'Stop, Dan. Pearse's awake.' Pearse turns away on his side and squeezes his eyes shut. A light comes on in a wee second and Da laughs. There's a slap and Da says, 'She's a grand fucken ride your ma.'

*

One shimmering summer's morning, Dad woke May-Belle and said, 'Come downstairs, May-Belle love, I have to show you something.' She got up, all yawns, and followed him. In the living room, Ma was sleeping. She was slumped over on the sofa. The heels of her shoes were on the floor, and her body to one side. Her skirt had ridden up her legs; the white of her thighs above the top of her stockings. She had no knickers on. Dad shook his head and he said, 'She's not long in. Come on.'

They went back upstairs, and Dad got May-Belle washed and dressed and then sat her down on the bed and said he needed to get out of the house for a wee while, that he couldn't stand being around You Know Who. He doled out a few coppers and a bit of silver from his pocket and said, 'Go get some sweeties and run about the estate and have fun.'

May-Belle and Dad walked outside and he said, 'I need money, honey. I'll be back as soon as I can.'

He walked her round to the neighbours and said to the lady next door, 'I have to look for a job – her mother is ill so can you please keep an eye on her if she needs anything until I come back at tea-time. She'll be out playing anyway, most of the day, as the weather's so nice. Wee May-Belle will be no trouble.'

Dad walked May-Belle down the street and he gave her his watch and said, 'I'll be back by eight.' He checked to make sure she knew where the big hand and wee hand were, and told her, 'Don't go disturbing the neighbours until you're starving, and meet me at the top of the big field near our house at eight o'clock.'

'Okay,' May-Belle said.

'See you soon,' he said, and he gave her a wee kiss on the lips.

There was a wild time had that afternoon. Chasing after feathers and building a dam in a stream – watching the water roll and rivel around the lip of the dam wall, pushing at its bank, trying to breach it. Each time the dam was ready to break, she'd mend the wall – putting pebbles into the packing to sturdy it. The work got boring after a while, though, so May-Belle sat and watched until the heft of the water overcame the dam and it cracked and caved in, the water flattening the entire construction, washing it away. There was no point in creating things any longer. May-Belle went off to look for the nests of hedge sparrows, but found none.

In the late afternoon, when the schools were getting out, May-Belle went back up to the neighbour's house and the lady said she'd make something to eat. She asked, 'Is your mother alright?'

'No.' said May-Belle, 'she's still poorly.'

The lady's two children came in from school. They were a wee bit older than May-Belle, the girl in P1 and the boy in P2, and were very shy, quiet types. The mother said, 'Get the three of youse into the living room and watch the cartoons.' Their house was bright and open; the air ran through it, so your breath felt fresh in your lungs. The boy switched the telly on. The white dot hummed in the middle of the screen, and then stretched itself out into a glowing line; the TV set blossomed into life. An English woman was reading the news and then the children's hour started. Jackanory told its story while the mother made dinner. The narrator was a guy in a rocking chair in a dark, dark room. His story was about a young boy from the frozen north who was haunted by an invisible spirit. The thing had killed his father, and he was half running from the monster, but half hunting it down as well. As the story-teller talked – and drawings of the poor boy came up on the screen showing this terrible adventure of his – the light, sifting into the room from the evening sun, faded; the invisible monster darkening the auld house. The first part of the story ended when the little boy made it to the hut of an old white witch who told him he was cursed and would have to defeat the spirit, otherwise his whole line would be haunted by the thing forever.

The show ended as the mother walked in with three plates of cheesy beans on toast and juice. She put the tray on the dark brown dinner table behind the couch, and said, 'Sit down nice and eat.'

'I should turn the telly off,' she says, 'but I know these two love their shows.'

When she walked out of the room, her son got up and pushed the buttons with a big thunk, changing channel from BBC 1 to UTV. Magpie came on. 'Pish,' said the boy, and switched the channel back. Blue Peter started.

'I hate that show,' May-Belle said. 'Watch Magpie instead.'

She'd watched both these programmes before in other neighbours' houses. Blue Peter was a terrible chore, whereas Magpie was all singing and daftness.

'It's my house, and I'll watch what I like,' the boy said.

'Who asked you round here anyway?' the girl said. 'You're not our friend.'

May-Belle chucks the plate of beans over the girl's yellow summer dress, and the boy, still stood in front of the TV, jumps over the back of the sofa and grabs her by the hair. The next thing May-Belle knows, the mother is dragging her off the boy. He's on the ground, on his back. He's somehow got a cushion from the sofa covering his face and most of his body. He's cowering under it, shielding himself, and May-Belle is stabbing into the cushion with a butter knife, trying to smother him at the same time. The daughter is howling in the corner like a beaten puppy, covered in beans. The mother takes ahold of May-Belle's arms and legs, picks her up, carries her through the house, and tosses her out the front door, saying, 'Get out of here, you fucken wee maniac – I don't care if that good-for-nothing mother of yours is sick, you can piss off, or I'll call the police.'

May-Belle goes down to the big field to wait for Dad. It wasn't even half five. There were bushes off to one side that were deep and dark. Only a wee thing like May-Belle could get inside. Once in, no-one could see you. May-Belle scrapped together some leaves and made a bed. It was cold in the bushes, and the change in temperature made her sleepy. She took off her cardigan, and snuggled down on the leaves, pulling the cardigan back over her. Lying on her side, she could see through the branches, out towards the road to the town. When Dad came back he'd be spotted long before he made it to the field. There was fun to be had staying hidden and then leaping out on him.

May-Belle fell asleep and woke up. Inside the bushes there was still just enough light to tell the time. It was coming up to eight. She lay on her belly, with her hands under her head, watching for Dad, and drawing shapes in the dusty earth with an auld stick: circles and stars and dogs and dicks and boobs and birds and knives and cows and people.

It got too dark to draw or tell the time. She clambered out of the bushes and walked up to her house. The light was on in the living room. The front door was open. At the entrance, a man was standing in the hallway, Ma was coming down the stairs.

'Where have you been?' she asked.

'Out.'

'To this time?' she said. 'It's nearly 11 o'clock.'

'Sorry. I fell asleep.'

'Right,' she says, 'well I'm off out to work. Dad's not home so I'll lock the door behind me. Don't answer it to anyone. Jump out a window if there's a fire.'

May-Belle had slept for so long, though, she couldn't sleep anymore once they left – the man without saying a word, and Ma with a puff of powder and perfume. She ate some bread with jam and drank a glass of milk and went upstairs.

May-Belle sat up in bed and sang till her tongue got tired. She sang about hundreds of green bottles sitting on the wall, and about the little mouse with clogs on going clip-clippity-clop on the stair. When it got bright outside, the song was:

I've got a handful of songs to sing you,
can't stop my voice when I long to sing you
new songs and blue songs and songs to bring you
happiness,
no more no less.

Ma came in early, about seven in the morning. The fella was still with her, and she must have heard singing upstairs, for she calls up, 'Get down here you.' She allows May-Belle a little sip out of a bottle of red wine she has with her, and says, 'The pair of us have had such a wicked night would you not sing now I've given you a wee drink to help us all relax.'

May-Belle sings 'This is the Way We Brush Our Teeth'. Before the bit that goes, 'this is the way we go to school', the man, who is sitting beside Ma with his arm around her shoulder – while May-Belle stands in front of them and performs – he says, 'She's got a great wee voice but what a fucken boring song.'

Ma clunks the fella on the side of the head.

'Get the fuck out,' she says.

'Darlin,' the guy says.

'Out,' she says, and she pulls him up by his collar and bundles him through the door.

'She was singing for you, you miserable cunt,' she says, and slams the door after him.

Ma walks back into the living room, laughing. She sits down and looks at May-Belle with a smile on her face, shaking her head slowly, like there's a child just too good to behold.

'Come here and sit on my lap and sing for me,' she says, patting her knee.

'What song would you like?'

Ma says, 'The one you were singing before that ignorant prick interrupted you.'

'Ok. Where's dad?'

'I don't know,' she says. 'He should be home soon.'

*

Not long after singing a few tunes for Ma, helping her doze off, a knock came to the door. On the step there was a tall, skinny policeman with this baby-bird head poking out of a green collar. He asked May-Belle if he could come in. He didn't wait for an answer but marched into the living room like he owned the place.

'Mrs Mullholland,' he says, with a bit of a bark in his voice, 'Mrs Mullholland, wake up, please, it's the police.'

Ma had fallen asleep on the couch. She sat up a bit, looking about her, with the slabbers all crusty round her mouth, and sleep-sticky yellow blears in her eyes. She made a walrus sound.

Ma had picked up some of Dad's Glasgow expressions and she said, 'Oh fuck no, not the polis.'

'Your man has been arrested,' the lanky cop says.

'What for?' she screams. 'Where have you bastards got him?'

The cop nods toward May-Belle and says, 'You should watch your mouth, love.'

Ma'd often come down with the hysterics. She'd scream and cry and lash around hitting folk and breaking things, and then take to her bed and sleep.

Once the cop left and she'd had her dose of the head-staggers, she sent May-Belle up the road to fetch auntie Mary – not a real auntie, mind, but a friend who went drinking with her – and sure enough, Ma was in her bed by the time Mary led May-Belle back to the house.

Mary, who had a bucket-shaped haircut, took May-Belle to the chemists to get a prescription to calm Ma down. Once she'd doled out pills and had a chat with Ma to make sure she was alright, auntie Mary made some sandwiches, left them on the living room floor and went home. And there May-Belle sat – in front of the food. There was no TV or nothing to do, so she dandered outside. It was around seven. There was a group of wee boys at the bottom of the street, playing with their toy cars. She wandered down and stood watching them. She picked a thick ribbed leaf from a patch of grass. Dad had shown her how to put it between her thumbs and blow so it made a mad kazoo noise.

Every time the boys pushed their cars fast along the pavement, May-Belle laid on the lips and this leaf gave out a big parp. The wee lads started laughing and May-Belle showed them how to do the trick and make the noise. One wee fella, with a mess of black hair, said, 'Race cars against me.' He handed over this crappy looking rusted yellow and black motor with a wee man sitting in the driver's seat, and took a new red sports car for himself, and the race was on.

The cars whooshed down the hill, swerving obstacles – twigs and stones and tin cans. The wee fella says, 'You're a good player.'

'Aye, aye,' says May-Belle, and as they start talking the wee boys all get called in for bed.

Back at the house – with Ma dead to the world – May-Belle sat on her mattress wishing the sun outside would finally set in the sky for it was stopping sleep from coming; and the night would never be over and the morning never return.

When the morning came, May-Belle wandered around the house like a fresh spirit, trying to be quiet but so bored and lonely she felt she might disappear into the carpet, just vanish off the earth as she had nothing to do or say. Later, Ma got up and gave her a slice of bread and a cup of tea and said, 'Tomorrow we have to go see your father in prison.' She took her pill bottle out of her pocket and shook it – it was a deep, black-orange colour; inside the pills were tiny and white.

She said, 'Swallow one. You need your rest before tomorrow – I don't care if you are not sleepy.' She poured a glass of water and took a gulp with her pill, then handed over the glass and watched May-Belle's tablet go down too. They went back to bed together and May-Belle fell into a black pit, lost for hours.

When she woke up she thought she was still in the black pit

but it was just the pitch black dead of night. Ma was sleeping beside her. May-Belle got up and went downstairs – her head felt slooshed full of thick gloopy water. The back door wasn't locked. Outside the stars were up high and icy. It was good to be made to feel so small as they twinkled.

It started to get light and cold. She returned to the kitchen and switched the radio on just to hear something, even if it was men's voices babbling in the corner of the room about nothing comprehensible.

Ma came down the stairs like the White Lady, drifting through the room, her blonde hair paled out by the sun leaching in through the Venetian blinds, her face wan, her eyes milky.

*

Pearse stayed with Gran, at her flat, the day Mum and Da buried auld Barky. No-one had hurt the dog much before he died. He just got sick, puked green, keeled over and that was it. Everyone, apart from Gran, had hit him in the past, though – he was a wild one for jumping up on the sofa and clawing at the skirting boards. Mum liked to bang Barky hard on the nose with a rolled up newspaper, and Da wasn't slow to put the boot into the dog. Pearse was taught to cuff him round the ear as well – for an animal needs to know its place and learn who's boss. The wee cuffs, though, were mild and weak, and Da shook his head at how soft Pearse could be, but said nothing. So, Pearse and Barky had spent years together, mucking about as friends, when Barky died all sudden in the Easter holidays of P2.

Mum and Da stuck dead Barky in the boot of the car, wrapped in a blue blanket, and drove off to Tardree Forest with a spade for the burial. Pearse was sad he couldn't go along, and cried for Barky, but Gran geed him up a bit, saying that a boy of seven had to be big and strong, that death happened and there was nothing anyone could do about it. It was better to learn about death through the loss of a pet dog, than the loss of a loved one. Living entails growing some calluses on your soul.

Mum and Da got back from Tardree Forest and collected Pearse from Gran's flat. The pair of them took Pearse to the Chinese in town for a treat. Pearse had chicken soup and banana fritters in syrup. There was a fish tank to look at. Mum had chicken fried rice, and Da had ribs in red sauce and a curry that was green with loads of onions in it, followed by ice cream with a wafer. They both had a couple of beers. Mum's in halfs, and Da's in pints.

Da asked Pearse what he wanted to be when he grew up and Pearse said an astronaut, of course, and Da said, 'Good – you'll be famous if you go to the moon and if you can't be famous be infamous.' Pearse knew what infamous was: the likes of Jack the Ripper or Hitler or Bonnie and Clyde. He'd seen Bonnie and Clyde get killed in their car on the telly. They were machine-gunned by G-Men and the bullets made their bodies dance. Even when they were dead they still danced when the bullets hit them. Pictures were everywhere of Nazi concentration camps – in the papers, on TV, in magazines. Pictures of skeleton Jews and their corpses piled up in mountains or burned in pits after they'd been gassed. Hitler and his SS boyos made lamp-shades out of their skins and chairs out of their bones. The Nazis were hanged for what they did – and Pearse loved the stories Gran told of the men in his family who'd fought the Germans over two wars. Most of them were sailors – some were from the east end of London where Jack the Ripper killed streetwalkers. He tore babies out of their stomachs and cut off their diddies and noses and put their insides all over them for decoration. He walked about in a cape and a hat with his leather bag, and drove a handsome cab. It was always foggy. In London, fogs are called pea-soupers or the City Particular. Jack was never found and is probably the most famous person who's ever lived as he killed all these people a hundred years ago and yet everyone still talks about him.

He wrote letters in blood to the newspapers, post-marked

'From Hell'.

*

There's not much remembered of the prison visit to see Dad – except one of the women guards running her hands over May-Belle's body, and the smell of sweat in the visiting hall. Dad had a bit of a cry, though, she thought.

After they left the prison, Ma took May-Belle along with some of the other women and their kids, who'd been visiting as well. They were all going somewhere for a laugh. This must have been 1974, and May-Belle's first time in Belfast. They walked for a few minutes and came upon some lads with wee hankies tied around their faces. The lads chatted to the women and allowed them to walk on up the road, past a burning car. The lads waved to May-Belle with their hurley sticks as she looked back at them over her shoulder. They all had shaggy hair and green jackets and bell-bottom jeans and boots – apart from one who was in a checked suit, but still masked. The biggest fella said, 'Bye, pet.' She waggled her hand and said, 'Cheerio.'

The group of women and children wound up at an end terrace house and Ma and the other ladies walked in through rainbow coloured strips of ribbon hanging in the open front doorway.

Inside, a few rooms were laid out with tables, and men drank whiskey and beer. The lady who ran the house gave the kids some cherry Creamola foam – only a few had tasted it before and everyone else thought it lovely, but it was nasty and gritty on May-Belle's teeth. The lady told them to run out into the street and get some fresh air.

The jelly gets runny here – and the past all cloudy – but May-Belle remembers a game of tig there in that lady's front yard with another wee girl about the same age and a couple of boys not much older, and the sound of shooting and sirens. A pair of big green army trucks definitely did whizz past at one point, though, and one of the men came out of the lady's parlour and said something about British cunts. That's sure.

One by one the other mothers took their kids home. May-Belle slipped back into the house as it was getting late and chilly. Only Ma was left, with a load of guys sitting around her, all laughing. The lady made a ham sandwich. May-Bell ate it. The lady said, 'How soon are you taking your child home?'

One of the guys tickled Ma and she giggled and squirmed.

'The poor wee dear is tired, you should take her home,' the lady said.

Ma smiled at May-Belle and said, 'Och wee darlin', and stood up and walked her outside by the hand. She pushed the door over behind them, and knelt down, pinching the back of May-Belle's neck – pressing her forehead right into May-Belle's nose.

'We'll fucken go when I say, you wee bitch,' she said. May-Belle sat on the step, and Ma went back inside. The men let a big 'yo' out of them. It got dark. May-Belle dozed against the door-frame.

A scrap broke out between two guys. They came whirling out the door, with the rainbow ribbons in the entrance flying behind them, skittling May-Belle. One trod on her hand as he threw a punch. She yowled and rolled away clutching her fingers.

Ma came out behind them – one of the rainbow ribbons, a yellow one, is caught in her mouth and there's her trying to spit it out – shouting for her guy to knock the fuck out of the other one. The bigger man fell down and Ma's guy started kicking him in the head. The lady of the house appeared and said she'd have both of them knee-capped if there was one more fist to fly. The guy on the ground was crying and holding his teeth. Ma laughed and spat at him saying, 'What kind of a fucken man are you?'

The lady of the house turned Ma around and poked her in the chest saying, 'Listen love, I haven't fucken liked you since the moment I saw you. Get your bag and get your coat and get your wean and get the fuck out.'

Ma started to square up to the lady, but a guy appeared and

said, 'Go, and take your boyfriend with you, or you'll be in trouble.'

May-Belle, Ma and the fella started off, walking for a few streets. There was rubble all over the road and a fire was burning somewhere nearby, beyond the house-rims, making the sky red with roiling black clouds.

Men came out of the lady's house and followed. May-Belle began to cry and Ma says, 'Shut up', hoiking her on by the hand.

One of the men shouts, 'Tell your wee girl not to be afraid. Just get back to wherever the fuck you came from. Get the child out of here.'

After a minute or so, the guy with Ma says, 'Thank fuck, there it is.'

He walks over to his car and says, 'You get in the back, May-Belle, love.'

The men behind turn around and walk back the way they came.

Ma gets into the passenger seat and she's touching him now like he's a prize-fighter.

'You fucken showed him, babe,' she says.

With the orange light from the street lamps and the red light of the fire in the sky, there's a trickle of black blood glistening under the fella's eye where the other man hit him.

Ma leans forward and puts her mouth over the cut, her lips open and close.

'Where do you live?' she says.

'You don't want to go to mine,' he says.

'Why not?'

'Just,' he says.

'Well, let's go to mine then.'

'That's grand,' he says, and he drives off, out of the city, past the check-points and soldiers and police officers – not one of them stopping to pull him over and ask who either of them are, or test his breath for liquor.

May-Belle falls asleep on the back-seat. When she wakes up, they're in a forest somewhere. It looks like this fella is murdering

Ma over the bonnet of his car. May-Belle screams for him to leave her alone, and Ma turns to look through the windscreen. She's lying on her back with the guy between her legs. Her left hand is wound round in his hair; she points with her right hand and shouts, 'Shut the fuck up and go back to sleep.'

Curled up on the floor of the car, May-Belle peeks through eye lashes at the window above her head and sees the trees and moon and houses go by as the fella finally starts to drive.

She plays possum – pretending to be asleep, even when they try poking and shaking her, saying, 'We've arrived home.'

'Carry her in,' Ma says. 'Put her upstairs then get that sexy arse down here.'

The man walks up the stairs with May-Belle crooked in his arms and says, 'Are you awake, wee girl?'

No movement. He puts May-Belle on her bed.

'Goodnight,' he says, and shuts the door.

Ma's voice rises up the stairs. 'Come on, boy,' she says.

'Shush, you,' he says.

She laughs, and then he laughs quieter, and he shushes her again. He walks down the stairs and shuts the door.

There's not a sound heard for the rest of the night.

*

After Barky, there weren't too many upheavals for Pearse for a wee while. Life mostly centered on Action Men, who are beezer. He had a German and two British soldiers and an American. The Germans had the best uniforms – the auld jackboots and lightning flashes on their collars, and skulls on their hats. On mad times, the Action Men would be taken for a bath and sadly all drown. The Allied ones got balded with Da's electric shaver and had their clothes ripped up and were interned in a concentration camp. The German bummed the British lads senseless at the bottom of the stairs. That was a wild terrible thing to happen. Then the

German tied the bare steel razor blade – which Gran used to pare the auld corns on her feet – he tied it onto a pencil and tortured the American. He cut his wee rubbery fingers off and slashed his back and chest. Later all the Action Men were bad so they were hanged. Men are hanged and pictures are hung, Gran taught. The Action Men were hanged on a step-ladder that Da was using to decorate the spare bedroom. The step-ladder looked class with the dead Action Men hanging from it. They were hanged by the neck until dead and God had mercy upon their souls. There was enough room on the step-ladder for more than just the Action Men so Kermit was hanged too, and some teddies as well.

Da came in and said, 'Jesus Christ, what're you doing?'

'I'm executing my toys,' Pearse said.

And Da said, 'There's something wrong with you, wee fella. You're not right in the head.'

Gran bought a lovely grand teddy bear once which was almost the size of a kid. It'd a stupid bow round its neck, though. One day it sat on the bed and gave lip so Pearse got a big knife out of the kitchen and snuck up on the teddy and murdered it, leaping on it when it wasn't looking and stabbing it in the stomach, then cutting its throat. It fought back but it died anyway. Pearse said, 'Here it comes – get ready to die.' Then he hacked off the big black nose button and stabbed its eyes out. He knifed Snoopy too but wished that hadn't happened because auld Snoopy was fun. Snoopy had chummed him along to school the first day so you couldn't very well kill the poor wee soul, could you?

*

It was a good few months before Dad got back home to May-Belle.

The day after the first trip to visit him, she'd come down with a bit of a summer cold.

May-Belle stayed in bed for a few days. One afternoon, Ma brought the doctor up the stairs. He wasn't the usual doctor from the clinic in town. He was an auld fella about sixty in a brown suit. It was a hot day and his hair was plastered over his head. Seaweed on a rock. He smelt of honeysuckle and damp.

Ma said, 'Sit up so the doctor can take a look at you.' The doctor pulled down the skin under her eyes to check if the sockets were good and red and healthy.

Ma walked over to the window. The doctor said kneel on the bed, and then he stood and took May-Belle's nightdress off. He put his palm flat on her chest and tapped the back of his hand with his fingers, the way doctors do. He said breathe in and out and open your mouth and say ah.

Then he sat down on the bed and stood May-Belle in front of him. He put his hands either side of her knickers and pulled them down. He turned her around – away from him. Ma watched and the sun shone in the window behind her. She said, 'Jesus, May-Belle – the state of your feet.' The man looked down. May-Belle's white socks were all dirty.

The man sat May-Belle on his knee for an examination. Then May-Belle had to examine him. When he laid her on her back on the bed, her head hanging off the side, she began to struggle and scream. Ma came over and said, 'Stop fighting.' She knelt on May-Belle and held her by the shoulders.

Afterwards, her head hung backwards off the bed and the sick poured out of her, down her face, and into her eyes, and onto the floor. Ma said to the man that he could clean up the mess, and then she took May-Belle into the bathroom to wash her and get clean clothes.

PART TWO

Dead Man's Fall

Even though they lived just a street away from each other, it wasn't until they were in P7 aged about eleven, that Pearse and May-Belle got to know each other properly – saying hello for the first time and all that; not just seeing each other kick about the estate. It was after this one night that the Creature from the Black Lagoon didn't come home till four in the morning. The auld devil had been out every night that week and this time Mum locked the door. He started off wrapping the letter box, then he chucked some stones up at the bedroom window. Pearse was sleeping beside Mum and woke. Da started hollering, 'Oi Josie, let me fucken in, will ya.' She opened the window and – conscious of the neighbours – whisper-yelled down, 'Fuck off.' Eventually he hammered so much she let him in as the folk across the street turned their bedroom light on, and peaked out through a crack in the curtains.

Pearse snuck off back to his trampy auld room and heard them going at it downstairs. He heard him hit her and her screaming back and then him shouting at her to get off. Pearse came out onto the landing, stood there and took out his wee fella, as he called it, his cock or whatever, and pissed all over the floor. Pearse finished pissing and yelled, 'I fucken hate you.' Mum came out and said, 'Get into bed, everything is alright', and Pearse said, 'No, it's not', and Da said, 'Get the fuck to bed before I break your jaw', and he took a big auld drunken charge up the stairs. Pearse ran. Mum grabbed Da by the collar and hauled him back and he fell on top of her. Pearse started screaming and opened his bedroom window and shouted, 'Police, police – murder.' Mum pulled him in and said, 'Calm down', and the front door slammed as Da left.

In the morning, Da still hadn't come back and Mum said, 'Go out to the front garden', which was just a square of patchy grass, 'and get some air.' Pearse sat on the wee wall that separated the Furlong garden from the garden next door, which had flowers in it and a tree, and he saw May-Belle, playing that girly game, throwing balls against a wall chanting icky-sticky dogs-dicky out pops pish. Pearse says, 'Hi', and May-Belle says hi back and adds, 'My name is May-Belle Mullholland.' Pearse says, 'Oh hi Mable, I'm Pearse Furlong. I live here.' She says, 'No – not Mable like table. May. Belle. Two separate words.' Pearse says, 'Sorry, May-Belle. That's a nice name. I've never heard that before.' She replies, 'Thanks, I've never heard of anyone called Pearse either. I live up the road a wee bit. I've seen you about.' Pearse says, 'Aye, I know, I've seen you kicking about too.' May-Belle said, 'Good', and then she jumped about six foot in the air when a woman's voice hollered, 'May-Belle get in here now, I need you.' Her face changed – Hammer House of Horror white. 'That's my ma,' she says. 'I've gotta go. Maybe you'd like to play later.' Pearse says, 'Aye, I would. It was nice to meet you, May-Belle Mullholland.' And off she went, skipping.

Mum came to the front door and said, 'Pearse, can you come inside a moment please. I have to talk to you.'

Mum packed their bags and off they went to Gran's again. This time, though, Mum put all of Da's dirty pants and socks in a black bin liner and grabbed Pearse by the hand. They walked across town to Greystone, one of the other housing estates that sit in a ring around Antrim. They wandered about until they found some ugly box-shaped flats and Mum knocked on a downstairs door and a blonde woman answered. She was pretty and seemed to have just woken up. She looked down and smiled and then went pale and opened her mouth and Mum said, 'Here you are, if you want him you can have his washing as well – and this is his son too, take a good look at what you are doing, you whore.' Mum had lived all her life before Pearse was born in England so said whore like more – not hoor like poor.

Mum stuck the bag in the woman's arms and was off. After about a week Mum took Pearse back to see Da, and the feeble auld slug – for that's what he looked like – the auld slug was in bed with plates around him and he smelt like onions and spuds; he was crying and begging Mum to take him back saying he'd kill himself without her. She said, 'Why don't you ask your son if he wants to come back.' Da said, 'Do you son? I love you and I want us all to be together.' Pearse wanted to say no but knew that wasn't supposed to be an option for him. Still, he said no anyway. Whatever he said, though, didn't matter as Mum went back that evening.

The next day when Mum was upstairs making the bed Da came into the kitchen where Pearse was drawing a wild curly sheep on a piece of paper at the table. He pulled Pearse up off the chair by the arm and shook him saying, 'I'm your fucking father and when I say you are meant to live with me then you are meant to live with me. Understand, ya wee cunt?' He slapped Pearse across the back of the head and kicked him and pushed him into the living room. Then he started to watch football. Pearse had to watch it in silence. He called Pearse a wee poof for not liking football. In his head Pearse called him a fucken bastard and imagined him dead. Bang. With a Colt .45, the auld Peacemaker.

*

Now, the day that Pearse and May-Belle became best friends forever was a few weeks later, or more, maybe – anyway, it was the day they played Dead Man's Fall. They'd nodded to each other a few times so far but because she was a girl and he was a boy they'd spoken only that once. The day of Dead-Man's-Fall – a Sunday – Pearse was at home and so was Da, and Da was in one of those moods where you'd be skelped for looking sideways at him, so Pearse went to sit on the front garden wall and work out what to with himself for the rest of the morning till Mum made breakfast. May-Belle was outside too – lounging around at the top of the street, kicking stones. Everyone knew May-Belle's lot, the Mullhollands, though no-one ever talked to them. Even Mum said the family were dirty tramps, but she said she felt sorry for the Mullhollands all the same too. Da said they were fenian scum, and the wife was a slut who everyone in Antrim had fucked at least twice. The father was hardly ever at home – probably in clink – and he was supposed to be a rotten auld thief from Glasgow anyway.

It didn't matter to Pearse, so he said hi and May-Belle said hi back. May-Belle was pretty with short black hair and a white face and red lips and green eyes and a pointy nose. Pearse loved girls with those noses. It's their noses that make them pretty. Pearse was nice looking too, to May-Belle's mind. Most boys are gangly and awkward like their bones aren't joined up properly. Pearse had dark hair and eyes, and pale freckles on his face. He always stood hitched to one side.

Pearse said, 'You look bored', and May-Belle said, 'Aye, I am', so he asked her if she fancied messing about. 'Aye,' she said, and then Pearse asked if she knew how to play Dead-Man's-Fall. She didn't, so he explained, and May-Belle said, 'It sounds a cracker of a sick game, lets do it.' So they did, and with just two playing it wasn't a competition game, it was a fun game – for voting and judging by others didn't apply.

Pearse and May-Belle were well-matched at Dead-Man's-Fall – though Pearse had assumed he'd easily beat a wee girl. Most girls can neither make a noise like a gun nor pretend properly when they are playing games. If a girl pretends to shoot she makes a really stupid noise like pee-yoo. When boys do it they make a PERRRAEKERRRR!!!!!! sound with loads of exclamation marks. The boys' noise is good like a gun. The girls' noise is just rubbish – wick, like you'd say in Antrim. Also, girls can't die properly when they're pretending. They'll ask to be done in with something dull like an ordinary gun not a bazooka, and then when they're shot they'll sort of topple over to one side, or even worse bend down, touch the ground, sit and lie back. As if that's the way anyone dies.

May-Belle picked being strangled and suffocated and then being stabbed in the back and her throat cut, and when she died she screamed and writhed around. When May-Belle took on the role of the executioner she made excellent noises like real guns and knives and killed properly with her hands, garrotting the auld Spanish Franco way.

Later though, May-Belle could not remember one damn thing about that day. Pearse recalled everything. That was fine by her, of course; Pearse always was a cocky little sod who said he knew it all.

*

The game only lasted a wee while as May-Belle got called in for her breakfast at about half eleven. Pearse dandered back to his house. Mum was in the kitchen washing the dirty clothes in the sink, and Da was downstairs watching one of those Sunday morning religious programmes that scunder your head. Da got up when Pearse came in and said he was off up to the top of the town to get the papers and would be back in an hour and wanted a bacon sandwich for lunch. Pearse went upstairs to find something to play with. Da had jammed his tool-box on top of Pearse's toy-box, though, and it was so heavy it was unshiftable, so Pearse took a wander into Mum and Da's bedroom and looked at the wardrobe where Da kept his army stuff. This army stuff called to Pearse like a mermaid. Inside the wardrobe, there was an entire UDR uniform. Trousers coloured all green, brown, yellow and black in camouflage. The jacket, camouflaged too. Webbing and belts and pouches. Big black boots that could kick your head in, with polished steel toe-caps reflecting your face. There were puttees that tied tight around a soldier's ankles, and a helmet. It all smelt like the army – a thick oily auld smell. There was also a gas mask. The

29

elastic strap pulled tight and hurt, ripping Pearse's hair when he put it on. It was frightening in the mask – hot and dark – and it steamed up around the eye-holes. There was a canister attached to the mouth which must have been a filter for poison gas. Pearse put his hand over it and he couldn't breathe; his lungs lurched, and he panicked and pulled the mask off, ripping a hunk of hair out.

At the bottom of the closet, there were some bullets and army food – special rations, KP, like dried beef stew in a silver packet – water purifying tablets, a billy can for cooking and a flat wide tube of brown pretendy mud to disguise your face when you're hiding out.

Pearse dressed up like a soldier. He had to roll up the sleeves and legs of the uniform. The giant's clothes hung huge on him. It took ages to get the puttees and the webbing on as they were very fiddly. The helmet and boots were wobbly too, making it hard to walk or move his head. The food and bullets went in the clip-on pouches, and all that was needed was a smear of the pretend mud on his face and Pearse was ready to march out the front door. One of the neighbours was walking his dog. He said, 'Hey, boy, are you off out to fight the Provies?' Pearse flashed the big double thumbs-up and ran along the street.

A road, on the far side of a big field that everyone called the common, separated this estate from Snob Hill where the posh folk lived. The common was the size of two football pitches. It ran down a steep slope and bushes divided it from the road and the rich families. In the bushes, Pearse pretended to be in a hide-out waiting to snipe Germans. He'd brought a beezer toy gun with him. It looked real and he was proud of it. It was meant to be an SLR, a self-loading rifle, like the army had back then, and it came with a magazine which held twelve wee grey bullets made from plastic that shot out of the barrel, and a bayonet. Pearse stared down the sights at folk out going for the milk and papers. He got a bead on them, and followed them as they walked, and then waited until they were just about to get out of his line of sight before pulling the trigger and watching them drop to their knees and fall dead on the ground. When he fired the gun the wee bullet flew out only a yard ahead and landed in the muck; Pearse had to crawl on his belly through the bushes – under the barbed wire and across shell-holes – to get the bullet back and put it in the magazine again.

About fifteen people died that day. Some were Nazis who'd been sneaking around corners to liquidate the Jews. Some were Japs with no idea there was a sniper lying in wait to pick them off. Others were folk just killed for fun. After a while the thought of assassinating SS officers and the like was boring, so the targets became monsters, the Sheriff of Nottingham or people he hated from real life like teachers.

Just shooting the neighbours was too easy, though. He changed the game and began playing bayonet charges up and down the hill, killing the fuzzy-wuzzies and the Huns with their pointy helmets at close quarters. The fighting was fierce and bloody when Da's voice clanged out over the common like a bad bell, shouting, 'Get over here, you fucken wee idiot.'

Pearse's goolies shriveled tight with fear. He pretended not to hear and carried on running around. Da came and grabbed him by the scruff of the neck and squeezed and shook him so much that the breath left his body. Pearse couldn't see anything properly anymore – just a burl of pushing and spinning, of air then fists then dog-toothed light; a halo of violence. He got a slap on the cheek, and a punch on his arm and another slap to the back of his head. Then a punch between the shoulder blades and a kick in the arse. Pearse fell. The army helmet slipped off. Da picked Pearse up by the hair and dragged him to the top of their street. There Pearse was, dressed up like a soldier and getting a leathering, and the neighbours must have seen it all. Da pushed and slapped Pearse down their street and threw him through the front door. Pearse landed in the hall banging his head off the telephone seat. He wailed, 'Mum', and heard her say, 'What's wrong, honey?' from the kitchen. Da leaned over and slapped Pearse clean in the face and punched him on the shoulder, then he poked him hard in the ribs, the stomach – wee diamond jabs. Ten good slaps must have flown and he was saying, 'What the fuck are you trying to do, you stupid wee cunt? Are you trying to get me fucken shot going out dressed like that? Do you want people to kill your fucken father, you thick wee bastard?' And he hit Pearse with punctuation, as he finished each clause and sentence.

Mum got in between them saying, 'What the hell are you doing? You don't beat your son like you beat a dog. He's only playing, for Christ's sake – just explain to him why it's so dangerous.' Da told her to fuck off, and then looked at Pearse, saying, 'Why don't you go and suck on yer mammie's tits, ya wee queer cunt.' Mum was kneeling down, holding Pearse's head against her. He'd kept his tears in so far, but he was close to crying now. He looked at Da and said, 'Get lost, you ugly wanker', and then before Mum could get in the way Da slapped Pearse across the face so hard that stars and tweety birds and wee white lights really did appear above his head. Da walked out the door saying, 'You're fucken killing that child by molly-coddling him.' Mum shouted after him that he was a fucken lunatic and that he'd be well advised to try and get himself run over on the dual carriage-way.

That night Pearse and Mum are lying up in her bed at about nine watching one of her detective programmes on TV and eating chocolates when Guess-Who came back home. He was a bit drunk but not nasty. Gran said that meant he'd been drinking beer, not vodka. When he drank beer he was okay, but when he drank vodka the devil came out in him.

Da said, 'Move over', and he lay down on the bed too, and watched TV with them and ate some chocolates and cracked a few jokes, saying things like, 'Moses supposes his arse never closes', which Pearse tried not to laugh at, but after a few rounds of this type of blether he laughed anyway because it was all so wild and dirty. 'That's better,' Da said. He ruffled Pearse's hair. 'You love your auld da, don't you?' Pearse didn't say anything. 'Well,' he said, 'don't you love your auld da?' Pearse's face still hurt and so did his legs where he'd been kicked and no-one had said sorry so Pearse said, 'No.' 'What?' Da said.

'No.'

Da kind of karate chopped Pearse across his hand and said, 'Well, I don't fucken love you either, ya cheeky wee guttersnipe, who the fuck could love a cunt like you?'

The pain went marrow deep. Pearse leaped up screaming, holding his fingers. Da looked scared and said, 'Aah, you're ok, son, now, calm down, it was only a wee slap. I'm sorry.' Mum had to take Pearse to hospital in their crappy yellow car with the black roof that looked like a dilapidated bee. Da wanted to drive but Mum said, 'No, you're drunk, you're a fucken disgrace.' At the hospital, there was x-raying and the doctor said, 'Your little finger has a hairline fracture.'

Truth be told, Pearse's hand wasn't that badly hurt by now – though it was still a bit sore. It certainly wasn't broken or fractured. He could move his fingers fine. Of course, he hadn't shown that to the doctor and nurse. He'd just been laying it on thick – pretending his hand was bust up – to scare Da. He had no explanation why the hospital people believed his lies and thought his hand was fractured. The doctor and nurse dressed his hand up with bandages and a metal splint.

On the drive down to casualty Mum said to Pearse, 'Tell the doctor whatever you want. Tell the truth if you think it's right.' When the nurse, who examined Pearse before the doctor came, asked what had happened, Pearse said, 'Me and my Da were playfighting in the living room and he karate chopped my hand by accident.' The nurse laughed and said, 'What a silly daddy you have.'

She was beautiful but brain dead.

*

May-Belle had watched the auld bastard knock seven shades out of Pearse from her front room window. The next day was a bank holiday Monday. She left her house at nine and walked up and down the street, counting her steps. Busted hand or not, Pearse had been grounded for a month. Mum let him go out anyway, though, that morning, as soon as Da left to head down the town to the pub. Pearse took the bandages and splint off his hand in the bathroom before he went out, and stuck the dressing in his pocket so he could put it back on when he came home from play that night. He'd probably have to keep up the fib for a week or so until he could say his hand was all better, and get free from the fakery for good. It was a price worth paying.

May-Belle stood at the top of the street in a wee black dress with a white collar and white tights and shiny patent black shoes. She gave the thumbs up as Pearse walked towards her. 'Your Da's a right wanker,' she said. 'Aye he is,' Pearse said, and asked what her father was like, and she said he was great when he was about but Ma was a fucken beast.

She said, 'Ma and Dad are out', so they went up to her house. The place was rotten. All the blinds were drawn so it was spooky and gloomy inside. There were only a few sticks of furniture about, black rings round the toilet and the sink, and a stink like chips and beans and onions. May-Belle slept under coats in her room. Upstairs, May-Belle opened a door and said, 'This is Ma's wee work room – it's a no-go area.' They walked inside and shut the door. The room was filled with a big auld bed decked out in a fancy red velvet eiderdown. The kind of bed you'd see in a Dracula film with red pillows and dark wooden panels.

There was a cupboard and a night-stand with a movie projector on it, and a pull-down screen about the size of a portable telly standing in the corner.

'Beezer,' said Pearse. He had seen an advert in the back of The Daily Mirror for a movie projector, and Gran had bought one for him too. It came with old silent horror movies like Lon Chaney in The Phantom of the Opera. 'Feast your eyes and glut your soul on my accursed ugliness!' That's what the phantom said.

Pearse asked May-Belle what movies she had and she said dirty ones. Blueys. Pearse said he'd seen dirty books before. Up at the Weary Woods, way to the back of Gran's flat, that's where loads of dirty books are to be found, all ripped and scattered. Pearse had divvied up some pages with a few of the lads from his school once and snuck them home. Addie's big brother, who's sixteen and left school, said, 'You lucky wee bastards – you've been visited by the Porn Fairy.'

Pearse asked May-Belle, 'Are you serious? I do not believe that you have blueys sitting right there.'

She said, 'I have. Wait till I show ye, wee fella.'

May-Belle opened the cupboard and took out a couple of spools of tape. She held the cupboard doors open and said, 'Take a look at all this stuff.' There was a whip which looked just class and masks too. Pearse said, 'Cmon let's dress up like Zorro. You can be the fat Mexican.' May-Belle said, 'Aye right, you saw what your Da did to you for messing with his stuff.' She pointed at the whip and said, 'I get hit with that when I misbehave.' Pearse said, 'God', and then was quiet. He stared at the stuff in the cupboard. There were three rubber cocks lying on the shelf.

'Are they pretendy dicks?' Pearse asked May-Belle. 'That's what they look like,' she said and shut the door.

She put on one of the movie reels. It was called Nun so Bad. It looked like it was made in the 1930s. A fella is done up like a baron, sitting in a room puffing on a big cigar and drinking wine. A servant opens the door and drags a nun into the room. She has the auld penguin outfit on, with the wimple and all. Words come up on the screen saying something like THE WICKED BARON ORDERS HIS SERVANT TO MAKE THE YOUNG NUN UNDRESS! After the words, the servant pulls the nun about a bit and then she's naked with the baron's chap in her mouth. The servant takes a whip and starts to beat her and then gets one of those big rubber cock-things and goes at her with it. She's still got the baron's lad in her mouth too, for God sake. The servant starts whipping her again and then the baron stands up and there's spunk in her mouth and up her nose and in her eye and all over the bloody place like serious snotters.

Pearse says to May-Belle, 'Holy Jesus, May-Belle is that spunk?' And she laughed. 'It's called cum,' she said. She was sitting cross legged on the floor. When she laughed she doubled over with her head in her lap, hiding her face, and she couldn't stop giggling. She said, 'My Ma whips fellas like that.' Pearse said, 'What?' And she said, 'My Ma whips fellas like that in this room.'

Pearse looked at the nun.

'If you're a pal you'll never tell anyone,' May-Belle said. Pearse promised. 'I wouldn't have told even if you hadn't asked,' he said. 'I know how to keep a secret. Never tout on a mate. There's nothing worse than a grass or a squealer.'

They went downstairs for some juice. Pearse didn't want to sit in Ma's creepy auld room anymore so suggested a game of Brides of Dracula instead. As they climbed back up to May-Belle's room, Pearse slipped because the stairs didn't have proper carpet laid down, just bits of auld lino coming loose from its tacks. He shot his hand forward to break his fall and stop the drink from spilling. May-Belle was in front – two stairs ahead. As he fell forward his hand ended up her skirt, between her legs.

Pearse said, 'Woops, sorry May-Belle.'

May-Belle laughed and said, 'You're blushing Pearsey. Were you trying to slip the hand on me?'

Pearse said, 'What's that mean?'

And she said, 'Trying to feel me up. Get a grope.'

Pearse laughed. 'I know what get a grope means, May-Belle.'

'I've got nothing to grope, though,' May-Belle said.

Pearse didn't reply and tried to carry on up the stairs. May-Belle blocked his way, though, and said, 'And anyway, you're The Back Street Groper for feeling me up.'

She laughed and ran to her room and he laughed too and ran after her. They chased each other around – him being Dracula and she one of the brides – trying to bite necks and wrestling. Pearse quit the Rowdy Yates stuff after a while and said he had to go to the toilet. He locked the toilet door and smelt his hand. It smelt lovely like perfume but also nasty like a rotten orange. Together, though, the two smells made him want it all the time. He washed his hand and smelt it again – the smell had died away, but was still there a little, not gone completely. Da, when he's having his rare funny half-hour, would sometimes stick his middle finger under Pearse's nose and say, 'Smell my new girlfriend, wee lad.'

May-Belle waited and looked in her dressing table mirror, humming to herself. Pearse returned. Her smile lit on his face.

May-Belle's house was giving Pearse the heebee-jeebees by now, however. He kept wondering if Monster Ma would come back and beat them with her whip or make them do something horrible with her rubber dicks like stick them up their arses so he said to May-Belle, 'I fancy going for a walk down to the factories.'

May-Belle felt a bit sorry for him as he looked guilty so she said, 'Grand idea.'

'Then c'mon,' said Pearse, 'we'll have a great adventure. I've got a hut down there, you can join and we can start a camp fire.' She thought that was a cracker plan and asked who else was allowed in the hut. Pearse said no-one – as no-one else had ever been there with him. It was his wee place – den and hide-out. They went downstairs. May-Belle fetched a box of matches and handed them to Pearse. He shook the box and put them in his pocket and May-Belle gave a wonky squint wink.

To get to the factories, it's a long walk to the other side of the estate. The destination isn't actually factories – they're just auld warehouses but the kids call them the factories. There's about twenty big warehouses, each the size of a school, belonging to a lorry company. Pearse said, 'Mum works there as a clerk.'

Neither of them were allowed this far from home. The factories were a couple of miles away and a little girl called Kelly had been murdered nearby about a year before. They'd found her body chopped up in a water tank in the attic of a local house. The man who killed her was supposed to be a mad slavering psycho. After he strangled her, he'd eaten dead dogs and had sex with wee Kelly's corpse. 'Serious,' said Pearse. 'No joke.'

On the way to the factories there's the hole where the killer's house used to be. When the cops got him, the people in his estate petrol-bombed his home with his mother inside, and then it was bulldozed. All that's left is a black gap in the row of houses where his home stood – an auld tooth that's been knocked from a jaw. They sent him to the nut-house up the road – Holywell Hospital, where all the adult loonies live. They keep the young ones at Muckamore Abbey.

Gran told stories meant to scare Pearse into never going so far away. One tale was about Katie Cloaky and Gulliver Riggs. These two were a man and a woman who weren't married and travelled around Ireland about the time Gran was born at the turn of the century. Guillver wore a green velvet suit and they drove a horse and cart like a gypsy wagon. They'd stolen children from the town of Toomebridge, where Gran was raised on a farm. Gran never explained what happened to the children but the guess was that Katie Cloaky and Gulliver Riggs were like Ian Brady and Myra Hindley up on their Moors.

Pearse was telling May-Belle about Katie Cloaky and Gulliver Riggs and how they kidnapped youngsters when May-Belle said, 'Aw Pearsey, don't be such a fanny. That story isn't scary at all.' Pearse said, 'It's flippen terrifying, and if I'm a fanny then you're an auld faggot.' May-Belle laughed and said, 'You're calling me a queer – a girl can't be a queer.' So Pearse said to her, 'Well, a boy can't have a fanny – so what're you talking about?' She flicked him on the ear and said fanny and ran off. Pearse chased after her and got her by the arm and swung her round shouting auld faggot. They raced each other across the fields on the way to the factories, shouting fanny and auld faggot and playing tig. If she caught and tigged Pearse she got to call him fanny and if he tigged May-Belle then he could call her auld faggot. The grass in the field was long and hadn't been cut by the council men and they kept tripping and falling over because they were running so fast. May-Belle was singing a song from Top of the Pops at the top of her voice.

Pearse got a stitch in his side and May-Belle said, 'That proves you're a weak wee fanny.' Pearse said, 'Fuck off, ya sick auld faggot', and fell back in the long grass – disappearing. May-Belle knew he was planning to pounce on her so she tried hard not to laugh. Pearse could hear her snigger though. She couldn't see him as the grass was about three foot high and he crawled on his belly towards her. He sneaked up hidden by the grass and got her around the legs and pulled her over. May-Belle was a champion at play-fighting. They wrestled with each other like they were the stars of Saturday afternoon telly. Pearse shouted, 'I'm Big Daddy and I'm gonna kick your arse.' May-Belle grabbed ahold of him and said, 'Fuck you – I am Giant Haystacks and I am gonna tie your balls round your neck.' Pearse managed to get her down and lay across her, pinning her to the ground. One two three she was out. 'I won,' he said. He told her he was gonna fart on her face but didn't and got up, and May-Belle leaped on him from behind knocking Pearse over onto his belly. She put him in an arm lock that hurt like buggery and said, 'Submission, do you submit Pearsey?' 'No,' he said, and she made the arm lock tighter and said, 'Submit, Big Daddy, ya bastard, you're beat. Say uncle.'

'Uncle, uncle, submission, you're killing me, Hay-Stacks, ya fat bollocks,' said Pearse, and May-Belle let him go. Pearse said, 'Well, that's a draw', and she said aye, offering a hand, but then Pearse spun her and pushed her so she fell over flat on her face and he ran off towards the factories shouting, 'Got ye, ya faggot.'

He was far in front of her and the wind was whipping her words – 'Oi, hauld up there, fanny boy' – whipping the words away out behind her to the sky and back to their streets.

To get to the hideout at the factories, you come off the road, cross an auld field, cut through some trees and slither down a ten foot trench. You're hidden on all sides by the factory wall, the trench and the trees. It's a grand place for making huts or just ya-ho-ing around because no-one can see you or hear you.

Pearse disappeared through the trees, and May-Belle pounded on behind him, looking for the secret entrance place.

Pearse stopped at the top of the trench – there was a wee boy down in the dip. He was about four and playing with his toy cars going, 'Brrmm brrmm', as he pushed them about in the muck.

The wee boy was covered in dirt and had bogies coming out of his nose – he kept curling his tongue up to lick the snotters off his lip. May-Belle crashed through the trees now.

'Who are you?' she said to the wee boy. He looked up and then looked down again and carried on playing with his cars. Brrmm. Brrmm.

'Oi, fuckface, who are you?' May-Belle shouted. 'You better tell me or I'm gonna go get your ma.'

The wee boy says, 'Martin.' And May-Belle says, 'Well, you should ask if you can play in other people's huts, Martin. This is our hut so fuck away off before I have your guts for garters.'

Pearse said, 'Aye, it's our hut. Fuck right off.'

The wee boy says nothing. May-Belle skittered down the trench on her arse to where this Martin lad was standing, thumb in his gob. Pearse climbed down after her and said, 'Say sorry to us, Martin, ya wee shite, and we won't hit you.'

'Say it,' says May-Belle. Then she says, 'Eugh, look at you licking your snotters, you dirty fucken wee pig.' The wee boy takes his thumb out of his mouth and starts to cry. May-Belle walks up to him and grabs him by the hair and slaps him and says again, 'Say it. Say sorry.' The wee boy is crying hard now and shaking and looking round him for grown-ups. Pearse says, 'Stop being such a fucken wee jessie, Martin, and just say sorry and you can play here if you're good.'

The wee boy says, 'I want my mummy,' and May-Belle hits him such a punch in the face that he falls over. 'I'm sorry,' he says, not properly but all baby-talk like 'am swowwy'. May-Belle aims a toe-pointer of a kick at his back and he screams out something that's meant to be, 'I want to go home.' May-Belle says, 'You aren't going home. You aren't going fucken nowhere, Martin. You wanted to play here so play,' and she picks up the toy cars and throws them at him. She kneels down beside where he's lying and says, 'Fucken play', and then grabs his cheeks with one hand and squeezes hard making a fish-face out of his lips.

He looks at her with poppy-out eyes and she screams, 'PLAY! PLAY! PLAY!' into his face, her hand slapping him each time she says the word. She starts hitting him all over, punching him in the head and the body, and his face goes red and he falls back flat on the ground. May-Belle gets on top of him and says, 'I'm gonna kill you, wean.' Her hands are round his throat.

May-Belle's face is strange – white, blank and still. She's looking at nothing and talking to herself while she's shaking him by the throat and his head snaps about. 'It stops the air getting into the lungs,' she says. 'It makes their throat go down.'

Pearse says, 'May-Belle let the wee fella go.' But she's vanished somewhere behind her eyes. Pearse grabs the wee boy and pulls him away from her. She falls to one side, like a short-circuited robot. 'Pearsey, what are you doing?' she asks without looking at him.

Pearse says, 'You'll kill the wee lad, May-Belle.' Then she sits up, and roars 'Fuck off' – and stays there crying.

Pearse gets the boy to his feet and ask if he's alright. Martin starts to cry and says he wants to go home. Or in baby-talk it's like, 'wanna go ome'. Pearse pushes him and says, 'Well, go fucken home then, ya wee cunt. Now. Before you cause any more damage.'

Martin walks off a few yards and then turns to come back and says, 'I want my toys.' Pearse picks up an auld stone as big as his hand and shouts fuck off and throws it at him.

It hits Martin square above the eye and he falls down like he's dead. There's blood pouring out of his head. May-Belle says, 'Shit, we've done it now, Pearsey.' Pearse says, 'We've not done nothing', and runs over to wee Martin lying tombstone. 'Why did you start this May-Belle?' Pearse said. 'What do you know about dead people? Is he dead?'

'You have to check their heart and their breathing and their pulse,' says May-Belle. Pearse laid his ear on Martin's chest but couldn't hear a heart-beat. He held Martin's wrist but couldn't feel a pulse. He put his hand to Martin's mouth to feel for air but there wasn't any breath. 'I think he's dead, May-Belle,' Pearse tells her. 'Oh flippen hell, May-Belle.' He stood up and walked about and started to cry a little.

May-Belle says, 'Don't you be a jessie too, Pearsey. Let me see.' She repeats the same actions, but this time deft and delf – checking his heart and his pulse and his breathing. She says, 'Aye, he's alive.' May-Belle shows Pearse. She takes his hand and puts it on Martins's chest and Pearse feels the heart beating. Then she puts Pearse's fingers on Martin's wrist, in a special way, and there's a wee fluttery patter and a sickening at the thought of the blood pumping through veins under skin. May-Belle holds the back of Pearse's hand to Martin's lips for ages and breath leeches out. 'He was just breathing slowly,' May-Belle says. 'You have to wait. Stop crying. You're ok.'

'I wasn't crying,' Pearse said. 'I was just scared a wee bit. Let's get out of here.'

'Wait,' says May-Belle. She lies the wee boy over on his belly with his head to the left and says, 'That's in case he pukes. He won't choke to death that way. Dad showed me that.' May-Belle grabs Pearse by the hand and says, 'Come on.' There's a stain on Martin's trousers where the wee boy has pissed himself.

'We better make a plan,' says May-Belle, 'let's go back to mine.' Pearse said, 'If you want.' He wouldn't have been able to take her spooky auld place after what'd gone on, May-Belle knew, so she asked if there were any other hide-outs round and about the estate. Pearse says, 'Of course, we should go to the railway carriages.' May-Belle says, 'Great idea.' They scramble up and out of the trench and head away from the factories towards the carriages – running, running.

If there's no dandering and dawdling, the four auld abandoned train carriages that kids from the estate use as a den are about a half hour away from where Martin's lying – a couple of miles, give or take. They're on waste ground near the railway station. At night, older boys and girls use them for drinking and sex. There's rubber johnnies and empty cans of beer and bottles of wine all over the place. In the daytime, though, they belong to kids.

Pearse and May-Belle have given it pelters, sprinting far away from the factories. They're almost there at the carriages already. All they have to do is cut through a wee woody glade and there's the wasteland by the railway station appearing. They haul up into the carriages as quick as Jack Flash. The old train seats inside are wet and smell like rats. May-Belle hunkers, and then smoothes the hem of her skirt across her thighs. Pearse stands and coughs and says a bit feebly, 'What are we going to do?'

May-Belle says, 'We have to get an alibi.'

Pearse had flicked through a lot of Da's detective magazines – like True Crime, with the tied-up ladies on the cover – and considered himself pretty smart when it came to words such as alibi. Most kids wouldn't have known a legal term if it popped up in their soup, but May-Belle did.

'What about the orchard up on Snob Hill?' Pearse suggests. 'We could go there and get caught stealing apples and then that'll give us our alibi.'

May-Belle sits thinking and then says, 'Well, why do we have to do something bad? Why can't we just be seen somewhere? If we go robbing apples we'll get in more trouble.'

'But no-one will remember us unless we get into trouble,' says Pearse, 'and no-one is going to think we did two bad things in one day – especially if one is a wee daft one and the other one's a big serious one.'

May-Belle says, 'Aye, you're right. Okay.' And then pulls Pearse down on his hunkers beside her and says, 'Pearsey, we can never tell anyone about this. We have to be the best of friends forever. It's our gang and we have to be blood brothers.'

'Blood brother and blood sister,' he says laughing. 'You can't be my brother.'

'Well, you can be my sister, you fanny,' she replies.

'Faggot,' he says back. 'Maybe brothers is right.'

Pearse gets a piece of broken wine bottle and says, 'Right let's do it then. You go first seeing how you suggested it.'

May-Belle says fine and takes the glass and cuts a nick in her palm about half an inch long. She hardly even winces. It goes in deep and red black blood oozes out.

She passes the broken glass and says, 'Now you.'

'I remember falling down a hill when I was about six and my knee landed on glass,' says Pearse. 'The blood poured out and a little bit of meat that looked like a bogey plopped out of the wound. When I came back from getting stitches in my leg one of the kids hanging about said a bird had eaten the wee bit of bogey meat. It made me want to boke up, May-Belle.'

'Pearsey, stop talking and don't be such a jessie,' says May-Belle, holding her slit hand up to the light to show off the blood. Pearse shut his eyes and tried to cut but he couldn't go deep enough even to break the skin. May-Belle took the glass from him.

'Here, give it here,' says May-Belle, a bit of testiness in her voice. 'Keep your eyes shut and I'll do it.'

'Don't cut too deep,' Pearse says, all pleady. 'I might bleed to death.'

May-Belle's skin went cold at the thought of nicking one of his veins and Pearse turning whiter and whiter; Pearse getting weak and dying like a feeble auld dog in the railway carriages surrounded by a pool of his own blood.

She says, 'Look at me', and holds his gaze, singing that Adam and the Ants song Kings of the Wild Frontier to distract him. Pearse feels a quare auld stab right in the palm of his hand and looks down. There's blood running over his wrist and onto the cuff of his shirt.

'Ahhh-fucken-ahhhh,' says Pearse, shaking his hand about – blood flying out. He stands up and hops from one foot to the other in pain and May-Belle takes a fit of laughter.

'Stop laughing,' he says. 'I'm in agony here. It's sore.'

May-Belle says, 'Come here before the blood stops. It wasn't too deep. We have to put our hands together while they're still bleeding.'

Pearse crouches down beside her, still saying ouch and oooh, and May-Belle pats him, and they put their hands together and say, 'Friends for life.' And May-Belle adds, 'Best friends forever. Blood brother and blood sister.'

Both have it in their minds to kiss the other on the cheek, but they hesitate and then stand up. Pearse coughs and says, 'Well, let's get out of here and go up to the orchard.'

'Wait,' says May-Belle, 'our fingerprints are all over this carriage, and your blood from your flapping about. If the police find them then they'll know we were here today and our alibi won't work.'

'But what's that matter, May-Belle?' Pearse asks. 'It doesn't matter us being here.'

'It might,' she says. 'How do you know it won't?' And she casts one of her wonky squint winks and an eye-brow waggle, and so Pearse nods and says, 'Fair enough.'

He takes the box of matches out of his pocket and shakes it at her. 'Okay,' she says and claps. Pearse jumps out of the carriage and fetches some wood lying nearby. May-Belle stands in the carriage door and hauls the beams and branches inside. They place them on top of an auld mattress, lying in there for teenagers to have sex on. Pearse gets the matches and lights the mattress with bits of scrap paper to aid the process and they wait for a wee second to make sure the fire catches. With the worn-out seats and wood and other bits of rubbish in the carriage it starts to go up something beautiful.

They jump down and run off. Half-way up the field from the derelict trains they stop and May-Belle looks back, like auld Lot's wife, the pillar of salt, and there's a huge trail of black smoke coming up into the sky from where the railway carriages are burning, burning. It looks like a bomb has been dropped. 'No-one will ever find our finger-prints now, Pearsey,' says May-Belle. He hollers out a big yo-ho of a laugh and hoists his sore hand in the air – at least now he'd have a reason to put the hospital dressings back on when he got home later. By the time they reach the top of the field, the fire engine sirens are sounding like the three-minute-warning has just been declared because Pearse and May-Belle are on the loose and out and about.

*

On the walk up to the orchard that day with the fire behind and Martin still further away, May-Belle was on wild scatty form, but Pearse was in no mood for games. When he turned his back on the fire, Martin was in front of him, hanging in the air, blood in his mouth and ears. May-Belle didn't see Martin. Instead, she was there codding Pearse on, her nippy wee feet dancing and jigging.

The orchard at the top of the town isn't really an orchard; not like a farm with hundreds of acres for supermarkets and cider. This orchard is just two dozen wormy apple trees owned by an auld git who's a judge or a magisgreat or something. He's like a character out of The Beano if he catches you on his property, wobbling about on a nobbly walking stick in a black waistcoat and bawling his baldy head off, shouting, 'I'll set my dogs on you young rascals you.' The apple trees are in the grounds of his la-di-dah house with the ivy up the sides and the white and black timbers.

A big wall stops you getting into the grounds of auld Judge Grumbly Posh Plumb's house. This wall is about twice the size of a grown man, but it's useless as any mongol with capacity in their limbs could climb over it as it's an auld fashioned thing with good footholds between ancient rickety bricks. The apple trees are close to the inside of the wall so once you're up on the top you just grab ahold of a branch and swing yourself down like Cheeta the Chimp. Then you can go robbing apples like billy-o. To escape – once the judge is on your tail – you just hoike your way back up a tree and scramble from the branches onto the wall and then you're off, lickety-split, damn.

May-Belle was rabbiting away on the walk up to the top of the town – going on about beating the bollocks of different wee lads she hated and saying that if she ever saw that wee bastard Martin alive again then she'd finish him off. Pearse wasn't much for talking. He was shivery shaky and felt like shitting with a stomach full of water. It might've been better to have just killed Martin and buried his body in the trench where no-one would ever find him because with him alive there stood more of a chance of getting caught and sent to prison for assault and battery.

May-Belle wouldn't stop patting Pearse on the shoulder or giving wee soft punches on the arm and saying, 'How's it goin, Pearsey?' – attempting a cheering up. Then she started singing that song from before that was on Top of the Pops. It was by that Kate Bush girl who jumps around waving scarves in the air and hollering like a banshee. May-Belle leapt about like she had St Vitus Dance and rolled her eyes and wobbled her face going, 'Heathcliffe, it's me a-Cathy, I've come home now.' Pearse wanted to get to the orchard, get spotted robbing apples, have an alibi pocketed and get home to bed for a sleep, but May-Belle was up for carrying-on like nobody's business. She'd walk quietly alongside for a minute and then out of nowhere jump in front and start that auld Kate Bush dancing again and yodeling and face-wobbling. After the third time, Pearse could do nothing but crack up and he called her a nutter and joined in. They went up the street whooping and singing Wuthering Wuthering Wuthering Heights until their throats hurt.

At the top of the town, there were policemen and soldiers on foot patrol. Pearse and May-Belle sat on a bench and watched them. The army and police were coming towards them from Snob Hill, heading for the centre of town. The army guys knelt down when they came to corners or garden gates and stared down the barrels of their rifles at cars or people walking their dogs – at Pearse and May-Belle. It brought on a tremble, those fellas looking at you through their wee rifle sights with their finger on the trigger. One sneeze or a fart or a car back-firing and they might have shot your head off.

The cops walked slowly up the street; their hands on their guns in the holsters on their hips. Others carried snub-nosed machine-guns in the crooks of their arms like wee babies. The army guys were in the usual auld camouflage that they wore. These boys weren't in the UDR or from round here though. They had those Scotch berets on. Funny long auld-fashioned looking hats that ran down the centre of their heads with white and red checks and a long black ribbon at the back. They looked a bit useless those hats; it was hard to reckon how they could stop a bullet if the IRA fancied shooting at them. The peelers wore their dark green RUC uniforms with the bullet-proof vests on top.

There was a great game to be had with a plateful of Alphabetti Spaghetti trying to get all the names of these different eejits spelt out on your toast.

'What a gang of wankers,' says May-Belle.

'Who?' Pearse asked. 'The Scotch boys or the peelers?'

'All of them,' she said.

Pearse asked her wasn't her auld fella a Scottish man and she said he was but that didn't mean she had to like this lot into the bargain.

'Fair enough,' Pearse says.

Two trucks pull up. A grey steel van for the coppers and a green steel Saracen for the soldier boys. Both had the auld iron grilles over the windows in case they got petrol-bombed. These trucks – pigs or paddy-wagons or meat-wagons, they were called – they could fairly burl round corners when they were on the chase.

The cops and soldiers got into their vans, slammed the doors and sped off down the town. It was getting on for about half four and they usually put up a check-point at tea-time on the main road to Toomebridge where loads of wild Provo gunmen are supposed to live. Surely, if you were an IRA man, Pearse and May-Belle reasoned, you'd just make sure you went out to plant your bombs or shoot folk a bit earlier, then the peelers and the British soldiers would never catch you. Easey-peasey-lemon-squeezy.

May-Belle got up and watched them all race into the centre of town. She put her hand up to her mouth and went, 'Keererch'– like a walkie-talkie noise – and said, 'Roger. Pearsey, this is Captain May-Belle, do you copy? Over.'

Pearse went, 'Keererch. Captain May-Belle, this is Major Pearsey, I copy. Over.'

'Keererch. Pearsey, since when did you get promoted to Major? Last time I looked you were just a smelly wee sergeant.'

'Keererch. Captain May-Belle, the Brigadier says you are such a useless bollocks that he's put me in charge of you. Roger. Do you copy? Remember to say over when you copy. Over.'

'Keererch. Sergeant Pearsey, I think you're talking shite. I'm going to have to have you shot for mutiny. Do you copy? Over.'

'Keererch. May-Belle, you wouldn't know which side of a gun to point at me and would likely shoot yourself in the face. Do you copy? Over. Keererch.'

'Keererch. Okay, you can be a lieutenant then. Over.'

'Keererch. Nope. We can both be captains. Over.'

'Keererch. Aye, alright then.'

'Keererch. Dead on. I copy. Over and out, Captain May-Belle.'

'Keererch. Roger that, Captain Pearsey.'

Neither of them spoke.

'Keererch. You didn't say over,' said Pearse. 'Are you over?'

'Yeah, I'm over.'

With the street pretty empty now, except for a few cars chugging about, they snuck across the road to the orchard wall – wee twinkly toes as sneaky-like as Wile E Coyote.

Pearse says to May-Belle, 'Do you want me to go up first and give you a hand over or shall I give you a leg up and I'll come second.'

She says, 'You go first and then give me a drag up, Pearsey.'

'Right,' says Pearse – and he gets his fingers into a crack in that wall. The palm-cut from the Blood Brother and Blood Sister routine opened up. 'Oh Christ,' he hollered.

'Aw, Pearsey,' says May-Belle. She took his hand and dabbed it with the cuff of her sleeve wiping the blood away. 'Are you ok?' she asked. 'I'll go first if you want and help you over.'

Pearse jiggled up and down for a second. 'No,' he said. 'I'll go, I said so.' He sat down and took off his shoes and socks.

'What're you flippen doing, Pearsey?' says May-Belle. 'Climbing the wall like the human fly in your bare feet? You fanny.'

'Shut up, you auld faggot. Watch.'

Pearse pulled lumps of grass out of the ground, spat on his hand and pressed the leaves down onto the wound like padding. Tie the sock around the palm as tight as it can go – and shazzam. Field dressing.

'The other sock's for you,' Pearse said.

'I don't need one of your stinky socks, mate,' May-Belle says, with the nose turned up on her face like someone just gave her a bum-finger moustache.

'Aye, you will,' he told her. 'It's sore. Think of how quick you'll need to be escaping from Judge Dick-Breath and his deadly nobbly stick and savage hounds.'

She laughs and says, 'Aye, whatever you say, Pearsey'; and lets him do her cut hand up just like his. 'Thanks Pearsey,' she says.

The pair scuttled up the wall and sat on the top surveying the mission ahead. 'What's the best way to go about this?' Pearse says to May-Belle. 'The auld boy's got to remember our faces so if ever anyone asks us about Martin we can say, but we were in Judge Whatshisknicker's orchard. And if they check with him he'll say, 'oh I saw those two wee bollockses alright, wait till I wrap my nobbly stick round their fucken heads.''

'Keep it all simple pimple,' says May-Belle. 'We should just go on the rob till yer man comes out after us, hang round for a wee second so he sees us good and proper, then skedaddle before he gets ahold of us.'

'Roger fucken dodger, May-Belle. That's a plan. Who's on the ground and who's in the tree?'

'I'd be better on the ground, I think,' she says. 'Your hand is more done in than mine and that won't help you climb back up fast once it's all on.'

Pearse swung over into the nearest apple tree and May-Belle scrambled down to the ground. She stood beneath the tree. Pearse tore off apples at the stalk and threw them down to her. She pulled up the hem of her dress with one hand and loaded the apples into it like a wee sack. Pearse could see right to the top of her tights, to the waist-band. There was a peek of white skin showing with red welts and bites where the elastic, maybe, had nipped into her belly and marked her up quite nasty. Beneath her white tights, she was wearing white knickers. A seam ran up the centre of her tights over the front of her knickers. Pearse took aim at the wee sack she'd made and tried chucking the apples directly into it. But her tights were wild distracting and he kept missing and even boinged her on the head a few times.

Every time he missed the sack, May-Belle would shout to him, 'you're a dick', or 'what an arse', or 'bloody Nora, Pearsey, are you flippen blind?' She revved herself up in delight at her daftness and the laughs of Pearse, and danced round the bottom of the tree, still holding up the hem of her dress with the apples inside, wiggling about and hooting, making it even harder for Pearse to aim his shots properly. Suddenly, she drops her hem, and the apples go skittering over the ground. She picks a few up, and then bop bam bing she pings them at Pearse, one two three. One skites straight off his head, one gets him on the shoulder and the other hits him on the chest so hard that he loses balance and slips down three levels of branches.

'You are the King of the Fannies,' she shouts.

Pearse is upside down in the tree with tears of laughter running down his face – trying to say, 'Stop May-Belle, you faggot, I can barely breathe.' Everything is topsy-turvy for him. May-Belle looks like she's standing on her head, resting her crown on the sky; her feet daggling towards the earth – slapping her thigh and chuckling. The auld farmer culchie bumpkin types would say she was having a hoot in a haybarn.

Then bingo, Pearse sees Judge Bollocks coming straight towards them. He's still a fair distance away as his house is so posh that you could put about ten ordinary homes in his garden alone. From Pearse's hanging upside down position in the tree it looks like the auld bugger is pelting towards them on his baldy head, with his nobbly stick and runty legs churning away above him. He's a wee beetle on its back running hell for leather.

Baldy-Bap lets a Red Indian style whoop out of him. 'Hiya-hiya,' he goes. 'Get off my property, you filthy wee beggars. Leave my apples alone, you dirty thieves.'

'Away to fuck, granda,' shouts May-Belle.

Pearse gets himself the right way up in the tree and shouts, 'Hey Geronimo, what's your fucken problem?' Then he spies a couple of big auld hounds come bounding out of the house.

'Aye, did the Apaches scalp your baldy napper?' May-Belle shouts, hopping about from one foot to the other knowing he's still too far away to catch her. She hasn't seen the hounds of hell galloping out of the house behind him though.

Pearse looks down at May-Belle and says, 'Get up here with

me – he's let the dogs out.'

May-Belle is up the tree like a chimpanzee and they fling the apples at the judge and his dozy dogs. The pair of them – without rehearsal or one taking the lead – they start singing this song which goes, ooh ooh ooh the funky gibbon, while pelting the auld bollocks with his scrumpers and bopping his ugly Dobermans on their noses with the apples too.

The judge is right underneath the tree now and his dogs are giving it serious barking and yalloping down below. Blap. Pearse gets the judge a cracker with a big doozie of an apple right on the top of his shiny chrome-dome, and a nice auld cut wells up with blood.

'You little fuckers,' he shouts. 'I'll shoot you.'

'Hey gorgeous,' shouts May-Belle, who is standing up straight in the branches now, 'take a shot at these apples.'

She turns round, pulls her tights and drawers down and shows Judge Geronimo her arse. Then she gives the bum cheeks a quare few slaps in his general direction and pulls her arse open so he could see her auld hole and waggles it at him. Pearse can't believe it. She says, 'Have a look in the mirror, granda. It's as handsome as you, ya arsehole.'

Pearse laughs till he can't breath and his sides hurt – sure he is going to die. He's never seen the like of it in his life. May-Belle wobbles and slips with all the arse-slapping and bum-pulling-apart and hole-showing behaviour and almost falls out of the tree with her knickers round her knees. Pearse grabs ahold of her and she gets her balance back.

'Holy fuck, Pearsey,' she says, 'if I'd have fallen my ass would have been grass, and they'd have been the sheep.' She pulls her pants and tights back up.

'You dirty beasts,' shouts Judge Baldy. 'What kind of parents raised you?'

Doink ding. Two more apples on the nut for His Worship and they hop out of the tree and onto the top of the wall.

'Don't mess with us Parkhall kids, you posh auld cunt,' Pearse yells to the judge, who's going mental down below, holding his bleeding head, and calling them brats and animals. 'And your dogs are shite.'They ping a couple more apples at the hounds, and May-Belle and Pearse stick a giant scruncher apiece in their gobs and slither over the wall.

Behind, Judge Slap-Jack is shouting, 'The police are on their way. I know your faces. I know where you live. You won't get away with this. It'll be borstal for the likes of you.'

'Good,' May-Belle hollers back at him. 'I fucken dare you to catch me.'

'You'll never take us alive, copper,' Pearse shouts.

They scoot across the road and race towards their estate laughing their arses off and flashing the fingers behind them – even though the judge couldn't see what they were up to now because of the wall and all that.

'Up ye, ya fucken wanker,' shouts May-Belle.

'Get it right up your hole with a big jam roll, ya baldy bastard,' Pearse yells over his shoulder.

PART THREE

Story-time

The stories Pearse told May-Belle when they were kids – all about these long dead relatives of his – the tales had her wrapped up in him for hours.

These people of his seemed to come swirling through the mist. You could see their outlines, away in the distance, vaguely, getting clearer though as the twentieth century approached and then filling out, each with their own history and feelings – not just auld cardboard cut-out people, from yesteryear.

The Mullhollands went no further back than her grannies and grandas. She'd never been told about anyone who lived before them. And none of her grandparents had ever done a remarkable thing in their lives. Her living grandfather – on Dad's side – had worked as a fireman in Glasgow during the war: that was it, from the Mullholland family vaults.

The weekend nights when Pearse and May-Belle were still little – the nights to come spent hidden in his room, wasting all the hours of darkness alone together, while the adults slept next door – these nights were filled up spinning yarns to each other. Apart from the handful of tales that were special to her, May-Belle's stories would mostly just recount what Pearse and her had got up to, or what they were going to do. His, though, were about this wild collection of relatives that had come before him. He'd been told these stories by Gran, time and again, for he loved to hear them – and he loved to tell them to May-Belle in turn, keeping the tales alive.

'It's best to start with my great-granny – though I never knew her,' Pearse told May-Belle. 'The way she's described, she looked just like you.' She had a pretty pale face, dark hair, green eyes and red lips. Wee and dainty. The family stories, handed down to Pearse, painted her as the belle of the ball. Her father was German, but her mother Irish, and the pair of them raised her in Belfast. Her name was Mila, but everyone called her Milly. She was a bit of a gadabout. Her parents were quite well off – her father being a jeweler – so she made the most of all those turn of the century parties, not knowing that in a few years her German family would be fighting her Irish family in France; though, she and her husband would be dead by then, leaving Pearse's poor auld Gran an orphan.

In the stories that Gran told Pearse and Pearse in turn told May-Belle, Milly reaches the age of 18 and finds herself betrothed, as they said back then, to one of the son's of the richest men in Belfast – it begins like a soft sort of novel full of bustles and bonnets. But then great-grandad – Bern O'Neill he's called – sallies forth into Belfast. This was a fella who'd made his money at the races in Scotland, buying and selling horses and running his own bookies.

He was back inspecting the auld country now, and there was no-one more desirable than Milly. A natural singer, she spent her evenings entertaining the posh people at the soirées held by her fiancé's mother – the type of event you'd hear described as 'the height of the social calendar'.

But Bern happens along and, regardless of being far below her status, he sets Milly mad for him, and they run away together – elope, as they'd say in those days; leaving her wailing raging rich fiancé behind to blacken her name in Belfast society. Her father dies – with a load of debts nobody knew anything about – and her mother follows not long afterwards, and, as she's an only child, like Pearse and May-Belle, Milly is compelled to sell the family home, and there's barely enough left over for the burials and a half decent black dress. Reduced to poverty, is how the family described it. A mighty fall from grace – for then and ever more.

So, Milly does what she does best – and while Bern is trading livestock and taking bets, she hits the music halls of Ireland, singing her songs as she travels along behind her husband to the horse fairs and races all round the counties. There was a music hall in every important town back in those nineteen-o days.

Time goes on, as it does, and after about seven years of these horse fairs and music halls, Milly has had a daughter and then another and then a third and final girl. 'That was my Gran,' Pearse told May-Belle. 'Born in 1905.' There had been a son born, also – first in the litter – but he was one of those infant mortality cases.

'You need to understand all the branchy confused lines in my tree,' Pearse said to May-Belle, when they skulked alone and out of the shadow of adults. 'Gran was a Catholic. Both her mother and father, the singer and the bookie, were Catholics. Her father's family – Bern's lot – back then they were what would have been called Home Rulers or something. They weren't anti-English, like, but they sort of saw the English in Ireland as a pain in the arse you'd be well shot of. How I end up with a Da who's as Protestant as King Billy, I'll tell you soon.'

May-Belle thought it a wild story that you could set to music.

*

Back in the days before she met Pearse, the way it seemed to wee May-Belle – the way she interpreted the passing of the weeks and the months – Dad spent about half the year inside and the other half of the year at home with his family. Life took on a pattern of familiarity. After that first summer, years ago, when May-Belle was about four and Ma took her to visit Dad, she never once went back to see him again when he got himself put away. Dad had decided that the Crumlin Road Gaol – for that's where he usually wound up – was no place for a child.

During their secret nights together, May-Belle told Pearse that except for the time Dad took her away on holiday to Portrush when she was nine to escape Ma, life was a tick-tock clock until he came along.

Tick, Dad would be taken to prison, and she'd be alone with Ma and Ma's friends. Tock, Dad would return and Ma would try to rein herself in and behave. Tick, she'd only manage to keep it up a few months, before vanishing again, off to Glasgow or Belfast or Dublin. Tock, Dad breathed easier, and the house took on a bit of order with regular hours kept and meals eaten together and bedtime stories and no madness.

Tick, Ma would return a bedraggled mess after a while, and she'd cry and say, 'I love youse both.' Tock, there'd be a few days of Happy Families.

Tick, it would start again, with her screaming and saying terrible things, and then there'd be waiting, knowing Dad would soon run low on patience. Tock, all the breaking down began, with her bringing people home at every hour of the day and night.

Tick, off Dad would go one day and he wouldn't come back; he was a thief. Tock, there'd just be Ma and her parties and visitors until he got out one more time and returned to May-Belle.

That was it – life was a slow train to nowhere; a never-ending dream about a sky fading to grey on a rainy twilight. The only kink in the structure was that one holiday to the seaside with Dad – it happened a good two years before Pearse materialised. That summer holiday when she was nine temporarily knocked time's pattern off course for a while. That year, May-Belle explained to Pearse, Dad had gone away for six months at the beginning of February. Each week Ma started her parties on a Thursday and let them run till Sunday.

As usual, men would visit – on Mondays, Tuesdays and Wednesdays. More and more seemed to be coming, that year, though – 1979. Sometimes two or three at a time. She'd give orders to stay downstairs or else throw May-Belle out, and then take these guys up to her workroom.

Other men would stay for weeks at the house. These ones were treated like she loved them, with their breakfast served in bed, and instructions issued to be polite, to treat them as if they were the man of the house. The others – the auld callers – barely got a smile.

She must've had around twenty-five regular visitors, and of those, only three ever called May-Belle upstairs. The old man who smelt of honeysuckle was one, of course; and then there was another – a nobody aged about twenty-five – and a very stern well-dressed fella who reckoned he was someone important, a gentleman, worth something. Each one looked as if he had a terrible end coming. May-Belle played the robot when they were around.

Ma had one last huge party the week before Dad was released from prison at the beginning of a beautiful August. The day before his return, she said, 'Don't go squealing to your father about all the fun we've been having. He doesn't need to know – it'll just make him sad.'

Out of nowhere, Ma decided on a shopping spree and bought May-Belle a cuddly Smurf. May-Belle had watched the Smurfs living in their wee blue town on other people's TVs.

They left the little toy shop, with its tiled black and white front – the prettiest shop on Antrim High Street – and went to Billy's Caff, next door, for lunch. Ma ordered two plates of rissoles and chips and two cokes. When the food came it sat in a pool of its own grease on the plates. Billy was about fifty, with a wild, bouncy, brylcreemed teddy-boy quiff. A couple of young lads were in the caff – baldy-bap skin kids – waiting for chips to take away. They were larking about and sitting on one of the tables.

Billy said to the biggest one, 'Hi boy, those tables are for rissoles, not fucken arseholes. Get up or get out.'

The boys got up and stood quiet by the counter until they were served. Once they'd got their chips, they started walking out of the shop, eating the food from the open bags – the oil pooled at the bottom, staining the brown bag dark and greasy. At the door, the biggest one turned around and said to Billy, 'See while I'm away, why don't you fry your fucken wig, Elvis. It's bound to taste better than this shite.'

Billy drew back his fist, but he was standing behind the counter, and there was no point in even trying to catch them. 'You're fucken barred,' he shouted.

He slammed his hands on the counter. Down one arm ran a tattoo of King Billy on a horse, with the words 'Quis Seperabit' and 'UDA' underneath; and across the muscle of the other arm was the red, white and blue of the Union Jack, and a scroll in weak green reading 'For God and Ulster'.

'How's your food, wee girl?' Billy says with a smile. He had a tattoo of a bird on his neck in pale, blue, faded, drab-sky ink.

The batter was hanging off the soggy rissole on the plate; the Spam fritter pink like a peeled face.

May-Belle said, 'Yummy.'

'She loves your chips, Billy,' Ma said.

'Aye,' said Billy.

Back home, Ma sat beside May-Belle on the couch and said, 'Well, back to butts then. Same old, same old. Make sure you tell your father about all the help I've been giving you with your singing.'

On the odd occasion when they were alone, Ma would find herself with nothing to say, so she'd put old Irish songs on the turntable and ask May-Belle to sing along with her. May-Belle had learned a load of these tunes and could recite them by heart – songs like The Mountains of Mourne, and Maggie, and Molly Malone. Sometimes, Ma wouldn't even bother to put the record on; she'd just ask May-Belle to sing to her and then applaud at the end and kiss her. She'd say, 'You are a star in the making, you'll see your name in lights one day, May-Belle.'

*

After battering Judge Geronimo's head with apples at the orchard, Pearse and May-Belle pegged off across the main road to their estate and headed for home. They split up at the top of the hill where they lived, and Pearse dandered down to his house. He could hear May-Belle's Ma shouting, 'Get in ta fuck, ya fucken wee bitch.' It must've been getting on for eight by then, and tea was ready at six. Da was out getting blootered so Mum didn't mind Pearse being a bit late. Gran was there – she said, 'You're a wee skitter for going out gallivanting around the countryside'; but then she oched and oohed and handed over a quid and said, 'You're a handsome wee darlin, run out to the corner shop and get me ten Sovereign and yourself a bottle of pop and some crisps.'

Tomorrow was a school day, a Tuesday after the May bank holiday. Monday night's tea was always tinned beans and sausages on two slices of buttery toast. Pearse ate and watched a bit of Dallas with Mum and Gran but couldn't concentrate. No-one hardly ever got shot on this show, and it was difficult to get Martin and the fire and the auld judge out from inside his head – the thought of being caught and sent to borstal where the older boys beat the shite out of you and give it to the wee lads up the bum and all that washed around behind the sound of the Americans talking on TV.

Da came in about ten and Gran got up and said, 'Right that's me, I'm off. See you all later.' Da said something like, 'Aye and good riddance.' Mum told him to shut up, and Gran called him a useless bastard and then he told them all to fuck off. Pearse sat there trying to watch the man on the ITV ten o'clock news – bong! bong! bong! Big Ben – talking about this fella from America who'd got out of prison that day after spending nearly seventy years in the nut-house and jail. He was called Paul Geidel, though on first listen the name sounded like Giggle. He'd killed his mate when he was fifteen for a laugh and then Giggle got sent to the funny farm. Later, the State moves him to the penitentiary when it's thought he's alright in the head again. After fifty years or so the authorities were all set to free him but he begs, 'No, I wanna stay, I like it here, I might do bad things again if you let me go', and so they allow the auld lad to remain. Ten years on, though, they get sick of him and tell Giggle to sling his hook. He leaves prison, with his hand over his ancient face, telling all these reporter guys outside, 'No pictures, please. No publicity.'

The story on the telly about poor auld Mr Giggle ended and then a report about bloody Northern Ireland came on the screen; one of those stories where nothing is happening – just a bunch of bollockses yapping away and loving the sound of their own voices. Maggie Thatcher was mouthing off about something and so were the other lot. Pearse got up and said good-night to Gran. That's enough for Da to shout, 'Shut the fuck up and stop talking when the news is on telly.' Pearse said something like, 'Jesus', or 'Oh my God', because it was stupid not to be able to say night-night to Gran when they were all yelling at each other in the first place. Da takes a swipe at Pearse and lays on a not-bad clip round the ear-hole. Gran pokes Da in the belly with her walking-stick, her auld nobbly stick, and Mum jumps in between everyone and sets to screaming. He starts in with the effing and blinding and you are all cunts and hoors and stuff like that. Pearse just walked out of the room and none of them saw him leave. When he got into bed, they were still at it downstairs giving off to each other and shouting and hollering. The back door banged and that was Gran leaving to walk home. Da shouted, 'Just shut the fuck up will ya, ya bitch', and Mum called him a good for nothing whore-master. Then there was a bit of a clattering noise from the kitchen and that would've been Mum in a massive strop making Da his dinner.

Mum had tidied Pearse's room that day and left the window open and thank God there was a cold clean smell. The night-light was purpley and drowsey. Pearse picked up a 2000 AD annual and started reading about the Judge Child being tracked across the Cursed Earth. He fell asleep but woke up when he let go of the annual and it hit the bridge of his nose. The clock, with a fruity looking Mickey Mouse on it for God's Sake, showed it was just after midnight. The auld witching hour. The house was quiet.

Pearse couldn't get back to sleep. He lay and looked at the wallpaper which had spacemen and rockets and planets on it and tried to make up a story about outer space and UFOs that'd help him drift off to the Land of Nod, but nothing would come to mind except a song by that Elton John guy with the glasses and some pretty girl in dungarees. It kept going round and round – stuck – and it would not get out. It was hooked into some part of the brain. He shut his eyes and screamed inside his head to make the song stop and it would for a few seconds only to start up again – the Devil running a continual play loop on his turntable.

It was nearing one o'clock and there was school in the morning. The police and their detectives would be in the school tomorrow asking about Martin and fires and apple stealing, no doubt about it, and they'd be caught – everyone would know it was them or they'd give themselves away. Hanging out with May-Belle would be risky too. It was honestly better not to see her again. Lie low for a while, play possum, then she might forget they were ever friends and not want to kick about together anymore; and Martin and the fire would go away.

Crying under the covers felt a shameful thing, but getting up to see Mum so she'd make it better and help sleep to come wasn't an option as Da would be there in bed beside her. So Pearse said to himself out loud, 'Right, you are taking tomorrow off, even if that auld bastard is about, just lay it on thick with a sore tummy.' A sick day would help keep a good distance between Pearse and the cops at the school, and from May-Belle too. Sleep came then, all of a sudden, once he'd made his decision, and a nest of darkness settled on his body.

*

Many years later Pearse wrote down the dream he had so he could one day tell it to May-Belle, perfectly – when they met again.

'I'm standing alone on an empty planet somewhere and there

is a huge interstellar tornado closing in on me from above, coming down through the atmosphere and sucking clouds and atoms into its whirling mouth – a galactic funnel. Before it takes me, I look up into its gulf and body, and see that light years away the funnel widens out like the base of a vase – and there's ground there on the far side, another planet, Earth. That's where I'm going. It sucks me up – my body stretches across space, streaks half way through the universe.

'Then I plop out on the far side, whole and reconstituted in a normal shape, onto the surface of this new planet, Earth; and the air has settled, the whirlwind funnel worm-hole has gone, and I'm sitting on a bench beside an old lady who is feeding ducks in one of the hundreds of ponds I have walked alongside in parks throughout this country of ours, staring into the water in case the woman walking several yards in front of me just might bear a reflection that is May-Belle's. And the old lady beside me is May-Belle. She hands me a slice of plain white bread from a polythene bag and smiles and says, "Go on, you feed them now, you've been sitting there saying nothing for ages, Pearsey". I get the loaf and tear it up and throw some to the ducks. She watches the birds eat. I roll some bread between my fingers making a wee pellet of dough, a wee bread ball, and I place it in the flat of my palm and flick it at her like a football. It pings off her nose and she puts on a face of mock outrage and slaps the back of my hand, laughing. I move a little closer beside her on the park bench and hold her hand, and lean in near to her ear, and tell her she's a beaut. She calls me a silly auld fool and says she loves me too. We get up and walk home together, her hand holding onto my arm; her on the inside of the road and me on the outside so no cars can splash her with a puddle or young lads bump into her as we make our way to our house. When we get to our house, I realise that we've never been rich. We've got a garden the size of a postage stamp – it's got pretty roses in it, though – and through the windows I can see decent but inexpensive furniture. It's a neat, tidy, well-kept respectable house. There are pictures on the mantle-piece, photographs of May-Belle and I. There's one of her in her wedding dress and it looks as if we're about twenty-five by the prettiness still in our faces. Then there's pictures of us on holiday in ordinary places like Spain or Scotland, and there are pictures of little babies, and those little babies going to school and growing up and getting married themselves; leaving us here and happy in the year 2050.

'May-Belle puts her key in the lock and we walk in through the front door and I see the stairs of our own home leading up to the bedroom above; as I look up the stairs the funnel closes down on my head again, whipping me across the universe and spitting me out once more on to the empty planet I started out on. I go bump, bump, bump on my arse as I land, and I stand and look up and the funnel's gone and the faraway planet Earth can't be seen or reached, and I open my eyes alone in my bed and then shut them again and then I'm asleep.'

*

In the morning, when Pearse wakes up, it takes him a sliver of a second to remember to play the dying duck so he can get off school because of the police and Martin – and to be away from May-Belle forever in case she gets him in deepy for keepy.

Pearse lies in bed for a while and thinks and then starts yowling and mewing. Roger the Dodger is always pulling a swifty and beaking off school – covering his face in his mammy's compact powder to make himself look all ill and deathly pale; using her lippy to put red dots on himself like he's got the measles. Pearse just screeches like a banshee and holds his stomach and rolls around on the bed. He thinks of Public Enemy Number One taking a slug in the guts and checking out the slow painful copper way – that helps him let big moans out of him like he's bleeding away, and cold and lonely.

Even the Unsettled Score falls for the scam. Da looks a bit

interested and worried while Mum stands over the bed hand on Pearse's forehead going, 'God, you're hot – shush my little dumpling, we'll get you to the doctors.' She's for taking the day off work to act nursemaid, but Da says, 'I'll drop him down at his Gran's on my way to work. She can take him to the docs.'

The Furlong family doctor is called Dr Graham. Pearse considers him a flippen dick-head. Whenever Pearse has to go to his surgery, Graham throws around words like malingerer and wonders if headaches aren't psychosomatic. Mum's work – the warehouse place where Martin played – is on the way to Da's work at a crappy textile factory. He won't even drop Mum off, though. That would mean he'd have to get up early as she starts work half an hour before he does – so she has to walk there alone every morning, and he tootles off to the factory all warm and cosy and covered in toast crumbs listening to the Dave Lee Travis Show and the news on the radio in the yellow car – the one with the black plastic roof – that looks like a massive ugly bee.

Mum goes to work and there's time to be filled with Da until he's ready to leave. Da spends the minutes scratching his nyerkins and eating Frosties. Sweet Fanny Adams is said. Pearse gives his belly a clutch every now and again to keep up The Death of Pearsey act.

In the car, on the way to Gran's, Da smokes like a trooper and has the heating on high, so Pearse is ready to puke when they pull up outside the flat and Da says, 'Get out and get inside.' Pearse walks up the front path of the block of flats. Da rolls down the car window, sticks his big bugle out and hollers, 'Make sure to do some maths today seeing as how you're off school, boy.' Then he blabbers something about the 11-plus coming up and how failure ain't an option. Pearse silently mouths, 'Get fucked, ya bum-hole.'

Gran takes Pearse to the doctors and they have to sit there for ages – as they don't have an appointment – with a bunch of sneezy auld miserable folk. There are no windows, just overhead electric strip lighting. It burns the eyes and brain. There's only a handful of comics for kids to read. Two wee girls with snotters hanging out of their heads have gathered most of the comics around them. There's one that they've dropped on the floor near them that they aren't reading – the Beezer, by the look of the drawings – but to get it Pearse would have to go near this diseased pair, and they'd likely give a body the bugs, so he picks up a copy of Women's Realm. It's all about periods and making ends meet and Pearse realises with horror that he looks like a gay wee sailor reading it so puts it down and studies the posters on the walls about rubella and mumps and washing your hands before eating. 'What,' he asked Gran, 'would a creature called Rubella be like if she were a person?' Gran looked worried and smiled and nodded. Rubella, Pearse thought, would be a big, red, fat, mad bitch who rides around in one of those Cinderella coaches and coughs on you, like your an auld pauper dressed in rags, as she goes whizzing by – that's enough to give you the lurgie and you die and she goes home to her chateau for a bit of a ball and a carry-on with her pals Scarletina and Infantile Paralysis.

A snooty receptionist in those funny glasses with the pointy frames, the type housewives in America wear, honks over her loud-speaker, 'Pearse Furlong for Dr Graham's surgery. Pearse Furlong.' Gran stands up and takes ahold of his hand and they walk through the tiled corridors until they get to this doctor fella's office. He is one stuck-up snob, with the wavy Mr Whippy-style hair that politicians have, and thinks he's the boy in his grey tweed jacket.

'Well, Master Furlong,' he says in his posho accent, 'what's up with you this time?'

Pearse has been writhing off and on in uncontrollable agony so Gran is sure he's bleeding to death internally. She says, 'Doctor, he's in a terrible way. He's been crying and clutching his stomach since he woke up this morning.'

'Let's see you,' the doctor says. 'Hop up on the couch, young man, and we'll find out if anything is really the matter you.'

Pearse drags his dogs over to this operating table or whatever it is that the doctor has in his white room, and crawls onto the long line of paper that covers its black upholstery. He shivers at the thought of lying on the leather itself, with no covering on it, where every dirty auld diseased monster in town probably sweated and died.

The doctor does some stethoscope stuff – breathe in, breathe out – and says, 'He's shaking, Mrs Flowers.'

'I told you, doctor.'

The doctor says, 'Well, tell me what the matter is, Sonny Jim?'

Pearse says, 'My stomach, doctor, is in agony.'

'Where,' he says.

'All over,' Pearse says.

'Here?' he says, and Doctor Graham pushes his index finger into Pearse's side like he's digging up spuds. Pearse lets a scream out of him, loud enough, surely, to be heard back in the waiting room, and starts to cry, saying 'Gran, don't let him hurt me again.'

Gran stands up and says, 'Doctor, what are you doing?'

The doctor's voice sounds a bit shifty and he says, 'Sorry, Mrs Flowers, he must be in a bad way, indeed.'

Pearse croaks and turns a teary face up to him and says, 'That hurt, doctor.'

The doctor takes Pearse's temperature and asks whether a bowel movement has been had or vomit produced and Gran says no, and so the doctor takes two fingers and starts tapping around the belly area, as if that's going to work out what's wrong. Then he says, 'I have to undo your trousers, young chap, as I need to feel your groin.' Pearse keeps an eye on the doctor while he has a poke about; at least he doesn't touch the lad or the plumbs, thank God.

The doctor turns to Gran, leaving Pearse up there on the couch pretending to be dying and with his trousers all skew-whiff, and says, 'Mrs Flowers, I'm not sure what is wrong, but it might be worth taking him to the Waveney Hospital to run a quick check in case it's an issue to do with his appendix.'

'Oh Christ,' says Gran, who has a wild fear of operations. She had all – every single one – of her teeth taken out in the 1930s without anaesthetic, and then in the 40s, after the war, she had both her knee-caps unscrewed, scrapped and re-fitted because she had house-maid's knee or tennis elbow or something.

'Don't worry about it, Mrs Flowers,' he says. 'I'm sure it's fine.' He takes a long auld look at Pearse swooning about in agony, and then adds – as if he thinks he's dead witty like Hawkeye out of MASH – 'and if he's not fine, ha ha, well, he'll be in the right place, won't he.'

*

So, as Pearse told May-Belle, this great-granny of his – this Milly Mila girl – she'd turned into one hell of a singer. Not Lilly Langtry exactly, but loved enough to get on any stage in Ireland and have the crowd excited by the thought of hearing her. She was almost famous in the north for doing a routine with a parasol, like a French madamoiselle, singing this lovely auld lonely song called If You Were the Only Boy in the World and I was the Only Girl. Or so Gran claimed.

Milly had contracted TB by now – as did everyone in Ireland, and most places else, it seems, in those auld Edwardian times. Milly was taking on that look: all fever-cheeked, hot with bright eyes; at the back of the damp TB-glaze there was a pale powdered dying white. And written across all of her symptoms was her cough. The blood from her ripped lungs and throat smattering up a white hanky with pink rain drops – like one of those dying poets Gran loved.

One Saturday in March of 1907, they were all set up in a hotel in Ballymena; the horse fair was on and Bern, her husband, was buying and selling – but also hooring and drinking by now. Milly was meant to be performing on stage at the local music hall.

The day before, they had been forced to trudge all the way from Magherafelt to Ballymena as the train from Derry broke down. It's a helluva way; and it was in the rain, and as they found out later – and it's better to give the story away now as it is too terrible to fall on a person's head as a surprise out of nowhere – and as they found out later, the poor woman was two months pregnant and dying.

She'd already had a baby girl, Pearse's own Gran, now aged two – and before that two other daughters: Maria aged three – who Pearse's great-grandad, Bern, carried on his back in the night to Ballymena; and Katy, a wild independent type of a child, who trod on in front by herself aged seven – only wanting her own company and ignoring the lot of them, in the blowing wet gale.

By half eight on Saturday night, when Milly was due to go on stage to do her parasol and singing routine, the woman is a ruin. She's lying on the floor in her dressing room, it's said, twitching with fever and spluttering blood over the carpet.

Her husband is called for. He tells the stage manager to get outside so he can see to his wife. No-one ever said the man was cruel to her with his fists – he was a just a terrible philanderer and drunkard. It's only a guess – and the guess comes from Pearse's own Gran, the dying woman's child – that he said, 'You've got to get on stage, girl.' For the love of children and money.

Sick to death or not, of course she did stand up and get on stage – and she sang her heart out. She sang till her lungs burst – and that became a line in the family story. She finished the performance and walked off, waving to people, who you would these days call fans, and she retired to her room. The children were taken to their mother in her dressing room, and she expired on the divan, Gran said, with the coal fire blazing in the hearth.

Gran would watch old films about glamorous Victorian ladies ruining their lives and dying beautifully on their beds, and say, 'She's just like my mother.'

So with the mother dead, the father decides that he's got to go it alone in the world if he is ever to become the man he dreams of being. He leaves Katy and Maria and Gran – who was called

Annie – in the care of his mother: Suzanna O'Neill, Pearse's great-great grandmother. Suzanna was a widowed farmer's wife who lived in Toomebridge, and was the most evil woman who ever walked the earth; a creature, Gran said, who would poison the family genes until the day when there was not one descendant left on the face of the planet to carry the guilt of her echo inside them.

*

It was a great shining summer day back when May-Belle was nine and Dad came home fresh from prison, a wee carrier bag under his arm, and inside his toothbrush and comb and a spare shirt and a pair of scuffed auld gutties, with no laces. May-Belle hugged him. Ma made dinner and they all went to bed early.

'This was long before the days of you, Pearse,' May-Belle said.

In the morning, Dad decided to take May-Belle swimming. Ma said, 'No, she doesn't have a swimming costume.' Dad reminded her indeed May-Belle did have a swimming costume, and he went upstairs to get it from the dresser.

When he came back down, Ma pulled May-Belle behind her. She said, 'You are not taking her anywhere. I won't let you.'

He said, 'Wise up, for Christ's sake. I'm only taking her swimming.'

They were going to the Forum – the big sports complex – on the far side of town, near the court house, and new police station, and the Castle Grounds, with its deep black ponds webbed in green-yellow slime, beneath dark trees.

'You can't take her,' she says.

'Why?' he asks.

'Because she fell and has cuts and bruises all over her.'

Dad put the swimming costume down on the arm of the sofa, and said, 'Come here, May-Belle.'

'No,' Ma said.

'If she can't go swimming I want to see why,' Dad shouted.

He tried to push Ma out of the way, but she held on tight to May-Belle and fended him off with her other hand. Dad moved suddenly – like a fighting mongoose, boy – grabbing Ma's arm, and turning her around, so he had her hand up behind her back. She was bent over in front of him, kicking down with her feet, trying to stamp on his instep.

He pushed her forward, face down onto the sofa, and said to May-Belle, over his shoulder, 'Go into the kitchen, love.'

May-Belle thought the words 'go Dad, go Dad' to herself, stepped back into the doorway, and stood watching them.

'What're you up to?' Dad said, twisting Ma's hand.

She went demented, struggling and wrestling, till she was turned round facing him, scratching at his eyes and spitting on him and calling him every dirty name that's ever been uttered.

He slapped her three times across the left side of her face. He hit her as hard as he could, and after the third slap, her face red with welts, she just gave up her struggle – sighed and dropped her arms and shut her eyes.

'You fucken move – and I go to the police,' he said to her.

He walked May-Belle further into the kitchen and pushed the door over. 'Where did you get hurt?'

'Outside,' she said.

'No, love – where on your body,' he said.

'Kind of all over. On the back,' she said.

He turned May-Belle around and hitched her jumper and vest up over her shoulders – it felt a fine and right thing to do, and Ma was quaking now; May-Belle was sure of that, even though she couldn't see her.

Dad turned and pulled open the door to the living room. May-Belle followed him. 'How the fuck did this happen, woman?' he said.

Ma didn't speak.

'How did this happen, May-Belle?' he said.

Ma's eyes opened and then closed again. 'I fell down a hill and fell on some nettles, Dad,' May-Belle said.

'I don't believe you, honey,' he said. 'Let me see your legs.'

He asked her to take off her tights and lift her skirt up. Her legs felt nice bare, and she turned around and ran a finger over a scar. The whites of his eyes darkened – blood filling them to bursting. He crossed the room like Spring-heeled Jack and dragged Ma off the sofa onto the floor. He sat on top of her, holding the sides of her head, and screamed into her face, 'What the fuck happened in my house.'

She didn't resist at all. When she spoke to him, her lips hardly parted and her eyes stayed closed.

'Nothing happened,' she said.

Dad lifted her up by the head – his hands gripping either side of her face – like she was a shop dummy, and he dragged her half-way to her feet, pulling her across the room, to the front door.

'Out you fucken go,' he said.

She began to struggle – her heels scrabbling at the ground; her hands trying to free herself from him – and it seemed her neck would snap; the bones pulled on till they ripped at the throat and her head came off.

May-Belle watched and thought, and then said, 'Dad, please.'

He stopped and looked dumb at May-Belle, and then threw Ma to the ground. He stood over her and for sure he thought about kicking her.

'May-Belle and I are going out for an hour. If you are here when I get back I will kill you,' he said.

He walked over to May-Belle, took her hand and led her out the back door.

He let a big breath out of him as they got through the garden gate, and said, 'Let's go to the swings.'

At the park, he pushed her on the swings. She rode up in the air, legs stretched out straight, the tips of her shoes appearing in front of her. He pushed more and she rode higher and higher. Her shoes rose to touch the lower rim of the sun, away out there beyond her. He pushed harder and her shoes came up and covered the sun. She laughed.

'What did she do?' he asked, pushing May-Belle harder.

'I was bad so she hit me,' she said, as she came rushing back down to him.

'What the hell with, May-Belle?' he said, grunting as he heaved her so high her feet went beyond and above the upper rim of the sun – its wee golden circle disappeared, and then popped out beneath her flying heels; she rode back down to earth again, looking at a clear blue sky.

'A belt or a whip or a whippy stick,' May-Belle said on the way up, once more. 'I can't remember which,' she said on the way back down again.

Dad stopped the swing. He picked May-Belle up, holding her around the waist, and spun her about like he was a handsome prince at a ball and she was dancing with him – and they both thought it terribly romantic. 'No more hitting,' he says, putting May-Belle back on the ground. 'She'll be gone by now – let's go home.'

And sure enough, when they got home she was gone. Apart from a few cigarette butts with lipstick on them in an ashtray, there was no trace of her in the house. She'd packed all her clothes, taken her white suitcase with the silver-snap buckles and red satin lining, and vamoosed. A fairy had come in while they were gone and cast its wee wand around and made her vanish.

Disappear for good, May-Belle wished.

*

Pearse's Gran, Annie – Grannie Annie – fascinated May-Belle more than any other of his relatives. Annie had a cursed fairy-tale quality to her. May-Belle had spotted her often walking about the estate – this was before Pearse and her became friends. She seemed the kind of old lady who knew everyone and everyone knew her – a bit of a stand-out, clad in her headscarf and tweed coat, scooting around on her bamboo walking stick. No-one dared mess with her – even the young folk who delighted in robbing and hurting the old. Annie had an aura which let you know she was metal on the inside.

Back during those nights, not yet spoken of, when the pair of them hid together in Pearse's room – and the adults had no idea May-Belle was even there – Pearse spun May-Belle stories about Annie, and what happened to her when she was left to the devices of her evil grandmother after her mother Milly died and her father Bern went off galivanting.

Pearse started to tell these tales of his family partly because May-Belle couldn't stand his ghost stories anymore, and partly because she couldn't think of anything to talk about, apart from her story about the holiday to Portrush with Dad when she was nine, or the things they'd done together or planned to do. She didn't have many true stories to tell.

Under the covers together, still dressed in their clothes, they talked – with May-Belle on the farthest side of the bed, away from the door, so if they heard any adult coming, she could slip out the side and under the bed and no-one would know she was there.

'Tell me a story,' she'd whisper in his ear.

He'd pick up where he left off.

Gran, he told her, was still a toddler when she arrived to be taken care of at the farm in Toomebridge, the property of her own grandmother – Susie O'Neill, a woman with arms like Popeye. This was Pearse's great-great-grandmother. She'd make a child go and cut their own switch from the Hawthorn tree before stripping them naked and beating them black and blue.

The three sisters – Katy, Maria and Annie – were put to work on the farm. There was little religion or politics in the house; the widowed farmer's wife, grandmother Susie, had one goal in life: money. She had wads of white pound notes stuffed into holes in the ceiling above her bed.

She had a rule that if the girls had been good all day – done their chores, stayed out of sight and out of mind, given no cheek – then they would still get a beating, although it would be the kind of beating that at least left them standing. They were beaten regardless, so they knew their place.

It was a cold dreary Ulster farm in the winter, but in spring and summer and autumn, auld evil Susie would be away buying and selling at local markets – this art for making money had been inherited by her son – and the girls would lark around in the fields.

They'd lie on their backs underneath the cows with lumps of sugar on their tongues and milk the udders into their mouths. They'd hide in hay-ricks, and go romping around the pastures flinging sun-baked cowpats into the stream, racing them down river.

Annie's first memory was of her sister Maria falling into the open hearth fire in the main parlour and setting herself alight. The farm hand, by the name of Joe, picked her up and ran with her to a horse trough, dunking her in to put out the flames.

The years went on, as they do. Katy, the eldest sister, would have been about twelve now, and she was doing very well at the local national school. She could paint, sew, speak a little French, recite poetry, dance, sing like her dead mother and generally act the young lady. She'd even taken to learning a little Gaelic from the hedge priests, but that was frowned on by her grandmother who wanted no representatives of the state snooping around her property. So Katy kept that secret to herself and her sisters, whom she schooled a little in Irish too.

At home, Katy was still wild though, despite her brains. One afternoon, when auld lady Susie, their grandmother, was out, Katy was meant to be looking after little Annie and Maria. Instead, Katy is up in her grandmother's boudoir bouncing on the bed, creaking its springs and reaching so high her head is nearly hitting the beams above.

She bounces high, then higher, and tries to bounce off the foot of the bed. The bedstead is one of those old-fashioned wrought iron frames with standing props at each corner. Katy goes boing boing boing as she gathers up momentum to leap right over the posts at the foot of the bed and onto the floor. Up she goes, bouncing forward, her legs flying in the air, and down she comes – the iron post at the end of the bed, going right up her skirt and right up inside her, pinning her to the frame.

She hangs there screaming – a body impaled – and Joe the auld handyman has to come and free her; clutching on to her waist and wrenching her off the bed post like a cork from a bottle. The blood, by all accounts, was up the walls and over the floor and staining the eiderdown red, making the bedroom a butcher's shop of the wee girl.

Katy survived, but she was never able to have kids. At 17, she set sail for America. The bishop who looked after Toomebridge got her a position with a well-to-do Catholic family in New York, working as the maid to the governess of their children. She planned to work her way up to being a governess herself one day. The last rumour the children ever heard of their father claimed that he was living in New York. Annie and Maria believed Katy'd had it with Ireland and was off to America maybe hoping to find the man one day.

She told Annie and Maria that she'd write to them always. They never heard a single word from her ever again. And so that line of the family died out.

Maria would go on to live the quietest life of the three sisters. Like Katy, she got free from their Granny's farm as quickly as she could. She didn't do it by running away, all she did was marry a boy from two villages up the road – a lad from Crumlin who got her pregnant.

The only problem facing Maria was that she was a Catholic and her boy was a Protestant. It was 1920. She was just 16, and the War of Independence was still raging around the country, so Maria had little option but to go for a quick conversion to the Protestant faith. It was no big deal for her as religion wasn't much of an issue for any of the family. As she got older, though, and as the hatred of Catholics grew more bitter in the new Northern Ireland, she quickly put a block between her and her past by becoming the most staunch of Catholic-haters – a Born Again. She encouraged her weak auld husband to join the Orange Order, she drummed the monarchy and loyalism into her children, and she went on like that till the end of her days.

Maria's children amounted to nothing. She had three. The firstborn, a boy, died in the war and never married. Of the two girls, one ended up an auld spinster who inherited the very farmhouse in Toombridge where Katy, Annie and Maria grew up. She died there years ago, alone. The last of Maria's children – the other girl – married and finally had a child herself, a son, but he grew up and died aged thirty, the year before Pearse and May-Belle met, without ever touching a woman in his life. So out went that line, too.

Annie lost contact with Maria for many years. 'It was my Da,' Pearse said, 'who brought them back together again.'

May-Belle shook her head in disbelief that her life would never have the wild romance of these cursed folk.

*

Snuckled down in Pearse's bed beside each other – back during those nights spent hidden together in his room – May-Belle told him that the day after Ma left, when she was nine, Dad took her down the town and everything changed for a wee while. They walked along the High Street, past Billy's Caff and the toy shop. Opposite the old church with the spire, there was a pub called the Ulster Bar. Holding her by the hand, Dad opened the door and called out, 'Jacky, is it ok if I bring my wee girl in with me? I need to see Big Stevie.'

May-Belle loved to hear Dad talk like a man with other men. A voice shouted back, 'Fine.'

It was eleven o'clock. The church with the spire was chiming its bells. The pub had just opened and inside it smelt like bitter stale chocolate. There were two auld fellas standing at the brown bar, ordering their first drinks of the day. Dad sat May-Belle at a table in the corner and said he'd be back in two shakes of a lamb's tail.

He saunters over to the bar, and says, 'I'll have half a shandy. Is he in?'

This Jacky fella pours Dad a drink – filling a wee glass half way with lemonade and then topping it up with beer from the pump. It fizzes over the sides and down Dad's fingers as he takes a drink, and wipes the bristles on his top lip.

'He's in indeed,' Jacky says, opening a door at the back of the bar between the rows of liquor bottles lining the wall. He shouts, 'Boss. A visitor.'

Dad says, 'Can I get my daughter an orange juice, please?'

Jacky cracks the top off a little bottle and pours it over ice into a glass just like the one Dad is drinking from.

'Here you go, love' the barman says.

May-Belle walks over to get the drink and the barman pulls a packet of peanuts off a strip of cardboard nailed to the wall and throws it, saying, 'Catch.'

May-Belle thanks him.

'And how old are you?' the barman asks her.

'Nine,' she says.

Dad says, 'Go back to your seat, love.'

A big man with white hair walks through the door at the back of the bar. His blue shirt is open at the neck. The grey hairs on his chest poke through – wee white spider legs. He moves his head in a sweeping circle of the bar, casting his eye over the world in one short movement.

May-Belle watches and eats peanuts and drinks juice. The white-haired man and Dad shake hands and go into a corner to talk.

May-Belle lays her head on her hand – faking boredom

– sneaking a look at them, snake-eyes, and trying to hear.

Only the odd word, here and there, comes through, though – holiday, readies, job, month. They seem to know each other well. The white haired man acts like he's Dad's boss – a boss who likes his worker, though. Dad's relaxed around him – sharp and quick and funny. He has the boss man laughing in no time; telling Dad he's a great fella.

May-Belle is still leaning on her hand, smearing her cheek up to her eye, when the white haired fella – who must be the Big Stevie chap – takes another one of his roaming-head looks around the bar, taking in creation, even casting a glance over his shoulder, despite the fact he's sitting with his back to the wall; then he hands over two large rolls of money, wound up with elastic bands. Dad puts the bundles of notes into his inside jacket pocket – smooth, like he's stroking a passing cat.

The pair of them shake hands. Dad says, 'Thank you, Stevie. Count the matter paid for already.'

Big Stevie slaps Dad on the back and walks with him over to where May-Belle is sitting, pretending to be bored to death. 'You're a good lad,' says Stevie. 'You and your wee girl have fun on your holiday.'

May-Belle cocks her head. 'Holiday?' she asks, looking up at them.

'Och, Stevie – you've spoiled it now,' Dad says, mock-angry.

'Sorry, mate,' he says. Then he bends over to talk to May-Belle, his hands resting on his knees. 'Sorry, love. I'm a silly auld bugger, but let me tell you, there's nothing like Portrush in August for having the time of your life.'

He straightens up, puts his hand in his pocket and takes out a fiver. 'There you go,' he says, handing it over. 'That should get you a day's worth of rides in Barry's to make up for me being a prick.'

May-Belle has no idea what the man is talking about. She looks blank at Dad, and he laughs. 'She hasn't a clue what you're on about, Stevie.'

'Barry's, love,' Big Stevie says. 'The best fun fair in Ireland.'

'Ooh,' May-Belle says. 'Beezer. Thanks.'

Dad walks her out of the pub, and she starts babbling on, asking him, 'are we really going on holiday', and 'where's Portrush', and 'what's Barry's?' – leaping around him and telling him, 'never in my life have I been to a fun fair – I could flippen die of excitement.'

By the time they come to the top of the town – where the posh houses are near the orchard – he's told her that he plans for them to head off to Portrush on the train that very afternoon. May-Belle tries to get him to race her home, so they can get packed and get going as quickly as possible. He says don't be daft, he's not running around Parkhall at his age beating a wee girl in a race.

May-Belle says to him, 'Och, away Dad, you'd never beat me.'

'Never beat you? I'd whip you,' he says. He wrinkles his eyes and stares down his nose, and adds, 'I'd be at our front door before you even got off the starting blocks.'

'Whatever you think,' she says. 'C'mon then. I'll even give you a head start.'

'Head start me arse,' he says. 'You'll be getting the head start. If we had to race a hundred metres, I'd let you run ninety-nine before I even started just so it'd be fair when I beat you.'

May-Belle jumps around him, poking him in the belly and nipping his bum.

'Away on with you, wee girl,' he says, giving her a pretend slap on the arse.

May-Belle starts to walk around him like a rooster, going 'Bwak-bwak chicken.'

'I'll chicken you,' he says. 'I'll give you friggen chicken.' And he gets down low to the ground like he's a runner taking his marks, and says, 'Right then, Smarty, let's see how you handle yourself.'

'Roger dodger,' May-Belle says, and gets down low too, beside him. They're at the big field now, down near the railway tracks where the abandoned carriages are – about five minutes walk from home, uphill.

'On your marks,' he says. May-Belle gets even lower, sleeking her body, so she can race out of the blocks like oiled fire.

'Get set,' she says, and he looks over at her and laughs.

'Go!' they shout together, and they're off – pegging it good-yins, up the hill, hell for leather. She's fast, but he's off like a cat with a dog behind it. He looks over his shoulder and laughs. May-Belle's not that far behind him, though, but she will never catch him. As they approach the brow of the hill – just a few yards from their front door – he lets a big 'ow' out of him and clutches his side.

May-Belle runs past him, as he slows down. 'I've got a bloody stitch,' he says.

She turns to look at him, running backwards. She slows down and stops.

'Go on,' he says, straightening up and waving forward. 'Go on, and win the race.'

'You're cheating, Dad,' she says. 'Trying to let me win.'

He laughs and says, 'No I'm not.' Then he takes to his heels, sprinting towards her; as he dashes past he picks May-Belle up under one arm and runs with her to the front door.

He's panting and out of breath when he sets her down and says, 'It's a draw then. Ok?'

'Aye,' she says, and jumps up and kisses him.

They go inside, get the big suitcase that had been brought over from Scotland with them years ago, and throw everything needed into it higgeldy-piggeldy. Fifteen minutes later, they're walking down the long winding black path that leads from the bottom end of the Parkhall estate, all the way to the train station. They pass the black hole in the wall where the murderer's house once stood; the man who killed the little Kelly girl. Dad stoops over and helps May-Belle climb up on his shoulders so he can give her a piggy-back ride. She hangs on to him for dear life as he struggles down the black-topped road, lugging the suitcase with one arm and toting her on his shoulders, the other arm across his chest, keeping May-Belle's legs in place so she won't fall.

He lets her down as they approach the station. He slips a tenner from a roll of notes and puts the rest back in his inside pocket. They buy some juice and crisps and a comic and a paper in the wee shop at the station. They walk to the station-master's window and buy two one-week returns to Portrush.

'A week,' May-Belle says. 'Is that how long we'll be away, eh?'

*

The ambulance men are on strike, so Gran has to take Pearse on the bus to Ballymena where this blooming Stone Age Waveney Hospital place is to be found. It's about twenty miles up the road, and the town this hospital is in is full of culchie bumpkins with an accent like dung under fingernails. It's only a short journey from Antrim, but the people there sound like they were raised in a barnyard. While folk from Antrim would say 'Ba-la-me-na', folk in Ballymena would say 'Baaa-laaa-meen-aaah' like they're retarded sheep. It isn't 'six o'clock' in Ballymena, it's 'sex o'clock'. If you had a really good meal they'd say 'that feed was quare handlin'; they call all cars 'motors'; plus, they are ugly – no-one from there is pretty or handsome; the women have straw hair and the men have hems at half mast, like their trousers have fallen out with their shoes, leaving a flash of tartan sock at the ankle.

Pearse and Gran walk up from the health centre to the bus station and wait for one of the blue and white Ulster Buses that go from Antrim to Ballymena every half hour. Pearse is pretty impressed with himself for managing to persuade a doctor that he's dying, so he eases off on the auld screaming-in-pain-in-public routine now that his scheme is a success. People are still looking at him, anyway though, thanks to his herpling and shuffling.

The auld fretting tremor Gran has in her hand is starting to shake a bit too obviously. She rings Mum from the phone box in the bus station and lets Pearse push the ten pence piece into the wee slot. He holds on to her shaky hand. He has a terrible need to tell her that there's nothing to get het up about. But that would ruin the ruse. Gran has a quick chat with Mum, who's at work, telling her Pearse has to go to the hospital. She passes the phone over. Her trembles are worse. Mum tells Pearse to be a brave wee soldier and that she loves him and will see him this evening.

The bus comes and they get on and Pearse lays his head against the window. The engine's chundering whine rattles his head off the glass and makes him feel sick and sleepy and sore all at the same time. He holds on to Gran's shaky hand, running his fingers over the soft skin on her palm to comfort her a wee bit. The trees and houses whizz past the bus window as they begin their Journey to Bumpkin Land.

As the road rolls onwards, Pearse imagines himself outside of the bus, on the pavement, running along beside it as it picks up speed, matching its pace, then bounding over hedges, springing off car bonnets, and using bus stop poles and lamp-posts to swing from and vault from, one to the other; jumping on to house-tops and racing across roofs, leaping towards fields and hurling himself from cow to cow, using their auld black and white backs as stepping stones, never letting his feet touch the ground – for if that happens you're dead, as the ground is electrified. Pearse only dies three or four times on the way from Antrim to the bus stop outside the Waveney Hospital.

The hospital is brown like a Victorian asylum or Poor House, its window-frames painted cream; set in a garden full of spring flowers – daffodils and sweet peas and hyacinths – rotted by the rain and dying now with the coming of the first days of summer. Pearse holds on to Gran, feeling the auld veins in the back of her hand move squishy-fat like worms under his fingertips. She has that worried eye-wandering expression on her face.

'Hey, gran-gran,' he says to her, not minding that he sounds like an idiot, as there are no other kids around to hear. 'I think I'm feeling a wee bit better.'

'Uh-huh,' she says.

'So we can just go home now.'

'We have to get you checked out, honey-bunch,' she says. 'It might be something serious.'

In the hospital, they're made to hang about in another waiting room, with the same tatty magazines and comics being read by other wheezy dying children, and the same posters on the walls. The air is alive with the bumpkin voices of nurses and receptionists and cleaners. The doctors are posh, though, either that or they are Indians or Vietnamese.

Stressed and worried or not, Gran will talk to anyone. If she has to endure more than a moment's silence in a queue she'll start yammering to whatever poor soul happens to be near her. She's been warming the ears of this aged auld dear in a headscarf beside her, who only responds in 'mmms' and 'hmms', for about twenty minutes when they get called to go see one of the doctors in accident and emergency.

'Doctor Ho will see you in cubicle sex,' says the bumpkin girl at reception.

Pearse looks at Gran and Gran looks at him. 'Dr Who?' Pearse asks Gran.

'I don't know, dear,' she says, and walks up to the bumpkin at the desk and asks 'Doctor who or what do we have to see, love? Which doctor? Where?'

'Doctor Ho,' says the bumpkin. 'He's a foreign fella. In number sex.'

'Oh, right then. Ta,' says Gran, and throws a wee wan smile at Pearse.

The bumpkin smiles too. She's quite pretty in a pale way, with a green silky blouse unbuttoned pretty far down so there's a bit of a busty eyeful on display. Still, Pearse thought, she should be in a field chewing straw with freckles on her nose, not sat here in a hospital.

In cubicle six, Doctor Ho is standing with his hands in the pockets of his white coat, smiling fit to break his face.

'Hello,' he says, 'and how is our young chap? Ill with a sore tummy, I hear.'

'Our doctor said it might be appendicitis,' Gran says, 'and we had to travel on the bus as your ambulance people are on strike, which is a bloody disgrace if you ask me. I'm worried sick about the wee fella.'

Doctor Ho gives a bit of a chuckle and says, 'Nothing to worry about. He's in the right place.' He smiles, and reaches out to shake Gran by the hand. 'Nice to meet you,' he says, looking at his notes to check her name, 'Mrs Flower. I'm Doctor Ho.'

'Flowers. Very nice to meet you too, I'm sure,' says Gran.

For a man who is going to do what he is about to do to Pearse in a few minutes, Doctor Ho is exceptionally nice, and even quite handsome. The doctor gets Pearse up on his examination table and starts checking his belly with the auld two-finger tap-tap routine, saying 'hmm' and 'ooh' to himself.

'That's some name you have there, doctor,' Gran says, after about ten seconds of silence. 'Where's it from?'

'Vietnam,' says Doctor Ho. 'Saigon.'

'Vietnam?' Gran laughs. 'Nice choice – from there to here.'

'Aye,' laughs Doctor Ho, who says 'aye' in a wild beezer way like Fu Manchu was from Bumpkin Land.

Doctor Ho looks down and says, 'Now, young man, we have to make a test for appendicitis. You know what that is?'

'Yes,' says Pearse.

'He's a clever boy, Mrs Flowers,' the doctor says, again looking at his notes. 'Pearse. Good name. Now, kindly pull down the trousers and pants and lie on your side facing the wall.'

Pearse looks at Gran, and she purses her lips and gives an auld eye-brow lift, making it clear that he is at the mercy of Doctor Ho, and unless Pearse decides to get up and run, there is nothing she can do to help him.

Pearse miserably pulls down his trousers and pants and turns around to face the wall like some poor, cowardly, shell-shocked soldier.

His eyes take a mad swivel to the side, and with a bit of a tilt of the head, he can see Doctor Ho donning a pair of blue latex gloves and smearing his fingers with some squirty clear jelly. Pearse has seen enough episodes of General Hospital to know what is going to happen.

Doctor Ho starts grunting around and pulling at Pearse's bum-cheeks like he's trying to find a lost sock in a drawer. 'We have to check inside to see if the appendix is activated. Yes? The fingers tell me if you need an operation.'

'I see,' says Gran, somewhere far behind and to the left.

Doctor Ho puts two fingers up Pearse's bum-hole and waggles them about. Pearse stares wide-eyed at the wall in front of him, terrified that he may shit himself and blast Doctor Ho and his white coat. The doctor's fingers do a wee dance and then go even further, cavorting around. Finally, he plops them out and the disturbance gathers itself together and settles into something resembling what it once was before Doctor Ho got his hands on it. Pearse counts the flakes of paint on the wall, with a big blushy beamer on his face.

'Young Pearse does not have appendicitis,' says Doctor Ho, delighted with his diagnosis. 'Nothing to worry about, Mrs Flower.'

'Flowers. Oh thank God for that,' says Gran. 'Thank you, doctor, so much.'

Pearse is trying to get off the table and pull his pants and trousers up and not let his bum-hole fall to the ground all broken and ruined, when Gran says, 'Well, say thanks to the nice doctor, Pearse.'

Pearse looks at her and then looks at him – still wearing the latex glove covered in bits of his dirty nasty – and says, 'Er ooh.'

'What?' says Gran.

'Ank ooh,' Pearse says, getting ready to cry.

'It's okay, Mrs Flowers. Pearse is still in a little pain in the stomach, I think. Probably just an ordinary sore tummy. Have you been playing sports? Running? Fighting? Boy things, Mr Pearse?' the doctor says.

'Well, he was out gallivanting yesterday,' Gran explains, ruffling his hair with her hand – her hand that's still now – and smiling at her wee angel, as his auld unmentionable seizes about in his pants like it's dying of a spasm attack.

'Maybe it is a pulled muscle. Young boys, growing and playing, they have lots of pains and aches. He should lie up till he feels well again. I will give a prescription for some pain-killer which is fine for kids. Yes?'

'Thanks again, doctor,' Gran says. Doctor Ho takes off his gloves and scribbles some medical words on a pad and hands it to her.

The doctor pulls back the curtain on cubicle six and Pearse walks slowly out of the room. Gran offers her hand. Pearse sticks his hands in his pockets.

'Next patient, please,' shouts Doctor Ho down the corridor.

'May-Belle Mullholland for cubicle sex,' the bumpkin receptionist calls out – her voice sliding up the corridor like liquid mud.

*

At the age of fourteen, on a spring evening – Pearse told May-Belle during one of their long night talks – Gran was returning from school, where she was doing pretty well herself now, so the story goes; not as flashy and talented as her sister Katy had been, but a good scholar with a love of poetry and music. It's 1920, and Maria has just married her Protestant boy, leaving Annie as the last child in the O'Neill's old Toomebridge farmhouse.

Annie is dawdling home beside the banks of the River Bann, scrapping her rein of books along the ground, sick at the thought of returning to her grandmother's farm where she'll be told what a burden she is, and how she was never wanted by anybody.

She hears a rumpus ahead of her, and looks up. The sound is

coming from far off, and she can see nobody. She gets closer to the noise and spies people up on the hump of the Toome bridge – the place the town is named after. There's an army truck idling in the road. The shapes are still wee dots in the distance, and her eyes blur to focus on them, but by the outline of the berets on their heads she can make out it's British soldiers. There's another figure, and he's cutting about like an eejit – making a fool of himself. It looks like he's dancing or jumping. By the carry-on of the man, she knows it's auld Joe the Handyman. She hears them laughing and there seems to be a bit of good-natured crack and banter going on. Annie walks on towards them.

Joe was the local simpleton. It was a shame for him, they all said. He'd not always been funny upstairs. As a young man, he was well read and a bit of a republican sympathiser, and when the conscription call-up went out during the First World War, this fella tried every ploy possible to avoid fighting for King and Country – at least that's what he claimed, though most were sure he was a plain coward who couldn't face the thought of taking on the Germans. Others said he joined up before the war – on the run from a bad debt or an angry husband – and the fool found himself caught up in another country's war.

Either way, auld Joe ends up in the infantry. His tactic for survival and snubbing the Empire is to keep pulling a backie – pretending to be sick so he'd get sent to the back lines. When word went out that there was an assault coming, Joe would get himself a bad case of diarrhoea or sit with his feet in water so it looked like he had trench foot. For a while this worked, but after a term at the front, he was had up on a charge of malingering and given a bit of flogging and had his pay docked. He cut it out for a few months; but then he heard the Royal Inniskilling Fusiliers were going over the top, and pulled another backie. This time he got lucky with a new doctor just signed up, and found himself sent rear to the kitchen stations. It seems the Germans knew about this attack by the Irish soldiers though, as they shelled not only the front-line but also the supply lines, the day before the assault. Auld Joe was no more safe at the kitchens than at the firing steps. A shell exploded near his position and as he wasn't wearing his helmet a blade of steel shrapnel hit him just above the left ear. He was invalided out of the army, with a metal plate in his skull, and none too right in the head for the rest of his life.

Annie's watching the soldiers joke with auld daftie Joe up on the bridge, imagining that he's keeping them amused with his carry-on. As she gets close enough to make out distinct voices, she sees the colour of their uniforms and realises what kind of soldiers these are. These soldiers were Annie's first sight of the Black and Tans – monsters of history – with their khaki military trousers and their dark green police jackets.

Annie – never a daftie – jukes off the road, gets down on her belly and lies in a ditch. Trees hide her from the soldiers on the bridge, but she's got a clear view of all that's going on.

One soldier, with a rifle slung over his shoulder, starts waving a piece of paper in Joe's face. There's shouting that she can't make out, and then the soldier unhitches his rifle, cocks it and shoots Joe square in the face. The sound of the bullet is still echoing in the trees when the soldiers pick up Joe's body and throw him off the bridge at Toome into the shallow River Bann. The army truck starts up and the soldiers drive off, and Joe's body floats past Annie – the green fingers of the reed-beds pulling at his hands and face.

There were old intelligence reports from before the war, it turned out, that had Joe labelled as a subversive. The Black and Tans were coming to the farm to take him in for questioning when they found him all by himself on the Toome bridge. And that was the end of that.

*

In the dark under the blankets in Pearse's bed as they spun their stories hidden from the world and the adults, May-Belle told him how the wait for the train to Portrush to arrive in Antrim station felt like the time that passed between the death of the dinosaurs and now.

It took her a while to read her comic, sitting on the iron track-side seats, and the cartoons helped distract her from the wait-ache a bit. Just as she finishes the Sweeney Toddler strip, the train finally chugs into view. They get onboard. Dad says, 'Sit facing the engine May-Belle so you don't get sick', and he sits opposite. Antrim whizzes away, as the train cuts through the green country-side, heading for Ballymena, Cullybackey, Ballymoney, Coleraine, and Portrush and the seaside. Antrim's bricks and houses replaced by fields and cows and trees. The sweep of the world going by brings on a doze.

When May-Belle wakes up the train is at a stand-still, and Dad is pushing her gently, saying, 'Hey, wake up, May-Belle. We're here.'

Salt smelt the air. May-Belle knew it was the Atlantic Ocean – though she'd never seen the seaside before – and she loved the romance of being on a holiday. They walked from the train station, down a sloping road. Halfway, the bottom of the street appeared, with two sweet shops that had once been old stone-clad fisher-men's cottages standing sentry on either side; the street opened onto a picture of dunes and waves and beach. At the bottom of the street, she looked left and right – there were amusement arcades, chippies, stores with hats and wigs and giant lollies and swimming trunks hung up on racks outside – and then directly across the road, sitting like the town's keep and castle was Barry's Fun Fair, with its towering glass front and the screams of children inside; off to the side was the red and white spiral of the Helter Skelter – a giant bleeding barber's pole – and looming behind the building was the iron framework of the Big Dipper Roller Coaster.

Dad said, 'The beach and Barry's and the Big Dipper will have to wait. We need to check into the hotel.'

The pair set off, marching up the road, away from the town

and beach. Tourists and day-trippers spilled about like skittles, and the street smelt of popcorn and candy floss and burgers and onions. They followed the road round a louring cliff, towards a big white birthday cake building, with towers and casement windows and ramparts. It sat high above the sea, like the lord of the manor, looking down on Portrush below.

'This is the hotel,' Dad said. 'The best hotel in Portrush. The best in Ireland. The Northern Counties Hotel.'

As they walked in through the grand wooden front doors, Dad leaned over and whispered, 'You have to act a bit posh in here – so behave.'

May-Belle looked up at him and nodded, and said, 'Of course, Papa.'

A butler or footman or some type of servant walked towards them.

'Can I help you, sir?' the lackey fella asked.

'We're looking to check in,' Dad said.

'Have you a booking, sir?'

'No,' said Dad, and the fella waved in the direction of the reception desk.

The receptionist looked at Dad as if he had just arrived to empty her bins, but when she told him he had to pay in advance and he took out his wad of cash, she became fluttery round the eye-lashes, asking him was it just himself and his daughter, or was his wife with him too.

'The porter will take your bag,' the receptionist said, and she waggled her fingers at the servant fella, handed over a key attached to a fob the size of May-Belle's hand, and said, 'Paddy will show you to your room as well. Second floor. Enjoy your stay. I hope to see you later Mr Mullholland – and Miss Mullholland.'

'She fancies you,' May-Belle whispered as they followed the porter up a wide brown staircase with green carpet.

'Shush, Miss,' Dad said, and elbowed her.

The hallways smelt of polish and linen and dust. They got to the room – Room 212 – and Paddy the Porter put the bag down between the two single beds. Dad gave him 50p from his pocket, and Paddy skedaddled.

'What do you think?' Dad asked.

May-Belle wandered round the room. The beds were hard but the pillows soft, filled with feathers. There was a little electric kettle to make tea and coffee, and a bathroom with a shower and toilet. A TV was on a shelf, high on the wall, in a corner above the dresser.

'Cracking,' she said. She opened the window and looked out, sticking her head around the sides to the left and right. Up close, the white paint on the skin of the building was peeling off in big flakes, the stone underneath grey and pitted. 'How old's this place?' she asked.

'Victorian,' Dad said. 'It used to be the poshest hotel in Ireland. It's still okay today.'

He walked over to the window. He stood beside May-Belle and pointed down at the people in jeans eating chips on the High Street, and the kids splashing about in the sea, while their parents watched them from the sand.

'At the turn of the century, this place was filled with the best of folk – all those ladies with parasols, and the men with moustaches in long-legged swimming costumes. They'd all be on the promenade, where Barry's is now, listening to brass bands and singers, and having afternoon tea.'

They unpacked and went out for a walk along the old promenade, where the black and red dragons of competing graffiti read 'Taigs Out' and 'Brits Go Home'.

'The carnival spirit hasn't abandoned Portrush,' Dad said.

*

Off Annie ran. 'After the shooting of Joe, off Gran ran,' Pearse told May-Belle, during their night talks. First to a great aunt's house. But the auntie turned out to be just as mean and fierce, and just as much the Wicked Stepmother, as her own evil granny Suzanna. Then she spent a year in a convent. Although religion was no big deal to any of the O'Neills, they still believed – and for that reason they made sure their children were baptised and confirmed and had taken their first communion, or whatever. So they deemed the church somewhere acceptable for a runaway to flee to and seek sanctuary.

By the time she got out of the convent, Annie was almost seventeen. And getting out of a convent in those days was a lot harder than getting in. It was a bit of a scrap for freedom, by all accounts. But she argued her way out, nonetheless – threatening court and citing her rights, given women were emancipated now and so on.

Apparently, if the nuns took the fancy, and could convince someone in authority that you were a girl of ill-repute or hopped up with the Devil, then you'd find yourself in there for quite a while doing the rosary and prostrating yourself as a bride of Christ until you were so cowed by God that you'd never contemplate getting out and surviving in the big bad world.

Annie would have none of it, though, so she barged her way out in a storm of rage and menaces, and made her way to Antrim. It's only fifteen miles at most from Toomebridge – where the convent was – but this was 1921. She's still a girl and the War of Independence is just about to end. Still, she's a half-way intelligent girl who dressed decently and could hold a proper conversation so she'd never be short of a job in those days if she was content to work as a servant. Annie got herself a position in a place called Hall's Hotel – a rambling auld affair on the old Antrim High Street. When Pearse and May-Belle were little, it was knocked down and a Wellworth's built in its place.

Annie holds the job down for a while, but then her story gets a bit frayed and faded. The history she told of herself falters at this point and skips ahead – for there was a shooting in the hotel. A massacre – and then the stories about 1921 would stop.

A whole squad of British officers – Black and Tans, so the tale goes – are staying in the hotel one night, and a flying column of IRA men walk into the lobby, hold the porter hostage and set about going silently from room to room, shooting the Brit officers where they found them. Some were shot in their baths, some in their beds, some with their Irish girlfriends lying beside them, or even saying their prayers. It was like the Twelve Apostles all over again. The volunteers knew precisely which rooms to go to. They never opened a wrong door.

She left Hall's Hotel and went to Belfast. She talked about her time at the hotel often, though: tales about the servant girls sleeping below stairs in their quarters and being chased by local boys – then she'd find herself mentioning the shooting; the story just went kerchika-a-chick-a-chick, like a car not starting properly. She'd restart the story and it seemed like a year had vanished in the telling, with nothing happening until she wound up in Belfast in early 1922.

May-Belle imagined her as a gunman's moll. Pearse said he wished the same, but doubted it.

*

Pearse held May-Belle's hand under the covers of his bed, in the dark of the night, with the adults deaf to their stories.

That first night in Portrush, said May-Belle, she was escorted down to dinner in the hotel restaurant by Dad. Scampi, chips and peas each, with tartare sauce – 'tar-tar', the waiter pronounced it, all Frenchified – and a lemon wedge. A glass of coke and a half pint of beer.

Dad clinked glasses with her, and said, 'To you, beautiful Miss May-Belle.' She thought what he said daft and put on, but sad-happy too, and then tears started up in her eyes, and that made the whole thing so real and so fake at the same time that she couldn't decide what mood was on her: good or bad or what. The bad vanished quick, though, with ice cream and more coke and jokes and a sip of beer.

They walked down to the prom afterwards, and went into Barry's as night was falling. The fun-fair smelt of smouldering rubber, ozone and diesel fuel from the grinding sparking machinery of the swing boats and dodgems. At the doorway, a Laughing Policeman in a glass case – a madman in a box – roared if a twopence piece was fed into a slot. They walked through the crowds; the place was full even though it was gone ten o'clock. There were kids dragging their parents around by the hand, and old folk bewildered – wondering why they were in a whirling, screaming asylum filled with blinding colour and shouts, and not out on the prom licking an ice cream and sitting in a deck chair. Teenagers were snogging the faces off each other, and newly-wed couples walked around hand in hand with teddy bears under their arms and hot-dogs in their mouths.

Barry's was about the size of a couple of sports fields put together. Most of the entertainment was inside, but the bigger, scarier, more dangerous rides – like the Big Dipper – were out the back. In the middle of the arcade, the gambling games and the shooting stalls were to be found. Dad clapped his hands together when he saw The Kentucky Derby and said, 'Let's take our seats.' They each picked a horse – along with ten other players. The horses were in a row in front of the gamblers – up on a platform laid out like a race circuit, cut from sheets of tin – and the jockeys' steel silks were multi-coloured. Each player had a ball to throw at a set of targets. If you hit the bull's eye, your horse would charge a length up the little electrified track; if you hit the outer rings, it would just lumber a few steps forward.

Dad's horse came in second last, and he said, 'Mine's was a bloody nag with three legs. They should take it outside and shoot it – put it out of its misery.'

They took a ride on the auld ghost train. Dad held onto May-Belle for dear life as the car punched its way through the entrance gates – the mouth of a giant spook – and into the haunted house. May-Belle thought she better pretend it scared her stiff. The only thing she didn't like was the hot smoky wind that blew through the tunnels. She couldn't understand where it came from.

Afterwards, the pair of them had a few spins at a game of tuppeny roulette, putting pennies in slots marked with different colours. If you put your penny in blue and the roulette ball landed on blue then you won 10p. Jackpot – you're the girl who broke the bank at Monte Carlo.

On the way out, they stopped at a fortune telling machine. Inside a glass case, set with stars and symbols, there was a dummy of a gypsy woman, her head wrapped in a scarf fringed with golden sovereigns, and rings on her fingers. Dad put 10p in the machine and she sprang to life, the crystal ball under her hands glowing and throwing off all the colours of the rainbow. The dummy shook from side to side, it's mouth opened and it said, 'Your fortune has been told.' The machine whirred and a slip of paper popped out of a slot. It said, 'Love is just around the corner. You will find your soul-mate.'

They walked down to the beach and strolled along the surf, dodging the tide running up the sand. When it began to get cold, they walked back to the prom. Dad slipped into a shop and bought a couple of board games – Scrabble, and a compendium of different auld past-times like Ludo and Snakes and Ladders – and some juice and sweets and crisps. At an off-licence, on the way to the hotel, he got a bottle of whiskey; cooked up at the Bushmills distillery just along the coast, he said.

'I'll have a wee nip while we sit up late talking and playing games,' he said, throwing his arm around May-Belle. 'What do you think?'

'Grandy-dandy,' she replied – and hemmed a cough. There was fakery in her voice.

*

Walking up the green-tiled hospital corridor towards Pearse and Gran is a wee wizened version of May-Belle herpling along with a limp – her arm in a sling. She's got a cracking shiner. Da has this saying about fellas who have it off with loads of girls – 'he'd buck a black eye'. May-Belle's lips are puffy and cracked; there's bruises on her cheeks and across her nose.

Gran has no idea who May-Belle is. She's never met her and never will. May-Belle keeps walking towards them, held up and helped along by a man beside her – she's able to totter a little on her own with short shuffley steps. The man is wearing an auld jumper and jeans and looks a bit down on his luck, like one of the down-and-outs you see in England or America on TV. He's watching May-Belle and seems as sad as any person can be for another human being. He's gentle with her, as if she were a wee egg that might break on the way up the hall to Doctor Ho in cubicle six.

Gran says, 'Dear God', under her breath. She glances down at Pearse and smiles and shakes her head. Pearse takes Gran's hand and tries to lead her quickly on as May-Belle comes slowly, slowly, closer and closer. Gran puts her arm around his shoulder. May-Belle is such a hobbledeehoy that she hasn't noticed them and nor has the man with her. Pearse wills May-Belle to look up but also wishes that she'll never look at him again. She stops, and starts to cry, and the man kneels down and hugs her. 'Do you want me to carry you?' he says in a Scottish accent. And May-Belle says 'No, thank you.' He kisses her on the cheek and says, 'Take your time.' She still hasn't noticed him, so Pearse – without knowing why – lets a cough out of him. May-Belle trails her eyes up, not moving her neck and head. She looks at Pearse, and looks at Gran, and the vaguest of lost wee smiles comes across her face and she braces herself, slowly pulling her shoulders back and straightening her spine, and starts walking towards cubicle six, licking the tears away from her top lip. Dad puts his arm back around her and she leans in to his tatty auld jumper with her black hair and they move painfully past Pearse and Gran.

Pearse was allowed the rest of the week off school – Wednesday, Thursday and Friday. Even the Man in the Iron Lung didn't seem too bothered once Pearse said to Mum in his hearing that he'd been playing footie and cricket and had ripped a muscle that way. Da called him a wee jessie for hurting himself playing sports, but laughed in a chummy way when he said it, and asked how many goals were scored or runs or whatever. Pearse limped around when anyone was about, giving it pitiful groans and clutching his side every now and again. When he sat down, he'd lay on with wee puffs of pain, and the auld granda-getting-out-of-a-chair routine every time he had to stand up. By Friday, he began walking more confidently but still slowly to show that the pain was lessening – as he was getting bored of the play-acting. May-Belle hadn't been back at her school either all that week, so they had both missed most of the prep for their 11-plus exams. In the mornings, Pearse would watch out his bedroom window – keeping an eye on the wee alley at the end of her row of houses. Anyone wanting to head down the town, towards the main shops or St Comgall's school – her Catholic school – would have to come out the end of that alley and turn left. He watched from before eight in the morning every day until gone nine, and she never appeared all that week.

Once Mum and Da had gone to work, Pearse would spend the day with Gran, who came round to look after him. He'd get the auld soft boiled eggy-weggs and soldiers in bed, and then tootle downstairs, a bit limpy like, and watch some schools and colleges with her. If there were no historical programmes on, like How We Used To Live, with this Victorian family getting all het up about their boy having to go off and fight the Zulus, then he'd just switch off the telly and read or draw. He knew he was a useless artist but he could wile hours away recreating scenes in his sketch book of 1920s style rat-a-tat-tat Chicago shoot-outs, the Battle for Planet Insecticus from Space 1999, Apache fights with the Seventh Cavalry, Nuclear War, Dracula's impalement, helicopters over Vietnam, Jack the Ripper on the foggy streets of old London town.

Other times, Gran would tell some of her stories about the Blitz and the war in Ireland when she was a girl or Granda fighting in the Battle of Jutland or about how Da's side of the family were all just useless wasters and liars and arseholes, and Pearse would usually drift off to sleep after tomato soup and toast for lunch. Then it'd be a bit of telly in the afternoon – a film like Bad Day at Black Rock or The Wicked Lady – and on to the cartoons. Pearse switched off as soon as Magpie or Blue Peter came on and read for half an hour from Great Tales of Terror and the Supernatural, or Ancient Celtic and British Myths and Legends. Then the telly went back on for the Clangers or Rhubarb and Custard before the news started.

When the news was on – unless there was some mad blowing-up behaviour happening – Pearse tuned out and finished off whatever story he was reading and by then Mum would be home anyway and cooking the tea.

He read two stories that week he was off school, one from Great Tales of Terror and the Supernatural called The Most Dangerous Game about this bonkers aristocratic lad with a scar on his temple and a twitch who hunted humans just for the crack and then put their heads in his trophy room. The other was from the Celtic and British legends book about this King called Lear – like Shakespeare and the guy who wrote the Owl and the Pussycat. He asked his three daughters which one loved him the most, and the youngest one, the daughter who really did love him, and who all the princes fancied the knickers off, she said she loved him like meat loves salt. Her da, the king, goes crackers – no wonder – and tells her to bugger off out of his castle. All hell breaks loose. The daughter flees and marries this charming prince type and the auld king is left to the mercy of his two other monster daughters who take over the castle and tell the auld king to bugger off himself in a nice wee twist-around. The auld king ends up sleeping in a ditch for a while and then gets taken in by the charming prince, but the King's daughter – the charming prince's wife by now – disguises herself as a servant so her da doesn't know she's knocking about with the charming prince. It all ends a bit weak and wishy-washy. The daughter serves up a meal of meat but deliberately doesn't put salt on the table, and the auld King near pukes up – as it's so minging for some reason that he can't stomach it. Then it dawns on him that meat really does need salt and his daughter rips off her auld disguise and shouts 'Daddy!' and he shouts 'Darling!' and that's it. Bollocks if you ask me, thought Pearse.

Come the evening, Mum would make a half-way decent dinner after Gran went back to her flat. They weren't eating beans and Smash anymore every night, so Pearse usually got a chop with a nice big slice of bread and butter and another eggy-wegg or something like that. Da would eat his dinner in the living room with them and then usually go to the pub till kicking out time, or else go up to his bedroom with his food, now that there was a second telly, and watch sport by himself all night if his drinking buddies weren't about. Snooker and football and golf – anything with people chasing after balls, with no plot or purpose, except winning the game.

Mum would crack open the auld Lucozade and get the crisps and Mintolas and she and Pearse would watch Dad's Army or Are you Being Served? or that daft retarded fella Frank Spencer.

On Fridays and Saturdays, Mum would let Pearse stay up late and watch the midnight movie or some odd show that was on the telly. They watched If…, about this suave posh lad who goes to a public school and machine guns the teachers in their mortar boards and gowns, like that Baader Meinhof lot. Another wild show that stuck in Pearse's head was a film about this Naked Civil Servant guy. The star was the weird looking fella who played that mental emperor Caligula in I Claudius that was on telly too. In I Claudius this creepy looking actor lad has it off with his sister and ends up thinking he's Zeus so cuts his own baby out of his sister's stomach and eats it. In the Naked Civil Servant, the same actor lad is playing at being a gay fella – a fruit on the loose, bums-to-the-wall type of a guy. Despite being a mad arser, though, the lad is pretty swift. He gads about wearing loads of make-up – this'd be back around the time that Gran married Grandad way before the war, when being queer was a surefire way off getting yourself a kicking or going to jail – but this fella, he couldn't care less, he just walks around, gay as you please. The men who hit him or spit on him – they just bounce off him. Finally, he becomes famous for being a bum-boy extraordinaire and happy and a writer – a fella who basically tells the world to go fuck itself every time someone demands he act different to how he truly is.

During these auld shows, when Da was upstairs or out, Pearse would sit and blether away to Mum about all sorts of nonsense, asking her questions about people and places and things that have happened in the world and why they've happened and what makes people do the things they do whether they are good, bad or indifferent. She had a blue silky blouse and skirt with cream edges to it, and he'd lie with his head on her lap feeling how cool and soft the material was, and look at her, and notice how she had funny flecks of orange colour in the green of her eyes just like his eyes and he'd tell her how she looked like that Elizabeth Taylor girl in Cat on a Hot Tin Roof. That film had a physical effect on him – it made him feel hot and sweaty and Mum had to get him a drink with ice cubes in it to cool him down because he thought he was going to be sick with all the howdyamado on screen.

Mum talked about actors and singers like Paul Newman and Gerry and the Pacemakers – though who has ever heard tell of that fella and his band – and what London was like in the swinging sixties. She talked about these boyfriends she had before she got married and how they were charming and handsome and loads better than Twinkletoes. She asked Pearse how he was getting on at school and if he had friends, and Pearse said he was best mates with that wee girl May-Belle up the street.

Mum says, 'She doesn't come from a very good family, darling.'

And Pearse says, 'I've never met her family, but she's lovely though.'

'Lovely?' asks Mum.

'She's funny and pretty and great crack to be around.'

'And what do youse get up to?' Mum had picked up some of the Ulster way of talking, in her English voice.

'Just dandering about, playing marlies and stuff. She isn't into girl games, so we just talk and carry on. Dead Man's Fall and all that.'

'Right,' says Mum. 'Sounds like you like her.'

'I do.'

And even though it wasn't on TV at that moment, every time he thought of that conversation later, a song and dance routine by Morecambe and Wise fixed in his head. Some pretty girl on stage, giving it big leg scissor-kicks, and the three of them singing a song – You're the Tops, You're the Queen of Sheba.

'She's better crack than any lads I know and she's never nasty.'

'Great,' says Mum. 'Bring her round. I think I'll need to meet my future daughter-in-law.'

'Mum,' Pearse hollers, leaping off her lap and sitting up. 'What you on about?'

She laughs and says, 'I'm just teasing, but if you react like that then maybe you must love this young lady.'

'Oh my God,' he says. 'Mum are you flippen mental?'

'Maybe,' she says, and then starts tickling him, calling him Mr Loverman and Casanova, and blowing auld raspberry farts on his belly with her mouth.

'Away on, mum,' he shouts, with the laughs making it hard to breathe – gasping for air the way Stan Laurel does when Oliver Hardy gets a smack in the plumbs or a poke in the eye. 'I'm eleven, you can't do that to me.'

'I'll be doing that to you when you've made me a granma,' she says.

They head to bed, and about half an hour later Pearse is flicking through 2000AD, when he hears Da opens the backdoor. In the next room, Mum sneaks out of bed to turn her night-light off, and then gets back under the covers, giving it wee soft snores – ahoo ahoo – as if she's been asleep for ages. Pearse keeps the night-light on and continues reading about Judge Death who nobody, not even Judge Dredd, can kill.

*

Annie stayed in Belfast for only a few months of 1922, Pearse told May-Belle – while dawn was still far off, and the adults slept, as the pair told their stories, hidden nose to nose beneath the bed-covers in his room.

Violence was on in Belfast, and lone Catholic girls were none too safe. Gran would laugh and tell Pearse that people actually used the word 'pogroms' about what went on back then when she was a girl – simpletons who hadn't a clue about the true brutality of human beings. Whatever went on in Belfast, it wasn't your European-style genocide. There weren't people stuffed into churches and burned alive. But with the War of Independence over, the loyalists up north had scores to settle with their Catholic neighbours in the new Northern Ireland and things were none to pleasant for Papes or whatever people called them.

Annie managed to get a job with an English family who lived on the leafy Malone Road in the south of the city. The head of the family was a professor of mathematics at Queen's University who had no interest in Annie's religion – thank God – a fact she was impressed by, as Catholics in their thousands were being turned out of work, by all accounts. He gave her a job as a scullery maid, and she had quarters at the top of the family's grand home, in the attic with another, more senior, maid. A footman and butler lived in the basement, and the gardener had a little lodge in the grounds.

She had every other Saturday free from work, and would head

into the centre of the city to the movie house, which had taken up residence in the old music hall on the Ormeau Road. Mobs were busy evicting families from their homes in some Catholic areas; those who wouldn't leave were burned out. There were shootings and killings; Protestant girls who'd fallen in love with Catholic boys were tied to lamp-posts and tarred and feathered, just as Catholic girls had been treated similarly a few years before – in counties that would now be south of the new border – if they'd had a fling with a British soldier or a policeman.

One night, Annie was making her way home from the pictures, and fires were burning across the city – of homes torched by these mobs. As she walked up the street, arm in arm with the other maid from the professor's house, who she'd become firm friends with, a shot snipped past her ear. The pair had gone for a drink in a Catholic bar. The bar stood on a wide road, facing a Protestant neighbourhood. Any girl or boy walking up that street could be spied on from the houses opposite, and it was obvious if you were on that street which religion you were. The city still has its lethal telling sectarian geography, Gran told Pearse.

As they ran back towards the pub, Annie looked over her shoulder and saw a man in shadow move out from behind a lamp-post and raise his gun. The Black Man Behind the Lamp-post, she called him in her stories. She grabbed her friend by the hand and threw the pair of them in through the door of the bar as another shot rang out, breaking the frosted glass window.

Lying on her belly in the sawdust of the public bar, she turned onto her back and kicked the door shut after them.

The police arrived and were none too sympathetic to anyone in the bar. They asked Annie and her friend the other maid, a 19-year-old by the name Teresa who everyone called Terry, what they were doing out on their own – were they looking for men? Did they have decent jobs?

When the police officers found out they worked for a Queen's University professor, they put them in the back of their wagon and drove them home, not uttering a word on the way except to say that if the pair of them were lucky enough to have the patronage of such a man then they would be well advised to keep to his house for the foreseeable future.

The next day, Annie and Terry told the professor that they thanked him for his employment but they couldn't live in the city anymore without fear of being raped or murdered. The pair of them were off to England, they said, as soon as they worked out their notice.

The professor said he understood and that the times were mean and illogical. They had a week's notice to work. The next day, the professor called them to his study and said that he'd arranged letters of introduction with a number of friends in London. If there was work going as servants, his friends would be sure to assist them. On their last day, he gave them an extra few shillings each and paid for a taxi to take them to the docks to catch the ferry to Liverpool.

It was the beginning of May in 1922. Annie got on the boat and said goodbye to Ireland for the next 48 years, not returning until the year after Pearse was born in 1970.

The London she arrived in overwhelmed her. Belfast had been huge, but London was a vast giant of a city, with a thousand neighbourhoods, an underground railway, palaces, more wealth and poverty in extremes than she'd ever imagined, whores on the street, threats to lone girls on every corner, and opportunities to make money appear out of thin air if you were of the right brutal frame of mind.

The first night, the pair of them couldn't find digs for love nor money. There were signs in the windows of lodging houses declaring 'No blacks, no Irish, no dogs'. For that was real, Gran said, no joke, and it was a sin of ignorance and cruelty to treat the people of Ireland as if they were no better than darkies. She'd never seen a black man before and to spy them in groups on the streets terrified the girl – sure that each one of them had the rape of a white woman on his mind.

They slept the night in a Salvation Army hostel, and the next day struggled for hours on the trams of London trying to find the addresses of the friends of the professor. At last, as it was heading towards dinner time, they located the first house on the list – it was near Regent's Park; as big and grand as the mansion they'd worked in back in Belfast, but this time only one of fifty or more such homes on a single street.

They walked up the front steps, rang the doorbell and presented themselves to the footman. He shooed them around the back to the servant's entrance, and sat them at the kitchen table while he fetched the Housekeeper. The lady examined the note, sniffed at the girls and said she'd speak to the mistress.

The girls didn't get a job in that house, but by the evening they'd both secured positions in other houses nearby as scullery maids. Annie impressed with her hard work and polite manner. She fell in quickly with the staff who thought her clever and entertaining, and the master of the house promoted her to full maid soon enough.

She had itchy feet, though, and no desire to stay in one job too long. She scoured the employment sections of the newspapers – moving in a year between seven jobs until she landed herself a position as a chamber maid. As a chamber maid, it was her job to tidy the bedrooms, lay out the clothes of the members of the family, turn down their beds, light their fires and bring them supper in their rooms.

She was a fairly attractive young woman by now – no oil painting, but buxom and healthy and with a sense of wildness about her. Soon the sons of the great men in these houses were chasing her about and wooing her, but she preferred the young men she met who came delivering groceries at the back door, or the footmen and valets – often soldiers who'd served in France and were shy and strong, so she said to her friends.

She went on like this for a few years until by the time she

was 23 – about 1928 – she'd become the personal maid to one of the grand society ladies of London, Lady Ellen Steiner-Price. Lady Ellen treated her well, took her to Paris and Rome with her, bought her clothes so she'd look accordingly glamorous, and encouraged her to fall in love. If she married a good man, also in service, there was no reason why she couldn't one day be house-keeper and he butler – positions they'd be able to retain all their lives and live in comfort.

When Annie was telling stories such as these she was prone to the odd diversion about morality and fate and the way of the world, so she often said to Pearse – and he had no idea why he was on the receiving end of such a lecture – that he was lucky to be a little boy; to be born male. A girl, she said, ran the risk of ruining her life if she fell in love – unwanted babies and unmarried mothers were the route to the poor house and prison; and a man would use a girl and walk away if he felt inclined.

Lady Ellen grew ill and Annie spent most of 1929 caring for her. The lady died and Annie stayed on in the service of the Steiner-Price family as the under-housekeeper. She was nearly 25 now and she'd had plenty of offers of marriage but had refused them all; not because of a want of money or looks on behalf of the men who ran after her, but because none of the fellas got into her soul, was how she put it.

Her story takes on another one of those strange breaks at this point. It derails again, stalling and skipping ahead in time. All she'd say was that she grew disillusioned with London, but had no desire to return to Ireland as there was nothing or nobody there for her. One of the friends of the Steiner-Price family was a high-ranking officer in the British Army in India, and with some string pulling and favours called in, they secured her a position in Rawlapindi in the Punjab at the Headquarters of the British Military Garrison, which sounds terribly grand but the place was a stink-hole par excellence.

Her stories about India were sketchy too. She was sad there, she said, and lonely; she missed England, and wasn't happy with what she'd made of her life. The job with the army in India had her working as a maid for the wife of a Brigadier. The garrison was a dirty empty hell, the people were brutes – both the whites and the wogs, she said – and the food more vile than the human tongue could imagine.

To sum the place up, she said, even the officers referred to going to the toilet as visiting the shit-house. And it was a shit-house – the NCO's outside lavatory block – which gave her the only story of her time in India that mattered to her.

One night, two sergeants went out to the shit-house, and never came back. Some Indian rebels crept into the compound, over the wall, heard the dreadful farts and noises in the toilet block, and leant over the rear partition of the cubicles – cutting the pair's throats as they sat on the plank boards with their trousers round their ankles, grunting and groaning.

The wallas who found them came screaming into the officer's mess, and a search party was dispatched to catch the rebels. As a squad of soldiers marched out through the front gates of the compound – a volley of shots star-pricked the night, and three were killed. There was a pitched battle fought around the fort that night. By the morning about a hundred Indians were dead – some had no more to do with the rebellion than Annie, and were just unlucky enough to be in the vicinity of the fighting – and ten more British soldiers were killed, with the same number again injured, suffering lost eyes and bullets in their brains and lungs.

As soon as it was safe, Annie demanded an escort so she could accompany the batch of wounded soldiers departing the garrison for the port of Karachi – to make their way back to Britain. Permission was given and off she went. She got back to London in January 1931. Her life ticking on.

*

In the dark, under the blankets in Pearse's room, as their stories wound on over nights, May-Belle told him that the Portrush week, for her and Dad, passed away through days of lying in bed till late, eating lunch on the beach, rooting about in rock pools with a net for wee sea beasties, swimming free in the surf, shopping for nick-nacks, dinner at the hotel, larking about in Barry's and chatting into the wee hours till they fell asleep. They hardly watched the TV at all – it sat up there on the wall doing nothing. When they talked late at night, May-Belle would lie in bed and Dad would pull a chair up by the open window, roll a cigarette and blow the smoke out into the night air. He'd sip his way through a couple of nips of whisky and listen to her rabbit on about Lord knows what. He wasn't a story-teller. He was a listener and a questioner. He'd get the conversation going with some mundane wee inquiry about Ma, or school, or life in general, and May-Belle found that she'd be off rambling at the mouth, putting together an out-of-synch tapestry of tales for him – thoughts that had never occurred to her before. He'd prod her back on the path he wanted her to stay on with a well-targeted comment or query, and so it would go, until May-Belle's tired out mind and mouth slowed down and shut themselves off for the night, mid-conversation.

On the the morning of the last full day of the holiday, Dad said to her over a late breakfast in the hotel, 'Do you fancy Barry's this evening?'

'To tell you the truth, Dad, I don't.' And she wasn't just saying that because she'd been watching his wad of money get thinner and thinner as the week went by, but because she'd been on every ride in the amusement arcade, and played every slot machine – she'd worn the fun out of the place.

'Well, I have an idea,' he says. And his idea is this: to go to the Summer Theatre in the centre of town – right on the promenade – to watch a play.

By now, she's got to feeling quite the lady of Portrush, and takes this thought of a night at the theatre in her stride.

The theatre looked like the Orange Hall on Antrim High Street – a heavy hewn stone building, put up before Victoria was on the throne. It sat fronting the sea – a squat auld sailor with a kind grumpy face.

On the way in, they were given programmes, explaining that before the main play, there would be light entertainment in the form of singing, recitals, variety acts and magic.

Inside, the theatre was like a school gym or assembly hall; there were even classroom chairs set in rows for the audience. It held about 500 souls. The lights went down and there was a lot of hushing and shushing from people in the dark.

A Master of Ceremonies type came on and a bit lamely began introducing the warm-up acts: a girl who could swizz 50 hula-hoops around her belly; a guy with a dancing dog; a ventriloquist and his evil dummy. Then a big handsome looking fella – who you could picture roaming across the countryside with his black hair flying behind him – this towering fella took the stage and began singing Irish songs. He kicks off with The Wild Rover and the people around about are tapping their toes and slapping their thighs in time to the music. Dad and May-Belle are sitting in the third row from the front. The man starts encouraging the audience to sing along with him.

May-Belle couldn't help herself. She'd been singing along with him in her head since he opened his mouth, so when he gives the audience permission she gets stuck in straight away. He's singing one of her favourite songs now, called I'll Tell Me Ma.

It goes:

I'll tell me ma when I go home
the boys won't leave the girls alone.
They pull my hair, they steal my comb
But that's all right till I get home.
She is handsome, she is pretty
She is the belle of Belfast city

She is courting – one, two, three –
Please, won't you tell me, who is she?

May-Belle shut her eyes and clapped her hands and sang out the first verse and the chorus. She gets to her favourite bit of the song – *Out she comes, white as snow, rings on her fingers and bells on her toes* – when she realises that all she can hear in her head is her own voice. She stops singing and opens her eyes, and the performer is standing still on the stage, a finger to his lips signaling to the audience to be quiet – a hand pointing down to May-Belle, his eyes dancing over her.

He smiles and starts to applaud, and all the people around cheer too. The man says, 'Ladies and gentlemen, we have a new star of the show.' May-Belle wasn't sure if she was in trouble, or if she'd made a living fool out of herself. It's all she can do to turn her head to look at Dad. He's clapping and smiling as well.

The performer says, 'Come on up and join me on stage, Shirley Temple.'

May-Belle looks at him and then looks at Dad. Dad says, 'Go on – have fun.'

He gives her a gentle push, and when she won't move of her own accord, he takes her hand and walks her into the central aisle, between the rows of seats. The performer walks towards the edge of the stage, still clapping.

The fear flows out of her, away from her, and the cheering sends her ten feet tall. She's the only girl in the room. May-Belle gives a wave to the audience. She can't make out individual faces, but the mouths are smiling and the hands clapping and the eyes happy; all the voices on her side.

The performer leads her up a flight of steps to the stage, and stands her beside him.

'Take a bow,' he says, 'that was some singing.'

May-Belle dips a royal curtsey, and says 'Why thank you.'

'So tell us who you are, miss,' he says.

'I'm May-Belle Mullholland from Antrim, and I love singing.'

'We can tell that,' the man says, turning to the audience and giving them a cheesey wink. They laugh along with him. 'Would you like to join me in a song?'

'If I know it,' she says. 'I'd love to.'

First they sing Maggie, with May-Belle throwing herself into the sadness of the song, and frankly making the man look like he only took up singing the night before. Hand on heart and with truth and certainty, when she looked out into the audience, as she sang the last verse, there were people crying, not because of the black-haired performer – although they liked him well enough. It wasn't him bringing tears to their eyes.

As she sang the words – *and now we are aged and grey, Maggie, the trials of life nearly done, let us sing of the days that are gone, Maggie, when you are I were still young* – she knew she'd made the people see auld Maggie sitting there in her chair by the fire, with her hair up in a bun, the beauty of her face lost in time and wrinkles; and she'd made them feel in their hearts just like her poor old husband, beat with age but as in love with his girl as he was when he was 18.

When they finished Maggie, the performer turns to clap her and a few of the audience get to their feet to applaud. May-Belle is starting to learn the rules of being on stage, so turns to clap her singing partner and then offer a little round of applause to the audience – just for being so great and loving her so much.

Off to the left of the stage, screened from the audience by the red velvet theatre curtain, a wee bald man makes a T sign with his hands to the performer.

The performer sees the baldy chap out of one eye and says to the audience, 'I'm being told it's time for me and Miss May-Belle to skedaddle so the show can start, but I'm sure if you all ask nicely, we'd have time for one more song.' He lifts his hands in the air, and as if by his command, they all start shouting 'more, more' and whooping. Dad is standing in the audience clapping away and beaming as if she'd made him a millionaire.

'Fantastic,' the performer says. 'The lady can choose. What would you like to sing, May-Belle?'

With no hesitation, she says, 'Why, The Mountains of Mourne, sir.'

'Och,' he says. 'A connoisseur. What a choice, Miss Mullholland. And would you be so kind as to sing it by yourself?'

'I'd love to,' she says, and he backs away off to one side, out of the spotlight to let May-Belle have the stage all to herself.

She hit that song as if it was her who had written the words and music. She sang the story about Mary's lover leaving Ireland and digging for gold in the streets of London, and how the only happy Irishman he ever met in England was Peter O'Loughlin, who'd turned into a policeman.

While the song has its funny side – with the lyrics taking the mickey out of Irish people lost and confused in the city – it's got a terrible sad side as well, as the singer misses home so much his heart could break, but he has to stay to earn enough money so that one day he can come back to Ireland and marry Mary.

By the end of the song, May-Belle knew how this showbiz game worked – so she saved up her passion and let them have it with the last verse:

There's beautiful girls here – oh, never you mind –
With beautiful shapes Nature never designed;
And lovely complexions, all roses and cream,
But O'Loughlin remarked with regard to the same:
'That if at those roses you venture to sip
Sure the colours might all come away on your lip.'
So, I'll wait for the wild rose that's waiting for me
Where the mountains of Mourne sweep down to the sea.

She hit and held the last note, and bowed as low as she could.

May-Belle maintained the bow, looking at the cracks and scuffs in the boards of the stage, and heard the audience stamping their feet and clapping and cheering – some people even howled. Her singing turned people into dogs. She straightened up and the audience rose to its feet, shouting 'encore' and 'more' and 'bravo'.

The performer stepped out from the shadows in the wings, clapping her. He walked towards May-Belle, lifted her hand and said, 'The star of the show, ladies and gentlemen. Miss May-Belle Mullholland from Antrim.'

He walked her to the steps and she climbed down from the stage with the audience still clapping and whistling. On the way to her seat, people got up and patted her on the head and shook her hand and told her what a wonderful wee trooper she was.

The audience made way for Dad to come to her. The man on stage said, 'A young lady I'm sure we will hear very much more from in the future.' Dad led her back to the third row. She sat down and people were craning to look at her from every side – front, back, left and right. They were saying, 'You were marvelous', 'Where did such a wee girl get such a big voice', 'Who taught you to sing?'. And they were saying to Dad, 'You must be so proud', 'What a talent you have on your hands there', 'Take her to London – she could be Bonnie Langford'.

The performer up on the stage, with the lights on him and the rest of the audience all back in the dark now, interrupted, saying, 'Okay, ladies and gentlemen. Let's have a bit of hush for the main event. Our last little lady was wonderful, but now we have an even greater show for you – The Portavogie Players present The Coachman's Daughter, an original drama by Robert Sand.'

Hush settled on the audience, and the play began. The actors took to the stage, but they may as well have been flies on a window sill for all May-Belle cared or noticed. She vaguely recalled there being a bit of romance and a ghost story of some sort – a spot of fighting and killing – but as to the plot? She was up in the white footlights in her mind, watching herself make a room full of people fall in love with her because of the noise her voice made when she played clever tricks with it.

From the moment the curtain fell, people came up to May-Belle and Dad, congratulating them again, telling her she'd be famous one day, saying she was the best thing they'd ever seen on a stage. Dad agreed. He said he knew she was a talented singer, but he had no idea she had star quality.

*

According to Pearse, the only happy marriage he'd ever heard of was the one between Gran and Grandad – and even then, by the time Pearse was born Grandad was dead, and so he'd never seen proof of its brilliance with his own eyes, just the reckoning of it through other people's stories.

May-Belle considered his granny to be a lucky auld girl. Pearse wasn't so sure – waiting to marry a man until your nearly 33 years old can't have been that lucky for a woman back in those days. Still, she found him and she kept him – so maybe that is what counts as luck in the world.

It was more than seven years after she came back from India to London that Pearse's Granny Annie finally met and married her husband. Annie returned to service, but this time rather than working below stairs, she took jobs in some of the swankier hotels in London – White's, Brown's, Claridges, The Dorchester. When Pearse was wee, he found coat-hangers stamped with the names of these grand places in her wardrobe.

As her 30s approached, she seemed to settle down to a more sedate life. She kept moving from hotel to hotel, though – always to increase her pay packet – but excitements mostly revolved around going to the movies with the few fellas who'd caught her eye. She never fell for one of them. She'd come to dislike men a little, it seemed, and it would have to be a diamond-souled man who'd make her love him.

Her stories from this period – from the 1930s – were mostly

about other people. Not much about herself. She'd tell tales of a porter called Tim Flynn who was an infamous London cat-burglar nicknamed Flannel Feet Flynn, because he never made a sound when he snuck into the bedchambers of the rich ladies staying in the hotels where he worked, and unclasped the necklaces around their throats and slipped the rings and bracelets from their hands.

Her wildest and dirtiest story concerned a young maid at White's hotel who was a great friend of Annie's thanks to her daft giddiness. She was a bit light-fingered herself, this young maid, and if guests were stupid enough to leave a few shillings here or silk hankie there, then the items would end up secreted in her knickers till she knocked off shift and could hide them safely in her room.

Back in those days, the very wealthy would often take suites in hotels and live there for months on end. There was such a man in White's Hotel, an auld lecher forever nipping the arses of passing maids and leering over the waitresses. Each morning, this auld rogue has his breakfast delivered to his room. Along with his bacon and eggs and tea and toast, he orders an earthenware pint jug full of ice cold fresh cream. Each morning, after he finishes his breakfast and goes out for his morning constitutional down Piccadilly towards Hyde Park, the giddy, light-fingered maid traipses up to his room to clear away the breakfast things and tidy the place up. Each morning, she sees this pint of ice cold cream completely untouched, and she thinks to herself, 'what a terrible waste', so takes a big glug straight from the lip of the jug.

This goes on for weeks until one morning, the young maid is not feeling too well – she's got an upset stomach and a rash on her face – so a new member of staff, a young porter, is sent up to the gentleman's room to clear up after breakfast. The young lad arrives at the lecher's door, and thinking the auld fella is out, just walks in without knocking. What does he see, but the auld fella with his trousers and pants around his ankles, dipping his red, pimply lad into the jug of cream.

The auld boy lets a splutter out of him, his whiskers flying up in the air in outrage and his face blushing more scarlet than the suffering chap in his hands. The jug falls to the floor, the cream spills, the porter screams and runs off, and the auld fella can be heard harrumphing around in his room, until he packs his case, gets the lift downstairs to the reception, settles his bill and leaves never to be seen again.

It seems that the auld fella had a bad dose of some kind of clap and his doctor had recommended soothing his boy each morning in ice cold cream, to help reduce the oozing and throbbing. The young giddy maid stopped her thieving after that and soon married, giving up a life in service.

In 1938, an ex-sailor, about ten years older than Annie, was given a job as the handyman and caretaker in one of the posh hotels where she was the head chamber maid. He'd been badly busted up in World War One, this sailor fella. He was 43 now, but back in 1909, when he'd been a boy just turned 14, he ran away to join the Merchant Navy. Within a few years, he signed up with the Royal Navy and became one of the first lads to sail on a British submarine.

His name was Harry Flowers, and he'd been born in the east end of London – in Whitechapel, Jack the Ripper territory. His mother was a drunk and an hysteric with an addiction to over-the-counter medicine, so the story goes, which in those days wasn't rare as half the population was hooked on cocaine and heroin. His father was a sign-painter. Both his mother and father came from rough, criminal families. His father's brothers ran with a gang of Jewish hoods who specialised in rolling coppers. They'd wait up an alley for a young police officer to pass by and then attack him just for the hell of it. The usual routine was to kick the copper unconscious and throw him down into the sewers, clanging the steel manhole cover behind him as he dropped.

There was a lot of gin drinking and fighting and singing. Harry was the runt of a litter of five. Of that five, three died – all girls.

The other, a brother, was a good ten years older than Harry. Before Harry reached his teens, this older brother of his, by the name of Wally, had taken up his mother's taste for cocaine and heroin, contracted during a stint in the army, and was last seen hitching a ride on a steam ship to the far east, on his way, they said, to fill himself up on Chinese opium. Never was he heard of again.

Harry's father, the sign-painter, was a decent man, if a little in the shadow of his mad wife. This mad wife's side of the family could trace their line all the way back to the beginning of the 1800s to a woman called Bobo, of all things. That wasn't her real name – that's been lost to time. She was a Russian Jew from Odessa in the Ukraine, according to family legend. Bobo arrived in London some time in the 1820s, it was guessed, when she was about 20 years old herself and on the run from jew-baiters in Tsarist Russia – all without a word of English in her head. Her strange name, it turns out, comes from the word babuskha – Russian for grandmother. She'd married an Englishman and her young gentile grandchildren corrupted her pronunciation of the word down to 'Bobo', and by the time of Pearse's birth all recollection of who she really was had died out long ago. She was just Bobo the dead Jewish great-great-great-grandmother.

Harry's mad mother was forever getting drunk and beating him, so his soft but kind father decided that as he was out painting shop fronts all day, the safest place for his young boy – and his only functioning child, now aged about 11 – was in a boarding school. The family were old-fashioned cockneys but as they ran their own business, they had enough money – despite the cost of all the mad wife's drugs – to send young Harry off to a lowly ranked church school in the Kent countryside. The hope was that his time away from the east end might make a gentleman out of him.

But this was a lad who'd been brought up around villains and street-fighters, and he did not take particularly well to the kind of discipline meant to turn the sons of drapers and clerks into model citizens of the empire. Young Harry had been taught to box since he could walk, so the first day that a school-master insulted him and beat him for being the urchin he was by nature, he took the teacher's cane, broke it over his knee and punched the master in the jaw.

He was expelled, but his father didn't give up hope. He tried another school and then another. At the age of 14, Harry ran off to sea, fed up with the beatings – joining the Merchant Navy. That same year he docked in Aden, his head full of stories told by his older shipmates about the veiled houris of the port, who beneath their silken masks were the most beautiful creatures to have ever lived. He'd been on shore leave for no more than a few hours, when a sashaying veiled lovely, smelling of frankincense and swaddled in silks and gold, caught his eye in the street. He walked up to her and ripped the mask off her face. Beneath, lay the face of an average Arab woman with a hairy mole on her lip. He'd no time to consider the lies of his crew-mates, as the local men turned wild with outrage, chasing him up the alleys of Aden to his ship. The daft boy had managed to spark something of a diplomatic incident, and found himself taken off the ship and flogged in the public square. His captain told him he'd been lucky that the shipping company and the British ambassador had begged the local headmen not to have his hands – or worse – cut off.

He transferred to the Royal Navy before war broke out. The Battle of Jutland nearly cost him his life. He was a stoker on a sub, down in the hot furnaces of the engine rooms, making the heart of the big underwater monster beat and steam forward. A German destroyer depth-charged the sub during this battle in 1916; the explosion blowing open the furnace – and the mix of heat and water steamed Harry alive. The sub rose to the surface and the British sailors threw him into the freezing North Sea to lower the temperature of his boiling skin – with a life-jacket tied to his one unburned hand. His best friend leaned over the side of the sub, and held Harry's head up by the hair, keeping his face out of the water, so he didn't drown. It was said he resembled one huge human blister. A German light cruiser opened fire on the foundered sub, shelling its slopping deck until the British ran up the surrender flag. By then, thanks to the bombing, Harry had taken pieces of shrapnel to his leg and chest. His mates barely bothered to get him out of the water, sure that he was dead, floating in a bloody green sea.

The whole lot were taken Prisoner of War, and Harry was treated by a German doctor at a hospital in occupied Belgium – a pioneer in reconstructive surgery, so the story goes; and not only did he save Harry's life, with ice baths and skin grafts and greased bandages, he also left him mostly free from scarring. Harry Flowers was flat-faced and broken-nosed, but he was also a near-handsome fella, and what was remarkable was that this German doctor nursed him back to health with no visible signs of the dreadful blistering. The only wounds remaining on his body – hidden by his clothes – were a fist sized shrapnel hole in his leg, the scars on his chest where the doctor had dug metal out of his ruined left lung, and the white spit of healed burns splattered from his neck to navel.

After the First World War, the German doctor and Harry wrote to each other until 1939 when war broke out again. From 1945, they continued their correspondence until the German doctor died in early 1960, aged almost 80. Pearse never got the chance to read the letters – and there is no recollection now of the doctor's name.

When he got back to London in 1919, Harry Flowers returned to the Merchant Navy, traveling around the world as a stoker or bosun. Come the early 1930s though, his wrecked lungs had caught up with him, and he found himself confined to a sanatorium with a case of TB – his career at sea over for good, it seemed.

While he lay in bed, alongside rows of other men lying dying in beds, on a lawn in the grounds of the sanatorium – the doctors hoping that this strange combination of bed-rest and fresh air might help alleviate their symptoms – Harry was visited by his old mates from the navy. They lined him up with job interviews in London. He tried his hand as a boxing coach, but his breathing was too weak to inspire the boys; he had a go at working on the bridges and barges of the Thames, but being so near to the water and so far from sea was depressing for him; so he eventually took up working in hotels, usually on the front step as a doorman, for he could still handle himself in a fight and take down the biggest of men before the strain got to his lungs and he tired; and he had a gentlemanly air about him as well. In search of better pay, he took up positions as chief handyman and caretaker in various hotels, and that is where he meets Annie.

One of his last great acts of manly virility and violence before falling in love with Annie and settling down to a life of marriage and fatherhood, was to take on some of the auld Nazi black-shirts in the east end of London town, when they came to intimidate and abuse his Jewish friends. He and a team of lads who ran with Jack Spot, the Yid gangster, made short work of half a dozen or so of these Oswald Mosley types in an alley near Brick Lane. It went biff, bam, boof, he said.

This shattered sailor, ten years her senior, with a face as weather-beaten as the surface of the earth that he'd travelled over, but with a fit strong figure still, and a taste for smart suits and jaunty hats and good leather shoes – this shattered auld sailor caught her eye the first moment Annie spied him, in the backyard of the hotel mending a busted boiler.

They went on a few dates to the movies, kissed, fell for each other, got married, went to Margate on honeymoon for a weekend, and were back at work on Monday in the same hotel they'd met in just a few weeks before.

It seems they were trying for a baby when war broke out again. Harry – with his auld salty sea-dog credentials – helped take part in the evacuation of the British troops from Dunkirk, along with hundreds of other merchant seamen in their little boats and tugs and transports. On the way back from France, a German shell hit the deck of the boat he was bringing soldiers safely home in. It exploded killing a few young infantrymen, and a slice of shrapnel, ripped into his back piercing his one good lung. When they got him to shore, it seemed sure he was dying – all over again. Somehow, though, he pulled through, and the sea did not take him down. By 1942, he was on his feet again, and Harry and Annie adopted a little baby girl who'd been orphaned in a German bombing raid. They called her Katy.

*

Come Monday morning, Pearse is back at school for the day of the 11-plus, to find out if he's intelligent or not, and Mrs Boatman is running through auld mathematical and logical questions in preparation for the test that afternoon. He needs the practice or else he will never pass the entrance for the Grammar School. She looks at Pearse over her pointy spectacles as she sets a mock question paper down, and says, 'This is perfectly easy for you, Pearse.' She walks off, with chalk down the back of her black jacket, and chewing gum on the heel of her shoe.

There are daft problems like 'what fraction in its lowest term is equal to 42 per cent?' Who cares. Or they show the alphabet, as if no-one knows it, and then say 'PP is to SN as KL is to [__]', and you have to fill in the blank. How? What does it mean? And if it does mean something, Pearse has been away sick and missed it.

Nothing much else happened that week except for those 11-plus tests, and a fight after school on Thursday with Brian Blackwell, which Pearse never started. He tried to cripple the wee clipe in the fight, though, by jumping on his knee-cap a few times after he'd got him on the ground.

He hadn't seen May-Belle all that week either. She wasn't out and about in the estate, and she was never around in the morning or evening going to or from school, so she must have missed sitting her own entrance exam for the Catholic grammar – though it was highly unlikely she'd ever have passed it anyway, even in a million years of swotting up.

The memory of Martin and the terror of the police had drifted away – for no-one seemed to give a damn what they'd done; it was never mentioned. No-one came knocking at home, there wasn't a word said at school. Martin hadn't died, so it was no big deal. Pearse kept wondering what May-Belle was up to, and if she was okay. He hated that he'd bailed on her and wanted to dump her. He still couldn't call for her, though. He didn't want to see her horrible Ma; and May-Belle might even hate him for being fly; he knew he shouldn't see her anymore, though, no matter what, but he couldn't resist playing with her either.

He wasn't going to go chasing after anyone like some love-sick wee girl, though, so come Saturday he spent the morning watching Swap Shop bored off his tits. Fed up, he dandered out the door and took a wander about the streets, not doing much, kicking stones around and whipping bushes with a bit of a snappy auld branch. He was idling outside the gate of the last house in May-Belle's row, which ran along the top of his street, at a right-angle – as the auld mathematical 11-plus types would say. The people in that house – the last on May-Belle's row – were never in and had no kids, but they did have two big dogs that were always chained up in their backyard and surrounded by mountains of their own shite and pish. A terrible sight. God knows what breed the dogs were – they were mutants, about the size of Shetland ponies and a smokey-blue-grey, with red tongues lolling a yard out of their gobs and big bleary eyes. Pearse was poking his stick through the slats in the fence and making them bark, when he heard a big, 'Hi, Pearsey, fanny-boy', right in his lug-hole.

He swizzled around and there she was, looking a bit puffy round the gills, but with her wee puckered up smile on her face and her eyes blinking.

Pearse says to her, 'What happened to you? I saw you at the hospital and it looked like you'd been in a car accident.'

She says, 'Ma beat the shit out of me for being late when we came in from robbing the orchard.'

'Jesus,' he says. 'She must have given you one hell of a hammering.'

'She did,' says May-Belle. They wandered about the estate not heading anywhere in particular or paying any heed to whether they are going left or right or east or west. 'She twisted my arm up my back and I thought it was going to break, and she held me by the hair and punched me in the face. That's why I've not been to school.'

'Was that your Dad with you at the hospital?' he asked.

'Aye,' she says. 'But he had to go away again, a few days ago, for a couple of months, I think.'

And Pearse said nothing, because he didn't know what to say.

'He wasn't there, though, when she hit me,' says May-Belle. 'He was down in Belfast. He can't stand the bitch, but she won't let us go away and live together as she says she needs us. She had one of her fellas at the house when she was laying in to me, and he did nothing to stop it, but when it was all over – and this fella could see that I could barely get up and I'd made a pretty bad mess of myself too – he goes to call the ambulance and Ma says, 'No, ring her useless fucken Dad instead', so this guy runs out to the phone box at the top of the hill and makes I don't know how many phone calls until he finds someone who knows where to fetch Dad, and Dad gets a mate to drive him up first thing in the morning, because by then it's late and he's no way of getting up here, and when he arrives I'm all fevery and being sick in my bed and near blind with a headache so Dad takes me to the hospital up in Ballymena.'

She pauses, and laughs, and says, 'Och, I'm outta breath talking. What happened to you? Why were you up at the Waveney?'

Pearse says, 'Oh, I was just swinging the lead and trying to get out of school.'

'Why?' she asks.

'Just,' he says, and she shoots him a look, smelling a fib. 'What did you tell the doctors?' he asks her.

'Dad said that I fell downstairs backwards.'

'Right.'

'On the way home, he said there was something wrong with Ma – that she was sick in the head and that's why he couldn't live with her.'

'Right.'

'When we got back, he threw one of her fellas out and told her that if she ever touched me again, he'd break her neck. He's said that loads of times, though.'

Pearse said nothing, and thought of the dot dot dot you see in books when someone is struck dumb.

'Ma told him to get the fuck out of the house, and he said he was staying. She said no court in the land would allow a man like him to have me.'

Pearse nodded.

'And she told him he better watch his mouth cos she had plenty on him. He said, 'Try me.' And then she got her coat and her purse and left, shouting, 'You can keep the fucken wee bitch.''

'Where'd she go?'

'Och, she went to Belfast. That's where she works sometimes, or even down in Dublin or over in Glasgow. Once she went to Aberdeen for a month, but said it froze the knickers off her and she'd never go there again.'

'So who's looking after you now?'

'She came back the morning Dad had to go, so I'm stuck with the auld bitch now, till he comes home.'

'I hate it when Mum goes out and I'm left stuck with my auld bastard too,' Pearse said.

They sat down on a wall and started spitting on the paving stones and throwing wee pebbles into the gutter. 'Sorry I never called down for you,' she says. 'I was feeling better the last few days, but I didn't know if you were ill and I didn't want to see that

Da of yours, to tell the truth.'

'That's alright,' Pearse says, 'you were sick.'

'I fucken hate her,' says May-Belle, and Pearse can see out of the corner of his eye that she's crying a wee bit so he doesn't turn to look at her.

'There's plenty of dicks I hate too,' Pearse says.

'That Da cunt of yours?' she asks.

'I'd love to kill him,' he says.

'Fuck, I'd love to kill her too,' she says back.

'What about the police?' asks Pearse.

'I'd poison her so the cops would never know. Make it look like a suicide.'

'No,' says Pearse, 'I meant about Martin and the fire and all that.'

'I never heard anything. No-one gives a fuck round here.'

Pearse has a Sherbet Dib-Dab in his pocket so he gives it to May-Belle, telling her he can't stand the way it feels against his teeth, and as he doesn't want it, she can have it. She sits there sucking the sherbet off the lolly. Pearse tells her, 'Mum's going to leave Da one day – two sures about that.' She says, 'Dad'll one day get custody of me as well.' May-Belle's dribbling fizzy red and yellow spit out of her mouth onto the ground. Pearse can't get a proper slobber out of him. He's been gobbing and talking so much his mouth is dry. His throat is spikey, like a blade of grass is stuck in it.

Pearse feels a bit of a cry coming on him now, and he'll start bawling if they don't change the conversation, so he says to May-Belle, 'Come on down to my house. Mum's in, and she'll give us a couple of auld jars to go catching bees.'

May-Belle's up for that, so they wander back to Pearse's house, and she waits outside the garden gate while Mum huffs and puffs a bit because she's been asked to tip a whole jar of coffee into a tupperware holder, and wash out the tail end of the jam from a jar that's nearly empty; but after a few minutes she's fine and dandy, and they've got the jars and are away out the gate again and going up the road towards the common.

Pearse takes his penknife out of his pocket and digs air holes into the top of the jars. He's got the coffee jar and May-Belle's got the jam jar. They put a wee bit of grass and some nice smelling petals in the bottom of each jar to attract the auld bees – they add in a gob so the creatures will have something to drink – and then they go hunting on the flowers hanging off the bushes along each side of the common.

Pearse always considered himself the King of Bee-Catching, but May-Belle is born for this game; it is in her blood. Like the most practiced bee-hunter, she's not scared. She knows that the big bumblebees, the auld hairy fellas with the fat arses, wouldn't know how to sting a human being if you paid them. They're like furry flying cows – they are that gentle. They aren't like honey bees or hornets who'd dive bomb the bollocks off you and sting you half to death just for looking at them the wrong way. May-Belle makes sure she targets the right type for capture.

She's fast too when she's hunting and uses pretty much the same technique as Pearse: creep slowly up on the auld Bumbler, with the jar in one hand and the lid in the other, when he's perched on a flower having a drink of nectar and getting the pollen all over his wee black legs, and just slowly slowly bring the jar up and the lid down on Bumbler, flower and all. Screw the lid shut, snapping off the flower at the head as you do it, and Bumbler and flower are now trapped in the bottom of the glass going 'zzzz-fucken-zzzz-what-the-fuck-happened-zzzz'.

Then the Bumbler will start blattering himself off the inside of the jar, and you can feel him zzzz-ing through the glass until he gets knackered and just sits on his wee flower – beat. Even if you don't roll them over and over again down a hill in the jar, or spin them around, making them dizzy and sick and wobbly, the auld bees will eventually just fade away and die, trapped inside. There's never been a captured bee last more than about three hours inside a jar, even with air holes, without it just deciding to die for whatever reason – sadness or boredom or fear or confusion. And they'll die despite having other bees in the jar with them – so it's not loneliness that's killing them.

After they've nabbed about six or seven bees apiece, May-Belle and Pearse wander along to a nearby street and sit on a wall that surrounds a big tree outside an end house and shake the bees about and give the jars a bit of a spin on the ground. That shuts the bees up. There's no more zzzz-ing and they lie quiet among their flowers, just waggling the odd wee sticky leg in the air or stumble-bumbling into each other. They wouldn't even imagine trying to fly now inside the jar, it's all shaky-slow walking about or lying still – sick, groggy or sleeping. If you opened the lid, they wouldn't know how to escape.

Pearse and May-Belle haven't said anything for a wee minute to each other. Although, usually, Pearse doesn't like the quiet and no-one talking, with May-Belle it's alright – and she prefers silence sometimes without the need for noise. A bit of a right bitey wind is getting itself whipped up now out of nowhere, so Pearse says to May-Belle, 'Do you want to come down to my house for a wee while to watch the telly and have some juice? Da's out down the pub and won't be back for ages, so it'll be alright as Mum's the only one in and she's dead on.'

'Aye,' she says, and then she picks up her bee jar and gives it a hell of a shake. 'What about these wee fuckers?' she asks.

'Just let 'em go,' Pearse says.

'Away on, Pearsey,' she says. 'Cmon, follow me.' And she races round the corner to a dark skinny path which runs up the side of a row of houses. Windowless bare brick back-walls line the tiny lane. Facing the bare brick walls are the big tall bushes that run down the length of the common. It's a secluded lane – the path no broader than a man and a woman walking hand-in-hand. This is the kind of place where older kids come to smoke and write graffiti as it's all in shadow and no-one can see. On the walls there's writing saying things like 'Gary W fucked Pauline M' and a drawing of a dick with pubes and pimples and spunk. Glass is smashed all over the place, and there's graffiti on the ground too, saying, 'Cunts look here'.

'You ready?' says May-Belle, twiddling the jar between her two palms real fast as if she's trying to warm her hands.

'For what?' Pearse asks.

'For chucking the wee bastards?' she says, and she mimes throwing the jar like a cricket ball or a bomb, right and loose and over the shoulder in an swinging arch.

Pearse gives the bees in his jar the auld twiddling routine to make sure they keep right groggy and tells May-Belle, 'Hauld on till they're sleepy.' Pearse usually keeps his bees outside on his window sill till the morning and then throws them away. Maybe if they're dopey and sleepified, though, the end will be easier for them. The landing won't be too painful – they'll be kind of anaesthetised from all the twiddling and won't suffer too much.

'Ready?' she says.

'Roger!' he laughs, and they pull back their arms like German grenade-men – aiming up the alley. They count to three together and then fire the jars in a big swoop over their heads. Both jars arc and collide in mid-air about thirty feet in front of them, smashing to smithereens; the silver sparkle of the shards raining to the pavement. Pearse lets a big whoop out of him when the jars kiss and explode, and spins round on his heel to race off before any adults come out of their homes – but May-Belle grabs ahold of him and says, 'Och, hauld on, Pearsey, come here.'

He hesitates for a wee second, and when he can't hear anyone coming allows her to pull him forward, towards the broken jars, by his sleeve.

'What you doing, daft faggot?' he says to her. 'Come on. Let's get the fuck outta here.'

'Wait a wee minute,' she says. 'Let's take a look and see what happened to them.'

'Flippen hell, May-Belle,' he says.

They scoot forward. The bees are lying among the broken glass and battered flowers. Some are well and truly dead – busted up or cut in two. Others, though, are wandering about, like survivors after a bombing raid; tottering around not knowing where they are going, a bit tattered and torn and shell-shocked but otherwise alive.

There's one who's made it away from all the wreckage, a good few inches from the glass and jar lids and flowers. He's heading for the bushes. May-Belle brings her big guttie down on the wee fella – bomp – and scrapes him about underneath her plimsoll. She lifts her foot and he's just a dirty wee hairy smear on the ground.

'Fuck, May-Belle,' Pearse said. 'Have you never heard of the Geneva Convention?'

Bomp. She splats another one. 'What you on about, Pearsey?' she says.

'You're not meant to kill prisoners. It's the law.'

'Bollocks,' she says, and wallops another one under foot.

There's only two left alive, so he says to her, 'Aye, you're right, I suppose', and he leaps high in the air, aiming down hard with his feet, and lands perfectly, flattening the last two survivors at the same time – one under each shoe. Blap. Blop. Squished.

She laughs like a drain, and the pair speed off towards Pearse's house yo-hoo-ing to each other. When they get there, they're just in time for The Basil Brush Show followed by the Pink Panther, the rinky-dink panther. Mum takes a good long look at May-Belle on the door-step and after a second says, 'Hello, come on in. I expect people to behave themselves in this house, so no carry-on, please. Sit down and watch the TV and I'll get the pair of you some juice and a biscuit.' Mum comes back with a couple of Penguins and some coke, and Pearse and May-Belle sit on the floor and watch Basil Brush getting up to his auld boom-boom shenanigins and the Pink Panther being suave.

When the sports results come on, May-Belle brings the dirty dishes into the kitchen, where Mum is making Spaghetti

Bolognese on the stove, and says, 'Thanks very much, Mrs Furlong.' Pearse is repeating the football scores to himself – trying to be like Mike Yarwood and copying the man's voice on the telly, saying the names of all the funny-sounding football teams – 'Heart of Midlothian 4, Queen of the South 6' – but he's also got one ear cocked to what's going on in the next room. Mum says, 'You're welcome, dear', and May-Belle comes back into the living room.

'I'd better be heading,' she says to Pearse.

'Aye, ok, then.'

Mum follows her in and says, 'Is that you off then, love?'

May-Belle says, 'Yeah, I'd better be going for my tea thanks.'

Mum says to her, 'Well, Pearse and I are away out tomorrow for a picnic up to the Six Mile River in Muckamore. Would you like to come along?'

Pearse goes, 'Are we mum? You never told me. Aww beezer, mum, beezer.'

'Shush, you,' Mum says. 'I just decided. It's meant to be a nice weekend, and your father is away tomorrow so I thought it'd be nice to get out in the sunshine.'

'Beezer, ma,' he says.

'Don't call me that,' Mum says. 'I hate that word. It's Mum.'

'Aye,' he says, leaping around on the sofa like a thing possessed. 'Brill, Mum. Can you come, May-Belle?'

'Your friend had better ask her parents if she's allowed.'

'Ok. Thanks,' says May-Belle.

'Can I go up with her, Mum?' Pearse asks.

'Yes,' Mum says, 'but don't be pestering her mother and father.'

They bomb out the door and peg it up the road. May-Belle says to Pearse, 'I like her – she's nice.'

'Aye,' Pearse says. 'Fuck, I love picnics.'

'Me too,' she says.

They get to the bottom of May-Belle's front path, and Pearse hangs back, waiting at the broken gate. May-Belle walks on, leaving him behind, glancing back as she rings the door bell. She waits twirling her hair round her fingers and swinging on her heels. The door opens and a blank-faced blonde woman stands there screwing up her eyes to shield them from the weak evening light. She's wearing a flimsy white top and no bra. Beneath are these wild vivid pink nipples that Pearse can't take his eyes off. May-Belle lets go her hair. The woman looks at Pearse and a clumsy uglified smile passes over her face. She pulls the door wide and May-Belle walks inside. A few minutes later the door opens again and out walks May-Belle.

She nods her head, as she pulls the door shut behind her, not looking at Pearse. She gets to the bottom of the path, and says out the side of her mouth, 'That's fine. I can go.'

'Top notch,' he says and they race back to his house, skidding down the flight of six steps that lead from May-Belle's row to Pearse's row – pushing each other and ya-ho-ing.

While they run May-Belle babbles, 'Ma even told me to say that it was very nice of youse to ask me along, and she'd like to return the favour one day.'

'Super,' Pearse says as they run up his garden path, and into the house.

'Grand,' Mum replies when they tell her it's all okay. 'Now weren't you meant to be off home for your tea, dear? I'll see you in the morning about eleven o'clock,' she says to May-Belle.

That night Da didn't get in till God knows what time. By the time he did arrive back Pearse was fast asleep. The evening had been top crack: Gran came over for her tea and told some of her auld stories; then she went back to her place at half nine, and Pearse and Mum settled down to watch the horror double bill on BBC2.

When they were going to bed, Pearse hid in the dark at the top of the stairs and leapt out on her – hissing 'vampyre, vampyre'. Mum screamed like he'd bitten half her face off, shouted 'you're a wee shit' and then laughed and chased him around his bed saying she'd eat him. Pearse hopped into bed and she gave him a kiss.

Pearse could smell her Harmony Hairspray as he fell asleep thinking about playing with May-Belle down at the river in Muckamore tomorrow afternoon. It was wrong to use the word playing, though. Daft, in fact. They were heading for the big school soon, so they'd be hanging out.

*

May-Belle found the story of wee baby Katy the saddest of all the stories that Pearse told to her back during those nights in his bedroom – out of sight and out of mind of the adults. The adopted baby was killed in an air-raid in 1942 – just a few months after Annie and Harry had taken her under their roof. She was blown out of Annie's arms as they ran down the street to the bomb shelter – her poor pink brains lying dashed in the rubble and dust.

Annie and Harry had married over the broomstick, as it were. The ceremony was in a register office as she was Catholic, and he Church of England, but neither cared a damn about God. After the little girl Katy died, though, Annie took back up with the Church. With bombs falling on London every day, there was some reassurance in repeated prayers.

Her prayers seemed to pay off too. By the beginning of 1943 – only a few months after Katy was killed – Annie fell pregnant with her own child at the age of 38. This was Pearse's mother, Josie. She was born as the tide of the war started to turn against the Nazis. Her first memory – surely one implanted by the talk of her own mother and father, and not a recollection she could truly dredge up from her mind – this first memory saw her lying on her back in her pram, aged about one, and a doodle-bug flying over the Edgware Road. She points to the sky as the engines cut – the deadly whine stopping so the people below know it's destined to drop there and then – and she waves up at the V2 bomb and shouts, 'Doggie, doggie' – for the shape of the machine moving between the clouds reminded her of a dachshund.

Annie took her child Josie from the pram, laid her on the ground and covered her with her body until the bomb fell and the ground stopped shaking.

Bombs were the background to Josie's childhood, and Pearse used to laugh because the sound of a balloon bursting made her leap in the air.

A bomb fell in their London street one day, near the end of the war, as the milkman was making his rounds. All that was found of him when the smoke cleared and the people came out through their splintered doors was one smoking boot with a foot and a bit of a leg to mid-calf – clad in a sock – still inside.

They were bombed out of their home three times in the space of a year. To keep the child Josie safe they shipped her off to Margate to live with friends for six months, but, barely out of nappies, she sickened in sadness and they came to fetch her after a few weeks. Homeless, they lived in tents in the Essex country-side with other bombed-out families, and then wandered back to London, missing their friends, stopping overnight at a lunatic asylum – that's what both Josie and Annie said in their stories, anyhow – and although it's fantastic and horrible, they bedded down in this lunatic asylum, on the floor of the operating theatre, but the inmates howling and slobbering kept them shivering awake till dawn, sure they'd be cannibalised in their sleep.

None of this was much help to auld Harry's war wounds – for he was old now – and by the time 1945 comes around, he's barely able to work. Harry stays at home to look after wee toddler Josie, and Annie becomes the main breadwinner in peace-time, taking on three jobs a day, sometimes, to make ends meet. By the time the 1950s have come and rationing is over, Harry's reduced to selling all his war medals, his naval uniform and souvenirs from his time as a PoW and the retreat from Dunkirk – even a keepsake bit of shrapnel from his back. Annie's hardening life turned her increasingly toward the church, and Josie was forced to attend every mass going, choked by the incense and terrified of the Latin drone. The rituals set her up for a life of hating the church – not helped by her time spent in the care of the Little Sisters of Mercy, at the convent day school Annie sent her to in the heart of the city of London; wicked auld nuns who walloped her with the school-bell and forced her to eat cold custard and cabbage when she didn't clear her plate; priests who threatened wee girls with Hell if the Holy Wafer touched their teeth during communion, or they even considered marrying a protestant.

There was a glimmer of good hope, though, when a middling win on the pools allowed Annie to set herself up running a bed and breakfast in Kilburn just as the Irish lads started to flock over to London to help rebuild Britain – the engine of industry running again. It didn't make the Flowers family rich – far from it – but it was their own business, and all that penurious scrimping was now well away from the family.

As the whirl of life spun around London and young Josie, her father Harry worsened – hacking up blood and struggling for breath. Josie was a shy retiring 16-year-old by the time 1960 came around, but her good looks and figure made her a honey-pot for lads with their drain-pipe trousers and brylcreemed hair. She liked all the doo-lang doo-lang music, but was such a naive girl that the drugs and sex of the decade passed her by. She had a few boyfriends and one lover by the time her father died in 1967. He was 72, Annie was 62, and Josie 23.

In the weeks leading up to his death, Annie sat by his bed in hospital and prayed to God and Jesus and Mary and all the saints she'd abandoned as a young girl, begging them to save her husband's life so he could live to see their only daughter one day marry and have a child herself.

Josie paled at home as her mother stayed by Harry's bedside, sleeping in the hospital chair, hardly eating, taking just a few sips from a cup of tea every so often. Annie sat with her hands clenched in her lap, praying and praying so hard that she started to tremble all over. The passion of her prayers shaking her body from hair to hem.

He died regardless of her prayers. When he breathed his last, Annie's body relaxed for the first time in a week. Her body stilled as life passed from her husband, and she remained peaceful and quiet for an hour, while Josie laid her head on the hospital sheets and cried her eyes dry over his dead body.

When Josie lifted her head, and the orderlies came to wheel the body away, Annie was sitting in the chair she'd made her home, looking perfectly serene, apart from a tremor in her left hand. The tremor never left her. It stayed with her from that day forth. When life was average and normal, without rows and madness or worry, it was just a little shake, like you'd see in the hand of a drunk or someone with stage fright; when she was angry or sad it reached a frightening pitch, rocking from side to side, often setting her whole body trembling. When she was beatific and happy, or asleep, the hand stood still; its endless pitching forgotten.

She put away her religion again – for good, it seemed – when her husband died. Her God and Jesus and Mary and the saints had forsaken her, and she turned on them with the bitterness of her daughter's modern hatred for all things holy.

Josie froze into herself, barely leaving her room except to work in the department store where she sold perfume and make-up – the running of the guest house falling to Annie alone. As they drifted further and further away from themselves, each other and everything else on the face of the planet, Annie received one of her once-in-a-decade letters from her sister Maria back in Ireland, still living in County Antrim, with her protestant husband, in the wee town of Crumlin.

The letter said there was a young man who she'd cared for as a foster mother when he was a child; he'd grown up and got bored of Ulster. 'He has itchy feet, just like you and Katy,' Maria wrote, 'and he wants to come to London to find his fortune. Would you be kind enough to maybe put him up for a few days till he gets on the right road? The lad has dreams of going to college in London and getting into the accountancy game.' For that was the business the fella found attractive.

A few months later in the mid-winter of 1968, this lad of 19 arrives at the guest-house door. This is the man who turns into Pearse's Da.

*

Dawn would always be coming up when May-Belle got to the end of her story about the holiday she had when she was nine with Dad – and then it would be time for her to get out of the warm bed beside Pearse and sneak home before all the adults emerged into the waking day.

Of course, Dad and May-Belle had to return to Antrim from Portrush at the end of their week away together. Ma was still gone, and life was just grand. May-Belle sang all the time and told Dad ideas about becoming a singer. He said, 'You don't need to dream, you're cut out to entertain the public.' He'd save a little money and by the time Christmas came he'd have enough stashed away to find a talent agent. The agent would engage the stage, and there'd be tours of Northern Ireland over the school holidays, performing at sea-side towns and summer concerts and country fairs.

'All you need then,' Dad said, 'is the right person to spot you – and you'll be on stage in the West End of London, on your way to Hollywood.'

Nevertheless, the police came for him early one morning, a few days later, and they carted May-Belle off to the barracks too, as there was no-one but him to care for her. Da shouted to her that he loved her and was sorry. They pushed him into the back of a Black Mariah. The police couldn't get hold of Ma and said to May-Belle, 'Then you'll have to be signed over into the state's care.' May-Belle wasn't sure if that was meant to be bad or not. She spent the afternoon with a lady cop in the station, reading comics and watching TV. At teatime, a guard came through from the front office and said to the WPC, 'Jeanette – that's the wee girl's mum in reception now.'

The guard looked at May-Belle and said, 'You're ok now, love – you can go home with your mammy.'

*

For May-Belle, it was the story of auld Bollock-Brain that was the strangest of all Pearse's night-time tales. Gran had always told Pearse that Da was the cuckoo in everyone's nest. An unwanted creature who turned and ate the ones who cared for him. Dan Furlong was a changeling left by evil fairies. Though, the story could be interpreted a different way, and with more pity, if you were foolish enough to look at it in that fashion. Maybe he was just a born bastard, May-Belle wondered. Pearse sniggered and said, 'That's exactly what he was.'

Dan Furlong's mother was called Maude, and Maude's family, the Furlongs, came from a small town, near the loughs of Fermanagh, called Culky. Her father was a local solicitor, and her mother the daughter of a minister. This was a family of stiff collars and church-going, long hours of empowering Protestant work and respectability – this was not a home for singers and show-offs. Down the ages the men had served with no distinction whatsoever in every war the Crown had fought. Maude's father – a man Pearse never met – was a regimental bean counter in one of the Ulster battalions in the First World War. He was invalided out of the army a week before all the volunteer boys from the north went over the top at the Somme. An axle on a cook's horse-drawn wagon broke and smashed his instep, leaving him with a limp for the rest of his life – an ailment he did not attempt to convince people wasn't down to a bullet from the auld Bosch.

There's little known about these quiet folk – and they've passed out of time, life and history. Dan's mother grew up in what you'd call 'the middle middle classes'. Her lot was to marry a well brought up young man with a career in front of him as a civil servant or village GP, and to have a few healthy Protestant children who could contribute to the status quo.

Pearse only met Maude a few times – by then she was an old, lean woman. She forbade him calling her grandmother, and Dan was forbidden from calling her mother. A beaky, lanky crane of a person, she loomed over Pearse and asked if he bathed regularly and went to church. She came to their house – Pearse, Dan and Josie were not allowed to visit her – had tea with them and left, pressing a pound note into Pearse's hand and telling him to grow up to be a good wee man.

As a teenager in the late-1920s she wasn't exactly a rebel, but rather than sit at home as plenty of young women did in those days waiting for Mr Right-ish to come calling, she got herself trained as a nurse and went out into the world. There would have been little hope for her if she'd not taken life by the ears. Gangly women with big noses, spindly fingers and Olive Oyl legs and arms seldom catch the handsome prince. She was not a woman men would bound over each other to woo.

Come the end of the war – when she's about 30, and, it's no surprise to anyone, still a spinster – she's working as a matron in the military wing of the Musgrave Park Hospital in Belfast. She'd done well for herself – with no love life to speak of, she quickly rose up the ranks of the nursing staff until she was more or less the boss-woman come peace time.

As spring 1945 approaches, a wounded artilleryman from the town of Omagh is brought to her wing. He's not in too bad a state. His unit had taken a hit from the last few Nazi planes still flying over the continent, and after being treated at a field hospital, he's sent back to England for follow-up surgery to his shattered legs. Once the most difficult operations are over, he's shipped home to Ulster to recuperate. He was a sergeant with a few medals, and a Catholic, by the name of Eamon Kane. If love had taken the path it wanted to Pearse would have been called Kane not Furlong.

Nobody knows what happened – whether she climbed on top of him in her nurses uniform and they made love in the hospital bed, or whether they waited till he was up and about and back in civvie street – but the pair of them started an affair and it went on until 1949, when Dan was born.

This fella Eamon Kane – another grandfather Pearse never met – was married. So here was Maude, an upright Protestant middle-class girl, having a long-running fling with a married Catholic, who, to be frank, was well below her social class, as he was a debt collector by profession. It's hard to work out what was worse back then: to be a adulteress and a slut, to be a fenian-lover, or to be an unmarried mother. Put together though, the sins were a recipe for suicide and social ruin.

In late 1948, she finds out she's pregnant, and her mother and father pack Maude off over the water to a private hospital in Middlesex. It's easy to cover-up – they merely say she's away for more training in the nursing profession. While she's gone, they warn Eamon Kane never to come near their daughter again. He vanishes from history and no-one ever heard tell of him from then on. Pzzf. Out goes that line of the family.

All alone in her hospital bed in Middlesex, Maude gives birth to little Dan Furlong in the Spring of 1949. Maude stays on in England, securing a position in a hospital in the midlands – claiming that her husband had died of his war wounds, and she was raising her young son on her own. She stuck it out lonesome for about a year over in England, and then decided to find a way to come back home without bringing shame with her. She asked her parents to place an advertisement in the Northern Whig Newspaper reading: 'Wanted, respectable Ulster family to raise baby. Excellent annual stipend in return for services.'

Maude's mother and father didn't need to wait long before they had at least six offers from young mothers with struggling families willing to take on the responsibility of rearing another woman's child for just over £150 a year – more than half the average yearly wage of a working man back then.

The young mothers seemed too flighty though. The Furlongs needed a serious woman who'd raise the boy as if he was being brought up in the heart of his own steady dependable family. They found just such a woman in the shape of Maria O'Neill – sister of Annie O'Neill, who went on to be Annie Flowers, Pearse's Gran.

Maria had by this time been married to her dour, dull, husband for more than twenty years. Her wedded name was Kilpatrick. They'd had their own misfortunes, losing their only son in the war, and Maria thought that with a little baby in the house, the pair of them might rekindle some love for each other; and of course, there was plenty to be done with a tumble down cottage in Crumlin on a salary of £150 a year, particularly with the mouths of two surviving children – two rather wan-faced girls approaching their teens – to feed as well.

The deal was done, with Maria under strict orders that she was in no way to mislead the boy into thinking that she was his real mother. She was a fosterer at best – a glorified servant. Maude would pay regular visits – inspections, often without warning – to Maria's Crumlin home to ensure the child was being reared according to her wishes, and her money well spent.

After the death of her son in the war, Maria had taken to drink, but kept the fact well hidden for a good few years. Her husband, a man named Billy, a usually quiet character, with little wit or charisma about him, would sometimes fly into fits of rage – when he could no longer take Maria's dominion over him – and administer beatings to his wife and the new child under his roof. He worked long hours as a labourer, and Maria, so it turned out, was not disinclined to the company of more entertaining men on the long afternoons when her husband was away.

Dan Furlong grew up being cuddled and cared for by Maria, a woman he was continually told was not his own flesh and blood. Yet he thought of her as his mother – his mammy – and she thought of him as her own baby. Every few months or so, his real mother, Maude, a cold unloving schoolmarm, would walk into his life, reorder it and then vanish again – leaving a few shillings in pocket-money on the table.

By the time he'd reached 13, he would rise up like a cobra when Maude came to the cottage in Crumlin. One visit, he called her a cunt and a hoor and tried to stab her with a screwdriver he was using to fix his broken bike – a bike she'd bought him on her last visit.

He took to strange behaviour too. Maude bought him some expensive shoes for school – shoes too grand for the village classes he attended – and they didn't fit. So, he got ahold of a razor blade and tried to slice off his heels in order to get his feet into the shoes. During another visit, he put gravel in his hair, and when he sat down to eat – alongside Maria, her husband Billy, his two older foster sisters who treated him like a prince, and Maude – he shook his head from side to side and the pebbles and grit went flying into the soup bowls on the table.

Maude decided that from now on Dan would be educated at the Royal Dungannon – a boarding school where the sons of generals and surgeons went to learn how to rule Northern Ireland and the rest of the UK. His behaviour had become vile, she believed, as he was mixing with the children of navvies and slatterns in the backwoods of County Antrim. During the holidays, he would return to Maria and her family. And of course, all of this to-ing and fro-ing meant Dan stood out clearly for what he was to the clever cruel boys in the posh school and the bitter youngsters back in Crumlin: a real born bastard with no true place to belong.

He didn't fare well at this public school. With a bumpkin accent and no manners, he was soon singled out for a spot of fagging – cleaning the boots and buttering the toast of the older boys. This didn't sit good with a lad who'd been brought up kicking tin cans around back streets, so he clocked a few of the bullies who called him the Bastard Boy, ran away and nearly got himself expelled. The only thing that kept his head above water was his willingness to thump those who humiliated him, and his aptitude for kicking, catching and throwing a ball. He arrived at the school aged 14 and within a few months was captain of the football team, and a star of the cricket and rugby squads. As for academic work, his only forte was numbers.

He left the Royal Dungannon at 16 with a few O levels in maths and science subjects, and went back to Crumlin to live permanently with Maria. Dan enrolled in the nearest technical college to try and gain the qualifications to become an accountant – for, honestly, that's what he fancied as his niche in life. He failed the course and re-sat it. Dan joined the Orange Order, at the behest of Maria and an accepting grunt from her husband Billy – by now a staunch Orangeman himself. They told him that membership of the loyal orders was a great way to get your name known and a sure route to securing decent employment. This was at a time when Catholics were nipping at the heels of the state and demanding a decent job and a house, and not to be messed about with anymore.

Tales of music and women across the water in London started to lure Dan, though – by now it's 1968 – and he informs Maria that he's had it with Ulster, and fancies trying his luck in the Big Smoke. Maria attempts to persuade him otherwise, but to no avail.

So, she picks up her pen and writes her sister, Annie, a letter, apologising for the long delay between correspondence, but asking if Annie would be kind enough to offer some help to the young man she'd been caring for as foster mother for many a year now. Annie agrees.

Dan arrives in London, a gawky 19-year-old, but he's got reserves of goofy Irish charm to burn, and to Josie – who's five years older than him – he's a romantic distraction in a life divided between a house of grief and the pointlessness of work. All Josie wanted to do was lose herself in a world of books, movies and music. She had no interest in the real world or real people unless there was some beautiful story to weave, but that was very seldom the case.

Josie was 24 and, in her head, enjoyed playing the role of the older vamp. As a young woman she had waves of dark hair, full lips, curves and soft white skin, flickering lashes over green and orange eyes. In her wedding photos she could pass as the double of Elizabeth Taylor. She spun this handsome-ish Irish country boy Dan elaborate lies about an imagined past; stories which made her even more alluring – claiming she'd had scores of lovers and even a husband who'd died just a few days after their wedding. When, of course, Dan later found out that this was all day-dreams, he let it slide. It would be a stick to beat Josie with in the future.

Within a month of arriving at Annie's guest-house, Josie and Dan were secretly sleeping together. Annie walked into Josie's bedroom one day and caught them – full steam ahead. She was sure from the start that Dan was evil. 'He is twisted, cruel and spiteful, Josie,' she said. 'A snake.'

It wasn't his religion that bothered Annie – and it appeared at the time that religion didn't bother him that much either. Annie had abandoned all that by then, and young Dan didn't say one word, when in London, which hinted or harked back to all the auld nonsense of Ireland. The fact was, Annie Flowers just didn't like Dan Furlong. She had a nose for bastard men, she said. As for Josie and her view of the differences in their religion – why, the thought didn't enter her head. She saw herself as English, and Catholic or Protestant meant nothing to her. She had no under-standing of the hangover and the bitterness, as her own mother had kept her away from all that history as she grew up in London.

With Dan still under the age of consent to marry – in those days you needed to be 21 – the pair of them eloped to Gretna Green on the train. When they arrived at the dreary wee Scots town it was raining and they were informed by the register of mar-riages that they'd have to wait three days for the ceremony. With no money, they used their return ticket to get back to London. A few days later, Josie found out she was pregnant. It was Annie who first suggested they call the baby Pearse if it turned out to be a boy.

In the face of Dan's rages down the telephone – and letters threatening that he would come to her village and shame her in front of her neighbours with his presence and her abandonment and her act of robbing him of a father and a family – his mother Maude relented and gave written consent for the pair to marry; she even came over to London for the big day itself. The word bastard haunted Maude as much as it haunted her son, and when Dan cried about it Josie comforted him.

Annie was content to say to her daughter Josie, 'You're a grown woman – on your own head be it.'

After their quiet wee wedding – for apart from Annie's friends they didn't have too many people in London they could depend on – they tried to settle down to married life in Josie's room at the top of the guesthouse. Dan, it's said, lied his way into an accountancy firm in the city of London, claiming not only to have a university degree but also that his own father was a captain in the navy during the second world war. He was rumbled, and dismissed in a shameful episode.

As a man who always looked for short-cuts, never the hard sure path, Dan threw in the towel and declared he wanted to return to Ulster. He begged Josie to come with him. He was still in thrall to this beautiful, voluptuous older woman – for a few years makes a big difference when you are young – and she was still smitten with him, for as yet he hadn't once raised his hand to her or belittled her or betrayed her. And the pair of them were enchanted by the idea of a new baby and a life of love-making before them.

Josie agrees to set off for Ulster with him; and so a few months after Pearse is born in St Mary's Hospital Paddington, they depart by plane – the first plane either of them had ever flown in – for Aldergrove Airport, just outside Antrim. Apart from burying her father, leaving her mother is the hardest task that Josie ever had to do. They said goodbye on the steps of the guest-house, Annie's hand shaking so much you'd think it would fly off her wrist into the gutter and grab Josie by the ankle to keep her held in London.

When the plane touched down, Josie was greeted by the sight of soldiers pointing guns at her, and Pearse just a wee baby in her arms. She'd promptly arrived in time for the return of the British army.

Josie saw these soldiers and she got on the next plane home to England, leaving Dan in tears at the airport. He returned to Maria's house and rang his wife from the telephone box at the end of the street every day, begging her to come to him, weeping till he couldn't speak.

In turn, Josie begged Annie to come to Northern Ireland along with her. She wanted to be with her husband, but couldn't face the prospect of Ulster without the shelter of her own mother.

Annie finally agreed. 'The only reason I'm doing this,' she said, 'is for the child. No boy should be brought up without a father.' She sold her guest-house – which barely earned its keep – and after the debts were paid had enough left over to buy furniture and fittings for the council flat she would need back in Ireland.

She told Josie that she hadn't set foot in Ireland for nearly fifty years, that she'd wanted to die without ever returning to the country. 'The north is cursed,' she said. 'I'm going to go back there and I am going to die there. I'll end up buried there, not where I want to be – beside your father here in London, where my home is.'

She'd distilled the Irishness out of herself over the last five decades. In her dreams she saw the streets of London and English friends, not the fields of Ireland or Ulster faces. 'It'll be nothing but trouble,' she said to Josie. 'Mark my words. If an Irishman has no-one to fight he'll take off his own coat and beat it with stones.'

By now, Dan had found his new wife a council house in Antrim – where they could make a home and a life for themselves. He'd got a job in a factory, and lined Josie up with an interview for a clerk's position. It was all there waiting for them, when she and her child arrived back in Ulster.

Annie got on the plane to Aldergrove with Josie and Pearse

– just a baby of six months by now. As the plane started, the stewardess came up to Annie and knelt down beside her. The stewardess, seeing Annie's shaking hand and pitying her as a first-time flyer, said, 'Are you frightened, madam?'

'For the first time in my life,' she said.

And the plane took her five hundred miles back across the Irish Sea, and five decades back into her past, to pick up where she left off.

*

By the time Mum wakes up that Sunday morning, Picnic Day as Pearse came to style it, he's already downstairs in his jammies making a fort out of a cardboard box, as there was sod all on telly except those auld Jesus Jones Holy Joe programmes with ugly types singing hymns. Praise the lord, and pass the ammunition.

Mum walks into the living room looking a bit baggy and saggy round the chops, says, 'Morning, Pearse love', and goes into the kitchen to have a cup of coffee with four sugars, and a couple of fags.

Pearse tootles on with the fiddly business of fort-making, using scissors to fashion wee battlements and a hinged portcullis.

A big holler comes down the stairs – Da shouting, 'Och, Josie, will you come here?' Mum grumbles to herself and walks to the foot of the stairs and shouts up, 'What do you want now, lump?'

He goes, 'Come here, Josie, please.' Pearse hokes his US 7th Cavalry men and some red indians – Crazy Horse and his Lakota Sioux braves – out of the toy-bag where he keeps his soldiers. He's arranging the cavalry boys and the Sioux in and around the fort for one helluva battle, when Mum comes back downstairs. Pearse ponders over whether or not he should take the fort and all the wee men into the back yard, allow the Indians to win the fight and then burn the fort to the ground with the Americans inside. Mum says, 'Your father claims he's ill and he's not going on patrol today.'

Pearse glances up and then goes back to playing because he couldn't have cared less. Lance-Corporal Limp-Dick usually spent his Sundays out with the UDR manning vehicle checkpoints, auld VCPs, on the road to Randalstown, which is a dump with one pub, no shops and a load of backward bumpkins. Gran says he hassles Catholics in their cars just for the hell of it and drags them out in the pissing rain to check their papers and call them fenians and such like, so he can act the big man in front of his Proddie pals.

Pearse is struggling to cut decent shaped sniper slots in the cardboard fort when a wee thought occurs to him that if Satan really is sick then that might mean they can't go on the picnic.

'We're still going on the picnic, right, mum?' he calls, while she's doing whatever she's doing back out in the kitchen.

'Of course,' she says. 'I have to go to the shops and get him a paper and some head ache pills and tomato juice cos he says he's got food poisoning. Rubbish. A hangover more like, and now the big soldier boy can't even get out of bed to protect so-called Ulster.'

Pearse asks her if she'll get a couple of Scotch eggs for the picnic because he loves those wee fellas, and she says aye she'll go when Gran comes round so there's someone to mind Pearse while she's away at the shops. Gran is coming to the picnic as well, though she says she hates the countryside as it's full of hidden cowpats and wasps and nettles, and she grew up on a farm and had her fill of the fields. The city is the only place a half-way sensible or civilised person would want to live, she says; even a town the size of Antrim is barbarian in her book.

Mum's moaning on – while she makes sausage sandwiches for brekkie – about having to take the car and go down the town because you can't get tomato juice at the local shops.

Crazy Horse and his Sioux braves charge the fort – in a big blood and thunder rush – and get shot to pieces by a volley of gunfire from the marksmen along the walls. They retreat and General Custer, Old Yellow Hair, sends out his dragoons on horseback

– but the braves ambush them, cutting them down with their arrows, scalping the survivors.

Pearse finishes his sausage sandwich, sitting cross-legged on the floor, taking the dead off the battle field and rallying the troops, and drinks a glass of milk.

Gran comes in about ten o'clock and says hi and sits at the table in the kitchen with Mum. Gran has a cup of tea, with loads of sugar too, and Mum another cup of coffee and they both have a couple of smokes and a bitching session about Da being a worthless waste of space who Mum should get shot of at the first opportunity.

Crazy Horse orders his braves to storm the fort again, and this time they scale the walls and slay nearly all the soldiers inside. Custer and his trusty lieutenant surrender and are captured. They're all that's left behind. Crazy Horse rides into the fort. He says to Custer, 'There will be no mercy for you, Paleface', and kills the pair of them with his tomahawk.

It would have been much better to go out into the backyard, stick pencils in the ground, tie the soldiers to these stakes and burn them alive, but Bagpuss was about to come on telly and so the war had to finish toot sweet.

Mum gets up and says, 'Right, I'd better be off, or we'll still be sitting here when your friend May-Belle comes round.'

She fetches the car keys and says, 'See you in a tick, love.'

And she kisses Pearse goodbye on the forehead. Her lips are soft and warm.

She walks out the back door and through the garden gate to where the car is parked in the wee concrete driveway. All the houses are the same: each one has a ten-foot drive, and each driveway is separated from the next one by a scrappy patch of thorny bushes.

From the kitchen Gran says, 'Damn', and then gets up from the table. 'I need ciggies,' she says. She hurries to the back door, saying, 'Hang on, Josie, will you get me twenty Sovereign, darling?'

Mum, it's supposed, didn't hear her, and Gran must have went outside after her. It seems she followed her all the way to the car and was talking to her through the driver's window about getting her ciggies when Mum put the key in the ignition and switched the car on.

From the living room, Pearse heard the car chugging to life – the battery half flat. The engine going kerchicka-kerchicka-kerchicka-kerchicka-ahhh-oomm as it tries to catch and start; and then it starts. And then instead of the rumble of the engine turning over, Pearse is picked up by a sound – the ground opening up and hell spewing out through it onto the earth – and flung across the room. As he spins through the air, he sees parts of his house flying in space with him – the windows of the kitchen blown in and glass whistling by his head. The garden gate sails in through a hole in the wall where the window was a moment ago, landing on the lino on the kitchen floor. All of that happens before his body hits the far wall of the living room, and his head catches the window sill just above the right temple and he's knocked for six. Down and out for the count.

When he wakes up, Da is standing in the doorway to the living room, the air sick with dust. He looks knackered and stubbly and dirty and panicked out of his mind. He's wearing a tatty auld woolen dressing gown, but the tasselly cord around the waist isn't tied and it's hanging open – underneath he's in his blue y-fronts with white piping.

'Are you alright?' Da says. 'What happened?'

Pearse's ears hum dull and vibrate. He shouts, 'What? I dunno. The house just blew in. I can hardly hear you.'

Pearse gets up, and Da screams, 'Fuck sake. Stay down.'

Da's trembling like a wee girl, and a breeze is blowing into the house through the hole in the kitchen wall. Behind the smoke and burning, there's the smell of summer in the air. Da crouches down, the way a soldier under fire would squat; he makes a hunched run into the kitchen. He rises up quickly to see what's outside and then ducks down again.

'Jesus God,' he says.

'What?' Pearse says.

'Jesus Christ,' he says. 'Oh son.'

He holds onto the kitchen door frame. From where Pearse is – kneeling in the living room – he can see all the way into the hallway. The living room, the kitchen and the hall are layered in dust, carpeted with bits of torn paper and pieces of brick and scraps of metal. Everything that was standing is knocked over. If Pearse moved he knew the world would give way beneath him and he'd fall forever – just a spiral of arms and legs, vanishing down a hole, screeching all the way to eternity, and never stopping.

'What's wrong?' Pearse says again. His mouth and brain feel like he's crying but when he puts his hands up to his face to wipe the tears away, there's nothing there – just a bit of blood and white dust.

'Son, son,' Da says and starts to walk outside. Pearse gets up as if he's just been switched on again and follows. The back door has been blown off its hinges, and is splintered over the hall.

Outside, Gran is lying in the back yard. She's got some of the fence under her body. She's on her belly, face down, and the top of her head is missing. So is her left leg. Her auld tweed coat is scorched at the sides and still smoking, and her right arm is twisted all the way around, with the hand lying palm up on the concrete as if she is waiting for someone to put a penny in it.

Beyond the remains of the fence – raggedy black teeth jutting out from the ground – sits the family car. A giant has taken his hands and ripped the roof off the car to get at what's inside. The chassis has shifted about a foot to the right, as if the giant had picked the car up and put it down again, only a bit skew-whiff and slanty, after satisfying his terrible curiosity.

Pearse walks down the back garden path, and looks to his feet – where Gran is lying – and then looks up. Inside the car, Mum is sitting in the passenger seat with blood covering her face and a big wound in her head. The giant had found her and tried to get into her skull with a tin opener. The car is squashed up into a crumpled pyramid; fire is playing round the wheels.

Pearse shouts, 'Mum', and runs to the car. Da says, 'Please, son', and tries to catch ahold of him, but Da is moving as if he's in slow motion – he isn't quick enough to keep Pearse back.

'Don't,' Da says as Pearse gets to the car. There's no glass in any of the windows. The top half of Mum's body is in the passenger seat. The rest of her, from the waist down, is still sitting in the driver's seat. The bonnet has been blown off and it's propped up against the neighbour's gate. The engine is pushed up, out of its block, and into the car. It is sitting on Mum's feet.

Mum's eyes are closed, and the light breeze catches the lapels of her jacket and dances them about in the bombed air for a moment. Pearse feels his head spin around and around on his shoulders, and Da's talking to him saying something that he doesn't understand and then he's just gone, out. Bang bang, you're dead.

PART FOUR

Fanny and Faggot Ride Out

May-Belle clearly remembered a noise which must have been the explosion. She was playing in her room with the baldy doll, and the bang rattled the house, and she jumped – her teeth clicking against each other. It came like a whump as the air was sucked away, and then a crashing and shaking as the air rushed back again.

Ma told her she was not to go outside – not even to look through the window – and that she would not be going to the picnic. May-Belle took her orders – without question – and had no idea, back then, what was really happening in her own street. It wasn't until a few hours later – when Ma said she'd better go take a look, and May-Belle walked down to Pearse's house, still thinking they might be able to go on the picnic together – that she put things in order and made sense of it all. The racket and the screaming, though, the wail and whoop of the police cars and ambulances – it's still gone from her memory.

All it amounted to was that the bomb went off and that was it. A body sat there in the car with the wind blowing its hair and clothes, and it had died; the old woman too; they both did. Sparks flash and then extinguish in blackness.

Much later in life, May-Belle would have a repeating dream that she was a police officer – it wasn't clear what sex she was in the dream as she could never see herself, but May-Belle suspected she was probably a man: the officer in charge. Then, with the logic of dreams, she was no longer a police officer, but an invisible eye in the sky, hovering over Antrim town – an omniscient creature, watching events from on high. Car bombs went off below, across

Antrim; roofs and doors flying in all directions, the bodies of cars flung in the air; pennies tossed by a giant's hand; a wave of car bombs exploding one after the other – a Guinness world record-breaking chain of dominoes – the bombs detonating in syncopation, from the police station, and then all the way up the town, on into the Parkhall estate – finally blasting and arriving outside Pearse's door as the key went in the ignition and Gran leant in the window to ask Mum to remember to buy cigarettes. The penultimate bomb went off; the omniscient eye found itself swept down into the back seat of the car, a few feet from the chestnut hair of Mum and the auld wrinkled face of Gran.

The car was blown apart and May-Belle – or rather what there was left of her, for she was just a point of view, not a human being – this remainder was hurled up into the air and hung there, in the sky, regaining its omniscient perspective, looking down on a sea of blood washing over Antrim – a tidal wave of blood running from Parkhall, down into the town, and climbing up the walls of the police station, flushing into the courtyard, mounting past the fifth floor windows, until even the communications aerials 200 feet above the roof of the barracks were drowned in blood, and the entire town lost beneath an ocean of red.

*

May-Belle wasn't sure if Pearse was alive or dead for more than a day, and took to her robot mode – sitting, staring, sleeping; switched off. When she was functioning, she watched at the window and saw funeral cars come to his house; but then later she heard he was badly sick – and was relieved then as he wasn't blown up and would live, even if he was mutilated or a vegetable – and it was weeks and weeks until she saw him again. Weeks when she took to a waking hibernation and let the events and decisions of life and other people roll over her like waves over the drowned while she waited to be reanimated and come back into the world again.

After the bomb went off – after the bodies – Pearse found himself lying on the couch in what remained of his living room, while people whirled around. He was there in flesh only, though, not spirit. He came to as the army left and detectives arrived. Doctors and nurses were there, wanting to look at him and administer injections for his nerves. As the police jotted notes in their little books, the ambulance crew took Mum and Gran away on stretchers with blankets over their heads. The day was endless. Immortal time. Builders turned up to mend the holes and patch up the windows. Distant distant relatives – that Pearse had hardly ever seen and didn't know – called at the house. Friends of the family came, and ladies made food that he couldn't eat and tea he couldn't drink. And men tried to talk to him about football and cars. A minister came and said prayers and Da knelt down with him on the living room carpet to talk to God. Da took Pearse's hand and pulled him onto his knees beside them and Pearse stared at the two of them there, with their eyes closed, asking God to forgive the repentant and bring vengeance on the wicked, and look after Mum and Gran.

Da kept telling all the people who came to see them that it was meant to be him. That the bomb was meant to have killed him once he'd put on his UDR uniform and got in the car and started it to head to the barracks that morning to go on patrol.

That first night Da asked Pearse to sleep in bed with him, and Pearse said no and went to his own room. His window had been blown in and boarded up, but peeking through the slit in the wood panels nailed over the shattered frame he saw burn-marks on the ground in the moonlight.

In the morning, he watched the news with Da – and their house was on television, with pictures of their car being lifted onto a flat-bed lorry and driven away and Da standing with his arm round Pearse crying. In the pictures Pearse is looking right into the camera, but he doesn't remember the TV people being there anymore than he remembers the second day which is blank and dead and gone.

Undertakers bring Mum and Gran's bodies back to the house on the third morning and put their closed coffins in the kitchen, standing on little fold-out support tables. Some woman arrives with two blacks suits and ties. And they change into these black suits and black ties. The same lady combs Pearse's hair and kisses him and starts to cry. Hundreds of people file in and out of Pearse's ruined home, shaking his hand and stroking the two coffin lids and saying they are sorry for his loss. Da stands nearby, blubbering and hugging these people. He never stops crying. A lady asks him if the boy is alright, why is he not crying, and Da looks at Pearse, noticing for the first time that there are no tears on his face.

He says, 'He must be a brave lad.' And pats Pearse on the head, saying, 'That's my boy.'

That night there's a wake – the auld Irish funeral party for the dead. People from all over the estate and all over the town and all over Ulster seem to have brought cakes and sandwiches and sausage rolls and beer and whiskey. Everything they bring is coloured brown when it should be black. Nothing is ever done right. Da has been drunk since six at least and is still crying but now he's singing too, that song Maggie, which goes:

I wandered today to the hills, Maggie,
to watch the scene down below.
The creek and the creaking old mill, Maggie,
as we used to long, long ago.

Everyone is in the living room crying and eating and drinking and listening to people sing and Mum and Gran's bodies are in the kitchen. Pearse walks into the kitchen and stands between their coffins and touches the wood and the name-plates on the lids. A woman comes in behind him and hugs him and says, 'What are you doing in here on your own, Pearse, son?' He lets her lead him back into the living room, and then walks out to the front hall and on into the wee mottled garden. It's about nine on a Tuesday night. The house is ablaze with lights. The rest of the street is quiet. Pearse sits on the garden wall and listens to the people singing and crying inside.

Now they are singing A Bunch of Thyme, which goes:

Come all you maidens young and fair;
all you that are blooming in your prime,
and always beware,
to keep your garden fair,
let no man steal away your thyme.

Pearse walks up the hill. One of the neighbours passes by, a right boring fella with a nose like a tea-pot spout who nobody really cares for, and he says, 'Hiya, son, how are you, son?' Pearse walks on till he gets to the row running across the top of the hill, the row where May-Belle lives. It must be getting on for ten now, but he walks up her path and knocks on her door. Pearse waits, hoping for a light to come on in the hall – even if it's just her auld monster Ma who appears, he wouldn't care, as long as May-Belle is in there somewhere. If she's in bed, there'll be foot stamping and that bloody woman will be told to go get her. No door opens though. No light comes on. There's no Ma or May-Belle. No-one appears. May-Belle is far away from Pearse. She's in Belfast – staying there for the night with Ma and her friends at a party; her soul unplugged, her mind at bay, her body on auto-pilot. Dad is far away from May-Belle too; and he won't be allowed back again until it is all over.

*

Pearse just stood there. Waiting. Half an hour maybe. Longer. Shorter. Uncountable. He caught back up with time when this rarr of noise came up the hill and filtered through his ears into his brain. It was folk shouting his name. A group of men and women were walking towards him – to May-Belle's garden.

'Pearse,' says one fella who he's never seen before, 'your father's demented with worry, we had no idea where you were.'

'I'm here,' Pearse says, coming back to life. May-Belle's garden is disgraceful – filled with weeds and mess, auld cans and crisp packets.

Two ladies take ahold of him, each grabbing a hand in theirs, and start walking Pearse down the path.

Pearse turns and says, 'Goodbye, May-Belle. I will see you soon.' The women look at him and then look at each other.

The people lead him down the hill to his house. Da is standing outside the front garden gate with a glass of whiskey in his hand. When he sees Pearse, he shouts, 'Where the fuck were you?'

'I went for a walk,' Pearse says.

'A walk? You went for a fucken walk? I thought something happened to you, for fuck sake.'

'I'm alright,' Pearse says.

Pearse and the folk who came to rescue him are standing beside Da now – he grabs Pearse by the shirt and tie. 'Alright?,' he says. 'Alright? Your mother and grandmother would be alright if it wasn't for you. Fucken running about in my uniform in broad daylight. If it hadn't been for you none of this would've happened.'

He shakes Pearse, and draws back his fist, but Pearse doesn't flinch, he just rolls his head back a little on his shoulders; pointing his chin up at Da and looking him in the eye.

'You did it,' Pearse says to him.

The man Pearse has never seen before pulls Da around by the scruff of the neck and says to him, 'What the fuck do you think you're doing? Get a grip on yourself, Dan, for Christ's sake.'

The man turns to the two ladies and says, 'Lorrie, Corinne, would you take the lad inside and get him a wee drink or something, please?'

'Aye,' they say together.

'Come on, sweetheart,' the prettier one says. The ladies lead Pearse indoors.

The other one says, 'Your daddy was just worried about you is all, darling.'

Pearse and the two women stand in the front hall, and the pretty one says, 'Your mother was a beautiful woman, Pearse.'

The other one gives Pearse a hug, and he folds into her, stiff like a plank – thinking its wrong to be between her diddies at a time like this. She says, 'You must miss them both awfully.'

Da and the man come in. The man says to Da, 'Dan?'

And Da says, 'Sorry, son. Are you ok? I was just scared about you, is all.'

The two women take Da by the cuffs of his shirt sleeves and lead him into the living room.

The man stays in the front hall with Pearse and and says, 'Are you alright, son? I suppose you don't remember me?'

He says, 'I'm Crawford Hinley. I was your Da's best mate in Crumlin. I used to come to your house all the time when you were a wee baby.' Now, he says, he's a sergeant in the UDR in the same platoon in which Da is a lance-corporal. 'We'll get the bastards who did this to your family,' Hinley says. 'Just remember what happened when you grow up.'

He tries to get Pearse to come into the living room where all the singing is back on now, but Pearse tells him he'd rather just sit on the stairs. Hinley says, 'Ok, lad', and goes into the living room, telling all the people there, 'The boy's ok, he just wants a wee bit of time on his own is all.'

The folk make twittering noises and wee 'oohs' and 'ahhs'. Every now and again, one of the women come out to check everything is fine and ask if Pearse needs anything, but after a while they forget as they drink on and soon no-one comes out and there are a few jokes getting told behind the door and a bit of chuckling, and the music and singing isn't quite as maudlin as before.

Pearse goes up to his bed and turns off all the lights and gets under the covers wearing his suit and tie and shoes. The pitch black makes the sound carry further, though, and the men and women can be heard downstairs, clear and hard.

Da and Hinley are singing this song to the tune of My Grandfather's Clock. The made-up song they are singing goes like this:

My grandfather's cock,
was too long for his pants,
so it spent ninety years down his leg.
Down his leg.
It was longer by half
than the auld man himself
but slightly smaller when it was floppy.
When it was floppy.

And when they finished singing, there were all these 'yo's' and 'what-about-ye's' and 'that's the crack' shouted from every corner of every room downstairs. People were clapping and you could hear tears of laughter in their voices. Then the men sang 'The Sash', and 'Derry's Walls' and 'The Queen', and a few people left, and there was a bit of tearful crying in the doorway. It started to get quieter by about four in the morning.

It was a wicked curse: to be relieved that Mum and Gran were finally going to be buried and free from this house by the morning. Pearse hadn't slept since Sunday, but sleep came easy then, and it was off to a dream-land where he didn't dream: not one damned thing.

*

People came around at eight in the morning – banging about and waking him. A different woman Pearse hadn't seen in the house before made bacon sandwiches and said she was Da's auntie Hazel. She wasn't a real auntie – just one of those ladies close to the family – a dear friend of Maria the foster mother, who'd been dead herself now a good few years. 'God love the wee man,' she said to Da, 'he's got nothing or no-one in the world now but you. Look after him, Danny.'

Da bent down and kissed Pearse and said, 'Sure, I love him, Hazel.'

Then another make-believe auntie arrived – this time a woman who called herself auntie Lucy from England. She'd been Gran's oldest friend in London. Lucy arrived about half an hour before the funeral men came to put Gran and Mum in the hearses. Aunt Lucy was a widow. She said to Da, 'I know what you're going through, Dan. I'm here for you.' And she crushed a tenner into Pearse's hand – telling him that he was all that was left of Mum's family now – and gave him one of those big squeezy tearful hugs that he'd had before from the other women who squashed him into their diddies.

He still had on the black suit and tie. Da put on his UDR uniform, not the auld rough and tumble one he'd wear on patrol, but the smart one worn on parade with shiny buttons and a peaked cap and trousers pressed so well you could cut your throat on them. On one arm he had his single lance corporal stripe and on the other he wore a black arm band. Some of the other men had uniforms and black arm bands on too. The women were all dressed the same in dark dresses with dark hats and dark bags and dark shoes.

Black cars and limousines and hearses pulled up outside, and Da and other men lifted the coffins onto their shoulders and took the bodies outside. They put them in the hearses, filled with every different colour of flower – rainbows inside the black cars. Pearse got into the back of the lead limousine, Da shut the door behind them, and the car followed the hearses the short drive into the centre of town to the church with the spire on the High Street. The church was brown, the seats were brown, the bibles were brown, the coffins were brown. It wasn't Catholic, but what did that matter now or ever. The minister said prayers and people sang hymns and Da got up to make a speech about how much he loved Mum and Gran and how heaven would be a better place for them in it and how the British people would not be terrified out of their own country by murderers and terrorists. He said how much pain he was in, and how destroyed Pearse was, and the people all turned to look at Pearse and he tried to look every single one of them in the eye, but there were too many.

The coffins were picked up again – Da taking charge – and carried out to the hearses once more, with Pearse walking behind holding his two fake aunties' hands, for another wee journey to the churchyard in Crumlin – Da's home town. Mum and Gran were going into the ground there. In the car, Da said, 'One day I'll be lying beside Mum and one day you'll be there beside us too.'

Gran used to tell a story of two ancient people – from long ago back in the lost history of Ireland, when Gods and spirits walked the earth alongside human beings – two early people, Gog and Magog, who hated each other: Gog, the head of one family, a man; and Magog, the head of another family, a woman. They were joined together in blood because their children married, and when they died the pair were buried together in the same tomb. At night, the tomb screamed, and in the morning the priests would open the gates to this underground crypt and find the two coffins standing tall in the cold stone chamber – off their plinths – facing each other; flowers and gifts for the dead strewn like trash all over the floor.

The coffins of Mum and Gran were carried high on shoulders again to the grave sides – two pits in the ground by a mound of mud. No headstones could be put up for weeks until the earth settled. A minister appeared again and pretend Aunt Hazel started to sing a terrible, mournful hymn with her eyes closed and her face held up to the heavens. Someone gave Pearse two roses and said drop one in each of the graves and say bye-bye. He did what they asked, but couldn't hear his voice.

TV people were at the gates of the cemetery when they all left, and there were police there too. Da took Pearse's hand, and Pearse wanted to say to them, 'No pictures, please'. They drove back to the house and the black cars and limousines vanished, and there were more sandwiches and people and tea and whiskey and cake and singing and crying. Pearse sat on the settee between make-believe auntie Lucy and make-believe auntie Hazel and fell asleep. When he woke up, he went to the kitchen and got under the table and tried to get to sleep again. Some people came and found him, but he kept trying to get to sleep, to stay asleep. The next day, their doctor, Doctor Graham came, and tried to talk to Pearse, but Pearse didn't say a word to him or anyone else. The doctor and Da talked about him, over the top of him, one on either side of his bed. He got an injection and went to sleep and the doctor came back the next day after he'd woken up, and tried talking to him again, and when Pearse didn't talk the doctor said, 'He better come with me.' The doctor asked if Da wanted to come along and make sure Pearse was safe and well where he was going for a wee while. Da said no, he couldn't face it, so the doctor gave Pearse another shot in the arm, and later – that's when he first woke up in a hospital that's white and cold and clean and calm. The auld looney bin.

*

Pearse ended up in Muckamore Abbey, a right Victorian looking place that was built to house handicapped children whose parents didn't want them, but there was also a small ward and a few private rooms for kids who'd just gone loop-dee-loo.

The handicappers were all in a terrible state. There was one who had to wear a crash helmet with a grille, covering his mouth and nose, as he kept walloping his head and face off walls and radiators and anything he could clunk himself against. Another lad had a head shaped like a cone and a tongue on him the size of a cow's. There were kids who couldn't move, and teenagers – with wee shriveled legs and arms – still in the pram, or ones pushed about on contraptions like carts; they were just massive misshapen babies really. The doctors tried to keep the few normal kids like Pearse away from this lot but you couldn't help bumping into them. You'd be walking from your ward to the therapy suite and you'd pass by the locked day room where they kept the cripples and crazies, and some of them would be standing there – their faces against the wire-mesh windows, their lips on the glass and the slabbers trailing out of them. Or the ones with half a brain in their heads would smile and wave or make noises like dirty wee monkeys. The older ones were no better than chimps, anyway, playing with their cocks and fannies in public and flinging their shite at the walls like they were on a dirty protest.

Pearse wasn't there that long in Muckamore Abbey. A month at the most. It was more like somewhere to go to catch a breath. Not like a prison with doctors talking, talking, talking, trying to make people open up their heads so they could look inside as if there was a map to be read. There was still a bit of talking here, at the Abbey, but if you didn't want to talk no-one forced you, or frowned on it. His room and windows weren't locked. No-one was made to take medicine, no-one man-handled. Da came to visit once to say, 'You're going home in two days. I'll be back to collect you.' Of the few normal-ish kids who were there, only one seemed worth getting to know. A girl called Cilla Dorey. She was so blonde and pale – a transparent see-through person. She was two years older than Pearse and hardly ever spoke, but when she did she had the most beautiful tinkly voice, even though she wasn't pretty; the voice of an old piano.

She could look after herself perfectly well – do things like tie her shoe laces and get dressed. She didn't want to though. She'd happily get pushed around in a wheelchair all day – then when she fancied it she'd just get up and walk about. Cilla and Pearse were the only two kids in the main ward for ordinary children during the time he was there. Cilla thought of the ward as her room, and kids like Pearse who came and went as her visitors. Cilla had been in the Abbey about a year.

When Cilla did talk she said the other kids, the deformed and retarded ones, weren't human beings at all. She said she was scared that they'd break out at night and kill her or eat her. She'd go on about hearing them moving around in the walls. And she'd say all this in a voice that was gorgeous – the Song of Songs.

A veranda was attached to the big room that Cilla and Pearse shared. On sunny days, the nurses would open the French windows and you could sit outside and drink juice and read books or draw or write or just look at the birds and sun yourself. This sanatorium of theirs was built in the countryside, a few miles from Antrim, and placed in the prettiest of wee spots, set on a hill, looking down on farms and the Six Mile River, although there was always a faint smell of dung in the air from the bumpkins muck-spreading their spud fields.

One warm day, Cilla and Pearse are outside on the veranda. He's going over a story called The Sun and the Maroon about a boy who accidentally blocks out the daylight when he reads one of his family's magic spells aloud, and starts to kill the whole earth off with shadows and darkness. Cilla just sits there. Pearse reads bits of the story to her, and if she likes it she raises her thumb, and if she doesn't she moves her hand from side to side. He goes back and changes the bits she doesn't approve of until he gets a thumbs up, and then moves on to fixing the next section.

Pearse is at the bit where the spell has blocked out the sun, when Cilla lifts her left hand off the arm of her wheelchair and holds it there, signaling silence. He stops and looks at her.

'There is a clegg on me,' she says in her quiet voice, throbbing now – like red blown glass.

The clegg is an ugly insect, with big green eyes and black shiny wings, that drinks blood. A dung-fly, the culchies call them.

Mostly, it'll feast on cows and sheep and creatures that can't hit them a whack and kill them, but sometimes they are stupid enough or hungry enough to take a bite out of a human. When you smack them on your arm or leg, they splat like a big blister – the red from the blood they've been drinking gorged out across your skin. They leave their mouth-parts in you when you kill them.

The clegg is on her right arm. It's completely still – digging its wee razor fangs into her and supping at a vein.

She repeats herself, 'There's a clegg on me.'

'Uh-huh,' Pearse says.

'Get it off me, please, Pearse,' she says.

Cilla doesn't look at Pearse, or the clegg; she stares at the hem of her white dress. Pearse gets up and goes to flick it away but she lifts her head and and says, 'No.'

'You don't want me to get rid of it?' he asks her.

'No, take it off me and put it in my hand,' she says.

He prises the wee bugger off Cilla, and drops it into her hand. It's fat and drunk on her blood. It can barely move and certainly doesn't look inclined to escape.

Cilla pets it gently on its wirey wee head, as if it's a kitten, and gives a faint smile. She licks her hand and puts her finger and thumb together like a pair of pincers and plucks the clegg's wings off its back. She rubs her finger and thumb together; the wings disappear into molten dust.

'Wee devil,' she coos. She flips him over with her fingernail and rips his legs off one by one, with her auld pincers; the wee black tendrils – horrible eyelashes – are flicked from her fingernail after each operation. When the clegg's left with no legs and no wings, Cilla turns him over and lays him belly down in the lap of her dress. He's a wee black dot on a wide flat plain – a solitary explorer dying in a desert seen from the window of an airplane.

The creature wriggles about a bit. Cilla says, 'I'll keep him for a while in case any more cleggs fancy biting me.' And Cilla sees herself with heads on spikes arrayed around her battlements.

She turns to Pearse and she says, 'This here is Jake the Clegg. Say hello Jake the Clegg.' She pokes the thing, as if that's going to encourage it to speak.

Cilla starts singing a made-up song to a lullaby tune. 'I'm Jake the Clegg, diddle iddle iddle um, with my lack of legs, diddle iddle iddle um.' And in her voice, the song sounds like an angel is talking to Pearse. He gives up trying with the story. A fly lands on his arm. He says to her, 'Look, I've got one too.'

Cilla looks over, and Pearse brings his hand down smartly on the insect, turning it into a wee brown stain against skin, and wipes his hand on his pajama leg. 'That's how you deal with them,' he says.

Not long afterwards, Pearse came back home, on a still and blank evening. The house was dirty and empty and cold. Da fetched fish and chips and six beers and allowed Pearse to drink the frothy foam at the end of each can, just a mouthful, and made a big deal out of how they were going to have a great life together, despite it all, and how they'd look out for each other and do amazing things. Pearse went to bed at eight o'clock. At nine, he heard a knock at the front door and some people came in. He could make out Da's voice, and another man's voice and at least one woman, though there might have been two, only they both sounded the same, with their identical droney tones. They were all still carrying-on when Pearse feel asleep about midnight.

A week of housebound nothing slid by – reading, resting. Da worked, came home, made ready meals, slept. In the evenings, Pearse watched TV downstairs. Da watched TV in his bedroom upstairs. Trappist monks talked more to each other. Come Friday night, Da went out. The doctor had ordered Pearse to stay indoors and recuperate until the weekend, so at ten he headed to bed and drifted off looking forward, finally, to calling for May-Belle on Saturday morning.

He woke up early and went downstairs. The place was pigging with dirty ash-trays and drinks spilt on the floor. It stank of booze and fags. Pearse got a bowl of corn flakes and ate watching those eejit Saturday morning kids programmes. He went back upstairs to get dressed. On the landing, he heard a woman's voice whisper from behind the closed door to Da's bedroom, saying something like, 'Is that him up?'

Pearse walked across the landing to his room, got dressed and then stood at the head of the stairs. He looked at Da's bedroom door and said, 'I'm away out.' There was a pause and then Da shouted, 'Right you be, son. See you later.'

Pearse walked down the stairs and could hear laughing. Not cruel laughing, mind, like laughing at him, just laughing; the sound of people giggling and having fun.

*

Every day, on the way up and down the stairs in her house, May-Belle saw the black mark of the man who wasn't there: a hand-print smeared on the wall. She knew it wasn't Dad who left it there, it was too small for his hand; and it wasn't Pearse's print either, the mark had been there long before he'd first come to her house. She knew it would probably be there forever now, even after she was long dead. It was the mark of the man from the horror rhyme – that was the only thing which could have left such a dark stain on the wall by the stairs. Her teacher had read the rhyme out in school, and the story – although it wasn't a story, just a few moments of some poor person's life – the story made her feel sick with the haunted lonely fear at the heart of it.

She would never say the words of the rhyme out loud, just in case, but May-Belle could not stop the recitation in her head when she looked at the smudged hand-print shaded like night.

Yesterday, upon the stair,
I met a man who wasn't there
He wasn't there again today

I wish, I wish he'd go away.
When I came home last night at three
The man was waiting there for me,
But when I looked around the hall
I couldn't see him there at all.
Go away, go away, don't you come back any more.
Go away, go away, and please don't slam the door.
Slam.
Last night I saw upon the stair
A little man who wasn't there
He wasn't there again today;
I wish that man would go away.

She first spotted the hand-print when she came home from school, after this poetry lesson. She needed to go upstairs to get some felt-tip pens from her bedroom to do her maths homework – colouring in squares and triangles, that kind of stuff; not that she bothered much with study, to be honest, but she was bored and had nothing else to do – and about three steps up, there it was: a black smudge on the wall in the shape of a man's hand. She had never seen it before. She tried to pretend that the black mark might've come from the hand of one of the men who often went upstairs – maybe he was a coal-man or a printer – or it could be the accumulation of years, from the hands of hundreds of men, and she'd only noticed it just now; the dirt finally built up enough over time to stand out and catch her eye. She knew, though, that it wasn't a smudge left behind by another person at all – it was the mark of something standing on the stairs right there and then, in front of her, something waiting for her and watching her; something that couldn't be seen.

*

This is what will happen next: now that Pearse is out of hospital

– one week since his discharge – and finally deemed fit to go out-side alone, he'll leave his house, walk up the hill and come calling for May-Belle. He'll knock her door as she starts sidling up the stairs, past the black stain, to go to the toilet. When she opens the door, it will be the first time in more than a month – since the day before the bomb – that they've seen each other. And they are going to go out playing, and then they are going to find Galen, and then it will all move towards an end.

May-Belle remembers him there on her doorstep – clear as day, as if it were yesterday. What a waste, though, what a fool back then, not to show just how overjoyed she was to clap eyes on him again. All she did was smile and say, 'It's cracking you are home.' They didn't even kiss or anything.

Pearse felt as if he was walking in a white fog. He was aware of calling for May-Belle, though. She came to the door and for a while nothing seemed to record itself, embed, on his inner tape – his memory; then they were playing marbles on a wee patch of concrete near the common when this kid who they'd seen around the estate every now and again came up to them. He was about six and looked like Galen the monkey doctor out of Planet of the Apes.

He asked Pearse if he was the kid whose ma had been blown up. May-Belle told Pearse later that he'd replied yes and then they took the wee boy by the hand and led him past the common and over the big road towards the posh houses on the far side. In a wee dip, a shallow valley, down from the main road, workmen were building new posh houses. It was the weekend so no work-men were about now. Nobody was about. There were lots of half built houses with no doors or roofs. The houses looked skinned and blinded; the outer walls raw plaster and brick, with no glass in the windows.

Pearse was still floating in a hazy auld mist, but as he breathed and walked with the wee Galen look-alike boy it slowly started to clear around the edges. When the three of them crossed the road, the wee lad began to pull away, trying to get his hand free, but May-Belle squeezed his fingers together, crushing them in her hand and knelt down to tell him to shut the fuck up. There was no-one there to see him crying as they wandered through the empty building site and entered one of the unmade houses. This one had a front door, so they led Galen inside and pulled it shut after them.

They walked into what would one day become the living room of some family's home. They stood in the middle of the room and May-Belle looked up and said, 'Wow, there's no ceiling.' There were just rafters, and you could see up into the room above – into one of the bedrooms. The living room was filled with workmen's gear. Paint tins and cement bags and bricks and rope, loads of funny tools and gizmos.

The wee boy, Galen, said something and May-Belle was nodding at him, but Pearse could make no sense of it – the boy was talking too slowly to piece the meaning of his words together. May-Belle let go of the boy's hand and he started to walk towards the front door. Pearse picked up a heavy spirit level, and swung it like a baseball bat at the back of Galen's head. He kept his eye on the liquid in the middle of the spirit level, and the little air bubble, as he hefted it through the air. There came a crack like a cap-gun going off and the boy pitched forward onto the ground.

Pearse turned him over and his eyes were shut. He didn't move even when Pearse slapped him a few times sharpish around the face. Galen had smashed his mouth when he fell, and his top teeth had gone through his lower lip making him look like Bugs Bunny now. There was a stanley knife near a bag of cement and May-Belle got it and cut the boy's clothes off. She carved an M in his chest to see if he was alive and the wee boy sat bolt upright like a body waking in a coffin and let a shriek out of him. Pearse kicked him in the face and the kick must have caught him on the tip of the nose for it broke over his cheek and he went out and away and down. May-Belle got Galen around the neck and started to strangle him, saying all that stuff she said before when she'd got her hands on Martin. Pearse helped her, wrapping his hands around her hands and pushing down so hard that she said, 'You're hurting me.' There was a snapping noise deep in the wee boy's throat, and something caved in, beneath their fingers. Pearse took his hands away, and covered the boy's mouth and pinched his nose shut and let May-Belle finish the strangling.

Pearse got up and watched May-Belle sitting on top of the naked wee boy, bouncing his head off the floor and saying, 'It makes the auld throat go down.'

'It's down already,' Pearse said to her.

In a few minutes, she rolls off the boy and lies beside him on the floor sweating and trembling with exhaustion. The wee boy's skin is blue and white; his face and mouth covered in blood. Pearse walks towards him and kicks him in the head to see if he moves. Galen just lies there. May-Belle laughs and sits up and takes hold of the wee fella's jaw and waggles it about so it looks like he's talking. She tries out a ventriloquist and dummy routine, saying, 'My mummy's gonna be very cross with me when I don't come home for dinner.'

Pearse picks up the stanley knife from the ground, where May-Belle put it beside Galen, and carves a P into the boy's chest, beside May-Belle's M. While he's doing this – amazed how the blood doesn't spurt, but the flesh just opens pink under the knife – May-Belle is fidgeting around somewhere behind him. Pearse can smell the washing powder that the wee boy's mother must use to clean his clothes, and there's a taste like grown-up sweat in his mouth. Pearse lifts Galen's eyelids and leans forward. 'His eyes are all the colours of the rainbow,' he says. May-Belle kneels beside the boy and looks down into his eyes as well. 'If I was forced to tell you his eye colour,' said May-Belle, 'I'd have to say they were blue, but when you stare deep into them, you can see green and brown and red and yellow. His eyes are gorgeous.' Pearse and May-Belle lift their heads up, slowly, still watching the boy's face – the pores in his wee nose retract away as they move back.

Pearse stands up and pushes the stanley knife blade back inside the steel casing and starts to rub their fingerprints off the hilt with his jumper.

May-Belle's got ahold of an electric plug for some power-tool and plugged it into a socket in the wall. 'Do you think we can bring him back to life?' she asks. Pearse looks at her and laughs. She turns Galen over onto his belly, takes the forked-end of the contraption and puts it inside the wee boy.

They stand him up and ask him if he is feeling better – the cable whipping around out of him, like a devil's tail – and then let him go to see if he can walk or talk now he's wired to the mains, but he just falls down dead on the floor again. The cable whirls on the ground beside him as he tumbles down. He lies in a wee crumpled heap, and Pearse says to May-Belle that they need to make it look like a child molester killed him.

She says, 'Well, leave the plug up his arse then.'

Pearse agrees, and turns him over again onto his back and looks at Galen's wee man, which is about half the size of a pinky, and says to May-Belle, 'So what do I do to him?'

She says, 'Pull the skin back and forward or something.'

Pearse tells her he can't touch him there as he's not a poofter, and she says, 'Move then.'

She takes the stanley knife, and pops the blade out and starts to make wee cutting marks around his balls; then she wipes the knife clean and puts the blade away and says she doesn't want to do it either.

They grab the wee boy – Pearse gets him under the armpits and May-Belle takes ahold of his ankles – and they shuffle with him up the stairs. Pearse then dutifully goes back downstairs – while May-Belle keeps the wee boy company on the top landing – and returns with a length of plastic cord and a tin of swarfega.

May-Belle and Pearse tip-toe into the main bedroom – which only has wooden beams laid, no proper floor beneath their feet.

They look down into the living room below where Galen's clothes are, and the spirit level. Pearse goes back downstairs again to wipe finger-prints away, while May-Belle ties one end of the cord around a beam in the floor. Pearse looks up and sees her walking like a tight-rope artist across the slats above as she goes back a few steps to the landing to fasten the other end of the cord around Galen's neck. She drags the wee fella a little way into the bedroom by his feet, huffing and puffing.

Pearse comes back up the stairs and helps her. They position Galen's body so he's supported by a couple of these auld floor beams – one under his shoulders and one at the back of his thighs.

They get their balance on the beams, and grab an arm each, hauling Galen into a sitting position. Pearse opens the cannister of swarfega and hands it to May-Belle. She pours the orange-green gloop over the wee boy's head.

'Bye-bye,' says May-Belle.

'Bye-bye, you little fucker,' Pearse says, and they push Galen forward. His body slides down between two of the beams, the plastic cord running after him like a snake down a hole. His chin catches one of the planks a terrific wallop on the way; his teeth click together and break, and when his body gets to the end of the cord, the beam he's tied to – one of the planks that Pearse and May-Belle are standing on – it bounces and cracks like it's set to break in two, as the body springs about down below them; an electrified puppet. The beam holds. May-Belle and Pearse laugh and leap out of the room like the whole house is going to collapse on top of them.

Pearse stops May-Belle on the landing and tells her to come back into the bedroom with him to make sure they haven't left anything behind. She says, 'Maybe we should burn the whole house down.'

'No,' Pearse says. 'We just don't want our stuff with his stuff.'

There's nothing bad that they've left behind in the bedroom – no fluff or fibres, even if forensics had the time to spot them, what with murders all across the land – but they do have this glimmering iodine stain of dried swarfega on their hands from Galen's head and shoulders. They go downstairs and the wee boy is hanging in the middle of the living room, with his bare feet about three foot off the ground, swinging round and around, syrupy snotters of swarfega dripping to the floor, in a steady drum-beat. May-Belle says, 'Let's go Pearsey. I don't like it here.'

'Wait,' he says, 'we have to check the living room and clean our hands.' There's turps and rags in the corner. Pearse pours the turpentine over their hands, and as they use two rags to get the splatters of swarfega off themselves Pearse looks around to make sure there's nothing dangerous left behind here in the living room either. There's not as far as he can see. They take the rags with them and walk out the front door. When they get back to the common, they go up to May-Belle's house, as no-one is home again, and burn the rags in the fireplace grate. Then they use soap and water to wash the smell of turps from their hands. It takes about four washes each. Pearse lets May-Belle sniff his hands and he sniffs her hands until they are both satisfied they are clean of the smell, and there are no tell-tale stains on their cuffs or fingernails.

*

Once the clean-up was done – no more proof of swarfega or turps – May-Belle and Pearse talked for a little while there in her house; about Ma mostly, about things that had gone on which Pearse understood when May-Belle explained them to him but that he'd never heard of before, and could never have imagined until they came out of her poor mouth.

Then she told him about Dad being back in the clink for thieving and how he was in jail more than he was out. Ma was working in Belfast tonight, May-Belle said. Pearse asked her, 'You're really all alone?'

'Aye,' she says. 'Thank God.'

Pearse told her he'd better go home now – it's about half four – get dinner and then come back out and hang about with her as long as he can till he's called in for the night. He tells her he'll bring her up some of his dinner if she wants, but she says she's got ham sandwiches and crisps so it's alright and not to bother. They give each other a pinky-pax handshake and swear silence.

When Pearse gets down the road to his house, there's a woman in the kitchen who was at the wake. She comes into the living room drying her hands on a tea-towel and says hi, and Da goes, 'This is Yvonne. She'll be helping us out now that Mum's away.'

Da goes upstairs for a bath. Pearse is pin-sharp – clear-headed, flushed clean. Da's left the television playing one of his stupid football games. Yvonne asks if it's alright to switch off the footie. Pearse says, 'Sure, I hate it anyway', and she laughs and says, 'Oh my god, a man who hates football. Pleased to meet you.'

She's quite pretty with blonde hair. She sits down in one of the two armchairs and starts saying what terrible shape Da is in, and how she's a dear friend of his and wants to look after him. 'Both of you, now that I've met you too, Pearse,' she says, and she blushes. Pearse is sitting on the sofa, cross-legged with his cheek resting in the palm of his hand. He smells turps. Down on his other hand, that's resting on his knee – just on the tip of the nail of his little finger – is a tiny orange-purple spot of swarfega. There's one or two other dibs and dabs on the hem of his right trouser leg too. Pearse has no idea how he could have missed these marks.

His heart bounds and binds in his chest – like one of those coronary things – and a cold flow from his stomach spreads out through his body. There's a pukey feeling. His face gets hot. Pearse looks at this Yvonne woman and her gob is moving and saying words, and there's noise, but he is not stringing the noises together to make linked-up sounds that can be understood. She could be sitting there barking like a dog or quacking like a duck for all the sense she's making.

'Squawk,' she seems to say. And then she's saying, 'Are you ok?

Are you ok?' She's leaning over the top of Pearse, strands of her blonde hair falling over her boob-crack where it's pushed up out of her jumper. He smells her sticky sweet yellow-scented perfume.

Pearse tells her he's fine, just fine – and he is now that he's calmed himself. Just a bit tired and a wee bit hungry. She says she'll fix something to eat and goes into the kitchen. Da comes down the stairs, all buffed and clean, and switches his football game back on and says, 'What do you think of Yvonne?'

'Nice,' says Pearse.

'Is that all?' he says.

'She's nice,' Pearse says.

The television plays football noise for a moment.

Pearse thinks of May-Belle all alone, and Galen, and can't stop a shudder coming over him.

'What's up?' Da says.

'Nothing,' Pearse says.

'You not well?'

'I'm alright.'

Yvonne brings in one of those frozen mini cheese and tomato pizzas, cut into fours on a plate, with a cup of Ribena. Pearse settles it onto his lap. He still feels a bit vomity sick, but when he takes the first bite he finds he's starving. He could eat a horse well brushed, as Gran always said. He wolfs it down, gollops the juice and sees by the clock on the mantle-piece that it's gone half five.

'I'm away out to play,' he says.

'Oh are you?' Da says.

Yvonne comes into the living room with a glass of something that is either vodka or gin filled up with ice.

'Was your tea alright, love?' she asks.

'Yes, thanks,' Pearse says.

'Well, you can head out for a couple of hours, but be in by eight at the latest,' Da says. 'And where are you going anyway?'

'Just round the square,' he replies. Pearse walks to the front door and this Yvonne person follows him and ruffles his hair, saying, 'Have fun, love. Back by eight.' And shuts the door behind him.

Pearse runs as fast as he can up to May-Belle's house as she's by herself and might be having to reckon with those wee twangy pangs and panics about the police – and you don't want to be having those when you are all alone.

Her front door's open, so Pearse raps it with his knucks and walks in. She's sitting in the living room; waiting and doing nothing. She's done nothing but sat there since he left; she didn't even sing to herself. He sits beside her, and they talk about all the people and things they hate.

'I wish we could just stay off school forever,' he says to her.

'Fuck school,' she says back.

'Fuck teachers too,' he says.

'Fucking cunts.'

'Fucking dirty smelly cocks,' he laughs.

'Wankers,' she shouts, getting to her feet.

'They're all wankers.' Pearse jumps up, hollering at the top of his voice.

She slaps her thigh, laughing, and then stills herself. 'Shush,' she says. 'We better not be too noisy. If the neighbours tell Ma then I'm creamed.'

'Okay,' he says.

'Anyway, fuck them all,' she says and does her wee jigging dance from one foot to the other and back again.

'We're ok.'

'I wish Dad was here,' she says.

'I know,' Pearse says, feeling like a div. Then, when she doesn't speak, he asks, 'Why?'

'Cos then it wouldn't be as bad as this shite.'

'You ever robbed anywhere?' he says to her when there's been silence for too long. 'Like your auld fella's done?'

'Naw,' she says. 'I've nicked things from shops like.'

'Aye, I've done shop-lifting,' Pearse says, trying to stop his cheeks from reddening because he's such a sly wee lying braggart. 'C'mon we'll go robbing then.'

'Where?'

'I dunno. A school. We'll go rip up a school.'

'Roger dodger,' she says. 'I'm bored out of my head.'

'I have to be back by eight or I'll get my cunt knocked in,' he says to her.

'Grand,' she says. 'Let's go then. Do you know what to do?'

'Aye,' he says. 'Do you?'

'Och, aye,' she says back.

They don't need to discuss where they are heading; they both know that Parkhall Nursery School is their destination. Five minutes walk away. On the way, Pearse asks her what she is going to do that night what with Ma being away and her in the house on her own. 'Sleep,' she says.

Pearse starts to tell her about this book he'd read when he'd been away, Abbey-wise, about two young lads, around their age, who go to some Pacific Island to help their father with research into sea creatures and end up meeting a tribe of real-life headhunters and cannibals. This was a true book, not a makey-uppy pretendy thing, but real life. The boys were never in any proper serious danger but the time they spent in the long houses of these cannibal boyos made for some cracking reading. The tribesmen had a special hut, filled with the shrunken heads of their enemies, and they believed that every time they killed and ate their enemies they got stronger, that they took their enemy's strength themselves.

'Jesus-weezus,' says May-Belle. 'Imagine shitting out a human being the way you would a sausage. That's wild. I suppose it's true though. Dad told me once about this fella who had a heart transplant from a French person and they were English or something and they woke up speaking French even though they'd never known a word of the language before.'

'Away on,' Pearse says to her. 'That's balls.'

'It's true. Dad told me.'

'Aye, whatever. How could that happen?'

'Anything can happen, Pearsey,' she says.

They're at the gates to this wee nursery school now. It's a flat one-storey building. No burglar alarms seem to be above the doors.

There's a chain around the gate. They climb over and get into the play-ground. It's still quite light, so they keep low and run around to the back of the nursery school. Back here in the rear, no-one would be able to see them. Pearse looks up and along the top of the windows and doors, checking again for those burglar alarm things, and May-Belle starts tugging on doors and windows to see if any are open. Everything is locked.

Pearse tells May-Belle to keep dick while he goes to see if he can find something to stove in a window. He waddles back, holding a head-sized stone between his legs.

'Good stone,' she replies.

Pearse lobs it through a window, and before it even hits the glass, the pair of them turn tail and hike it for some nearby bushes. The glass goes in – the noise of a thousand bottles breaking. They hide in the bushes.

They lie still and Pearse whispers, 'We'll wait fifteen minutes. If no-one comes by then the coast'll be clear.'

Pearse lays his head down wishing the time to pass. May-Belle says, 'What if they come with sniffer dogs?'

'Then we're nicked as they'll smell your dirty hole,' he says.

May-Belle starts her laughing.

'Shush,' Pearse says in a whisper.

'My hole. Your arse more like,' she says, rolling on her back, holding her sides. 'Oh, my belly,' she says, almost crying.

'Okay, be quiet,' he says.

She's silent for about five seconds and then starts to snigger again and says, 'Dirty hole. Oh holy fuck, Pearsey.' She bursts out laughing, louder than before.

'May-Belle, please shut up,' he says, laughing too – and he puts his hand over her mouth.

She bites down on his fingers and he cries out. She lets go and says, 'Get the fuck off, don't do that.'

'I'm sorry,' he says, and turns around onto his belly, putting his bitten hand under him because the pain is sharp and hot.

'I'm sorry too,' May-Belle says.

A couple more minutes pass and no-one comes. 'Right, Dirt Bird, let's go,' Pearse says. 'The coast must be clear by now.'

When they get up to the window, most of the glass has been put in. It takes ages to remove the rest of the spikey shards sticking in the window frame, though, so they can climb inside without getting the guts torn out of them.

Once they're in, they stand stiff as pokers and listen. No noise comes. They're in a fairly big classroom. Pearse picks up a stick of chalk, pushes all the teacher's books off her desk, and draws a massive dick on the wood. He draws a big face with an open mouth beside it and writes 'Suck Me, ya tart' underneath.

May-Belle laughs and says, 'Brilliant.'

She goes over to a book shelf and starts picking up books, like Little Red Riding Hood and The Three Billy Goats Gruff, and rips the backs off them; she shreds the pages too, turning the fairy-tales into confetti.

Pearse is drawing on the walls with felt tips and crayons, writing things like 'All teachers must die' and 'You are all fucking cunts'. May-Belle says, 'Gimme a go.' She writes 'Lik my fanie you smely basterds' and 'Eet shit and di'.

There's a nature table – which they smash to pieces; busting all the eggs and firing the leaves and conkers and feathers around the room. They tip a fish tank out onto the floor. May-Belle and Pearse watch the wee goldies die one by one on the ground, gasping their last.

'This place is fucken shite,' says May-Belle.

'Course it's shite, all schools are shite,' Pearse says.

'I'm gonna shite all over this place,' she says.

'Uh?' he says. 'Shite in here?'

'Aye,' she says. Pearse laughs and says, 'Right you be then, you're on. Do it.'

'Turn away then,' she says to him.

Pearse turns around, and carries on drawing cocks and tits on the wall. He can hear that she's squatting down now and straining and then laughing to herself.

'You dirty wee bitch,' he shouts over his shoulder.

'Shut your fucken mouth,' she says back. 'You can't slag me off if you won't do a shit yourself.'

'Fuck it,' Pearse says, and he ducks behind the teacher's desk so May-Belle won't be able to see him. He gets his trousers and pants down and manages to produce a bit of a meagre shit in the corner, and pisses on himself by accident. While he's at this business, he catches a noseful of his own smell and then May-Belle's smell too and he starts to get the dry heaves.

'Euugh, human manure,' May-Belle half laughs and half gags, and Pearse hears a big stream of piss coming out of her too.

He hitches up his britches and says, 'Are you decent?'

May-Belle scavenges bits of crispy-crunchy ripped up storybook paper to wipe herself with and then pulls up her pants and straightens her skirt, 'Aye, that's me,' she chuckles.

She walks forward holding a turd – a monster-sized shit – on a sheet of paper.

The smell hits Pearse like an warm open oven full of dark brown stink and he pukes on the floor. He waggles his hands through his hair – it feels like the smell has wrapped itself around his head.

'Oh fuck,' he screams as she laughs and wafts the shit near him. 'That reeks. What the fuck are you doing with it?'

She runs up to the front of the class and pushes the paper and shit against the black-board. Then she smears it all over.

Pearse goes outside, into the hallway, to spew again, and May-Belle says, 'Where'd you think you're going, Pearsey? I need the shite you did as well.'

'What?' he say, and vomits a bit more in the doorway.

'I've run out of shite, I need your one. Spread it on the black-board.'

'Fuck sake, May-Belle,' he says.

'Please, Pearsey. Do it.'

He holds his breath and runs back into the classroom, grabs a baby's storybook and pushes it under the wee turd he created earlier. There's sick in his mouth and he can't stop it from running out of him onto this specimen he's carrying on the book – Rumplestiltskin.

May-Belle looks at the shit and says, 'What the fuck do you call that? It's a midget.'

'What the fuck shall I do then?' Pearse says nearly crying.

'Och, I don't need it. It's too wee. I'll just make do.'

Pearse smears the book and the shit and the puke and the spit all over the teacher's chair and walks back to the doorway, where even there the stink would knock you for six.

May-Belle pulls the neck of her jumper over her nose and breathes through her mouth. She takes a ruler and uses it to scrape some of the shit off the black-board. It takes a few seconds to work out what she's doing. She's writing something. In the shit, the words appear. 'Tis is not a blak bord it is a brun bord.'

'Fuck me, May-Belle,' Pearse say. 'It's spelt brown. B. R. O. W. N.'

'Och, who cares,' she says. 'It's still shite.'

'Cmon, let's go,' Pearse says, and starts to walk away, down the corridor.

She runs out of the room and shuts the door behind her.

'I need to go to the bogs,' Pearse says. In the toilets, there are wee tiny piss-pots for wee tiny lads with wee tiny winkles. Pearse bends down low over a wee tiny sink to wash his hands and splash his face and puke up and rinse his mouth.

When he comes out May-Belle is doing something to the door of the shit-stinky classroom. He puts his hand over his nose, for the reek is creeping out from inside, and comes close behind her to see what it is she's up to.

She's pushing a drawing pin into a big sheet of paper which says, 'Fuck you mista. We distroy so we can liv agin. Fanie and...' And the rest was blank. She handed Pearse a felt tip and said, 'I signed for you, and left a space for you to sign for me.'

Pearse takes the pen from her and writes 'Faggot'.

They're off and away then, like hares in front of dogs, out the window, through the play-ground, around the streets and up to May-Belle's place. It's gone half eight by this time and Pearse says, 'Mary's Hairies, I better go, see ya later', and pegs it down the road to his house. May-Belle stands in the road and waves bye-bye.

*

As Pearse comes down the hill, Da's coming up it, dressed like he's Daddy Cool or the flippen Fonze, with his shirt open to show off the three wee hairs on his chest, and the collar of his jacket turned up. There's a beezer red sky at night blazing away behind him – with wispy long Ribena coloured clouds and fluffy swatches of strawberry blonde crimped hair, swooping in the sky and criss-crossing; flacked with white puffs like the trails of jet engine burns – the body, blood and bone shades of the sunset.

This Yvonne girl is a few feet behind Da, and she's dressed to the nines too with her hair in thick matted waves flopping down the side of her face, and her jeans so tight she must have had to lie down to get them on. She looks like an auld pro, if the truth be told.

And it's her who says to Pearse, 'Where have you been?'

Surprised, Pearse says, 'What? I said I'd be back at eight.'

She says, 'We were meant to be going out at eight, it's gone half past now.'

'Get the fuck into the house,' Da says.

'I didn't know you were going out,' Pearse says, and he's pushed from behind as he gets to the garden path.

'It's Saturday night – what did you think we were going to do? When you say you are going to do something, you do it,' this Yvonne woman says.

'Fucken right,' says Da.

The clouds are pretty-pinked even deeper now, and wispy trails far off in the sky, throb glowy orange – the electric element of a three-bar fire. Behind the clouds, the sky's washed deep blue and dusty yellow. Low down, near where the distant houses meet the sky, the background is a fiery blaze, and the farthest farthest horizon, closest to the earth, is a sickly yellow, almost burned to white.

Da gives Pearse another clunk in the back as he steps over the threshold of his own house and says, 'Get into the living room you.'

He puts his face right in Pearse's face, with an expression that looks as if he'd like to eat him alive. He shouts into Pearse's gob, with his dirty spit flying on to him, telling him that he's a lying wee cunt who can't be trusted.

'What are you?' he says.

Pearse says nothing.

'What are you?' he says.

'Answer your father,' says this Yvonne woman.

'I'm late,' Pearse says, hoping for her sake that Yvonne is smart enough to decide not to hang around this house very much longer.

Bang. Da calls him a cheeky cunt and banjoes him under the chin – a sharp wee uppercut that you'd lay on a guy if you were fighting in a bar. Pearse catches the tip of his tongue between his teeth as they crack together, and ends up lying across the sofa. It's like his jaw has been injected with dentist anaesthetic and won't move properly from side to side or open far to let words out. The bloody point of his tongue feels as big as a pyramid and pulses as if someone had put a match to it. Pearse sticks his tongue out a little and put his fingers to his mouth and there is blood all over him, in his mouth and on his chin.

'Dan,' the woman says, 'a clip round the ear or a slap on the arse was all you fucken needed to do.'

She comes over to Pearse and says, 'Let me see you, love.'

Pearse opens his arms out to the side, like he's surrendering in a half-arsed way and couldn't really be bothered – showing himself to her. She looks at his teeth and says, 'Well they aren't broken.' Then she turns to Da and says, 'You better watch those hands of yours. There's ways and means, you know.'

Da goes, 'We haven't got time for all this shite, c'mon, we gotta go.'

Yvonne takes another look at Pearse and says, 'You're alright, son. There's a few sandwiches on a plate and some juice in the fridge.'

Da says, 'You can watch the telly till ten, but then get to bed. I'm fucken warning you, boy. Last chance. No more fucken about. Do you understand?'

Pearse looks at him.

'Do you understand?' he says.

'I understand what you are saying,' Pearse replies ventriloquist-style, trying very hard not to move his mouth, lips or teeth.

'Just do what your father tells you and life'll be a lot easier,' the Yvonne woman says.

She grabs her coat and puffs some perfume round the front of her diddies, and the pair of them waltz out the back door. 'I'll lock this door,' Da says. 'The key's in the front door if there's a fire and you need to get out or something. We'll be home late. Remember what I said.'

Ker-lunk, the door closes after them, and Pearse sits for a few minutes dabbing the tip of his cut tongue, licking and touching until no more blood spots appear on his fingertip. The pain remains, burning raw, but he can wiggle his jaw again slowly.

He waits half an hour, like a wee stone statue, not moving even an eye muscle and hardly breathing, until he feels it's safe and they won't be coming back. He walks to the front door and unlocks it and goes outside and bolts the door behind him. He puts the key in his pocket, walks down the front path and goes straight up the hill to May-Belle's house. He raps her door, and she opens it dressed in God know's what kind of an outfit.

Pearse mutters to her, though his clenched sore mouth, 'What have you got on ya, ya daft faggot?'

She's wearing Ma's red high heels and one of her dresses too, a green spangly one which May-Belle's rolled up in the middle so it'll fit her, and a face full of make-up.

'I'm just playing at dressing up,' she says, 'I've nothing to do.'

Pearse tells her to come on down to his house – Da's out for the night, just like auld Monster Ma is, and won't be back till the wee hours probably.

She's up for it right away, and they beak off, on down the road, as quick as they can, her still dressed up like Lady Muck.

'What's with the way you're talking?' she asks on the way down.

'Dah thmacked me in the fathe for being late,' he says, laughing and exaggerating the damage done to him. 'Hurt my thongue.'

'I fucken hate that bastard,' she says.

'I'd like to do the cunt in,' he says.

'He's near as bad as my bitch by the sounds of him,' she says back.

No-one sees them on the way back down to Pearse's house. They get in the front door and Pearse locks it behind them. May-Belle starts chattering on about what'll happen if auld Evil Bollocks comes back; and Pearse says, 'Him and the woman will be so pissed, May-Belle, you'll have time to run out the front door when we hear them returning, and scarper off home.'

May-Belle ponders and says, 'If we stay in the living room, we'll easily hear them open the back gate and that'll give plenty of time, ages in fact, for me to get off-side and for you to peg it up the stairs and pretend to be giving it big auld zeds in bed.'

'He won't hit you,' Pearse says. 'Don't worry.'

May-Belle says, 'I wouldn't give a shit, even if he tried. I'd just kick him in the balls and run like fuck.'

Pearse says, 'I'd love to see that.'

Some detective show is on telly; it's a British one, so there's little shooting and lots of country lanes. Pearse turns it down a good wee bit and says to May-Belle that they should play this cracking board game he's got.

Pearse runs upstairs and gets the game, The Fastest Gun in the West, out from under his bed and takes it downstairs. He sets the board up and tells her the rules are a bit like Monopoly only you have to kill everyone into the bargain, so it's like Monopoly Murder.

'What's that?' she says.

'What?' Pearse asks.

'Monopo-thingy. What you just said.'

'Monopoly?' he says.

'Aye,' she says.

Pearse stares at her like she's the biggest eejit on the block and asks her, 'Are you pulling my leg, May-Belle? You don't know Monopoly?'

'No,' she says. 'I flippen don't. What you going on about?'

'Alright, alright,' he says. 'Keep your wig on. Never mind, I'll just show you the rules to this one.'

They play a fake game, a dummy run, one where no-one is allowed to win, but where the person who knows the rules takes the other by the hand, and shows them what to do.

Pearse explains to her how they have to get around the board where this Tombstone kind of town in the wild west is laid out. They have to move about buying up the saloon, where all the hoors in swirly dresses with ruffly knickers live, and the stables and the sheriff's jail and the Pony Express head-quarters and the telegraph office. They've both got a pot of money to start and if Pearse lands on one of May-Belle's properties or she lands on one of his then that's like someone taking off their buttoned-up gloves and slapping you in the face, boy – that's cause enough for a gunfight. The way the fights work is that you both hire a gunman and the two fighters square up to each other at high noon on the dusty main street. It's a bit like Russian Roulette. If you throw a six, blam, you've killed your nemesis. Once you run out of money and can't afford a gun for hire, then you have to put yourself up for the next bout of gunplay. If you lose that fight – you're dead, on your way to Boot Hill, and out of the game. Your opponent wins.

After Pearse has shown her the ropes, he turns the gas fire on, and flicks the big light off, so they can play by the picture of the turned-down TV.

'Right, who you gonna be?' he asks her.

'Dunno,' she says.

'Well, I'm gonna be Doc Holliday.'

'What are you gonna be a doctor for, fanny?' she says.

'He's not a flippen doctor, May-Belle,' he says back. 'He was a cowboy, or rather a doctor who was also a cowboy. No that's wrong, he was a dentist, I think, and then became a gunslinger – that's not the same as being a cowboy. He just had gunfights for the crack, and caught that auld TB thing that makes you cough up blood in a hankie.'

'Oh. Right,' she says, 'well who am I gonna be?'

'Who do you want to be?'

'You choose.'

'Umm… Wild Bill Hickcock?'

'I'm not having no name with a cock in it, Pearsey, thank you very much,' she goes.

'Well, Buffalo Bill?' he suggests.

'Do I look like a flippen buffalo person?' she says. 'Are there no girls?'

'Oh flip aye, of course there are.' he says remembering. 'You can be Calamity Jane.'

'Tip-top,' says May-Belle. 'Who's she?'

'A mad gun-fighting bitch who wore cowboy clothes and shot the shit outta any guy that got in her way.'

'That's my girl,' she says clapping her hands together.

'Do you know Doris Day?'

'No, who's she? Another one of these cowboy girls?'

'It doesn't matter,' he says.

So Doc Holliday and Calamity Jane move into Tombstone and start to buy up the town. The first showdown comes when they cross swords at the iron-mongers, over May-Belle trying to muscle in on Pearse's property. Pearse tells her it's a no-good two-bit piece of crap and it ain't worth no bullets flying, but she says she ain't gonna be hornswoggled outta what's hers by right.

They send their boys out to fight with the town bell tolling twelve and May-Belle takes two in the guts. The undertaker scuttles out from the swing doors of the saloon, and carries the body off to get it measured for a wooden waistcoat.

'I don't want no more feudin,' Pearse tells May-Belle. 'Put your shooting irons away.'

'You hush up, Doc, before I fill your belly full of lead,' she warns. Pearse has been teaching her the lingo.

The peace is held for a while, until Pearse tries to stake a claim at her gold mine. This time he's got him one of the best sharpshooters in all the prairie states, while she's got a greenhorn who's no more than knee-high to a grasshopper. But that young'un claims Pearse's man with a clean shot right to the head, whipping his Widow-Maker outta his rawhide holster faster than a rattler hunting conies.

May-Belle starts clearing up, bumping Pearse's men off left, right and centre. Pearse says to her to hauld on a wee minute and let him earn a bit of extra cash as if he doesn't get some money then the next time they fight it'll have to be him – Pearsey, Doc Holliday – that goes up for the shoot-out as he hasn't the funds to afford a hired gun.

'Tough titty,' May-Belle drawls, her faced scrunched up like a cow-poke.

'Fuck sake,' Pearse says, and rolls the dice.

The roll takes him right into May-Belle's provision store. 'I only came to buy me some grits,' he says. 'I don't want your shitey store.'

'Let's take it outside,' May-Belle says. 'You got a reckonin with Calamity a-coming.'

'Back off, pilgrim, I ain't fighting ya,' he says.

'Get your gun, boy.'

'No,' he says, getting a bit tetchy as she won't stop arsing about and pretending to be some dude out riding the range. 'Bollocks, May-Belle. If I die then the game's over.'

'Ain't that the truth, pardner,' she says. 'And then this here town is mine.'

'Away to fuck,' he says back. 'I'm not fighting, May-Belle.'

May-Belle takes the funny look off her face, and asks, 'Are you pulling a huff?'

'No, but I don't want the game to be over.'

'Oh don't be such a baby, someone has to lose. It's only a game,' she says.

'But I don't want to lose now.'

'Och away and cry then, Pearsey. It's only meant to be a bit of crack.'

'Fuck off, May-Belle,' he says and gets up and half-runs half-staggers into the front hall, like an hysterical eejit, and belts up the stairs, locking himself in the bathroom, and starts crying – for the world, a wee toddler who's dropped his sweeties.

He's balling his fists in the bathroom and his head pounds like it's going to blow the crown off his skull. There's a horrible thick green taste in his mouth and it just gets thicker and more sickly sweet the longer he cries; the tears are spurting out of his eyes now, not even bothering to be half-way civilised and roll down his cheeks.

'Pearse,' May-Belle shouts from the bottom of the stairs. 'I'll go home if you want.'

'No,' he calls from behind the door. 'Sorry. Don't do that. You can't do that.'

'Well, are you coming down?'

'Yeah, gimme a second,' he says, and starts drying his eyes – splashing water on his face and rinsing his mouth out and drying himself off. In the mirror, he's a wee puffy damp tomato.

'I've put that auld game away,' May-Belle says to him when he walks out of the bathroom. 'We'll call it a draw.' She turns on her heel and goes back into the living room.

'Naw, May-Belle. Sorry. You won.'

'Doesn't matter,' she says. 'Let's watch a bit of telly. I never get to watch telly.'

'No?' Pearse says. 'There'll be some cracking programmes on – let's check.'

It's near ten and there's nothing but arse-aching cricket on for another half hour until the Horror Double Bill starts. Tonight, Dracula's Daughter is the black and white movie – that comes on first; up afterwards it's The Masque of the Red Death.

Even before the start of the first film – which is nearly 45 years old and wouldn't scare a nun – May-Belle's clinging to Pearse's arm. When it gets to the part in the second movie where a dwarf burns a fella in a gorilla suit to death, she's nearly crying and asking Pearse to unplug the television and make it stop. She lies with her head in a cushion while Death himself lays waste to the castle of the evil Prince Prospero.

May-Belle says to Pearse that there's no way on God's good earth she's walking home alone now, and reckons she'll go mad by morning if she has to stay in her house by herself after watching those films. So Pearse tells her it's no sweat, no need to have a crap attack, just sleep here. It's fine to stay up in his room – and when they hear Bastard-Face and his Bitch come in from the pub May-Belle can do the auld duck-under-the-bed trick and hide till the Pishy Pair have hit the hay. Bip bop. Tick. Tock. Wait a wee while, and then come back out, and stay till the dawn is up – then she can run away off home again.

'You're mad game for it, Pearsey,' she says laughing.

'Aye, and you're not?' he asks back.

*

It's getting on for half one now the horror movies are over, so Pearse turns off all the lights and tidies up a bit downstairs. May-Belle gives him a hand putting dishes in the sink and unplugging stuff. He checks the windows are shut. Neither of them have said a word to each other about Galen or the Nursery School. Wrapped up in one another, thoughts of such things are far far away out in the rest of the world – a place which has nothing to do with them and never will as long as they are together, alone.

May-Belle stands at the foot of the stairs. 'Give us a carry-up,' she says, as he closes the living room door behind them.

'Away on,' he says, 'you're flippen massive. A heifer like you'd break my back.'

'Och, listen to the shite of you, Pearsey,' she says. 'I'm a skelf, there's nothing of me. Cmon, give us a carry-up. A piggy-back, ya weakling. I never get a carry up the stairs.'

'Aw, Jesus,' he says, bending over a wee bit and making his back a saddle for her, 'get on then, quick.'

She grabs ahold and hurls her legs around his hips like he's Red Rum and she's a silky wee jockey. 'Yee-ha. Giddy-ap,' she says.

The wind goes out of his lungs – he's a punctured beach ball and she's a fatty sitting on it. 'Hauld on, May-Belle. Christ you are heavy, Count Pigula.'

Pearse starts a staggery walk up the stairs, nearly bent over enough for his nose to scrape along the carpet, and finally drags her and himself to the top landing.

'Right, get the bloody hell off me, you're killing me,' he says.

May-Belle goes into the bathroom and Pearse turns off all the upstairs lights and stands outside the bathroom door, hiding there, waiting for her.

She comes tootling out after taking a pee – and gazing at her reflection in the bathroom mirror for a moment – and Pearse leaps on her, hissing, saying 'I am a Wampyre – I vant to sook your bloood!' May-Belle gives a scream – a grave opening – and starts slapping him, all flappy-wise, saying, 'Don't do that, Pearsey. Why'd you do that?'

Then she's crying and he says sorry – that he didn't mean to scare her – and puts his arms around her and gives her a bit of a squeeze, not a cuddle.

She says, 'That's alright', and after a wee second they go into his bedroom. May-Belle's still wearing her ma's green dress and red high heels and Pearse says to her they'd better take their shoes off in case they rip the sheets. He tells her to get into the far side of the bed, so he's nearest the door.

They hop in, and with the lights off there's just an orange glow shining around the edges of the curtains from the lamp-posts outside. It's quiet too – only a few drunks singing in the distance somewhere, and the groany auld rumble and fade of a couple of cars dopplering by.

They're lying on their sides facing each other almost nose to nose. 'Flippen hell,' Pearse says. 'I hate that auld scary singing in the middle of the night.'

'Waddayamean?' she says, pulling her knees up to her chest and moving closer.

'Never mind,' he says, thinking of things to scare her with. 'I tried to tell that Katie Cloaky and Gulliver Riggs story before but you thought it was gay so I won't bother.'

'Tell me,' she says, edging away from the side of the bed – which is just a wee single one.

'No. It gives me the willies,' he says, and his arse feels too near the side of the bed as well, so he shuffles his body over into the middle a bit too.

'Tell,' she says, so he tells her how Katie Cloaky and Gulliver Riggs were caught for the murders of all these children in Ireland long long ago and sentenced to death. Katie escaped from prison but before she fled she gave Gulliver a drug that would make him appear dead. In the morning, the hangman came to get them and found Katie gone and Gulliver as dead as your doorknob. They take Gulliver to the edge of the city walls and dig a pit and put him in a mouldy auld box that'll have to make do for a coffin and throw the box into the grave. Lime on top. Katie has to wait till nightfall to get to the grave and start digging Gulliver out with her hands. When there's less than a foot of soil covering the coffin, Katie Cloaky hears Gulliver's nails scraping against the lid and murmuring prayers to the Devil probably. The potion she gave him was only enough to keep him asleep for about eight hours, so Gulliver has been awake in the box for a good nine or ten more. She gets him out, covered in grave dirt, and if Gulliver Riggs wasn't mad before, with all his child killing and kidnapping, he was mad now. From then on, he and Katie take to killing adults, and their modus operandi, as detectives would say on telly, was to hide in fog, waiting for some unsuspecting passerby to come along and then they'd pounce and slit their throats and make off with their wallets and watches and so on. On nights when Katie didn't want to go out killing because she felt they had enough money, Gulliver would walk about town in the fog on his own, waiting for a woman to come along. He'd hide in an alleyway once he heard a lady's feet come clip-clopping up the cobbles in her wee satin heels. When she'd gone twenty paces on in front of him, so the fog swallowed her up, Gulliver would emerge and start slowly walking behind her, whistling auld Irish tunes, echoey songs like Molly Malone. As he closed in – the girl terrified by now; an invisible stranger somewhere behind her in the fog whistling like a ghost – Gulliver would start mournful singing in a low voice, going:

She died of a fever
and no-one could save her
and that was the end of Sweet Molly Malone.
Now her ghost wheels its barrow
down streets broad and narrow

crying cockles and mussels
…Alive alive oh.

When he was almost upon the girl, he'd stop singing, and just before the fog cleared between them, and she could see him once and for all, he'd break into song again. This time louder. Then he'd slit the poor doll's throat and leave her bleeding to death on the foggy cobbles of the street and make his way back to the house where he lived with his lover Katie Cloaky.

May-Belle's holding on to the front of Pearse's shirt and jumper now, saying, 'Is that true? Did that really go on?'

He tells her, 'It's as true as the pair of us lying here in this bed together.'

'Fuck,' she says.

He asks her if she wants another scary story, and she says, 'Holy shit no', but then has a bit of a think and laughs a frightened wee titter and goes, 'Aye alright then, but don't blame me if I have a brown hemorrhage in your bed.'

'Have you ever heard of the Monster of Massereene Castle?' he asks her.

'Naw,' she says. 'You mean down the Castle Grounds?'

'Aye,' he says. 'It lives in that big deep black pond that's shaped like the letter O in the middle of the park.'

'Oh fuck off, Pearsey,' she says, nearly lying on top of him now she's so scared.

'Okay, I'll stop,' he says. 'I'm scaring myself.' They've wiggled over so far in the bed to get away from the sides that their noses are just about touching, even though they are trying extremely hard to stop any nose-touching at all; their knees are pulled right up to their chins as they don't want their feet anywhere near the bottom of the bed where something could get ahold of them and wheek them under with its big black scaly hand.

'No, no, go on,' she says. 'I like it. Do you believe in all this stuff?'

'Not sure,' he says. And then he starts to tell her the story of the Massereene Monster. Pearse asks her if she knows the history of the Castle Grounds and she says no, so he explains it to her.

Today, the Castle Grounds is nothing but a public park, but years ago, up until the end of the First World War, all that land made up the gardens of an ancient stately home owned by these Viscounts or Marquesses or something – who went by the family name and title of Massereene. In 1919, the IRA burned the castle to the ground, and now all that is left is a bit of the medieval walls, with its Norman keep and gate, and one crumbly old tower. Two deep, dark, stagnant ponds covered in green bubbling algae are the only remnants of the original manor's landscape gardens. One pond is long and rectuangular, and the other wide and circular. The Monster of Massereene lives in the circular pond.

No-one knows what it is, or how it got there, although some think it's the living remains of a witch who was burned centuries ago and managed to free herself from the stake. She ran aflame through the town and before the locals could catch her, she dived into the circular pond, the monster pond, to put herself out. She sank to the bottom – and it is deep that pond, about twenty foot down in most places – and no-one ever saw her again.

All we know is that people have disappeared when they've been walking along the edges of that pond, alone. It's said that a black, gnarly hand, with the skin hanging off it, hoys up from the water, gripping the victim around the ankle; pulling them down and carrying them off for God knows what watery behaviour.

Pearse takes a divergence from his main story now, and is just starting to tell May-Belle the legend of Galloping Thompson who haunted the Seven Mile Straight – and how his ghost and the ghost of his horse were captured and put in a spirit bottle – when they hear the back garden gate open, and Da and his woman laughing as they come up the path.

May-Belle slithers out of bed without standing – turning into liquid and flowing off the edge as if she were mercury. From beneath the bed she says, 'Cut the flippen scary stories till I'm out from under here.'

'I'm gonna start pretending to be asleep. Shush.'

'K.'

May-Belle concentrates on the iron mesh lattice of springs beneath the bed and stays still, ready to run, jump out the window, find a weapon and commit murder if needed. To be convincing, Pearse tries to sleep. He drops his brain down a few levels, relaxing and kind of going into a brown study – losing himself in a cave in his head. He breathes slowly and heavily. The blackness starts to spiral red behind his eyelids; multi-coloured dots and whirls move around and pulse in different directions but with a rhythm and purpose. May-Belle counts seconds in her head.

The bulb comes on in the hall as Da and his woman make their way to bed; the light-shine under the door changes the pattern of the spirals behind Pearse's eyelids, and draws May-Belle's gaze to its glimmer on the carpet. Ma's high heels are sitting a few feet away from her – on the floor, by the wall, near the bed, near the door.

Da says, 'You head in to bed. I'll be in in a minute.' He opens the door and Pearse feigns stirring to the coming of the light – fractionally. May-Belle prepares to move – out from under the bed, away between the auld bastard's legs, through the door, down the stairs and off before anyone's had time to blink. Ta-da.

The air shifts as Da comes close. It moves again when he leans over and strokes Pearse's hair. There's a muggy smell of beer. Da stands there until the count of one hundred has passed, and then it sounds like he blows a kiss, and walks out of the room. The light in the hall goes off, and Pearse opens his eyes. May-Belle shuts her eyes. The light in the next bedroom goes on and then in a wee minute it is off and the house is back to darkness.

In the pitch black, Pearse whispers to May-Belle, 'Stay there.' From Da's room, they hear the bed squeak and spring for a few minutes and then there's some giggling, and then it's quiet and that's it – there will be no more noise till morning.

When it's been silent for about ten minutes, Pearse hangs his head over the edge of the bed and whispers to May-Belle, 'Are you alive down there? No big beasties or witches got you?'

She sticks her head out, like a mechanic from under a car, looks up at him, and whispers, 'I'm alive, but I could have done without the thought of your big arse bouncing around above me up there.'

'Shush,' he says quietly. 'Don't start me laughing. Come up into bed.'

She wiggles out from beneath the bed, all mousey, stands up, pulls back the covers and gets in beside him. 'No more scary stories now,' she says.

He asks her to hand him his wee alarm clock – with that fruity-looking Mickey Mouse on the face. Mickey's fluorescent arms show the time is now gone three in the morning. Pearse winds it up and sets it for half seven. He says to May-Belle that they need to be up and about early in case this Yvonne woman rises with the dawn chorus. If Da's been out on the piss he won't be up till gone one at least, though.

'Right you be, Pearsey,' says May-Belle.

Pearse shuts his eyes for a wee moment and sees a rock, a giant rock that's been carved by hand, standing in the middle of a desert. He opens his eyes and then shuts them again. There's a mighty dog bounding across a field. Then there's a hut with glowing torches on the walls. A hand lifting a roof off a doll's house. Huge footsteps on a beach – deep enough to stand in.

He opens his eyes. 'Do you ever see things when you are sleepy,' he asks May-Belle.

'Mmm,' she says, sounding far away. 'Sometimes. Like what?'

'Strange things. Things your mind just makes up.'

'Mmm,' she says. 'Sometimes. Like what?

'I just saw a big stone that people worship on a faraway planet.'

'I don't see shit like that,' she says.

'What do you see then?' Pearse asks.

'I just saw a big foot, there, as you started talking, coming down and stamping on people. Just one big foot, all by itself.'

'I saw its foot print,' he says, and laughs so quietly that he's not even sure if he did laugh or not.

May-Belle chuckles. 'Get to sleep. No more games.'

'See you in the morning, May-Belle,' he says.

'Aye,' she says, and starts giving it wee snores before the word has fully left her lips.

He turns on his side to look at her. Her ma's green dress is bunched up around her face. Even though it's dark, the freckles scattered on her nose stand out. Her mouth moves a little – like the two lips are slow-dancing.

Behind her eyes, May-Belle sees herself standing inside the big footprint in the sand. She considers trying to climb out of this huge hole, which is the depth of two people. She's stood right at the spot where the big toe has made a massive dent in the beach; she's standing in this bowl looking up at the edges of the footprint. The sea water runs in a little, over the rim through wee channels above. She worries now that she might drown if she arses about down here too much longer and does nothing to get out. She takes a leap in the air to grab ahold of the ridge above her in the sand – to haul herself out – but the walls give way and the sand falls down on top of her face. Then salty water is pouring in, filling the footprint and rising so fast that it's up to her neck by the time she struggles to her feet. The water turns the ground beneath her gooey and sludgey like quicksand, and she can't lift her legs to swim. The water is up to her lips and then over her nose, closing in around her eyes. Stuck in the sand, she's swallowed by the sea – her head tilted to the side so that just one ear and half an eye and a wee sliver of breathing nostril are left shown to the sky; she hears the sea water zhoozhing her from every side, all around, like the sound of a shell, and then she awakes with the auld alarm clock brrr-ing-ringing and Mickey's arms pointing to half seven. Pearse is saying, 'Shush you, you are making a quare

PART FIVE

The Weary Woods

May-Belle went back home, and a few hours apart from Pearse got her thinking and frightened. Later that morning, the pair of them meet up again, and sit like two old men muttering at the base of the old oak tree, at the end of the street. He's drawing lines in the earth with a stick, trying to prove some theory, and she's pointing out mistakes – re-assessing.

May-Belle wants to know 'if this happens, will that happen' – they did this, so therefore might that befall them – 'how do we know we won't get caught'.

'Don't feel bad about it,' Pearse said.

'I don't,' she said. 'I'm scared, is all.'

'I'm telling you,' he said, 'it will be fine.'

'Promise,' she said.

'I promise,' he said.

'Swear.'

'I swear.'

'Say it definitely will be so.'

'It definitely will be so.'

'And you aren't just saying that.'

'I am not just saying that.'

'Cos I feel sick all the time at the thought of the police taking me away.'

'They will not take us away.'

'Swear.'

'I swear to you.'

'And you know that?'

'I know that, May-Belle. They'd never have a clue.'

'I can't help it,' she said. 'It's driving me mad.'

'Forget about it. It will never happen. Think about it. Be logical-ish.'

Pearse had watched quite a number of films that Mum and Gran termed melodramas. They were wild shows – hot sweaty American carry-on mostly. People whipped themselves into a storm of words and feelings and then unleashed sentences and expressions that destroyed life and happiness and home with as much power and timing as the hand of God in the Old Testament – Sodom and Gomorrah style; Pearse hated the pain but loved the passion. This moment – right now – felt like judgement and drama for May-Belle, and Pearse wanted to try to use words in a way that would make her feel safe, just as he did.

He patted the auld oak tree they sat beneath – a terrible sense of fakery welling up in him, but he was able to press it down so he could make his point – and he started in on one of the stories Gran had told him: this one about something May-Belle had never heard of before, the Battle of Antrim.

The Battle of Antrim went raging around this town back in 1798, he told her, in the time of britches and muskets and pow-dered wigs. The main bloodshed happened outside the gates of the castle in Market Square. The killing carried on up High Street, with Irish rebels hiding in the walls of All Saints Parish Church – still there today, with it's spire and clanging hour-bell – shooting at the Redcoats and men loyal to the Crown.

There was whooping and gun smoke and cannons and bayo-nets, and in the end the rebels – who were called the United Irishmen and were meant to be a proper mix of Catholics and Protestants, folk who didn't give a tinker's curse for religion, but were inspired by the French and the Americans instead – they got hammered into the ground. The mass graves of the executed lie under the black tar top of the road that runs from the court house in Market Square up High Street. No-one knows how many folk are under there, in their wee green waistcoats, with their hair cut short in the revolutionary Croppy fashion, or in their red petticoats and bonnets. Some say it's a couple of hundred at least, or six hundred at the most. A half decent sized war crime for the times, anyway, no matter what way you count it – and both the killers and the victims were just the same type of people who live in this town today: hoors and monsters and liars, and the innocent, decent folk who should never be near the rest of them. A judge, one of those black-capped boyos, gave the official order from King George himself for the state troops to round the traitors up amongst the townsfolk, have them dig their ditch, set them in a line and shoot them so they filled in their own grave.

'When was all this?' asked May-Belle.

'Hundreds of years back,' said Pearse – and he gritted himself for how false he would feel at the point he'd come all this way to make. 'About the time this tree went up.' And he patted its trunk again.

'What's with you and this tree?' she says. 'The town's full of murder – so what?'

'Blood's everywhere,' he says – back to the beat of his poor wee sermon, and free from the blushes of the moral he's trying to put on the story. 'And no-one is ever punished. Most people don't get punished. It happens and it's forgotten. This battle in Antrim and all the things that people got up to back then – it was just life. Like now. No-one ever won or lost if you count it all up, and so it's forgotten.'

Pearse thought it best – because his last speech had been so lovely and powerful and off the cuff, in his opinion – to look away and just nod to himself. He plucked at some weeds in the roots of the tree.

May-Belle shook her head in disgust and said, 'But fuckers catch you – that's the way it goes. Wise up. Didn't all the good guys die in your wee story.'

They sat under the tree – her to the left, and him to the right

– and stared at the dividing network of brown and white and black streets. Police officers appeared on the brow of the hill – they came around corners into the main road – emerged at the bottom of the street; all of them walking towards Pearse and May-Belle.

May-Belle said, 'Well, this is it, then. Cheerio.'

Pearse said, 'See if we are caught – you better meet me when we get out.'

May-Belle said, 'How long would they put us away for?'

Pearse said, 'Life – I dunno. I think that means 20 years. We'll be 30 ish.'

May-Belle said, 'Fuck it, don't move or say a thing.'

'Don't run,' said Pearse. 'Hauld our ground till we need to go.'

May-Belle counted the cops – twelve in all, coming from all sides. The cops were rapping letter boxes – women cops going inside; men cops poking around hedges with sticks, speaking to local guys, pointing and laughing. The police inched their way along the streets towards Pearse and May-Belle – letterbox by letterbox, house and hedge.

Two police-women walked right up to them.

'Hello, kids,' the prettier one said. 'Have you heard about the wee lad who we found at the houses over by?'

'No,' said May-Belle. 'What happened?'

The auld one said, 'We think a bad man hurt him – someone who wants to hurt children. Have you seen anyone around here who has scared you or talked to you that you don't know?'

'No,' said May-Belle, 'Though there are always fellas riding around in cars.'

'Like who?' the auld one asks.

'No idea,' says May-Belle.

'Kids,' says the pretty one, 'you should be keeping yourselves inside. We want to look after you.'

'Do you need any help searching?' asks May-Belle.

'No,' the auld one says, 'we found the wee fella. His parents are in a state. You two should get back to your mummies and daddies.'

'OK, we better,' says Pearse and gets up, dusting off the seat of his trousers. 'That sounds scary.'

'Kids,' says the pretty one, 'don't worry – we don't mean to scare you – you are safe. We are just here to see if we can find clues to the man who hurt that wee boy.'

'Yes, don't worry,' says the auld one, 'the man doesn't live here – he probably came from far away and hurt that wee boy and then has gone off somewhere else. So don't you two worry.'

'We'll go home,' says Pearse.

'OK, kids,' says the pretty one.

'Bye,' says the auld one.

'Bye-bye,' says May-Belle.

And Pearse and May-Belle walk off – pretending they are going home; they are not going home, they are on their way to the common where Pearse will tell May-Belle that the behaviour of the policewomen proves they have nothing to worry about, and May-Belle will say, 'Aye, it really does, doesn't it? The fucken eejits.'

*

And so they plodded on for the next few weeks until school ended – the last day of Primary – and they were freed from their daft, boring, cowardly classmates, and the empty lunch-breaks and sneery teachers, at least for the two hot months of the summer holidays. They'd shamble through the week, hanging out with each other after class for a few hours Monday, Tuesday and Wednesday; May-Belle fighting the odd fit of fear – Pearse quelling the bad worries down as he knew in his heart there was no risk; they were invisible to the authorities and the world at large – and come Thursday when Da went out drinking with his Yvonne floozie, May-Belle would sneak down to Pearse's house, as Monster Ma would be out hitting the town too; May-Belle would stay till about ten at night. Every Friday and Saturday, when all the grown-ups were out partying late, May-Belle would sleep over, in Pearse's bed, till dawn – the pair of them telling stories to each other, about ghosts or his family line or her favourite memories – and then she'd scamper off home in the early morning, before Ma came back from a night on the tiles or Da and his woman woke up. On Sundays, they spent the afternoons running wild in the fields.

It would have been the Tuesday or Wednesday before the last day of school, that the pair of them first had any dealings with Campbell McDonald. They were gadding about on the common one evening when they saw this lad, who was about fourteen, wandering up towards them. Campbell McDonald was a big ox of a fella. Everyone knew him, but no-one gave a damn about him. He didn't have a friend in the world, and his family were tramps. He and his mother and his sister had a ground floor flat a few streets away. He had no father. His sister was called Donna and she was one of those Down's Syndrome mongol types, that everyone called Ma-Don-Ja, because of the way she spoke. His ma was a fat shouty cow. They'd never so much as passed a word with this Campbell McDonald boy in their lives, but as he walks towards them, he shouts out to Pearse, 'Hi Furlong, ya fucken wee poof, playing with girls now are ye?'

May-Belle and Pearse had been chasing each other around and about through the bushes embarked upon a pointless endless game of tig. They stop running when McDonald shouts, and stand beside each other looking at him.

'Get fucked, fat-boy,' May-Belle shouts back.

'Fuck off, ya wee hoor,' says McDonald. 'We all know your type.'

If May-Belle hadn't been there, Pearse would have taken to his heels and ran. McDonald was a foot taller than Pearse – and it was Pearse that McDonald was gunning for, paying not a thought to May-Belle who was just a girl. McDonald was about four stone heavier than Pearse too. But Pearse stood his ground as McDonald advanced, looking once to the side to check May-Belle wasn't scared.

She caught Pearse's eye and nodded her head at McDonald. 'Follow me,' she said, out the side of her mouth – but she didn't move.

'Come on, fat cunt,' says May-Belle, 'what ya gonna do, smack a wee girl about?'

McDonald was right up by them now and he stopped still. 'No,' he says, 'but I'll smack Auld No-Ma here.'

He slugged Pearse a hay-maker to the side of the head. It knocked Pearse over, but he'd sure as hell been hit harder than that before. Pearse heard McDonald say, 'Where's your mammy now, cunt? Oh yeah, fucken dead – I forgot.'

Pearse rolled away from him on the ground, expecting to get kicked in the head when he was down. As he turned to get up he heard a horrific holler come from May-Belle. Then he caught sight of what was happening. May-Belle was climbing up McDonald's body. Her plan was to eat him alive, rip him to bits, and the power of hate in her made her shake and salivate. She had one hand squeezed around McDonald's balls, the whites of her knuckles showing, and the other clawing at his eyes; her legs were wrapped round his – he couldn't shake her off; he stumbled, foundering; she bit his body, trying to tear chunks out of his tits and belly. A sleek wee mongoose killing a fat lazy python.

He struggled to punch her. Pearse jumped up and ran towards them, just as McDonald caught her a hard rap on the head. May-Belle didn't loosen her hold on him, though, she just let out a yowl of anger and mauled him harder. Pearse got behind McDonald – on his shoulders – pulling his head back by the hair. The pair of them dragged him to the ground, biting and punching and kicking and laughing. There was no-one about and they kept on for what seemed an age but was probably only a minute – though that was surely enough for Campbell McDonald.

When McDonald was flat on his back and gasping, May-Belle stopped hitting him and climbed on top of his body, kneeling on his throat and holding on to his hair. Pearse sat astride

McDonald's knees, stopping him from struggling, punching him in the stomach and balls, and biting his legs. May-Belle giggled when McDonald squealed like a pig. 'Apologise for what you said about Mum,' Pearse shouted, between bites and punches, 'and we'll let you up.'

McDonald was desperate to say sorry, but with May-Belle's kneecap in his Adam's Apple he couldn't get a word out.

'Say sorry and it's over, you useless bastard,' says May-Belle. The way she's positioned, kneeling on McDonald's throat, Pearse can't see his face – but he hears a terrible gargled scream.

May-Belle looks back at Pearse over her shoulder, and wiggles the tip of her thumb. 'I really went for his eye that time,' she says.

McDonald must get a rush of mad panic, thinking his number is up, for he somehow manages almost to free himself – half-rising with them still hanging on to him; burrs clinging to his clothes. May-Belle feels like she's a wee bronco rider taming and breaking a dying mustang.

'I'm sorry,' McDonald moans. 'About your mum.' And he lies back – done in. Pearse thinks McDonald looks like an auld wounded moose on a nature programme.

Pearse and May-Belle get up. She looks at Pearse and winks, and then says to McDonald, 'Get up. We're quits now. No more fighting.'

McDonald gets to his feet and he stands there, white and shaking, like a dummy, looking at them. 'No more fighting,' says May-Belle, holding up her hands, palms out. 'Once a fight's over folk should be friends. Let bygones be bygones.'

She turns her right hand to the side and offers it to him – for shakes.

McDonald takes it and shakes it. Then he looks at Pearse. Pearse puts out his hand as well and McDonald shakes with him too.

'You're a good fighter,' says May-Belle. 'If there hadn't been two of us, you'd've murdered us.'

McDonald smiles – there's lines of blood rising on his face from the scratches and bites – and says, 'You can't beat two people.'

'Wanna join our gang?' says May-Belle.

McDonald just looks at her.

'We get up to all sorts – fighting and wild high jinks and all that. Ever went shoplifting?'

'Aye, of course,' says McDonald.

'So do you want to join our gang – we could use a fighter like you.'

'Aye,' he says, starting to gather himself together and breathing more normally – watching the pair of them.

May-Belle doesn't look at Pearse once while she talks to McDonald. Pearse has no desire for this fat bollocks to start hanging around and getting in the way. But he lets her carry on, thinking he'll tell her after McDonald goes that she can just explain to the lump later that there isn't a hope in hell that he'll be joining their gang.

'So are you in a gang yourself yet?' May-Belle continues. 'Who do you hang out with?'

'Just folk,' he says, and Pearse can't help but let a laugh out of him, as everyone knows McDonald is the most friendless creature that ever walked God's earth – even lepers have more buddies than the likes of Campbell McDonald.

He looks at Pearse and then looks back at May-Belle and says, 'Folk.'

'Great,' says May-Belle, 'so are you in?'

'I am,' he says.

'Grand,' says May-Belle.

'So what's your gang called?' asks McDonald.

'We'll tell you that and give you your membership card and all the other stuff when you join properly,' says May-Belle, and Pearse looks at her, and she smiles a fairy smile.

'Fab,' McDonald says. 'When can I join?'

'I'm not really able to get out much again this week until

Saturday,' says May-Belle. 'Why don't we do it then? First day of the summer holidays and all that.'

'Beezer,' he says.

'That'd be cracking,' Pearse says, smiling at McDonald and deciding to join in the fun. May-Belle reckons that later on she'll tell Pearse how good he is at playing catch-up.

'We've got a hide-out down in the Weary Woods,' says May-Belle, and the three of them start walking away from the common towards their houses. 'That's where we'll do it.'

'Great,' he says. 'How many other folk are in your gang.'

'Loads,' Pearse says.

'Loads,' says May-Belle. 'Loads of mates.'

The three of them walk on a little further until they get to the corner where McDonald has to go right to get home, and Pearse and May-Belle have to go left.

'Is your face ok?' says May-Belle. 'Your eye?'

'Aye,' he says, rubbing his cheek. The rusty blood like peeling paint against his fingers. 'I'm fine.'

'Sorry,' says May-Belle.

'Sorry too,' he says.

'Aye,' Pearse says.

'Why'd you start all that anyway?' says May-Belle.

'I was bored,' he says.

'Oh,' she says.

'I hate being bored,' Pearse says.

'Aye,' McDonald says.

'See you on Saturday then,' she says. 'Meet us about twelve on the bridge over the stream before the Weary Woods.'

'Grand,' he says.

'Bring your sister if you want,' says May-Belle.

'My sister?' says McDonald. 'What for?'

'She can join our gang too. Be like our mascot, if you want.'

'Right,' he says. 'I will. She'd probably love that.'

'Grand,' says May-Belle. 'I'd love to play with her too.'

'See ya,' says McDonald, and he heads off to the right to go home.

'See ya,' says May-Belle.

'Aye, see ya, mate,' Pearse adds.

May-Belle and Pearse walk on a few dozen yards without speaking. Pearse looks over his shoulder to check McDonald is nowhere to be seen and says, 'Well?'

May-Belle says, 'He's a fucken dead man.'

*

May-Belle is ready to leave for Pearse's house on Friday night at nine, as usual. She's put on her red tracksuit with white piping. She shuts her front door and jogs down the street – on Her Majesty's Secret Service. It's mizzly, and the misty drizzle glazes her clothes with rain-water.

Pearse has already found the two sports bags that he keeps his toy soldiers in, and tipped out all the wee infantry men and fusiliers and commandoes.

When she arrives, they pack the sports bags with the things they've discussed. She's brought a kitchen knife from her house and a towel, and some rope from Monster Ma's work room; Pearse has got a knife and a towel too, and he's also snaffled a hammer and black tape, from Demon Da's tool box, along with a couple of screw-drivers, and turps from under the sink. They divvy up the stuff between them.

They watch late night telly together – Dave Allen and Parkinson – and cook a couple of frozen pizzas under the grill. After they've eaten, they play a game of Mousetrap. It takes an age to set up, but once you spring the trap and watch the mechanism run – the ball dropping, the diver diving, the cogs turning, the boot kicking and the cage falling – the theatre of the wee doomed mouse and its inevitable capture and death is frankly hypnotising.

'The mouse should move,' says May-Belle.

'It can't,' says Pearse. 'That's not allowed.'

They get to bed about one. There's not a lot of talking or sto-rytelling tonight. She asks him if he wants to kill the IRA men who did what they did.

Pearse says he'd be happy to kill them but he has no idea who they are – and anyway, aren't they all as bad as each other. They were trying to kill that nasty fucker Da, and his lot are trying to kill them into the bargain. Everyone seems hell bent on bloody murder for no reason – just because someone's a Catholic or a Protestant or believes in this flag or that flag or this piece of land or that piece of land.

'They're all a bunch of dicks,' Pearse says. 'I'd like to blow them all up. Blow the whole fucken country up.'

'Aye,' she says, and snuggles in beside him.

Soon May-Belle is giving it wee zees as she falls asleep, and Pearse drifts off as well. At six o'clock in the morning, May-Belle wakes Pearse to say she's heading home as Ma will be back in an hour or so. Pearse starts to get out of bed to walk downstairs with her and let her out.

'Don't worry,' she says. 'I listened at your Da's door already – they're both still fast asleep – and I know how to let myself out by now. Bye-bye.'

'Call for me by ten, May-Belle, so we can get to the woods long before Fat Boy.'

'I will,' she says, in a voice all soft. 'See you soon, Pearse.'

May-Belle leaves, walking quietly out of Pearse's room and off to her quiet, still, dirty wee house where she sits and sings and arranges matches into squares and triangles for hours until the time comes to meet up again. Pearse doesn't even hear her move down the stairs. There's the faintest click, though, as she pulls the front door closed behind her. He curls up in the warm bed, mov-ing into the dip in the mattress where her body was, and starts dreaming again.

Pearse returns to consciousness about nine o'clock, gets up, washes his face and cleans his teeth, combs his hair and goes downstairs. Da and Yvonne are still sleeping. He pours some Frosties into a bowl and eats them while watching Swap Shop. Noel Edmonds is banging on about the summer hols. Pearse washes his bowl, and goes quietly upstairs to fetch the water bottle from his room – it came in a set of survival equipment he got last Christmas, with a compass, a whistle, a torch and a first aid kit. He decides to take the whole lot as who knows, he just might need a compass or a torch – though, touch wood, not a first aid kit.

He goes back downstairs with the whole kaboodle and the two sports bags. He fills the water bottle with diluting orange and packs all the survival equipment away in his bag. Then he makes some jam sandwiches and wraps them in polythene – these go in the bag that May-Belle will carry, along with three packets of Tayto Cheese and Onion, a dozen Jammie Dodgers and a couple of Wagon Wheels. He hefts the bags – his is heavier, so that's good.

It's a quarter to ten. He turns off the telly and sits on the sofa – waiting a few minutes, doing nothing. He hasn't drawn the blinds yet, and the room is dusky with wan yellow light trying to creep in from outside – wee motes of dust floating in the air.

He gets up, opens the Venetian blinds and sees May-Belle sitting on the garden wall waiting for him. He shouts up the stairs as loud as he can, 'Da – I'm away out.'

There's a long pause, and he shouts again, 'See ya later.'

A noise like 'fer-er' comes muffling out from behind the bedroom door.

'I've got my key,' Pearse hollers again – so loud he nearly deafens himself.

'Right, fuck sake,' Da shouts.

Pearse goes out, pulling the door quietly behind him.

*

May-Belle waits and watches for Pearse to emerge from his house – running over the plot in her head, trying to think if they've missed any wee hole that might be in the plan. She nibbles her thumbnail and inspects her fingers.

'Hiya,' Pearse says to May-Belle, as he walks down his front path.

'Hey,' she says. And they set off on the two mile walk to the Weary Woods.

They walked through Parkhall, along the rows of houses and grave-sized front gardens, towards the local shops. There's a hair-dressers, a newsagents, an off-licence, a post office, a chippie and a wee supermarket. The shops overlooked Pearse's school – his old Primary now, as P7 was over and they were bound for the Secondary, or the Grammar if they were smart, once the summer ended.

The shops were grey concrete henges clustered together around a central square with a few trees set in cement and a couple of seats for auldies in the middle. Nearby there's a banjoed kids' play-ground: a set of swings with the chains tied in knots, a rusted see-saw that couldn't see or saw, a slide with gunk all over it and broken monkey bars.

On the far side of the precinct, a long hill opened up, lead-ing down through the Steeple estate – this estate was even a bit rougher than Parkhall. The Steeple was nearly all Protestant. Parkhall was mixed back then, with Catholics and Protestants still living side by side more or less. The town was beginning to divide though. Rathenraw – an estate on the other side of Parkhall – was home to just Catholics. Protestants were no more likely to live in Rathenraw, than Catholics were to live in the Steeple.

Beyond the Parkhall shops, on the brow of the hill, there stood one of those wee single-storey ugly buildings that the Free Presbyterians use as churches. It looked more like a bomb shel-ter than a place of worship. A white board outside the church displayed the times for prayers and Sunday school in black and red stick-on letters; on the wall by the front door a banner reads: 'It is appointed unto men once to die; but after this – the JUDGEMENT. Hebrews 9:27'.

They walked down the hill, down the wide road that split the Steeple in two. Half-way through the estate, the Steeple common appeared – laid out just like the Parkhall common – where the local kids played, but here the field was filled with wooden palettes, car tires and old furniture. It was still more than two weeks away, but the Steeple youngsters were already beginning to gather in all the garbage they'd need to build the bonfire for the Twelfth of July. There was a painting on a nearby wall of King Billy astride his horse, the white charger rearing back, and auld William of Orange is waving his sword aloft, above his tricorn hat, the black curls of his wig beneath. Painted scrolls surround the mural with the words 'Rem 1690' and 'For God and Ulster'. On another wall graffiti reads 'Up the UVF' and 'Fuck the Pope and the IRA'.

At the bottom of the long, straight road, the Steeple estate gave way to a small gathering of posh houses, where some of the bosses lived – the men who ran the textile factory and the warehouses where ordinary folk worked, and teachers and police officers and the like. Opposite these homes – with their big front windows and nice long gardens – were the council offices, sitting in the middle of the Steeple Park. The park was a grand place to play; it had fairy rings and gnarly trees, squirrels, and right in the middle – the Round Tower. This tower, Pearse told May-Belle as they walked, dated from before the time of the Vikings, when Ireland was the Land of Saints and Scholars – the only place in Europe not plunged into the Dark Ages; keeping the light of civilisation alive. Or so Gran had said.

The tower was a perfect brick cylinder about one hundred and fifty foot high, with a coned roof sitting on top – a giant dick topped with a tit, said May-Belle. It had no doors at ground level. The entrance-way was a gap in the wall about thirty foot up. When Eric the Red or Olaf the Hairy or whichever Viking it was who first came raping and pillaging from the sea and along the rivers of Ulster arrived in the town, the monks, who had a monastery right here in the grounds of the Steeple Park more than a thousand years ago, would run from their bee-keeping and herb-gathering and bible-illustrating, and they'd climb up into the tower – through that wee high narrow arrow-slit door – and draw their ladders after them, hiding from the Vikings and praying for dear life. During the first few raids, the Vikings were happy enough to ignore the monks and just loot their monastery for gold and paintings, but soon there was nothing left to steal and the only fun to be had, on the return journeys, was a bit of murder. So, they smoked the Irish monks out of their tower and butchered them at the foot of the building. More than one hundred monks, flayed alive, decapitated, dismembered and eviscerated – given the Blood-Eagle treatment – by Berserkers right here on this spot. Auld ravens cawing in the rainy background.

May-Belle and Pearse walked on past the Steeple Park and the Round Tower – with the sun splitting the rocks, hot enough to do the famous egg-frying routine, May-Belle claimed – and they made their way towards the Weary Woods.

*

There was a good while to go until noon, when Campbell McDonald was due. They stood on the little bridge spanning the stream before the Weary Woods and ate some of their lunch. They finished, and chucked the wrappers over the side into the water so they could race the litter like Pooh-sticks. May-Belle's wrapper appeared first. She leapt in the air letting a big 'yo' out of her. Pearse waited to see his emerge. A minute passed and nothing happened.

'Where the hell could it have got to?' said May-Belle. They walked back to the civilisation side of the bridge – the opposite bank to the Weary Woods – and down the incline to the lip of the river. The bridge was low and the river shallow at this point in its course – although it got deeper and wilder as it wended its way through the Wearys. They bent down and looked under the bridge to see if a troll was there with a wrapper in his hairy hand.

There was no troll, just two supermarket trollies. Leaves and branches and all sorts of rubbish – including the wrapper, they guessed – were entangled in the steel bars. May-Belle's had slipped through. They went back on to the bridge and waited.

McDonald arrived a few minutes later. He was wearing a white pull-over – a design of blue snowflakes across the chest. His Christmas sweater was tucked into the top of his stone-washed jeans, which came with no belt and dirty grass-stained knees. He had his leather school shoes on – scuffed and the soles hanging off.

'Here comes the Billy Goat,' May-Belle sly-mouthed to Pearse.

'Hiya,' McDonald said, as he walked onto the bridge, the heels of his hard shoes sounding clip-clop clip-clop on the wooden slats.

'Hi,' said May-Belle. 'Where's your sister?'

'She couldn't make it,' says McDonald.

'What a shame,' she said. 'I'd've had great fun with her.'

They crossed the bridge. McDonald and May-Belle couldn't stop yakking on about the initiation ceremony and what role he'd have in the gang and all that. Pearse lagged behind, watching the roly-poly way that McDonald walked – waddling from side to side as if he was a sailor on deck in a hurricane, or a fat bitch. May-Belle was at McDonald's side, turning her head to him with every comment, skipping in front of him as she talked – casting an eye Pearse's way now and again.

'We'll explain everything once the other gang members are here,' May-Belle said.

'How many are there?'

'A brave few,' said May-Belle. 'Half the kids in the estate, to be honest – some older than you, some younger than us.'

'And youse are the bosses?'

'No,' says May-Belle, laughing. 'There's bosses much higher up than us. Older than you even.'

'We're just prominent members,' Pearse said. May-Belle and McDonald looked around at him. 'That's all,' Pearse added.

'The bosses listen to us as we're good operators,' May-Belle said.

'What'll I be?' McDonald asked.

'That's up to the bosses,' said May-Belle. 'We need to get you ready for the initiation ceremony. Once that's done, you'll get your membership card and they'll decide what you should be.'

'We can give them some advice, though, if you want,' Pearse said. 'Sort of help them pick a good job for you.'

'Grand,' says McDonald.

'Well, what would you like to do?' Pearse asks.

'I dunno,' he says.

'Well, have a think about it,' says May-Belle, 'We'll have a word in their ear for you.'

They'd come to a clearing in the middle of the woods. They were far, far away from civilisation now – out in the Weary Woods with nobody next or near them.

'Let's sit here and have lunch,' says May-Belle.

Pearse looks at his watch and says, 'Yeah, there's still a good half hour before anyone turns up.' Pearse points to May-Belle's bag. 'Shall we eat and then get you ready?'

'Aye,' McDonald says.

All three of them sit down and May-Belle brings out juice and biscuits and sandwiches. Pearse is full up so nibbles his food. May-Belle chews steadily, and McDonald gobbles his grub down pig-style, crumbs flying out between his lips, bits of jam in the corner of his mouth, bread stuck in his teeth.

He chews with his mouth wide open, like a bumpkin, and talks at the same time. 'What happens in this initiation?' he says. There's a white splat of sandwich across his tongue.

'Och,' says May-Belle. 'It's meant to be a bit scary, but it's fine. It's just meant to make you realise that you are in this group for real and you have to stick with everyone and be loyal. It lasts about five minutes is all.'

'What happens?'

'I shouldn't really tell you as it'll spoil it.'

'Please,' says McDonald.

'Och, tell him, May-Belle,' Pearse says. 'It won't do any harm.'

'Alright then,' says May-Belle. 'But promise you won't tell them I told you?'

'I promise,' says McDonald. 'Cross my heart and hope to die, stick a needle in my eye.'

'A needle?' says May-Belle. 'That'd be horrible.'

Pearse passes McDonald the water-bottle filled with juice. He takes a slug of the orange, without wiping his mouth, and hands the water-bottle back. Pearse reminds himself to pour the juice out as soon as he has a chance – and not to drink it no matter how thirsty he gets.

'Well,' says May-Belle. 'You have to be tied up, to a tree, then the leaders ask you some questions about whether you'll ever squeal and what you'd be prepared to do for the gang. Then you get untied and you get to share a bottle of wine with us. The bosses – the older kids – will bring that with them. It's our job – me and Pearse – to get you ready, that's all. We won't be asking you any questions or anything like that.'

'As soon as you've finished eating, we may as well get started,' Pearse says, looking at his digital watch. 'They'll be here soon, but they'll stay hidden in the woods until you're tied up and good and ready – that's the rules.'

McDonald throws a couple of Jammie Dodgers into his gob. 'Okay,' he says, a shrapnel attack of his dirty auld crumbs hitting Pearse. 'What job should I ask for? What jobs are there?'

'Well, if I was you,' says May-Belle, 'I'd ask to be one of the lieutenants – that's a job for older kids like you. It makes you a bit higher up in the gang – and there's a post going as one of our lieutenants, Tommy Magill, had to leave as his family moved to

Magherafelt.'

'Aye,' Pearse says. 'And it's better than being a runner like us. We sort of organise things, but there's a terrible lot of work.'

'You could become a shop-lifter or a fighter if you wanted,' said May-Belle. 'Jobs like that only go to the best thieves and scrappers, though. If you looked a bit older you could be the person nominated to go to the offie and buy booze for us all. It all depends on you and what you can do best for the gang.'

'A scrapper. I could do that,' says McDonald, his mouth finally ceasing its grinding and munching and swallowing.

'Right, so,' says May-Belle getting to her feet. 'Shall we?'

Pearse looks at his watch again, 'We'd better.'

'You ready?' she says to McDonald.

'Spose so,' he replies.

The three of them walk away from the clearing, back into the deep quiet woods. McDonald lets a fart out of him as he ganders forward and then laughs. May-Belle says, 'Pardonez-moi, you let off a corker, monsieur.' Pearse says nothing, disgusted. They walk on a little further, until there's not a sound to be heard from anywhere.

'Here'll do,' Pearse says.

A sturdy tree stood in front of them. May-Belle walks over to it and wraps her arms around it. Her fingers can't quite meet. 'This tree is fine,' she says to Pearse.

Pearse and May-Belle set their bags down. May-Belle says to McDonald, 'Okay?'

'Spose,' he says, his mouth and his tongue moving like a cow chewing the cud.

Pearse fetches the black tape from his bag and throws it to May-Belle. 'Catch,' he shouts.

She catches it and says to McDonald, 'Hold your hands behind you, please.'

He obeys and she tapes his hands quickly behind his back.

'Great,' she says. 'That's perfect.'

She takes ahold of his elbow and escorts him towards the tree.

'What time is it?' she says to Pearse.

'We've got about five minutes before they come, so let's hurry,' he says.

'Five minutes?' says McDonald. 'Hurry up, then.'

'Okay,' says May-Belle. 'I'm going as fast as I can.'

Pearse takes the rope out of his bag. 'Catch,' he says again.

They stand McDonald against the tree, and wrap the rope around him a couple of times, looping it over his body and under his armpits, tying it at the front and back; they wrap the rope around him another few times, just to be sure, and then tie it once more at the front and back.

'That's a bit tight,' says McDonald.

'Needs to be,' says May-Belle, giving the knot a tug.

Pearse takes the black tape and wraps it around McDonald's body and the tree a few times too. He ducks down, taping McDonald's feet at the ankles as well, and then stands and says to him, 'We also need to tape up your mouth.'

McDonald nods and leans forward. Pearse circles the tape around McDonald's head – it sticks to his hair. Pearse tears the tape off, biting it with his teeth – his nose touches McDonald's cheek.

'Can you speak?' Pearse asks.

McDonald mumbles something behind the black matte gag.

May-Belle goes to her bag and takes out the smaller of the two towels.

'We need to put this on you like a hood. Okay?' she says.

She doesn't wait for an answer, but flings the white towel over his head, then brings the edges together, pinched around his neck. She takes the tape and wraps it around his throat and the towel three times, until it's safely cinched in place.

They stand back. McDonald's head looks like a marshmallow.

'Wait,' May-Belle says to McDonald. 'They'll be here in a minute.'

McDonald nods. The towel sucks in and out from his face as he breathes beneath the hood.

May-Belle and Pearse skirt around the nearby trees, looking, listening, making sure there's not a sinner in sight.

They return to the tree and McDonald, and take the knives and screwdrivers and the hammer out of the bags.

McDonald is still as a statue, leaning back against the tree, his weight on his heels. Pearse and May-Belle undress and lay their clothes on the ground. All Pearse leaves on is his white pants, and May-Belle, though flat-chested still, wore a pink bikini vest and a pair of red-spotted knickers.

'No-one's coming, you dopey fucker,' Pearse says.

McDonald doesn't respond.

May-Belle walks up to him and softly presses the point of the knife against his belly. 'We're talking to you, fatty. No-one is coming.'

McDonald's head moves from side to side and his chest rises and falls under his bobbly jumper. He's making a noise like 'na-na-na-na' behind his gag and hood.

Pearse takes the hammer and walks forward. He draws back his arm and hits McDonald on the right knee-cap as hard as he can. Before the pain has reached McDonald's brain, Pearse has skipped to the side and shattered the other knee-cap as well. May-Belle steps close and slides the knife she has into his belly. McDonald wriggles and moans and starts to slip down the tree, lunging forward, trying to tear himself free – maybe to get at them.

Pearse hands May-Belle the hammer and takes the knife from her. She wallops McDonald over the head. Pearse stabs him in the stomach one more time.

His weight drags him to the ground; the tape puckering and gathering around his armpits as he slips to the floor of the wood – in a sitting position.

Blood is trickling from two wounds in his side like little forest waterfalls, and there's a red stain on his hood. His head is slumped to one side, but he's still breathing. Pearse pulls the towel away from McDonald's face. There's a bloody dent about an inch above his left ear. His eyes open and he starts to struggle, shouting something through his gag, trying to loose himself from the rope and the tape – but he's a helpless giant worm.

Pearse reaches for one of the screwdrivers and digs it into McDonald's right thigh to the hilt. He roars behind his gag. Pearse punches him in the face and May-Belle sticks the other screwdriver into his left arm – it goes into his bicep and out the other side, poking through the wool of his jumper.

They both lift knives and hold them up to McDonald. He shuts his eyes and squirms, tears running; his body shaking – and pissing himself. Pearse runs his knife across McDonald's cheek, making a criss-cross pattern in blood and cuts. May-Belle fills in the grid with noughts and crosses. Pearse slits him under his nose, leaving one huge nostril, instead of two. May-Belle pushes her knife slowly into one eye, mindful of the depth so as not to touch the brain and kill him. Then she pops the second eye-ball into the bargain. McDonald pants and groans and moves slovenly – a dumb animal dying without a clue what is happening to it.

Pearse hits him on the side of the head with the hammer again to knock him out properly.

'We should have brought petrol to burn him,' May-Belle says.

Pearse rips the taped gag from McDonald's face and then he starts to moan, saying, 'Please. Please. I want to go home to my mum.' Pearse hits him in the mouth with the hammer, breaking his front teeth. McDonald makes a noise like a duck – a quacking sound. He moves his head to look around him, but with no eyes he can't see. Blood gloops from his mouth. Then he starts to scream – as if they really had set light to him.

They picked up their knives and quickly went about it, stabbing McDonald in his face, his chest, his belly; in his balls and legs. He hardly struggled at all; the only noises coming from him were way back in his throat – not attached to thoughts or words. Pearse broke the blade of his knife against the top of the skull. May-Belle shoved her knife down his throat, leaving it there. He was more or less finished off by now. Pearse hit him in the face with the hammer until his jaw came loose. May-Belle pulled one screwdriver from his leg and buried it in the left eye, deep enough to touch the brain this time, and then she pulled the second screwdriver from his arm and stuck it in his heart.

Even then he died slowly. They sat down and watched as McDonald twitched, looking more like a pile of old clothes than a human being. He slumped over, and behind him, his bound hands stuck out to one side. The fingers seemed to trace wee pictures in the dirt. His foot moved in a slow unconscious perfect circle.

When he finally died about ten minutes later, it came with a lazy hiss of breath through his nose and a little quiver of his entire body as if he'd just gotten a fright or become incredibly sad – they couldn't decide which.

They untaped and untied him, and tidied everything away – the knives, the food, the towels, the used tape, rope, the screwdrivers, the hammer. Nothing was left behind, except the heap of Campbell McDonald lying dead at the bottom of the tree.

They walked off, a few hundred yards into the wood, until they came to the river again. It was deeper here and faster. They burned the towel, and the tape and rope they'd used to tie him up – throwing the ashes in the water. Then they cleaned the knives and hammer and screwdrivers and threw them into the deepest whorl. They washed themselves – their hands and faces, across their chests and down their arms and legs – dried each other with the spare towel. Finally, they poured turps on the towel and used it on the hard to remove stains on their skin and faces and fingers. Then they burned that towel too, and scattered it. They were finished and they checked each other over. They put their clothes back on. The remaining spotting wasn't that bad, and what signs that could be seen might easily have been passed off as the result of a mild auld nosebleed.

*

They returned to the bridge and travelled back into civilisation – towards the Steeple Park and the Round Tower and the rest of Antrim.

Pearse looked at his watch again. It wasn't even two o'clock. 'Shall we have a bit of a dander in the park?' he asked May-Belle.

'Aye,' she said. They walked through the gates, towards the Round Tower. There was a grassy bank nearby and they sat down. They were tired. They both lay back. The sun was high in the blue sky, and it made their eyes heavy. Pearse turned to look at May-Belle but her lids were already closed. Some kids were playing football a few hundred yards away, and a couple of young mothers were pushing their babies in prams alongside the hedgerows and flower beds. A few dogs were running about, rooting their noses in mud and leaves.

'Don't go to sleep,' Pearse said to May-Belle.

'I'm not,' she replied. 'This is lovely here.'

'Come on,' he said, 'get up. There's something we can do for luck.'

'What?' she says, opening her eyes. 'Can't we just lie here for a while?'

'The Witch's Stone,' he says.

'Of course,' she says, alive again. 'Why'd we never think of that before.'

They picked up their bags and walked over to the foot of the Round Tower. About twenty yards from the base of the tower, there is a giant boulder – ten foot wide, five foot high and six foot long. If it fell on a man he would be crushed, lost, and never seen again – a pancake. The stone has a stubble of green moss on one side. It's as old as the earth. On it's top, there are two deep indentations – one about the size of a fist, the other the dimensions of a human head.

At school, Antrim kids were taught that the stone was prob-ably used by ancient pagans to worship their Gods, or by the first christians to baptise children – or maybe both the pagans and the christians just used it to grind wheat and corn for bread, some said. Any of those options may indeed have been the case, but everyone in Antrim knew that this stone was in fact the site of the downfall of the witch Enthrumnia. And it is from the witch that Antrim got its name, Gran told Pearse – through a corrup-tion down the centuries that turned and distorted the name of a heathen sorceress into the name of the town in which May-Belle and Pearse found themselves living: Enthrumnia became Enthrum and Enthrum became Antrim.

At the time of the building of the Round Tower, this local witch Enthrumnia swore that the Christians would never erect their monument while she was alive. They ignored her – much more impressed by St Patrick and his ability to read, and drive the snakes out of Ireland, than by Enthrumnia and her threats to their cows and crops. St Patrick, who only lived up the road in Ballymena, was dead some two hundred years by this time, but nevertheless his influence was far greater than Enthrumnia's dying breed of tree worshippers.

The tower goes up, regardless of the witch's warnings, and on the day the long vertical brick cylinder is finally capped with its stone cone, the people come out to sing the praises of the Lord in the fields and eat and drink and have a bit of a carry-on. The Vikings are still just a rumour, so the people of the valley have plenty to celebrate.

As it gets on for night-time – the party fearlessly raring away – the witch Enthrumnia comes hurtling out of her secret place; some say that in those days, the Weary Woods was a magical grove for Druids, and it may well be that this is where she leapt from to wreck her revenge on the peasants and monks.

Suddenly, the people find her amongst them, shouting them down and swearing death and disaster on all who disobey. Up she takes her broomstick – for pagan priestesses really did employ such things as part of their magic – and she rides through the air to the very top of the Round Tower, stands on the newly fitted cone roof, points down at the men and women and denounces them to her Gods, casting curses and spells over their terrified heads. The monks fall to their knees and the people follow suit, praying for deliverance from this woman of the woods who could fly through the sky on nothing but a stick and make the air darken at her command.

She shouts to the kneeling throng that she is going to get back on her broomstick, and ride down amongst them once more, bringing death to whoever she touches. The crowd shivers and the people start to cry, and even the monks quake and falter in their faith.

The people look up, and they see Enthrumnia swing her leg over her broomstick, readying to launch herself against them like an eagle on a flock of lambs. As she pushes off with her feet – the tip of the broomstick twitching in readiness to be about its business – a tremendous clap of thunder rings out and a fork of sizzling white lightning hits Enthrumnia just as the broomstick rises and wheels, preparing to dive.

Of course, those Antrim people back then had never seen a rocket or firework go haywire, but if they had, that is how they would have described the sight of Enthrumnia struck by lightning: first, careening up, then down, then left and right; trying to regain control of her broomstick, with smoke billowing from her singed hair and clothes. The broomstick found itself in a dreadful downward spiral – the corkscrewing screaming priestess wildly riding it to earth.

She hit the giant stone below, lightning flashed once more and the world stood still. There she was: her broomstick shattered on the ground; the witch crumpled atop the stone, in a twisted broken heap. She'd landed on her head and her right knee – and it was both the head and the knee which left those two deep indentations that remain in the stone to this day. The two holes are filled with water – they always have been since the day she made them.

If you dip your hand in the water and touch your head and then your right knee – in memory of The People's Victory Over The Witch – you will be granted the best of luck, and any curses that sit upon you will fade away entirely. A man should use the big hole – the one Enthrumnia made with her head – for the ritual; and a woman should use the little hole – the one made by the witch's knee.

May-Belle and Pearse stand by the Witch's Stone, and wet their hands – Pearse places his fingers in the big hole; May-Belle puts her thumb in the wee one. They bring their hands up to their heads and then lower them, bending a little at the waist, touching their knees. They pick up their bags and walk back home.

*

Over the next few days, Pearse kept an eye on the six o'clock bulletin and flicked through the papers Da left in the toilet; he watched the news bills posted up outside the shops change every morning. May-Belle thought he was wasting his time – for there was nothing to worry about; she was certain of that by now, and free from any of the auld creeping pangs of fear she'd suffered before. Pearse wasn't really that worried either, he said, he just wanted to find out if the world had a reaction. 'We might learn something useful for the future,' he said to May-Belle. The day after McDonald, the news bills outside the shops read 'Body found in woods'. The local paper, the Antrim Guardian, had a story the following morning headed 'Missing teenager tortured to death'. On the third day, the big papers said that McDonald was believed to have been killed by loyalist paramilitaries – a cop was quoted saying he was the latest victim to be rompered, for that was the expression used when Protestants mutilated and murdered Catholics for fun. McDonald wasn't a Catholic, though – which showed how much sense these cops and journalists had.

'What are loyalist para-whatsit-thingys?' asked May-Belle.

'It means a murder gang,' Pearse said.

'Well, at least they've got that right,' she said.

They laughed.

Apart from a short wee story in the Antrim Guardian on the fourth day about his funeral, the papers and the news bulletins said nothing more about Campbell McDonald ever again – the journalists and TV men had plenty more stories to keep them occupied up and down the land, it seemed.

*

It was a good summer that year – with dewy mornings, drowsy afternoons and dusky evenings. Their routine continued uninterrupted: weekdays spent playing in the woods and fields, and weekends kept aside for their secret sleep-overs and nights of talking at Pearse's house.

One Saturday, though, in early July, around dawn – half an hour before May-Belle was due to get out of bed and head back to her own house – the routine, and the quiet of the early morning, was broken by this crackling sound of what must have been a firing squad. Somewhere, not too far in the distance, there had been a rumbling roar – the report of maybe twenty rifles going off. The sound of pop rocks on your tongue. Then it came again – another firework of guns. And yet another. But after the fourth volley, the sound rolled out longer, taking on a rhythm and repetition. And it was an old sound, that everyone knew. It wasn't guns going off, it was drums, tight snares reverberating all over the estate. Drummers from the local loyalist bands were out early getting some practice in before they started to gather in the town for a parade.

The drums were joined by flutes – tweetering birds at dawn chorus, singing from their wee trees to other nearby flocks, letting them know they'd woken up – and then the sharper and deeper, more ancient, beating of the Lambegs came in: the loudest sound in the band, a sound meant to make fenians like May-Belle run shaking to hide under their beds.

May-Belle looked at Pearse and whispered, 'It's not the Twelfth.'

'No,' he whispered back. 'It's Saturday. It must be the mini-Twelfth.'

'The what?'

'The mini-Twelfth.'

May-Belle shrugged and shook her head; she rolled her eyes and held up her hands in bewilderment.

'For God sake, May-Belle,' Pearse whispered. 'Do you not know anything? It's like a daft warm-up celebration before everyone goes buck-mad next week for the proper Twelfth.'

'Mental,' May-Belle whispered. 'Why can't they just have one flippen party?'

Pearse nodded his head and was about to speak, when they heard the floor-boards creak in Da's room. Footsteps padded over the carpet and there came the sound of Da's bedroom door slowly opening.

May-Belle slithered beneath the bed in seconds – gone; the flash of a serpent. Pearse lay still, pretending to sleep.

Tick. Tock. Pearse's bedroom door opened. Da shook him and said, 'Come on, get up. I've got a surprise for you today.'

Pearse opened his eyes, and pretended to stare at him, dumb and half-conscious.

'Hmm?' he says.

'I'm taking you to the parade,' Da says, walking out of the room, leaving the door open, 'get up and get ready.'

Da walks into the bathroom, and leaves that door open too. He starts to piss, and Yvonne walks past Pearse's room, now, yawning, her hair a mess, and dressed in some silky auld negligee, with half of her hanging out of it.

'Up you get,' she says, walking down the stairs. 'I'll make brekkie.'

Once Da's washed and shaved, he walks back into Pearse's room and says, 'Come on. Get up. We're going out to see the bands.'

May-Belle remains under the bed while Pearse washes and cleans his teeth – he tries not to think of her. He walks back to his room and shuts the door so he can get dressed. He kneels down near the side of the bed, tying his shoelaces and whispers to May-Belle to stay hidden and leave once they go out. She doesn't answer. He leans down and peeks under the bed, she's lying on her back, staring up at the bedsprings and crying. She looks at him and waves her hand, like she's telling him to get lost and leave her alone. He walks out of the room, shutting the door behind him.

Downstairs, the three of them – Pearse, Da and Yvonne – gobble down a bacon sandwich each. Pearse has a glass of cold milk and the other two drink tea. Yvonne has three cigarettes. The sound of the small snare drums and the flutes and big lambegs is closer now – the bands are walking from every side of Antrim to the top of the town where they will begin their parade, down the High Street, past the Castle Grounds and then on to The Field – which this year is off the Randalstown Road – where ministers and Orangemen will give their speeches and the lads in the bands will lie drunk in the grass, with their berets over their faces and girls beside them.

When the three of them get to the top of the town, the parade is just setting off – and May-Belle is creeping out from under the bed, angry as a wasp. There are hundreds of people in the streets, lining the route. Pearse, Da and Yvonne stand for a few minutes and watch the lead marchers begin, keeping time like soldiers on parade, while the bands come to life behind them. Drums are beating out a three note repeat rhythm. At the front is one of the local Orange lodges: fifty men in dark suits, with bowler hats and orange sashes, who head the parade. Some have white gloves on, and others carry umbrellas. A few young boys – the sons of these Orangemen – are holding a big banner; they are the vanguard of the march. The banner shows yet another King Billy crossing another Boyne holding another sword aloft wearing another tricorn hat astride another white horse. There are words on the banner. In thick scrolled black letters at the top and bottom of the banner it says 'Standard of the Cross, L.O.L 1412, Antrim District No 5'; in the middle, on either side of King Billy and his horse, is the motto, 'Per Angusta, Ad Augusta'.

The snares and flutes and lambegs start their battle-march and as the Orangemen lead the parade off from the top of the town down into Antrim, a big whoop – a yo – goes up from the watching crowds. After the Orangemen comes a band, The Steeple Defenders. They're dressed like they're off to fight the Napoleonic Wars. The boys wear bright blue jackets with red piping and white buttons and belts. Their trousers are red, and the lads are topped by little red berets with blue pom-poms. At the front, a big farmer-looking lad in the same uniform is twirling a band-pole between his fingers, hurling it up high high into the sky and catching it behind his back, dropping to the ground to do press-ups, back-flipping and dancing in the street – always rolling and tossing that baton round his neck, between his legs and under his arms. The teenage girls watching on the pavement cheer him on and wave to their boyfriends in the band.

The lads in The Steeple Defenders fell into two groups – the older ones, some of whom might even be near forty; and the younger ones in their teens. They all had short hair, they all walked the same way – legs wide apart, swaggering, almost dancing as they strode on, with their drums on their hips, or their flutes to their lips. At the back came two lambeg players, the massive drums strapped to their chests with braces, the men beating the skins for all they are worth with sticks like a headmaster's cane.

A few more bands and Orange Lodges followed – The Ballycraigy Young Volunteers; L.O.L 1589, Bearers of the Holy

Light of God, Ballymena District 8 – then there was a small group of women marchers: ladies in Orange sashes with pink hats and pink gloves and wee blue eyes.

'Let's follow the bands,' said Yvonne, all smiles, and the three of them took off at a slow pace, walking down the High Street along the side of the parade. Some families, lining the road, were wearing little Union Jack hats – mum, dad, their weans and even the baby in the push-chair. Loads of them were waving Ulster flags. As they got down into the centre of town, there was a group of men and women singing and dancing in the street and drinking wine out of bottles – they clapped their hands together and linked arms and sang songs about guarding auld Derry's walls and the Battle of the Shankill. A queue formed outside a van selling burgers and chips, and a few police officers looked on from side streets and corners. There was no army about. Some of the big lads who follow the bands were stripped to the waist, their tops tied around their hips. They were showing off their tattoos to one another, and shouting about fenians and the IRA. It wasn't hard to notice that all the shops owned by Catholics – you could tell by the names – had grilles and wooden shutters over their windows.

In the heart of the town, the Arch had gone up. All the bands and marchers and Orangemen had to pass under it. This Arch, made of hardboard and steel, was the biggest to be built for years. It was much higher than the roofs of the local shops and banks – a good two floors higher – forcing your eye up to the sky and sun above it. Across the top, the arch was decorated with motifs and symbols: the cross, a ladder to heaven, an open bible, two swords, the Red Hand, a star, a crown and, of course, right in the middle, auld King Billy on his endlessly rearing horse. Down the sides of the archway there were mottos and phrases – For God and Ulster, No Surrender, Rem 1690, God Save the Queen.

The crowd cheered as the lead marchers in the parade – the local Orange lodge and the Steeple Defenders – passed under the arch. Da asked Pearse if he wanted to follow the bands to The

Field near Randalstown. Pearse said no.

'Right, you be. Well, do you want to head home then, son?' he asks Pearse. 'I think we'll skip the prayers at The Field too. Me and Yvonne were just going to meet up with some mates for a quick drink.'

Pearse looks up at the clock on top of the church with the spire and sees it's just gone eleven; the pubs are open.

'Okay,' he says. 'I'll go home and maybe head out to play.'

'Grand,' says Yvonne and she leans down to kiss him. 'What a great day. Makes you proud to be a prod.'

'Okay,' Pearse says and he heads off. Da shouts after him that they might not be back by tea-time.

He doesn't make the return journey up the High Street – the quick way. Pearse doesn't fancy running into any of those lads who follow the bands – not when he's on his own, especially now that the off-licences are open.

He takes the long way home, past the clinic and the train station, towards the warehouses at the lorry depot – the factories, as the kids called them, where Mum worked – and then up the black path through the Steeple and Parkhall. There's a smell of frying onions and sweaty marchers stuck in his nose. When he gets to his old primary school, he hops over the wall and takes a walk through the Nature Garden. He passes the giant sunflowers and the dainty wee roses. He hops back over the wall and there he is – at his own house in less than five minutes.

He opens the door and shuts it behind him, snibbing the lock so no-one can get in. 'Hello!' he hollers.

It's as quiet as a church. 'Hello!' he shouts again.

He walks up the stairs and checks under his bed. She's not there.

'Hello,' he says much quieter, 'are you there, May-Belle?'

He starts to walk back down the stairs when he hears a creak above him. May-Belle's head pokes out from the trap-door in the ceiling leading to the attic.

'Up here,' she says. Pearse pulls the draw-string that brings down the folded-up ladder to climb into the attic. He heaves himself inside.

'I've been up here since you left,' she said.

'Are you mad?' he asks.

'Ma won't be home all weekend. I may as well stay here as go home and stare at four empty walls.'

'What have you been doing?' Pearse asks. 'I'm never allowed up here.'

A light and an electric socket had been rigged up in the attic, so they weren't in the dark. Mum's old gramophone player and records from the Sixties had been put up into the loft years ago. May-Belle had been looking through the LPs in the low yellow light from a covered standard-lamp. Boxes and bags, old rolled up carpet, a dilapidated sink, some heavy tea chests and a metal foot locker took up most of the floor. On the far side of the attic was the water tank, a metal square lump covered in cobwebs.

'Can I play some records?' asks May-Belle.

'Sure,' Pearse said. The gramophone was a solid piece of furniture – the size of an average sideboard. There were two doors on the front which opened to reveal three compartments. One held the gramaphone; in the second was an old radio set with the names of towns like Paris and Rome and London and Brussels written on the dial; the third compartment contained all Mum's old records. They'd not been played in years.

May-Belle and Pearse flipped through the records. Most of the singers and musicians they'd never heard of, but there were a few Pearse remembered. He put on Edith Piaf, and her trill voice rose out into the air of the attic through the scratchy old needle and the dusty speakers.

'Creepy,' said May-Belle. 'But she sounds beautiful.'

She picked one – a girl singing, You don't have to say you love me.

'I like that,' she said.

Pearse said to her, 'Wait till you hear this.' And he put on an American band singing a song called Bad Moon Rising.

May-Belle loved it from the stompy start. The pair of them danced around on the wooden boards which sprung and lifted as they moved.

'Great song,' she said when it ended.

Then she asked if she could just put on any old LP and let it run through to the end, so they could listen to all the songs. Pearse said, sure, and she picked some old Beatles album – the one where they are all looking over a balcony in a scabby block of flats somewhere.

They started to hunt through the boxes and bags while the Beatles sang all their auld love songs, which Pearse didn't rate very much. May-Belle, though, was singing along at the top of her voice – and she sounded brilliant. They found old suits of clothes and dresses, scores of magazines about the empire and murderers, broken christmas decorations and all the garbage and junk that the Furlong family had collected over the years and never wanted to see again, even though they couldn't be bothered to throw it out.

Twist and Shout came on and May-Belle insisted on dancing the jive with Pearse. They jerked and threw each other around the loft, and Pearse nearly slipped through the hatch, but May-Belle grabbed him by the hand and yanked him back and they kept on dancing and laughing.

The record ended and Pearse asked May-Belle if she'd ever heard jazz, and she said she'd heard of it, but never listened to any. He put on some old jazz record and they carried on rooting about. Pearse opened what looked like a grey-green military foot locker. There were some maps and a compass inside, and two army pamphlets about field craft. May-Belle found a tied-up bunch of old books in the tea chest and started reading them. Some, she said, had dates in the margin from the turn of the century. They were old school books.

Pearse was about to come over and see if he could work out

who they'd once belonged to, when he lifted the maps and saw something underneath wrapped in a chamois leather. He picked it up and – he didn't need to take the chamois off – he knew what it was even though his hand had last felt it years before. He turned to May-Belle, but didn't speak. He felt the heft and balance of it in his hand. He held it, still wrapped up, in his palm. He called May-Belle over and said, 'I want to perform a magic trick.'

She looked at Pearse's hand and said, 'What's that?'

Pearse said, 'That's the magic trick. When I count to three, you whip the cloth away, okay?'

'Okay,' she says. He counts to three and she plucks the chamois leather off with her thumb and forefinger. She lets a moan out of her, like she's just eaten chocolate after ten years on a desert island.

'Is it real?' she says.

'It's real,' he says. He turns and rummages in the foot locker again. There are ten small bullets lying at the bottom.

Pearse sits May-Belle down and tells her the story about how, when he was a very little boy, he was playing out the back of his old house with his dog Barky and he found a mound of bricks in the yard. The bricks were shaped like a bee-hive and when he picked a few of the stones up off the top of the bee-hive shaped hiding place, he was able to put his arm inside, and he found a gun. A shiny black gun with a butt with the wee-est of wee knobbles all over it and a revolver barrel that spun if you flicked it with the palm of your hand.

'That was the last time I saw it, till now,' Pearse says.

Pearse passed the gun to May-Belle, and she squeezed her hand around the knobbly butt, and made the barrel spin with a quick flick of her fingers.

'When I found it, Mum told me it was a toy gun,' he said, 'that Da had hidden it for play – for a joke on me. I always believed it was real, though. I remember at the time – when I walked into the kitchen with it, showing it to Mum – I couldn't hold it properly. I couldn't grip the butt and get my Peter Pointer round the trigger at the same time.'

May-Belle gave the gun back to Pearse. He said, 'Mum took it away, and I never saw it again. I thought I'd made the memory up, but here it is – real as you like it.'

'Fanny, you star,' May-Belle said.

Pearse wrapped his hand snugly around the butt and put his index finger on the trigger at the same time.

'Aye-aye,' he said to May-Belle. 'I am indeed, Faggot.'

He put the gun back in the locker and told her that this wasn't an honest gun – that Da's not just hiding the gun from children. The man isn't allowed to have it by law. It's not an army gun.

'Gran always said he was mixed up with bad men.'

'Like who?' asks May-Belle.

'The bad men,' Pearse tells her.

*

There were still hours to go before the adults returned. Pearse went down to the kitchen to make some soup and toast and May-Belle stayed in the attic. She switched on the radio. She loved radio. The idea of a wooden box talking like a ghost in the corner of a room was to May-Belle as fascinating as a spider in a bottle. Television showed faces, radio hid them. Ma said telly stole time away from being alive, and Dad was never home long enough for him to get round to hiring a set.

A talky channel came on – not the usual one May-Belle some-times listened to with the English voices and comedians and plays and tales of real people and their adventures and miseries – but an Irish one, where the speakers spent too much time banging on about gunmen and killers and politics that made a body's head swim.

There was some kind of discussion – chat leading up to a point – about prisoners, and what's good for them, and whether jails should be slimy dungeons or holiday camps like Funlins or somewhere she'd never heard tell of, when the radio people skipped on to a story so wild to May-Belle that she could see it unfold in her mind. The tale was of these Collister boys.

Solly Collister was the oldest prisoner in either Britain or Ireland and he'd just died in Long Larrikan jail aged 94. The radio people were telling the story of his life. Apparently he spent his last days in almost total isolation – the auld fella seldom talked; was never in the recreation areas; he either sat in his cell or was wheeled around in a chair by a warder. Once in a while, he'd be chuntered into the library and left there all day, depending on half-decent cons and screws to take him to the bathroom when he needed to go, or fetch him a cup of water if he was thirsty.

He was a rare but gifted speaker, and the few folk who knew him had pieced together his life from snippets of his own memories, as well as court and prison records – and this was now being recounted by the people on the radio.

Back in the 19th century, Solomon – Solly, as his family called him – and his brother Robbie were born in the wee township of Gallagh, in the depths of the Antrim glens. They were twins and their mother died giving birth to them. They were reared by their father, in a farm house called Cargin that sat on a hill, and they met no-one until they went to school aged eight.

They left school at twelve, and returned to the farm to work with their father, barely coming across another solitary human being from one year's end to the next. Their father died in 1916. The boys were too odd and weird and shuffly to be called up for fighting. As a result of their father's death, though, they were forced to have a few more dealings with strangers from the township of Gallagh. It was their father who'd done all the buying and selling of goods. From then on, though, Solly Collister took on the role of paterfamilias, a man on the radio said. Being the first born, by an hour and a half, he was considered the older and wiser of the pair – and in fact, he was just that: Robbie being too soft for the world full-stop. Still, these dealings of Solly's with the outside world were of such infrequency that it would amount to abject isolation for even the most determined hermits or agoraphobes; for Solly, though, it was as if the world wouldn't leave him and his brother alone.

They lived like that for decades – through the second world war and the 1960s. Nobody knows, and Solly wouldn't say, what the brothers got up to alone in their tumble-down farm on the hill. Robbie was the sick one, always ailing. Solly got on with sowing and reaping their potatoes and cabbages and carrots and raising their cattle and chickens. The big brother looked after the distant commerce. Robbie cooked the meals.

The calendar goes by till it reaches 1971 – ten years before Pearse and May-Belle got together – and then, maybe two days before it all comes to an end for the Collisters, a social worker is dispatched by the state to visit their farm at Gallagh. Other farmsteaders nearby, who barely knew the brothers, had heard screaming and hollering a few nights before, and seen one of the Collisters running around the fields in the moonlight.

The social worker never returned to her office in Antrim. A local bobby is instructed to look for her, and he never returns either. Solly wasn't some cannibal or monster. He was a lovely auld man – but he had no understanding of what it meant to be truly in the world; he feared and hated the world: a crash-landed alien who didn't know the code of the planet on which it was trapped.

When the authorities finally moved in whole-sale on the farm – armed police, hostage negotiators, paramedics and fire crews in case of siege or multiple deaths – old Solly Collister was shivering behind his front door. The Collisters lived in a large brick farmhouse – grey stone walls, licked all over by tongues of moss. A gaping maw of a hole on the left side of the roof, made half the house uninhabitable. The police walked forward with guns drawn – they could see Solly peeking through dirty lace curtains – and ordered him to surrender or they'd break down the door and come in shooting. Auld Solly opened up, and let the officers into his house, which no stranger had set foot in for nigh on eighty years.

The house was filled to bursting with every sort of rubbish you could imagine. Whole rooms were piled with old papers. The two brothers had made tunnels through the mounds of papers to get from one room to another. The main room in which Solly and Robbie had spent most of their waking hours, had been reduced to a cave made from yellowed news-print. Stacks of old papers were layered high from floor to ceiling; the sheaves even formed a make-shift wall and archway in the room – on one side was the easy chair in which Solly sat, and on the other side his brother Robbie was propped up in his own comfy seat, dead. Robbie must've been there a few weeks as he was a bit green round the gills and flies were starting to breed on him.

The rest of the house was an equal jumble of junk; fetid, some-one on the radio said. One upstairs room contained hundreds of machinery parts; the brothers had never thrown out anything containing an engine – instead consigning it to a living death in their mother and father's old bedroom. The toilet had long since ceased to work, and when it was too cold to go outside, the brothers used a bath in what had been the pantry. Under a pile of bicycles in a lean-to workshop they found the social worker's body. Solly said he shot her as she wanted to take his brother Robbie's body away. Robbie had died in his sleep one night, weeks ago, and Solly decided to keep Robbie just where he was, until he too passed away. Solly used the same shotgun to kill the first police officer when he arrived to make inquires about the whereabouts of the social worker. The cop walked up through the mud-splattered front yard, and before he got halfway, Solly opened the door and let him have both barrels right in the chest. The cop tried to crawl away, his ribcage blown open and his right hand hanging off. Solly reloaded and blew the cop's head from his shoulders – policeman's helmet and all, smashed to smithereens. The officer's body was found, folded over on itself, in a cupboard under the stairs. Solly showed the police where his gun was and came quietly.

At his trial, the judge said that this may be a different kind of shooting tragedy for Ulster, but it didn't matter how old or lonely or confused someone was, if they weren't legally mad then they were going to jail for a very long time. Solly served just under ten years of his life sentence and died in Long Larrikan prison after a short illness, the report said.

May-Belle turned off the radio. Pearse popped his head into the attic opening, and said to her, 'Food's ready – do you want to come down?'

*

Ten bullets in total. That meant they could keep six and practice with four. The six would make up a full chamber. To practice, they needed to get as far away from civilisation as they could. Much further than the Weary Woods. They needed to get somewhere where a gunshot wouldn't be heard by another living soul.

So, the next day, they set off for Tardree Forest. It was a good five mile walk, to the north west of town, mostly uphill. The forest had beauty spots placed to capture the view of the lough glistering over the valley of Ulster. When they got to a safe lonely spot in the depths of Tardree they were faced with the task of trying to understand how the gun worked and not waste bullets with too much experimentation.

Neither understood the mechanics of guns, but the job fell to Pearse as he had a TV and watched lots of war movies and westerns. He had no clue how to shoot it, how to load it; he just looked at it. May-Belle sat under a tree while Pearse started to explore the revolver, keeping the business end well away from his face.

He played with it, slowly and patiently, for more than two hours. May-Belle fell asleep, woke up and went for a paddle in a stream, made daisy-chains for their heads and had both their names carved into three trees by the time Pearse was confident enough to stop tinkering and tell her that he was pretty sure he knew what he was doing now.

The gun was a Webley, that much was obvious from the name stamped on top of the nobbly butt. A Webley, Pearse had discovered, after half an hour of trying to push the cartridge cylinder out the side of the gun with his thumbs, is a top-break loader – although, of course, he had no sense of such technical terms back then. You don't push the cylinder out in a top-break loader, you crack the gun in two, pulling down on the barrel. It opens on a wee hinge offering up six oily holes – just waiting for the bullets to be slid inside.

Once he'd figured out how to put the bullets in the gun, he took them all back out again. He shut the gun up, then cracked it open one more time just to check that he hadn't accidentally left a bullet inside that might fire and blow the nose off his face.

He looked and felt around the body of the gun, searching for some wee switch or lever that might be the safety catch. He couldn't see a thing. He took it over to May-Belle and said to her, 'Can you find the bloody safety catch on this?'

She took it from him and started studying its body, and shrugged. She turned the gun, and looked up the barrel.

'Jesus, May-Belle,' he said, 'Don't.'

'I saw you take the bullets out of it,' she said. 'There's nothing here. It mustn't have a safety thingy.'

She'd been in an off-on dirty mood since he'd told her they couldn't just go shooting the gun, they had to learn how it worked first.

'Bollocks,' Pearse said. 'All guns have safety catches.'

'Fair enough, Doc Holliday,' she says. 'You're the one who knows all about guns.'

'At least I'm trying,' he said.

'Quit mumping your gums,' she says.

'Quit mumping yours,' he replied.

Pearse holds the unloaded gun at arm's length, pointing at a tree, and tries to pull the trigger. It's hard and tight, with the resistance of a magnet. He releases his grip on the trigger, and pumps his index finger a little bit. May-Belle thinks it looks like a puny wee man doing sit-ups. Pearse aims at the tree again and treats the trigger tough as he can. The hammer cocks back, the cylinder clicks round and the hammer falls – clink. A Webley doesn't have a safety catch – it's a double action revolver; not that Pearse knew that kind of gun lingo yet either – the shooter just needs to pull the trigger like they mean it, and off it goes: click, click, boom.

'I think I've got it,' he says to May-Belle.

'Good,' she says, 'call me when you're ready.'

He plays around with the gun for another forty-five minutes or so – learning how to pull the trigger and not shake, using the sight blade at the end of the barrel to aim at targets, taking the bullets in and out – and still not live firing it yet.

Pearse calls May-Belle over and shows her what he's learned. Within five minutes it's all as clear as day to her. 'It's not that hard,' she says, pursing up her mouth.

'That took me two bloody hours,' he said.

She holds his gaze for a few moments, and then pulls her hands up from her hips, her fingers pointing six guns at him.

She takes the daisy chain off his head and laughs, 'You can't be a gunman with that on you.'

Pearse tells her they need to go even deeper into the woods now that they're in a fit state to practice their shooting skills.

*

Tardree wasn't exactly Robin's Sherwood or the Black Forest. It covered maybe five square miles, high on two hills. From their vantage point, looking down on Antrim, the countryside staggered to the shore of Lough Neagh; the water silvering away to the other side of Northern Ireland.

They turned their backs on the view, and walked through the

tall pine trees. They'd only seen a couple of hill walkers and three women on horseback all day. The place was supposedly more active by night when gunmen buried their weapons and couples came to lovers' lanes.

They dropped down into a gulley; the pines a closed arch over their heads. They were as far in – as deep and as dark – as they could go: right in the heart of Tardree.

A fall of boulders lay down one side of the gulley, velveted with centuries of moss. They hunted about for a log roughly the size of a man's body – from hip to throat. It took them a while. They found one, dragged it back, and stood it up on a low lying boulder, so the top of the log was more or less level with their heads.

Pearse got the gun out of his back-pack and loaded one bullet. A couple of deep breaths calmed him down, and he took aim, lining the sight blade up with the dead centre of the log. He held his free arm behind him like a sword-fighter.

May-Belle stepped back, dropping out of his eye-line.

'Ready?' he said.

She mumbled, 'Uh-huh, D'Artagnan.'

He pulled down hard on the trigger, and the gun went off: click, click, boom.

His shooting hand flew up in the air and he staggered backwards on his heels. A spiced metal smell filled their noses as the gun smoke bloomed in front of the barrel.

'Did I shoot in the air?' he asked.

'No,' said May-Belle, who hadn't flinched, 'you hit the damn thing, man.'

'I can taste the gun-powder,' he said, walking towards the log.

'The steam of Satan's piss,' she replied.

There was a hunk torn out of the right side of the log. Pearse rubbed his finger through the gash. He'd aimed for the heart. If this was a man standing before him, he'd have shot him in the side, taking out half his ribcage.

'Not bad,' says May-Belle. 'Gimme my go.'

Pearse hands her the gun and they walk back to the firing position, very quietly, listening now, in case anyone is coming, in case anyone heard them.

They stand like statues for five minutes, only their eyes moving. A crack of twigs in the trees, though, had them clawing at each others arms, but it must have been a bird or a rabbit or a fox for no other sound is heard and no person comes either.

May-Belle loads the gun herself, stands sideways on to the log, levels the barrel, squeezes one eye shut and takes aim.

She fires. There is a sound of iron hitting iron – the mad ding of a blacksmith at work with his anvil and hammer – and twenty feet off to the left a clod of earth goes flying in the air from the bank of the gulley. The bullet had ricocheted off the boulder beneath the log.

'Fuck sake,' says May-Belle.

'Hang on,' Pearse says, and leads her forward.

'Look,' he says, pointing at the finger-length chip in the rock. 'If that was a man you'd have shot his balls square off.'

'I suppose I would have,' she smiles. 'Or shot a woman in the fanny.'

They wait again – another five minutes passing until they are sure no-one is coming for them.

On Pearse's next go he hits the log in the belly. After another wait, May-Belle's shot blows off half the upper rim of the log. 'That one would've taken the head clean off her shoulders,' she says.

'We're grand then, aren't we,' Pearse says.

'Well, I know what I'm doing. I could blow the foreskin off a fly at fifty paces,' she laughs.

Pearse puts the gun back in the nap-sack and hands it to her. 'Do you want to carry it home?' he says.

'Aye,' she says. 'Sure, mon amigo.'

*

Poor May-Belle had never been to the ruins of Shane's Castle – a shattered auld giant lying sprawled along the banks of Lough Neagh – so a few days later Pearse decided it was essential she see one of the best sights in her home town in case she never got the chance again. Shane's Castle was four miles west from Antrim Castle and the Castle Grounds park, which were open to the public and free all year round. You had to pay to get into Shane's Castle, and it was nearer to Randalstown than Antrim, if the truth be told. Antrim Castle, with its monster in the pond and ancient graveyard, sat at the heart of the town. Shane's Castle still had some Lord or Baron or Earl or something living in a modern private stately home in the grounds. The stately home was shut off by an electrified fence, far away and secluded from the places the public were allowed to roam after they paid their entrance fee; the ruins of the original castle were barely visible to the nobility behind their new walls. Fifty pence paid for a ticket at the gate of Shane's Castle and a ride on a tiny old steam engine around a deer park. At the end of the train journey – which lasts no more than fifteen minutes – the driver lets the passengers off at the banks of Lough Neagh where the ruins of the medieval castle lie.

'What's this town doing with two castles anyway?' May-Belle asks Pearse, as they walk down the Randalstown Road towards Shane's gates.

He tells her that there are two castles because in the olden times Antrim had two grand families. The grandest was the O'Neills – the owners of Shane's Castle. They could trace their line back to the High Kings of Ireland and the boys of the Red Hand, lost in the mists of time. There's a family tale that has it that Pearse's line is descended from the O'Neills on Gran's side, with some maid getting herself pregnant by one of the Lord's sons way back in the 1500s. Or so the story goes, Gran told Pearse.

'Sounds bollocks,' says May-Belle.

Antrim Castle, in the Castle Grounds was owned by the Massereenes, the other grand family. This was a richer clan than the O'Neills but a younger one with less history. They pop up about the 1600s and built their castle on the site of an old Norman fortress.

'Both castles were cursed,' Pearse said. 'And both burned to the ground.' Shane's Castle went up in smoke in the 1820s when a rook's nest, high up on top of one of the kitchen chimneys, fell down the flue and set up a blaze which burned the old stone battlements to the ground. In the early 1920s, Antrim Castle burned to the ground as well. Some thought a silly maid let a fire start in the kitchen, but everyone knew it was the IRA settling scores for the Massereenes supporting the British during the War of Independence. The Massereenes didn't rebuild on a new nearby site like the O'Neills. They upped and left for England, and all that remained was the tumbled down scorched tower of their castle, on the shore of the Six Mile River, and the gate of a keep which the people of Antrim have to walk beneath to get into the Castle Grounds, the town's main park. The walkway under the keep smells like a toilet and every teenager in town has written their name on its walls.

'Both Castles have their ghosts too,' Pearse said. Antrim Castle has its witch in the pond, of course – as everyone knows – as well as the White Lady wandering the grounds; Shane's Castle was supposed to be home to the original Banshee – Maveen; the lost child of Shane O'Neill; who was stolen by raiders a thousand years ago. She escaped the bandits' clutches and threw herself into Lough Neagh as they chased her, preferring death to rape. Any time since, when there is someone descended from the O'Neills on the point of death, she'll call out in the night from the water behind the castle, welcoming them to the spirit world and telling their loved ones left behind not to fear, that she'll care for them. But her voice can't be heard by the dying, and her wail only terrifies those left to live rather than reassuring them.

The Hound of O'Neill – the Hound of Hell – is another of the supernatural creatures to be found at Shane's Castle. An Irish

Wolfhound from the middle ages that still exists in ghost-form till this day. One spring morning, the youngest daughter of the then Lord O'Neill was out walking in the grounds when a wolf tore through the bracken to rip her throat out. From nowhere leaps a wolfhound, standing in front of the petrified young girl, guarding her from being eaten alive. The pair of giant dogs roll in a ball of hair and teeth and slabbers on the ground, the wolf and the wolfhound locked in a fight to the death. At last, the wolfhound tears the belly from the wolf, and staggers away, bleeding, its own throat gashed and ripped. It walks over to the young lady and collapses at her feet, dying there in front of her.

A week later some guards see a giant glowing white dog – a white wolfhound – walking on the battlements by moonlight. They fire arrows at it – but the arrows go right through the creature's ghostly body. A few months on, a group of invading Englishmen try sneaking up on the castle by night, with the intention of blowing off the portcullis doors so they can rush their hidden troops into the breach and start the plantation of Ulster by ousting the toughest most fearsome warrior chief in all of Ireland. As they approach the gate, a glowing white wolf hound appears – taller than a man – standing before the gates, growling and bristling.

A wail goes up from Lough Neagh at the rear of the castle, and the giant dog sets up a howling at the front of its walls. The combined wailing and howling alerts the sleeping castle and the guards pick off the advancing Englishmen with crossbows, before chasing the rest of the invaders, hiding in the trees, through the woods and polishing them off with swords and hunting dogs. Thanks to Maveen and the Hound, the only O'Neill to die that night was the chief's son, Hugh.

Finally, there's the Hairy Boggart.

'Hairy Boggart, my arse,' says May-Belle. 'Get on with you, Pearse.'

That's the last of the spirits and creatures at Shane's Castle on the banks of Lough Neagh, he tells her. 'The Boggart is just a beast,' Pearse says to May-Belle, 'about eight foot tall, covered in coarse black hair, with long arms and spindly legs. He's a bit like a troll, only this fella lives in the underground passageways beneath Shane's Castle and steals and eats children. He's a curse set on the O'Neills for all the murder they committed in their years of governing Ulster. Either that, or some say he was a deformed monster born from one of the O'Neill women who had sex with the Devil himself.'

'Away,' says May-Belle. 'Your stories don't add up. You told me before that the Banshee was older than time – a fairy with the faces of dead children hanging in her hair – and now you tell me the Banshee was some girl from this castle. And as for the Boggart – that's just a rubbish story, by the way.'

'There's different legends but they all mean the same thing and the creatures exist no matter what the story.'

'And I've never heard tell of the White Lady either,' she goes on.

The White Lady is a ghost that is mostly seen at Antrim Castle, but also sometimes appears down this way at Shane's Castle too. It's believed that she was a young girl who had fallen in love with both the son of Lord Massereene at Antrim Castle and the son of Lord O'Neill from Shane's Castle. Some say she was a beautiful young novice nun, and she ran away from Holy Orders and lived wild in the woods that flow for miles between the two castles, waiting till night to see the two young men. She loved both of them secretly, and neither knew the other was sworn to her as well. One night, meeting her lover O'Neill; and the next night, her lover Massereene. They both discovered that she was cheating, though, and went to her together, chasing her through the night forest and cutting her down, killing her. It seems she drifts more towards Antrim Castle as a ghost, for young Massereene repented of his crime and later became a monk himself, whilst O'Neill went on to father countless children by dozens of local women – one of them, the legend goes, Pearse's own great-great-great-great-great-great-great grandmother. All these wee bastard children living outside the gates of his castle in poverty.

By now they'd come to these gates of Shane's Castle. Pearse said to May-Belle that he'd pay them in. He'd nicked a pound fifty out of Da's pocket that morning. 'I'm not paying in,' she says. 'Bugger that.'

They'd walked from Parkhall, through the centre of Antrim and then on towards Randalstown. The Randalstown Road was straight and grey. On the far side there were yellow fields and the red barns of farms, rolling over hills all the way to Ballymena. On their side of the road there was a high grey wall which kept people who didn't want to pay out of the grounds of Shane's Castle.

'It's fine,' Pearse said. 'I don't want to be getting chased today, and if we don't pay in we can't get a ride on the wee steam train. You need the ticket to get on it. I'd love you to have a go on it.'

There was a man dressed like a prison guard on the gate – wearing a black uniform with shiny buttons and a peaked hat with a harp as the crest. It was the same sort of hat badge the UDR boys wore on their berets. They paid him and walked inside the gates through a turnstile. About twenty yards away there were the thin twin tracks of the railway line and an old-fashioned waiting room and platform.

It was a blissful summer's day now so there were a lot of mums about with their little kids in tow. Pearse and May-Belle, at eleven, were the oldest children there by far; they were the only youngsters on their own – free from the watch of parents. There were a few elderly couples as well, probably up from Belfast sight-seeing. The track disappeared to the left, bending into the forest where the deer roamed. The engine and wagons came round the corner, from the right, with an auld steam locomotive hur-chuh hur-chuh noise. The train even had a cowcatcher grille at the front as if Casey Jones was the driver.

They hopped on board with the rest of the folk. The train was open-topped and went very slowly – at a jogger's pace. Halfway through the journey they must have passed some swamp or a dead animal for they were suddenly eaten alive almost by filthy midgies; a hail of living black in the air around them. May-Belle panicked and jumped up from her seat, wiping her mouth and flicking at her ears and ruffling her hair. She pulled her top over her head and got down on the floor of the carriage and tried to hide from the bugs. Pearse leaned forward and covered her with his body; she shivered on the floor until they got away from the polluted spot. She wouldn't get back on the seat till the journey ended and the train stopped down by the lough and the ruins.

Once the train came to a halt, the people all went their separate ways, and Pearse and May-Belle walked over to the battlements to look at the old cannons, pointing out over the lough – keeping watch for any rival's ships on the horizon. Away in the distance was Ram Island. It was there – oh, it must have been nearly six hundred years ago – that the then Lord O'Neill kept captive the local beauty of Antrim, Aoife. She had raven hair and eyes like moss, lips as dark as blood and skin so white it shone silver in the sunlight.

Aoife was the daughter of a local tradesman, an innkeeper or blacksmith – no-one can remember which; one day she goes walking in the woods, along the banks of the Six Mile River, singing to herself, so the legend goes. The last person to see her was the local priest. He stopped and talked to her, for even a priest couldn't resist the sight of Aoife.

The priest said goodbye and walked towards his church – Aoife singing through the trees behind him.

And then she disappeared. Of course, back then, everyone assumed the fairy folk had taken her. In fact, when she first bloomed into her beauty as a girl, some people reckoned that she herself had been left behind by the fairy folk in place of a real human child – a changeling, they called it – for no living mortal could be so beautiful. Perhaps, the fairy folk had just come back for her this time, some thought.

Around the time that Aoife vanishes, the then Lord O'Neill begins building himself a little house on Ram Island. No servants helped him. He said it was a lodge for meditating on God, and he built it with his own hands out of wood. No-one else was allowed to set foot on Ram Island. He rowed his boat over to it almost every other day – it lay a good five miles or more out in Lough Neagh – and sometimes he'd spend up to a week there, praying, at a time. His wife and daughters grew lonely for him, but they couldn't very well come between their Lord and his God, so they simply contented themselves with the fact that O'Neill would be at the right hand of Jesus once he left the living world.

O'Neill died suddenly in his seventieth year – one of the longest living earls in the family – done in by an apoplexy. On the night of his burial, harpists and torch-bearers lined the funeral route from the gates of his castle to the family tomb in the centre of the O'Neill lands – and the common people, his servants and tenants and soldiers, wept their eyes dry as he past on his way to the grave.

A few days later, his son – his heir, now the new Earl – took a rowing boat, just as his father had done almost every day, and made his way to Ram Island. No other man had set foot there for nearly fifty years, since it had become his father's retreat. Now, though, with his father dead, the new Earl felt he should make a pilgrimage to the sacred spot at least once, to honour his father's holy nature. When he got near the shore he heard a muttering and chattering, like monkeys had learned speech. He stopped the boat in the shallows and clambered through the surf to the land. With his sword drawn he made his way through the trees lining the shore and found himself in a clearing, with a few wooden houses surrounding a small fire, over which hung a large cooking pot.

A striking old lady with long dark hair, streaked with grey, came towards him. Peeking from the doorways of the houses, were middle-aged women, young women in their stunning prime, girls just flowering – and some of these pregnant with big bellies

– then there were youngsters with the look of beauty just breaking on their features, little girls and bonny baby girls. All girls. No men at all.

'Where are your men?' the new earl asked.

The old lady said, 'There are none.'

The old lady led the earl to an open patch of ground some way through the trees. There the earl saw upwards of thirty small graves, all marked with a cross.

'These are our sons,' the old lady said. 'All dead before they reached one year.'

'How?' asked the new earl.

'Killed by their father,' she said. 'In this land, there could only be one man.'

The young earl asked the old lady her name and she said, 'Aoife.' Then she added: 'Go before he comes and kills you too. He hasn't been here in days and we expect him any moment.'

The young earl said that yes, indeed, he better flee right away, for fear of his life. Later that night, he returned to Ram Island with his three younger brothers – all of military age – and they put every living soul there to the sword. They burned the houses and hunted the women through the woods until they were sure not one was left alive. Two tried to escape – a girl of sixteen and her four-year-old daughter. They ran into the lough, swimming the great dark stretches of the water, pushing out far from the island – the nearest land, though, still miles away across the surf. A wail of death rose from air – circling and whipping around the island and lough. The brothers stood in the shallows and watched as a spinning spout of water shot up from the lough, fifty foot in the air; it captured the swimmers, the girl and her daughter. The wail howled on – up close, far away, everywhere, but with no source; no man or creature visible as the possessor of this cry of pain and anger and warning and despair. The girl and her daughter spun around the sides of the spout – their arms and legs sticking out, their mouths screaming – and just as quickly as it appeared, the spout vanished, taking the mother and daughter down into the depths. The wailing cut out as if the one crying had gladly died.

'We can thank Maveen for that,' said the new earl. His brothers agreed. They crossed themselves against the Banshee and they wiped their swords, got back in the boat and returned to their castle and the rest of their lives.

*

May-Belle and Pearse walked away from the shore battlements towards the main ruins – a few towers and some crumbled walls. They wandered through what was once the banqueting hall and looked up. There was no roof and seagulls flew overheard. Ravens sat on the ramparts, hunched over and silent, despite the warmth of the day.

Pearse tried to persuade May-Belle to come down into the caves and cellars and dungeons beneath the ruins. May-Belle asked why in the name of God she'd want to go down into some pit where, half an hour ago, he'd told her the Hairy Boggart himself was waiting to rip her arms and legs off and eat her.

'The Hairy Boggart disappeared a hundred years ago,' Pearse said. 'You don't have Hairy Boggarts in the twentieth century.'

She still refused, but he begged her and said all his stories were lies, so she relented. They held hands and walked into the mouth of the main cave, the path inside dropping down deep toward the centre of the earth and then leading off to caverns north, south, east and west.

'If we keep taking the left-hand path, we'll eventually find our way back out again,' Pearse said.

'Shite,' said May-Belle. 'Let's see what happens anyway.'

On the walls, the modern owners of Shane's Castle had placed glowing orange electric lamps, surrounded by wire mesh. They sat where in olden times a flaming torch might have been placed. May-Belle squeezed Pearse's hand and didn't let it go. They walked on, hearing people deep within the caves and dungeons laughing and screaming as they played tricks on each other and hollered out to hear their echo. They came to a long sunken path that carried on straight for maybe fifty yards underground. There were little alcoves off the path, that had probably been cells in years gone by.

'They'd've hung people in there by their arms to die,' Pearse says.

'Poor bastards,' says May-Belle.

A few paces along, there's a young couple, sixteen or seventeen, kissing in one of the alcoves. The boy's hand is under the girl's top, pulling it up – showing off her soft white bare flesh. The girl's hand is squeezing the boy's auld bulge. They bite each other on the lips with their eyes closed, heedless of Pearse and May-Belle, who may as well be ghosts.

May-Belle pulls Pearse back and whispers, 'We'll get lost in here.' They about-face and walk backwards, retracing their steps, this time taking all the right-hand turns. The light from the sky glimmers down as they come to the foot of the path leading up and out of the caves and dungeons to the fresh air. They stop and look around. They are alone. 'What were they up to?' says May-Belle. 'The da-do-ron-ron?' Pearse laughs and leans forward, putting his hand around May-Belle's waist. She laughs and puts her hand on his shoulder. They both whisper-sing 'da-do-ron-ron', swinging their hips, and move closer to each other and put their lips together in the softest kiss. Pearse lets her go and May-Belle lets him go and they walk up and out into the sunlight. They lick their lips.

As they get up into the mouth of the cave, there is a blue five pound note lying by a small bush. The pair of them breathe in at the same time as if they've just seen an angel rising from the waters of Lough Neagh. Pearse drops to his knees and scoops the fiver up, sticking it in the pocket of his jeans before anyone can see.

They hurry on to the lower ramparts of the castle, finding themselves a quiet place to sit by the lough shore, far away from the caves in case whoever had lost the fiver came hunting for it and tried to search them. They lay on the grassy bank and a family of swans float past – their elegant bodies barely breaking the surface of the water; their ugly feet paddling like hell below the slow rippling waves.

Pearse asks May-Belle if she still wants to go through with it.

'What else is there left for us to do?' she asks.

'Run away.'

'Where to?' she asks. 'Who to?'

'I dunno.'

'They'd just keep taking us back. We've got five more years till we are sixteen and free and can get the fuck away from here without anyone stopping us,' she says, pulling the seeds off a long blade of fluffy-headed grass with her fingers. 'I can't wait that long.'

'Fine,' Pearse says. 'Let's go back home and eat and get on with it then.'

She leans over and kisses him again – this time on the cheek. He turns his face while her lips are still on him, and his mouth slides over her mouth; their stupid teeth clink. They taste metallic – like the iron in blood.

They get up and hold hands, walking like that until they come to the gates of Shane's Castle. When they catch sight of adults they break off holding hands and walk through the turnstile, back onto the grey road, and set off in the direction of Antrim High Street. It's a Tuesday afternoon in July – as quiet and calm and pleasant as could be, even though the history books show that all bad things happen on a Tuesday.

*

Their route took them past the Black Chapel – the night-stoned Catholic church at the foot of the town; pale cream saints and Marys set in alcoves up the length of its indigo bricked rectangular bell-tower; white crenellations across its roofs and turret. A fastidious grave-yard, sprinkled with Celtic Crosses, circling the House of God.

Dandering, as they did, it took them an hour to get to the bottom of the High Street. They walked up the incline of the High Street. When they came to the crossroads in the middle of the town by the old stone Victorian library, Pearse asked May-Belle to follow him, over to the other side of the road. He wanted to see the old curiosity shop in Pogue's Entry.

Pogue's Entry was a wee cobbled lane, dipping down off the High Street towards the Six Mile River. There was a tiny museum there and a shop, which sold antiques, called Chimney Corner Antiquaries. The place was famous because some chap called Alexander Irvine had lived there when he was little in the middle of the last century. There was a plaque on the wall saying that the author of My Lady of the Chimney Corner had been born in a back room of what would now be the antiques shop. There was a sundial beneath the plaque and on the face of the dial it said, 'Would that all us would realise, like the son of this house, that love and not dogma is what makes the world turn.'

Pearse looked in the window of the antiques shop and saw military binoculars, an old German officer's hat, medals, china plates, tattered books, swords, figurines and statues, music boxes and all sorts of gorgeous trinkets his hands had never touched before.

'Look here,' he says to May-Belle.

She stared in the window too, leaning forward until her nose pressed piggie against one of the small glass panes between strips of lead. It steamed with her nose-breath.

'Let's go on in,' Pearse said.

He opened the door, a little bell jingling somewhere, and May-Belle came behind.

'Hullo, hullo, welcome, welcome,' came a kindly holler from the back of the shop. A man in a waistcoat stepped out from a rear room, took one look at them and said, 'Get the fuck out of here.'

He picked up a violin, which was lying on a fancy dresser, and chased them out of the shop.

'Cunt,' Pearse shouted, as they got to the head of the lane.

'Queer cunt in your waistcoat,' May-Belle chimed in, jumping up and down on the spot.

They walked on, until they saw her sitting on the benches at the top of the town. She was as fat as a barrel and dressed in a greasy auld grey coat and headscarf. Her tights were laddered and her shoes bust at the seams. It was Sadie.

Sadie was the local maddie. She looked as old as the hills but was no more than fifty-five or so. Her hair was white and beneath her bushy brows, her eyes were crossed – one looking for you and the other looking at you. Her glasses were as squint as the eyes behind them, and her tongue curled out of her mouth while she talked to herself.

Sometimes you'd come across her talking to trees or lamp-posts or shouting at the fruit and veg in the supermarket before the store detective chucked her out. On a few occasions she'd walk up to people's doors and try to get in, believing she lived in the home herself, and the family inside had dispossessed her.

May-Belle and Pearse are still a good fifty yards away but they can hear her shouting about the police and the IRA and people stealing her identity.

'It must be day-release,' says May-Belle.

Pearse didn't say anything.

'Scary auld bitch,' May-Belle goes on.

They get closer and Sadie looks at them. Her face fixes itself into an blackguard's scowl – an enraged baby.

Both of them have always kept a wide berth of Sadie, unnerved by her rambling shouts and hollers. They haven't seen her in months, though. The sight of her now spooks May-Belle as usual – Pearse, however, doesn't feel the fright of Sadie anymore. He walks towards her and says, 'How you doing?'

Sadie says, 'Ah, they are fucken everywhere.'

May-Belle laughs and says, 'What're you doing, Pearse?'

'Come on, Sadie,' he says. 'You can't sit there shouting all day. Where do you live?'

Sadie gets to her feet and looks at May-Belle. 'Are you my wee sister?' she asks May-Belle.

'Aye,' says May-Belle laughing. Sadie starts to cry, and sits down again, saying, 'Oh, Betty, Betty.'

May-Belle stops laughing, and steps behind Pearse.

'Come on, Sadie,' he says, 'we'll walk you home. Where do you live?'

'Pearse,' says May-Belle. 'No. Let's go.'

'It's fine, May-Belle,' he says, then he turns back to Sadie. 'Shall I take you home? Where do you live?'

'I live in Antrim,' she says.

'I know, but where?'

'Everywhere. All over. In the houses. Up the lane. At the top of the town. Up here. The bottom of the road. There's holes in the trunks of all the trees,' Sadie says. Her eyes rolled back into her head, the whites showing, as if she's dead or hypnotised or sleepwalking.

'Don't you have a house?' he asks.

'Are you children?' Sadie replies.

'Yes,' May-Belle says.

'Good,' she says. 'Children are all we've got. Look after yourselves.' And she leans back in her seat, smiling.

'Come on, Sadie,' Pearse says. 'Let's get you home.' He walks towards her.

May-Belle says, 'Whatever you're planning, forget it.'

Pearse stops and looks back towards May-Belle and says, 'I'm planning nothing. I feel sorry for her. She should be somewhere safe.'

He turns to Sadie again and walks a few steps nearer. 'Sadie, let me take you home. You can't sit here staring at the traffic all day.'

'All the drivers try to kill me,' she says. 'The food's poisoned, the water's poisoned, the air's poisoned. I know you all have it in for me.'

'Not me,' he says and reaches out a hand to help her to her feet.

She wallops his hand away with a stinging slap. 'Fuck off. You're not going to kill me, you little bastard. Fuck off and murder someone else.' She looks away from him, towards the road and the passing cars.

Pearse feels that cold flush of fear that comes in your stomach. May-Belle takes his cuff and pulls him towards her.

'Sorry, Sadie,' she says.

Sadie's head swivels back in their direction.

'Are you friends?' she says.

'Yes,' says May-Belle.

Sadie starts to cry again, water wells up behind the lower rim of her wonky glasses. 'I love you both,' she says. May-Belle feels good, happy tears in her eyes, but not on her face. Her throat is spikey, and hot and dry.

Sadie reaches out her hands towards them. May-Belle and Pearse look at each other. May-Belle walks forward, pulling Pearse along with her.

Pearse offers Sadie his hand and Sadie takes it; then she reaches out for May-Belle, who looks at Pearse and then offers up her own hand. Sadie holds on to both of them, softly, then pulls them hard towards her. May-Belle whimpers but holds her nerve as Pearse holds his. Sadie says, 'Don't be scared. Nothing can harm you when you are with me or you have each other.'

She looks at them. 'If you are my son and you are my sister, why are you the same size?' Sadie asks.

'I don't know,' says May-Belle.

'Are we?' Pearse asks. Sadie pushes them away. They both totter back a bit; then Sadie drops her head, and takes on a saintly auld expression. She brings her finger to her lips and then taps the side of her head as if she's just remembered where she'd left a lost key.

'Here,' says Sadie, 'a secret for you both.' She takes Pearse's hand in hers, and turns it so it is palm up, then she brings it to her mouth and whispers words they can't hear into it. She lets Pearse go, and then does the same to May-Belle. May-Belle feels Sadie's breath against her wrist, across her palm and over her fingers.

'Never be apart,' she says.

She drops their hands and returns to staring at the road.

They walk away without saying goodbye. A few yards on, May-Belle stops and sticks her hand in the pocket of Pearse's jeans – making him yowl. She takes the fiver they found at Shane's Castle from his pocket, and runs back – putting it in Sadie's lap, squeezing her hands around it.

'We don't need it,' she says, trying to give it to her.

Sadie screams, 'Get away. Who the fuck are you, you murdering wee cunt?'

'You have to take it,' May-Belle shouts, turning on her heel to run. 'You're like a fucken gypsy.'

When she gets to Pearse's side, May-Belle looks back. Sadie has torn the five pound note into pieces and thrown it over her shoulder. The shreds sweep along the grass towards them.

'Let's get this over with, May-Belle,' Pearse says. 'All we've done is put it off for days.'

*

It was a bad Tuesday, as they'd planned – July the eighth – so in May-Belle's house that meant Ma was all alone, still recovering from the weekend. Dad was in the Crumlin Road jail – just as he'd been for the past month or so.

For Pearse, Da would be in at nine o'clock. He was out on an early patrol with the UDR; it was the same routine every Tuesday. His Yvonne woman didn't stay over on Monday or Tuesday nights – spending those evenings at her mother's instead.

They'd ran from Sadie at the top of the town and not slowed till they got to Pearse's front path. May-Belle stopped, panting, and pointed up, saying, 'Oh my God – not another one of those bloody things.'

A flag – the Red Hand of Ulster – fluttered from a fitting below the main bedroom window. It must have been put up while they were away out. Such a thing had never been on display when Mum and Gran were alive.

The pair of them sat on the garden wall – getting their breath and gathering their wits.

'The most stupid fucken story ever told,' says May-Belle.

'What?' asks Pearse – feeling all jangly from the lactose acid bubbling in his muscles.

'That flag.'

'It's a great story.'

'Bollocks.'

The flag isn't even legally a flag any more though, apparently, or so some statute or other must claim – it is now just called the Ulster Banner, and has been for years, for it represents no recognised government or people. It is a bloody hand on a white background, adorned with a red cross, crown and star. The Red Hand is more than just bloody, however. It is the root of a story known in the heart of every child in Parkhall, or Antrim or Ulster or Ireland. They were raised on it.

Back when bears still ran in the forests, Ulster was ruled by a High King called O'Neill – the very man, Shane, who spawned all those Earls and ghosts and monsters for Antrim. The High King of Ulster had two sons born at the same time from two different mothers, and he couldn't decide which one should rule after him. When the lads grow up, the big tall lanky one suggests they run a race for the Crown. 'Bollocks,' says the wee fat stocky one – they should fight for it. The High King decrees that they will take part in a swimming contest across Lough Neagh as that'd be fairer to all concerned and less violent. The first one to touch the far shore will be the next High King of Ulster, once the current monarch – their da – has wound his way to the afterlife. The boys hit the water, mashing it to a foamy froth, and are neck and neck most of the way. They're swimming like the eels in the lough which make its green water look alive with leaping and wriggling on a sunny day; the bugs hovering just above the waves. When they are about one hundred yards from the far shore, the lanky one makes a break for it. He puts in a wild burst of energy and stretches ahead of his brother. The fat one sees this and knows he's beat, and stops dead in the water. He takes his dagger out from his belt – for these lads were both dressed in their breeches and whatnot, carrying their wee draw-string purses and bodkins and so forth – and he gets ahold of the fingers of his right hand with his teeth, and hacks the hand off at the wrist with one chop. He grabs the bloody right hand with his left and flings it as hard as he can for the shore. Plop. There it lands, boy, right at the feet of the King, his father. And His Majesty declares his fat son the next High King of Ulster, while the tall lanky one is still wading out of the water trying to appear all handsome and unfazed.

'Who'd do such a thing?' asks May-Belle.

Pearse shrugs.

*

They let themselves into Pearse's house, have a bowl of cornflakes each and make their way upstairs. They pulled down the ladder to the loft, climbed inside, but left the hatch open, so it was obvious someone was up there. Pearse went to the military footlocker, where they'd replaced the gun after practice.

May-Belle selected the record, put it on the gramophone and waited. Light shone up through the hatch from the hall below. Pearse looked at his watch. It was just before nine o'clock. He checked the gun; made sure it was loaded; held its muzzle down between his legs.

They heard the back door open and close. May-Belle looked at Pearse and he nodded. She walked over to the gramophone, turned the volume dial up as far as it would go and put the needle on the record. The opening bars of her new favourite song, Bad Moon Rising, blared out of the speakers; the music flowing through the hatch into the hall below, making its way downstairs into the living room where Da was standing in his UDR uniform.

Pearse stood back a little from the hatch. Anyone climbing into the loft would see Pearse once they'd popped their head through. May-Belle walked to the rim of the hatch, making herself visible too; and waited.

Da stormed into the downstairs hall. They heard him holler, 'What the fuck is that? Who's up there?'

'We are,' they shouted over the music.

He ran up the stairs three at a time, saying, 'I'm gonna fucken kill you, boy. Who have you got up there with you?'

He was directly below them now. 'What are you doing up there, you wee cunt?' he screamed. 'Turn that fucken music off. Get down here this instant.' Pearse put his finger around the trigger and shouted, 'Come fucken make me, big man.'

May-Belle looked out of the hatch, down onto the landing. She spat at him. 'Come on up, you cunt,' she hissed.

Da let a roar out of him. The loft trembled as he grabbed ahold of the ladder and started to climb his way up, to get at them. 'You hoor,' he said.

Pearse stood back a little more, so the trajectory was right, and aimed down onto the square of yellow light that shone up from below. He was shaking, so he held his shooting hand by the wrist to steady it – the way cops do.

Da was almost at the top of the ladder. The rim of his head – the UDR beret – crowned in the hatchway. 'You're fucken dead the pair of you,' he said.

His head and shoulders rose into the loft. He placed his hands inside, on the flooring, to haul himself up. The low light meant he couldn't see them clearly; just their still silhouettes against the black canvas of the walls.

'Oi,' Pearse said. 'Look here.' And he waggled the gun at him.

Da's eyes must have acclimatized to the dark quickly for his gaze ran down Pearse's face, along his arm, to the hand holding the gun.

'What the fuck?' he said.

Pearse steadied his hand again.

'Bye,' Pearse said.

The gun clicked once as Pearse started the long heavy pull on the trigger, and the cylinder swung into position.

'Bye,' said May-Belle.

The gun clicked a second time as the hammer swung back to its furthest point.

'Son,' his father said.

Boom went the gun.

Of course it happened quickly – a bullet leaves the muzzle of a gun at a velocity of something like two thousand miles an hour; and it only takes the time to blink to pull a trigger. All they were able to catch was a blaze of light, Da's head flying back and snapping against the far edge of the hatch – with a tremendous dull thump after the roaring blast of the gunshot – as he disappeared to the floor below making a muffled thud.

His beret had somehow ended up by Pearse's feet. Pearse stepped over it. May-Belle turned smartly on her heel to switch off the record player, and then reverse-pivoted, changing her mind. She wanted the music to keep playing, fantastic and loud. She looked over the edge of the hatch. He was lying on his back in a strange position, as if he was trying to walk like an Egyptian, but completely still. There was a hole in his head where the bullet had hit him just above the eye. A flap of skull was hanging to the side – it reminded her of a bin lid; a pool of blood spread out around his head in a red halo.

Pearse handed the gun to May-Belle and started to climb down the ladder. 'If he moves, shoot him in the face,' he said to her.

He stepped onto the landing on tippy-toes, fearful in case

Da's hand flashed out to grab his leg. It didn't. Pearse reached up and took the gun from May-Belle and kept it pointed at Da as she climbed down.

She kicked the body. 'Is he definitely dead?' she asked.

Pearse knelt down and put the gun against Da's teeth. His eyes were closed. The pressure of the barrel against his mouth made the flap of pink skull move like a creaky door. His brain looked like jam inside.

'Are you dead, auld cunty?' Pearse asked.

Pearse stood up. 'He's dead,' he says.

He hands the gun over to May-Belle. 'One shot, May-Belle,' he says. 'That's all it took me.'

As they walk down the stairs to the front door, May-Belle puts her hand, holding the gun, up her jumper, to hide it. They step outside – the music still clanging from the loft – and run quickly with their heads down, up the hill to May-Belle's house. They didn't even shut the front door behind them. The night is a dark orange; it's still too light for the stars to be seen, but the sliver of a Turkish moon is high up behind the trees.

They race around to May-Belle's back door. May-Belle pushes the handle and walks in; Pearse creeps slowly behind her. They stand in the hall and listen.

May-Belle turns and signals to Pearse to shut the door quietly. He does.

There's music playing from somewhere. May-Belle stands to one side, and motions for Pearse to walk forward and open the kitchen door. He takes a breath, smelling the oniony tang of the house, and does so.

In the kitchen, Ma is standing in her bra and knickers ironing a skirt. A transistor radio is playing some pop song he'd never heard before. Ma looks up at Pearse and says, 'What the fuck are you doing here?'

May-Belle pushes in behind him, going past him, holding the gun in front of her and fires. The bullet hits Ma in the shoulder and she falls backward. The ironing board crashes to the ground. Ma pushes herself up on her injured arm and, still holding the hot iron, hurls it. Pearse puts his hands up to shield him and it catches him a glance on the elbow. He moves to the side, stepping into the doorway of the living room, as Ma, still slumped on the floor, grabs the end of the ironing board and takes a swipe at May-Belle, knocking the legs from under her. May-Belle's spun in the air and lands on her back.

'No,' screams May-Belle.

Ma leaps on her, holding May-Belle's shooting hand down and gripping her by the hair, banging her head off the floor. Ma brings her knee up and whams it between May-Belle's legs. The air goes out of May-Belle and the gun skitters from her hand across the kitchen floor; dying at the hands of Ma would make her a beaten nothing; May-Belle feels the beast move in her and pushes Ma up and off her. Ma moves to get the gun. Pearse draws his foot back and kicks her square in the face. She doesn't go down though, instead throwing herself in the direction of the gun again – a relentless milky blob. Pearse jumps with her, landing on top of her. The gun is beneath her and she is trying to bring it out to shoot them.

Pearse bites down into the back of her neck and she fights like he's her exorcist, pushing him off her and rolling away from him. She aims the gun at Pearse's face.

May-Belle shouts, 'Die cunt.' Ma looks towards her. A split-second. Pearse kicks the hand holding the gun. May-Belle throws something at her – the iron, it seems, as it lands – hitting her on the face. She's stunned but fires a round in Pearse's direction anyway. The bullet burying itself in the fridge behind him.

Pearse picks up the iron and clonks her on the head again. May-Belle dives on her, grabbing Ma's gun hand, pushing it away from them and trying to wrestle it out of her grip. Pearse hits her again on the top of the head with the iron. She screams and tries to point the gun at May-Belle – her wrist wriggling to get a shot

– but she can't see to aim because of the hold the pair of them have on her, and her finger is no longer on the trigger.

May-Belle is pushing the gun from her grip, the way you'd roll a glove off, easing it slowly up and away from her fingers. Pearse hits her one more time with the base of the iron across the bridge of the nose and she makes a gargling noise and falls backward. The gun slips from her hold.

'Pick the flippen gun up, May-Belle,' Pearse screams.

May-Belle lifts it and moves backward, aiming at Ma.

Ma pushes herself up on her elbows – her face split open, blood running across her hairline from a gash in her skull.

'Shoot her,' Pearse says. 'Kill her.'

May-Belle looks at him.

'Kill her,' he says. 'Kill the bitch.'

'You hoor,' Ma says. 'What the fuck do you think you are doing?'

May-Belle pulls the trigger, a furl of fire leaves the muzzle and a bullet hits her mother straight in the heart. She falls back and sighs, as dead as you like.

'Fucken hell,' says May-Belle, trembling – so pale her lips are as white as her skin.

The body is lying on its back – right knee crooked; eyes open.

Pearse holds out his hand for the gun. 'Come on,' he says.

'Where?' May-Belle says, passing it to him.

'Out of here,' he says. 'We've got two bullets left.'

They walk through the house and out May-Belle's front door to the hill leading down to Pearse's house. Most of the people in the street have come out of their homes. There are bings and dings and drum rolls and clangs, distant distant – coming from Pearse's house, issuing down the stairs from his attic; a rectangle of yellow electric light in the open front doorway; the notes and octaves of the song that's still playing running out into the hot night.

A man a few houses up from May-Belle's shouts, 'What the fuck happened?'

Pearse lifts the gun in the air and fires once. 'Get back in your homes,' he shouts, 'or I'll kill every fucken one of you. It's nothing to do with you.'

The people jolt back like mice into their holes, doors slamming; some people gleeping out through their letterboxes or the side of their net curtains.

May-Belle laughs, and whispers, 'Gimme the gun a moment.'

He hands it to her. She turns in a circle, pointing the gun at every home.

'Stay inside or we will kill you,' she shouts. She turns and aims at her own front room window. 'Like this,' she screams, and she fires the very last shot at the glass. It explodes in a silver burst and silence stands tall while Pearse and May-Belle stand in the street. The song playing from Pearse's house is over.

'We've no bullets left now,' says Pearse.

'Fine,' says May-Belle.

May-Belle hands the gun back to Pearse. They walk down the hill. He points the gun slowly to the left and right. The sky has darkened now; the night almost fully black but still orange-licked. From the dual carriage-way and the top of the town and from the Steeple Road and Snob Hill, the wailing red and blue flare of sirens and cop cars flash over the tops of the looming houses, gathering around them on all sides.

They walk towards the square. The wailing and the lights grow louder and brighter and a half dozen police cars and paddy wagons pull into the road in front of them. Pearse and May-Belle stop. The doors of the cars and vans fly open – and stay open. Beneath them, black-toed boots hit the tarmac, as the cops shield themselves behind their bullet-proof doors.

'Drop the gun, son,' comes a voice.

May-Belle and Pearse keep walking towards the flashing lights of the cars. Drop the gun, comes the first voice again. Put the fucken gun down, says another. Stop, remain where you are, a third tells them. All the men are talking at once, ordering the children to stay still, drop their weapons, put their hands on their heads.

One shouts, 'One more move and we shoot.'

May-Belle stops walking and Pearse stands still beside her. He looks at her and then looks at the gun and lifts his shooting hand a shaking centimeter. There comes the sound of two dozen cops cocking their pistols and machine guns simultaneously – the riffle of a deadly deck of cards.

May-Belle puts her hand around his hand and takes the gun from him; she bends forward, keeping her eyes on the cops, and lays the gun on the ground.

A few police officers come out from their hiding places, behind their steel-plated car doors, their guns aimed on Pearse and May-Belle and walk forward. When they get to within a few feet, Pearse says, 'Come on then.'

The cops rush them. One cop rugby tackles Pearse, throwing him backwards – as they fall through the air the cop clocks Pearse on the chin with the butt of his revolver. The blow turns Pearse's face to the side and he sees May-Belle, below him, on the ground, on her belly, knocked out and dead cold, a cop with his knee in the small of her back, cuffing her. Pearse lands on his spine and the air rushes out of his lungs. The base of his skull catches the concrete. He drops down into the darkest, quietest place; the cops and the orange lights and the shouting and the pain – the pain just rising in his head from the punch of the pavement – all washed away in a warm bath of sleepiness; a drowsy nothingness that isn't broken or interrupted, until he comes round in an ambulance with three cops pointing their guns in his face.

'Where's May-Belle?' he asks them, the howl of the ambulance siren splitting his head open.

'In the wagon behind us, son,' one of the cops said.

Another cop said, 'You are going to jail forever and so's your wee mate. You fucken monsters.'

'You cunts,' the last cop said.

Behind them, on her stretcher, May-Belle swam in the orange

lights of the cars; lights that came beating in through the moving window, washing through the ambulance cabin – and Pearse swam with her, she saw. The pair of them: two wee orbs of white light on opposite sides of the planet; separated for now, but soon rising up in beams from the earth into the sky – roaming through the dark and each keeping search for the other. Two pillars of fire – raining down on below from on high – cutting through the land in fiery gouts until one found the other at last – no matter what; no matter no-one. And that would be it, then – over and done with for good. Forever.

The End

Acknowledgments

Erin Vlack, Frances Corr, Ulrich Hansen, Harry McDonald, JL Williams, Elinor Brown, Michael Schmidt, Laura Marney, Kei Miller, Iain S Bruce, John Burnside, David Hayman, Alan Bissett, Lucy Luck, Jonny Jobson, Colin Campbell, Adrian Searle, Rodge Glass, Moira Mackay, and Niamh and Caitie Mackay.